Praise for

The Farm at Peppe

'Kelsall is a bold and fearless writer who is unafraid of presenting her readership with a plethora of darker style themes . . . authentic, insightful and sensitive in the right places.' **Mrs B's Book Reviews**

'Léonie Kelsall's skilful portrayal of life on the land and the people who live it comes alive. An absolute gem of a book!' **Blue Wolf Reviews**

'. . . moves from foreboding, funny, breath-holding, sad and sweet. I loved the way Kelsall unwrapped the secrets slowly throughout the story—little teasers that kept me glued to the pages.' **The Burgeoning Bookshelf Blogspot**

'It's a mark of Kelsall's unique storytelling ability that she is able to combine both the dark and light elements of this story to create something so appealing.' **Jackie Smith Writes**

'A fantastic tale with relatable and loveable characters.' **Happy Valley BooksRead**

'. . . told with plenty of heart and humour . . . a charming book full of strong, unforgettable characters that you'll fall in love with.' *Glam Adelaide Magazine*

Raised initially in a tiny, no-horse town on South Australia's Fleurieu coast, then in the slightly more populated wheat and sheep farming land in the Murraylands, Léonie Kelsall is a country girl through and through. Growing up without a television, she developed a love of reading before she reached primary school, swiftly followed by a desire to write. Pity the poor teachers who received chapters of creative writing instead of a single page!

Léonie entertained a brief fantasy of moving to the big city (well, Adelaide), but within months the lure of the open spaces and big sky country summoned her home. Now she splits her time between the stark, arid beauty of the family farm at Pallamana and her home and counselling practice in the lush Adelaide Hills.

Catch up with her on Facebook, Instagram or at www.leoniekelsall.com.

LÉONIE KELSALL

The Farm at
Peppertree Crossing

ALLEN&UNWIN
SYDNEY • MELBOURNE • AUCKLAND • LONDON

This edition published in 2021
First published in 2020

Allen & Unwin
83 Alexander Street
Crows Nest NSW 2065
Australia
Phone: (61 2) 8425 0100
Email: info@allenandunwin.com
Web: www.allenandunwin.com

 A catalogue record for this
book is available from the
National Library of Australia

ISBN 978 1 76087 961 7

Set in Sabon LT Pro by Bookhouse, Sydney
Printed in Australia by Pegasus Media & Logistics

10 9 8 7 6 5 4

The paper in this book is FSC® certified. FSC® promotes environmentally responsible, socially beneficial and economically viable management of the world's forests.

For Taylor,
Who knows what she wants

And will get it.

Chapter One

Roni closed her fist around her keys. The longest metal shaft protruded between her fingers, a perfectly legal weapon. She'd sensed the presence behind her about five blocks from the train station, where the streetlights were spaced farther apart. It paused when she paused. Hurried when she hurried. And disappeared into the shadows when she turned.

Most women were smart enough to travel in pairs around here.

But most women didn't have to work late in the city on a Wednesday night and then hike two klicks home from the train station.

The guy who dogged her footsteps was an idiot; any woman who risked walking this neighbourhood at night was no stranger to his type. Roni dug bitten nails into the key as it slipped between her fingers. Tightened her hand on the cracked leather strap slung across her chest. The self-defence instructor had insisted bags should only ever be carried on one shoulder, and surrendered instantly on demand. Better a handbag than your life, he'd said, handing out printed memes.

Whoever spent their Sunday coming up with that little gem had far more disposable income than Roni did. No way was anyone getting her bag without producing a knife.

She broke into a jog as the back of her apartment block came into view, the few unbroken streetlights along the cracked pavement flickering beacons in the gloom.

A chill gust slammed the smeared glass of the rear entry door behind her. Dead leaves and empty chip packets scuttled inside to join the damp mound against the wall of letterboxes. She pinched her nose at the dank smell; once spring arrived properly, the rubbish would still blow in, but at least the mould would retreat. One eye on the external door, she keyed open her box.

Eight lung-cramping flights of stairs separated her from the further safety of her fourth-floor apartment. Each landing had once boasted a window, a deception to make the structure seem less prison-like. Now, urban art decorated the boarded-up holes.

She paused on the third landing, holding her breath as she made certain there were no sounds of pursuit from below. Her racing heart slowed a notch, and she took a second to compose herself before she hammered on door three-four-seven. Footsteps thundered from above, then a couple of kids pushed past, leaping down steps three at a time. Beyond the door she could make out Mr Edwards' familiar shuffle, his ever-present carpet slippers sliding on the gritty tiles. She dug into her bag, pulling out the prescription she'd had filled for him.

'Come in, Roni, come on in.' Lonely pleading was evident, as always, in Mr Edwards' tone as he tugged open the door and held out arthritic claws for the package. And, as always, she shook her head. It was one thing to run minor errands for her long-term neighbours but quite another to enter their homes, their lives.

'Let me get my wallet, then,' Mr Edwards mumbled, rubbing at the patchy grey stubble on his liver-spotted cheeks. He turned to make the laborious trip back across his tiny apartment.

'No rush. You can fix me up tomorrow.' This time she would have to make sure she accepted the money, though. Not that she'd ever had money to burn, but now she was definitely not in a position to hand out charity.

Over Mr Edwards' shoulder she saw a can of baked beans perched on the tray table alongside his tattered recliner, a fork dribbling orange slime onto the plastic surface. She grimaced. Mr Edwards' scripts didn't cost her much—he was on the PBS—and if he insisted she take the money tomorrow, she would use it to pick him up a loaf of sliced white to go with his beans.

She backed away, waving a farewell, then gripped the handrail to haul herself up the final flights. Groaned as chewing gum sucked onto her fingers. As Rafe loved to say, no good deed went unpunished. After more than a dozen years, she could just about hear her boss's voice in her head.

Her door was one of many identical rectangles in the beige corridor of dozens of apartments, but it at least had an operating lock. The barrel rattled as she keyed it and shoved open the door, reaching for the light switch.

Lips pursed, she squeaked through her teeth. 'Scritches?' she called, again making the high-pitched squeak he always responded to. Her nose wrinkled at the ammonia waft. There was a reason pets weren't permitted in the block, but Scritches had been with her eight years—ironically, from the week of her twenty-first birthday, as though he'd been some sort of cosmic gift. The only gift she'd received that year—or any other. Roni would resort to living under newspaper on a park bench before she would part with him. Greg had found that out last weekend. For years he had been keen for her to move in with him and split the rent. With her lease ending, it seemed the timing was right, despite her reluctance to give up the smallest fraction of her independence.

But then Greg had made it clear that Scritches wasn't welcome.

And she had made it clear that she was through with Greg.

He hadn't been worth fighting for. Not much in her life was.

She hadn't even been truly disappointed in him. Because disappointment would mean she'd had expectations—and she'd learned long ago never to allow that to happen.

The cat responded to her call, instantly underfoot and rubbing against her calves. Then he hooked his claws into her jeans to stretch to his full, impressive height against her thigh.

'Hey, you daft thing. How's life in the castle?' Certainly better than it had been years back, when she'd found him cowering behind a dumpster at the back of the apartment block. Each time the local kids approached, the scruffy kitten had erupted into belly-rumbling purrs, thrusting his broad nose into their outstretched hands. Then bemused hurt would take over his expression as they pelted him with rocks and yanked his tail.

Roni had chased the kids off and left the kitten to fend for itself.

She had done the same the next day, pretending not to see the graze across his pink nose where a pebble had found its mark. Pitiful mewing followed her footsteps as she headed for the train, but she had hardened her heart.

The next day, repeating the intervention, she had refused to wonder how long the kitten would search for love from those who abused it. Or how it would escape the arctic wind that cut through the littered, empty carpark.

On the fourth day she had shoved the scrawny, wet bundle of malnourished fluff under her coat, where he had immediately set to kneading her with tiny, sharp claws, his purr vibrating through both of them. Against her chest he had felt so . . . alive. So trusting and willing to give affection, without expectation or demand.

She had been wrong on that score; it turned out Scritches was a demanding little ass.

He wove through her legs now as she made for the bathroom. 'Okay, I get it. Priorities.' She slid down the door jamb, feet shoved against the base of the bed, and clicked her fingers. The cat bounded heavily into her lap, butting her chin so hard her teeth knocked together. As she scratched the base of his spine he arched ecstatically, and Roni tugged on the ragged ear that lent him the appearance of a street brawler. 'We're both fakes, aren't we?' Sure, she'd talked tough to herself on that walk home, been prepared to face off with a potential attacker for the second time this year, but that didn't mean her heart wasn't still thumping hard enough to make her feel sick.

God, she hoped that was why she felt sick.

Because apparently the cat wasn't the only thing Greg wouldn't tolerate in his life. After half a decade together—years where she'd pretended to herself that maybe what she'd found was love, not just someone to provide the safety that seemed to come with familiarity—she thought she knew Greg. As much as either of them, both products of the foster system, chose to let anyone know them. But she'd been broadsided by his boast last week that he'd been skipping out on paying child support, denying responsibility for at least two kids somewhere in Sydney.

Two more children who didn't know their father.

Although, maybe they were better off without him. Was it worse to know the parents who hadn't wanted you, or to always wonder who your family was and why they hadn't loved you enough to keep you? She shook her head as she hauled herself up and retrieved her handbag. That wasn't something she'd ever have an answer to, so there was no point letting her mind wander that way. She tossed the mail she'd collected from her defaced letterbox onto her bed and grimaced as she took out the chemist's package. The grease from the patchily translucent paper bag crammed alongside it slicked her fingertips. 'You're in luck, Scritch. Beef steak.'

Stepping over the instantly ravenous cat, she put the chemist's parcel on the cracked pink laminate vanity, then shoved aside the curtain across the shower alcove. As usual, Scritches' bowl was empty. Juvenile abandonment haunting him, he would always wolf down whatever food she offered. She split open the pies and dumped the gelatinous mass into the bowl. 'Nope, no pastry.' She fended off his sneak attack with her foot. 'Rafe gave us this lot free, so they're not exactly fresh.'

As she rinsed her hands, water splashed the chemist's bag. Her gut clenched. She shook her hands, as though the nervous tingle would disappear from her fingertips along with the droplets, and then she shoved the test into a drawer. Until she peed on that stick, the problem wasn't real. Which meant she could assess the hypothetical altern-atives of the hypothetical situation with hypothetical clinical detachment.

Abortion.

Adoption.

Acceptance.

Fingers wrapped around the drawer handle, she closed her eyes, focused on tamping down the surge of despair. The thing was, although she pretended she had options, she knew the truth. If she was pregnant, it was her own fault. She was an adult, and she hadn't been forced, cajoled or coerced. Not this time. So there was no way she would allow the child to be torn from the one place that should provide unquestionable safety.

Adoption? Supposedly vastly different to the foster system she'd grown up in—she would never consign any kid to a repeat of her life—but still she was wary without an iron-clad guarantee.

So, that left door number three. If she'd screwed up, she would have to keep the baby. Not only that but she would have to find a way to provide for it, because any hope of help from Greg was out of the question.

Scritches jumped as she slammed the drawer.

Leaving the bathroom door partly open, she took the six steps through the bedroom, pausing to scoop up the mail she'd tossed on the bed, and into the kitchen. She pulled a stool from beneath the bench that served as food prep area, desk and the cat's bed when he could get away with it. His favourite spot, though, was the window ledge. For almost a decade, his experience of the outside world had been in shades of grey, filtered by grime-covered glass. Plastered against her window like a furry starfish, perhaps he occasionally caught sight of his family skulking around down there and realised how much better off he was without them.

She and Scritches only needed each other.

Roni perched on the stool and flicked through the stack of mail, frowning at the fifth item. Her thumb rubbed the thick parchment, unease worming through her stomach. Nothing good ever came in a window-faced envelope. Especially not one embossed Prescott & Knight, Solicitors. What could a solicitor want with her? She'd done nothing wrong.

She ripped the envelope open.

Dear Ms Gates,

We act on behalf of Ms Marian Nelson. We have tried, unsuccessfully, to contact you via telephone regarding a personal financial matter. We would be pleased if you could call during business hours on the number listed above.

Sincerely,

Derek Prescott

She snorted. Either a luckless investment adviser who could tell her what to do with her whole twelve-hundred dollars of savings, or a scammer so basic they still used snail mail. At least it explained the unknown-number calls she'd recently ignored.

The fridge gave a geriatric wheeze and she lurched from the stool, her gaze flying to the door. Deadlocked, as always, the second she stepped inside.

But that didn't mean the street-creep hadn't followed her, wasn't waiting in the stairwell. Or on the street.

She shoved the mail back into her bag, jerking the zip across as though she could contain her fear within the leather prison.

Hell, didn't she have a right to feel safe in her own space? Not that rights had ever counted for much in her life.

Chapter Two

She liked seeing the same faces each day. After more than ten years, the nameless people were family. She had invented their stories without needing to leave the security of her mental solitude, had kept them safely at arm's length while enjoying the feeling of security that came with their familiarity.

The arrival of each train and ferry at Circular Quay saw a fresh crowd engulf the takeaway shop. First in were the tradies in orange or yellow hi-vis vests and white hard-hats, breakfasting on bacon-and-egg rolls washed down with cartons of iced coffee as they headed toward the city building sites. Most days, Roni would cop the same chat-up line. *Hey, sweetheart, how about you come hang at the pub this arvo?*

And every time she would silently refuse, sparing them only a tight smile.

At 6.17 the pinstriped businessman would appear, his shoes reflecting the fluoro overheads. After four years, she had forced herself to allow their hands to touch as she shoved his latte across the counter, inhaling a caffeine-eclipsing jolt of expensive aftershave, and he shoved five bucks, never waiting for his change. Impeccably groomed and polite, the guy should be everything a woman would want.

But Roni only made the contact to prove to herself that she could, a daily reminder of how far she'd come from being the kid who'd flinched from Rafe's gaze when she'd come in here begging for an after-school job. She had her shit together now, her memories under control.

Waves of office workers, schoolkids and then, finally, the unfamiliar faces of tourists, populated the rest of her day.

She rang up a sale on the till and raised her voice over the thunder of a train on the platform above them. 'Rafe, I'm taking lunch, okay?'

'Sure.' Her boss glanced at the clock above the cake counter. Not yet ten-thirty, but he liked her to take her break before the rush. They'd fallen into a routine over the years since she graduated. At first she'd juggled two jobs, but once Rafe discovered she was working nights at a service station, he'd opened up a full-time position for her.

He paid poorly and worked her hard, but he was quick with a laugh and a sympathetic ear on the rare occasions she chose to share. She liked to tell herself he was what a dad would have been like.

'Was the sun up when you got in?' Rafe slid the cake cabinet door shut. 'Heading for the gardens?'

'Not today.' She often spent lunch sprawled beneath the parrot-filled Moreton Bay figs in the Royal Botanic Garden. Other days, she would dangle her legs over the edge of the quay, admiring the rainbow petroleum slicks as ferries beetled past the white sails of the Opera House. She rummaged in her bag. 'Scritch reckons crumbs aren't a patch on fish-shaped biscuits, so I've got to shop.'

'Crazy cat lady. Y'know that animal doesn't actually have an opinion, right?'

'Y'know you don't actually have a right to an opinion?' She threw his words back with a grin as she scooped a handful of change from the bottom of her bag. The envelope she'd stuffed in the previous night fell out and she waved it at Rafe. 'How old-school is this? Scam-by-mail.'

Rafe took it, tapping his thumb on the return address. 'Inner city. Doubt any scammer could afford that bit of real estate.' He handed the grubby envelope back, turning to a customer. 'Morning, mate. What can I get you? Must be a fake address.' As usual, he carried on two separate conversations without missing a beat, despite the customer's confused expression. 'Why don't you head up there, let whoever's at that address know they're being used as a front? Could be a reward in it.'

Roni rang up the price of the cake the customer had warily pointed at. 'Three-sixty, please. Figures you'd think that way, Rafe. Guess the exercise wouldn't hurt, though.'

Rafe bagged the cake and flipped the paper to twist the corners closed. 'Reckon it *will* hurt. It's all uphill, mate.'

A few minutes later, bag slung across her chest, Roni emerged from the shops beneath the train station, blinking to acclimatise to the glaring sunlight as she trudged up the sidewalk. It took only seconds, though, to lose the sun in a forest of highrises. She walked slowly as her antiquated phone loaded the address she'd keyed into maps.

Despite the hour, she couldn't maintain a straight line on the pavement for the crush of pedestrians. Or she could, but unlike the woman who faced off with her, she wasn't that rude. Also, she wasn't wearing ten-centimetre heels that could double as weapons. Maybe that's what Roni needed for her evening commute. Her life had been a reluctant creep toward the western suburbs for twenty years, despite the random memories that insisted her first foster parents had lived east, where manicured lawns edged with rose bushes bordered double-storey homes on tree-lined streets. But who knew the truth of it? Childhood was tricky like that. There was no way to sort out which memories were her own and which belonged to Saturday Disney.

And no reason to want to.

She halted at the base of a fanned flight of sandstone steps. Neither they nor the glass-fronted façade of the building to which they led were unusual in their overt ostentation. But the business nameplate, stencilled in austere black letters on the chrome-framed doors, lifted her eyebrows. Prescott & Knight, Solicitors.

So she'd scored a ballsy scammer who'd pinched the company name along with the address?

The stairs led to an expansive polished-stone landing. A wall of reflective glass prevented her seeing inside the building but provided a disturbingly clear view of her own approach. At school she had aspired—if dreams counted as aspiration—to be as perfectly presented, well-dressed and beautifully groomed as the young businesswomen on the pavement behind her. Instead, despite the elegance lent by her height, her work uniform of black pants and T-shirt permanently reeked of grease, and her pale skin, a curse from her unknown genes, necessarily remained naked: a session over the deep fryer dissolved make-up rated less than nuclear-apocalypse-proof, a lesson she'd learned the hard way on her first day.

She ran a hand over her hair, the humidity frizzing her light-brown ponytail into wild curls. Pulled her shirt straight, as though that would disguise the cheap, casual clothes. The door swung open as a woman about her own age exited. Heels, pencil skirt, white blouse. No flyaways.

Roni took a hasty step back. No, she did not need to do this. The scam, or identity theft, or whatever, was none of her concern.

'Going in?' The woman held the door wide.

'Ah, sure. Thanks.'

The industrial sole of her flat black lace-ups squealed on the white marble tiles, the noise echoing endlessly in the six-storey hollow core of the building. The reception desk lay on the far side of a vast foyer dotted with lush greenery.

Cheeks warm, she squeaked past the sudden lull in meetings convened on chrome-and-leather lounges. Past a cluster

14

of people waiting for a glass-fronted lift. Past coffee-toting minions. Everyone wore business attire. No one squeaked.

Rafe had better be right about a reward.

She coughed as chilled, pine-scented air caught her throat. The receptionist looked up from his computer screen, quirking an eyebrow as though he'd been unaware of her trek. 'May I help you?'

'Sure.' She fumbled the letter from her bag, wishing it looked a little less crumpled and didn't have a paw print in a distinct gravy shade marring the address, and held it up. 'I received this yesterday, but it's a . . .' The word *scam* sounded foolish in this rarefied atmosphere. She crossed her arms over her chest, crinkling the envelope further. 'It's a mistake.'

'May I see it?' The receptionist leaned forward, all shine and sparkle. Manicured nails gleaming, chrome nametag glinting. Tristan.

She pulled the letter from the envelope and handed it to him, trying to remember whether Scritches had also wandered over that. As the receptionist skimmed the words, Roni scanned the back of it and saw no evidence of her cat. Tristan held the page up. 'And you are Ms Gates?'

'Well, yes, I am. But obviously, that letter wasn't intended—'

'You don't have an appointment with Mr Prescott today, though, Ms Gates?' Tristan frowned, his focus shifting between the page and his computer screen.

'No, I don't need one. I mean, I wasn't aware that Mr Prescott is a real person.'

Without moving his head, the receptionist flicked his gaze up at her. Eyes as grey as the midwinter harbour. 'A real person?'

Roni shuffled closer to the chest-high counter. 'I mean, I don't have any business with Mr Prescott.' She waved toward the page, as though it would somehow exonerate her. 'I assume the letter isn't really from him. Not your Mr Prescott, anyway.'

Tristan reread the letter. 'It certainly is from Mr Prescott. I'll schedule you in.' He tapped at his keyboard, craning toward the monitor as though an intent gaze would produce the desired result. 'Ah. I've nothing available for some time. Can you give me just one moment?'

'No, you don't understand. It's not me he wants to see. I don't even know—'

A finger raised for her silence, Tristan lifted the ivory telephone receiver alongside him and punched two numbers. 'Good morning, Pauline. Would you please check scheduling for Mr Prescott. I need an appointment slotted in.' His lips tightened as he drummed his fingers on the countertop. 'Yes, I can see he's full, but this is with regards to Ms Nelson. Marian Nelson. Yes. Tomorrow? Wait a moment, I'll check.' He cupped one hand over the mouthpiece and looked up at Roni. 'I can get you in at eleven-thirty tomorrow, Ms Gates, if that would suit?'

'But I don't need to—' She sighed. It would be quicker to accept the appointment so she could make her escape. Then she would ring back and cancel, explain the situation to someone with a lot less pretty and a lot more brains. 'Sure. That'll be fine.'

Tristan smiled, and she winced at the flash of white teeth, either the product of the most amazing genes or, more likely, a bucketload of cash and a fine orthodontist. She ran her tongue over her own teeth, aware of the slight overlap of her left incisor. Tristan returned to his keyboard. 'So the address we have on file for you is correct?'

'Well, correct for me, but I'm not—'

Tapping at his computer, Tristan wasn't listening. 'And allow me to confirm your phone number, please?'

She briefly considered asking how they had obtained her number but figured that, like most anything, it would be available for purchase online. Except it wasn't her information they had meant to buy. Someone's head would no doubt roll over this mess. She gabbled the numbers, silently daring Tristan to be swift enough to check them against those on his screen.

He took a pencil from a pewter mug on his desk and scribed neat, rounded letters on the back of a cream card. 'Excellent. I know Mr Prescott will be pleased to have located you.' He handed her the heavily embossed slip, along with her letter. 'Here's your appointment time. We'll look forward to seeing you tomorrow, Ms Gates.'

∞

Early Thursday knock-off meant a train full of kids. Roni squeezed against the scratched glass, trying to look beyond *Shazza sux* and *Climate change KILLS* to the humdrum of suburbia flashing past. The sun occasionally broke through cloud cover to spotlight the graffiti-tagged fences bordering the tracks. Missing iron sheets created a gap-toothed grimace, allowing voyeuristic glimpses into houses, streets, other peoples' lives.

Not that she ever saw anything she wanted.

She craved nothing more than familiar patterns, constrained by certainty and routine. The life she had created made for the safety that had been impossible to find in her youth. She'd thought Greg was part of that security, that she'd found someone who intuitively understood her need, without asking the reason. A rare relaxation of her tee-total rule five years ago had seen them become more than friends—slightly, and very occasionally, more. On those occasions, she would throw back a can of whatever Greg had brought over, dulling her thoughts. After, she would worm from beneath him and scurry to the bathroom to scrub away the memories. The evidence.

A product of the system himself, Greg knew better than to ask what her hang-up was.

And she had never asked about his. If she had, she would have realised he had no intention of being a responsible adult. Ever.

She drummed her fingertips on the filthy window, blowing out a long breath. It didn't matter; Greg didn't matter. She hadn't taken the test yet. She could be wrong.

She needed to be wrong.

Chapter Three

Roni paused briefly at Mr Edwards' apartment to drop off the bread and a box of the bitter Yorkshire teabags he liked, which she'd spotted on sale. Then she dashed up the stairs before he could insist she take more money. A few cents from him wouldn't make any appreciable difference to her situation, but the slow smile that spread across the elderly man's face went a long way to smoothing the sharp edges of the day.

The floral curtain plastered against her legs as Scritches forced his way into the shower cubicle. He appeared slightly offended by the water splattering him—possibly due more to the sporadic bursts and changing temperature than the dampness—but he always insisted on sharing her shower.

After drying off with a threadbare towel, she dropped the faded fabric on Scritches and gave him a quick rub down. His purrs echoing against the tiles, his fur stuck up

19

in spikes, the tiger pattern darkened to a deep, rich rust by the water and the white blazes on his chest and face pristine.

Until she met Scritches, she had never liked ginger cats. The stupid *Garfield* movie had ruined them for her.

No, not so much the movie, but what had happened when she watched it.

She thrust the memories aside, dragging on sweats and a T-shirt. Scritches pattered after her into the kitchen, where she spread paperwork across the kitchen bench. Lease agreement, pay slips, rental reference, tax returns, budget calculations. As though laying it all out there would make any difference. She couldn't afford the new rent on this place, but nor could she afford anywhere else. Finding somewhere for her and Scritches would have been problem enough, but if she had to work the possibility of a baby into the equation, her options changed.

Or not so much changed as disappeared.

She scratched at her arm, peppered by a history of tiny deep-fryer splatter burns, her gaze repeatedly sliding toward the bathroom door. She sighed heavily; procrastination wasn't helping. Time to find out for sure how screwed she was.

Leaving the papers for Scritches to turn into confetti, she strode to the bathroom, pulled the pregnancy test from the drawer and scanned the instructions. Already bored with destroying the paperwork, Scritches shoved his way in. 'Back off, buddy. You can't help with this.'

Pee and wait two minutes. There was no point staring at the white plastic stick she placed on the bathroom counter, so she stared at the cracked and mouldy ceiling instead, her hand absently caressing Scritches' head.

One hundred and twenty elephant-seconds.

The last ten she counted super slowly, willing her frantic heartbeat to the same pace.

Finally, she looked.

Two pink lines.

She'd read the instructions. Knew what that meant. Yet she read the page again, to make certain.

Her stomach cramped, but not the way she wanted it to. Needed it to. Instead, it knotted in fear and denial.

Pregnant.

Still dressed, she crawled into bed, cupping her hands over her belly. Scritches hauled himself up with a characteristic lack of grace and burrowed under the covers, butting against her until she hugged her arms around him. Stretched full length along her side, he purred until the bed vibrated. She buried her face in his fur. 'Holy crap, Scritch. What now?'

The enormity of the situation filled her head, muting the noises of the crowded apartment block. Her chest ached as though she could breathe in but couldn't expel her breath. There was nothing familiar or safe about this situation, nothing she could cling to, nothing to stop the sensation of the earth shifting beneath her, the world tilted and out of kilter. Two pink lines changed everything.

No home, no boyfriend. But a baby and a cat.

She was so screwed.

They were so screwed.

Scritches nudged her with a wet nose until she rubbed her thumb over the velvety expanse. The motion calmed her. Scritches hadn't fared too badly since she rescued him. She had never wanted a pet, had baulked at the thought of anything being dependent on her. But they had worked out okay.

Obviously, a baby was a whole different level of commitment—though realistically, how much more demanding than her neurotic cat could a child be? Her hand paused on Scritches' nose. She'd been alone most of her life, looked after herself, even screwed this up by herself—because she couldn't blame Greg, as that would mean she'd relied on him—so why did she instantly assume she couldn't do this alone?

The fact was, she had to do it. There were no options.

She was going to be a mother.

She reached under her head and punched the lumpy pillow into submission, staring at the ceiling as though it were the movie screen of her life. Deep inside her, rare excitement tingled. For once, the threat of the unfamiliar didn't reek of darkness, alcohol and strange men. For the first time, perhaps it held a little potential. Busy surviving, she had never bothered to dream, but now she would be responsible for more than just herself and Scritches. Maybe a new life could mean a new beginning, because, if she could pull this off, she would have the thing she'd always craved: a family of her own. One no one could ever take away.

Unplanned didn't have to mean unwanted.

∾

The next morning, she dressed and hurried through the ritual of ensuring Scritches had supplies enough to last the day. Every thought and mundane action seemed imbued with new meaning. Zipping her jeans over the slight curve of her stomach became tucking her baby up safe. A plan to grab breakfast at work changed with the realisation she now had to improve her diet. Briefly, she considered finding a GP who would bulk bill, but quickly discarded the thought. The appointment would be loaded with questions about her family medical history, questions for which she had no answers. And would the doctor also question her living circumstances, her casual employment, her non-existent bank account, and judge her unfit to be a parent? Perhaps suggest her baby would be better off with someone else?

She stroked a protective hand over her belly, calming her fear, knowing it was ridiculous. Still, her experience had given her no reason to trust the system; she was better off handling this alone, at least for now. She'd spent much of her life hiding between the pages of books at the library. Now she'd switch to non-fiction and use their computers to research all she needed to know about her baby.

Maybe it was the hormones, but instead of the dread it would probably be smart to feel, optimism surged through her. Pregnancy would be the catalyst for change, proof that life could be more than the routine existence she had cultivated. She would allow herself a little time to enjoy the thrill, then knuckle down to sorting out the mess she had created. Her hand stilled on her abdomen. No, not a *mess*. She would never let her baby be thought of that way.

The *opportunity* she had been given.

The smells of humanity crowded beneath a layer of smog, humidity and grime as she arrived at the station to see the rear carriage of her regular train disappear between the tall weeds bordering the track. The first crack in her routine, but she could handle it. Good practice for weaning herself from her obsessive need for familiarity and control. The next train would still get her to the city on time—she had only to dash down the stairs to reach Rafe's lower-level takeaway shop. A grin tweaked her mouth. Lower-level in every sense. She would remember that line to share with him; Rafe loved a good joke. Hell, he loved a bad one. His sense of humour was part of what made him easy, non-threatening company.

As she pulled the commuter pass from her bag, the solicitor's card spiralled to the cigarette butt-pocked ground. Retrieving it, she clicked her tongue. She had intended to cancel the appointment yesterday but had been totally distracted by her discovery and new plans. Too early to call the office now; she would have to sneak away from Rafe to phone through later.

The crowded train wheezed asthmatically into the station. She boarded and stood in the aisle, rising onto her toes to keep her balance each time the train squealed to a stop, then rocking back on her heels as it lurched off again. The vibration of her phone startled her, and she clutched her bag against her hip to silence the tune.

Like Scritches' yowl when she took too long to open his food, the phone rang louder every second it went unacknowledged. She scrabbled among the pens and crumpled tissues in the bottom of her bag, retrieving the phone as the other commuters frowned at the interruption to their sleepy journey. She hung up on the caller, but the phone rang again immediately.

'Yes?' she hissed, her cupped hand creating an oasis of privacy.

'Hello, who is this?'

'Who is *this*?'

'Derek Prescott from Prescott & Knight, Solicitors. Am I speaking with Miss Gates?'

She winced. Add a snippy response to her less-than-groomed appearance yesterday and no doubt Prescott & Knight had her pigeonholed. 'I'm sorry, yes, this is Roni.' She didn't add her surname. Not that eavesdroppers could do much with it, but she valued her privacy. There was none in foster homes.

'Miss Gates, I apologise for contacting you so early, but I wanted to make certain you are coming in to our office today.'

Prescott's voice was deep and self-assured, but he had to be joking. 'Mr Prescott, as I tried to explain to your receptionist yesterday, you have the wrong person.' A couple of passengers had tuned into her conversation, watching over their phone screens, or more discreetly from behind newspapers.

'As I have a personal interest in this matter, I'm quite certain we do not, Miss Gates.'

'And I'm equally certain you do.'

'Then, although I wouldn't normally do this by telephone, let me confirm. You were placed in state care, with the unusual objective of having you fostered, rather than adopted, twenty-nine years ago?'

Caution and irritation tinged her response. 'Sounds like you know rather more about me than I know myself.'

'And you were subsequently fostered by three different families?'

'I'm sure those records are accessible to anyone.' Hopefully not the reason the final placement had been terminated, though.

'Quite,' Prescott agreed smoothly. 'And, in the final year of high school, you won a competition you do not recall entering, the prize being rather exorbitantly priced driver's education and licensing.'

'What?' Her grip on the phone tightened.

'Immediately upon graduating high school, despite somewhat mediocre results, you received an offer of a fully funded university scholarship.'

'But that was a sc—' A scam. She'd thought it a scam, like the letter from Prescott & Knight. *What the hell?*

The train disgorged passengers, pulling her along with the human detritus. She made for a low wall, hugging the safety of stone as she stared through the open arch at the monochrome rainbow of the Harbour Bridge, the phone still pressed to her ear.

She hadn't pursued the scholarship because she'd known it was bogus.

Dear God, please let it have been bogus.

The life she could have had flashed before her eyes. A life that didn't smell like week-old hamburger. A life where she had a career. A home. A future. A life that didn't involve worrying about whether she could make the rent.

She closed her eyes, shutting out the view. 'Yes,' she said reluctantly. 'That's me.'

'Then I shall be immensely pleased to make your acquaintance this morning, Miss Gates.'

The call clicked off, and Roni bolted down the escalator, hurdling the steps rather than wait for the mechanism to grind to the bottom. The lower level was crowded with commuters as passengers jostled their way off ferries. She angled across the flow of workers headed from the dock into the city and shoved the heavy glass door.

'Door open or shut, Rafe?'

Her boss looked up from behind the workbench, where he had about forty slices of white bread laid out, his hand working in a steady rhythm as he buttered each with a single, practised sweep of his knife. His bald head glistened. 'Shut. Too humid. Don't want my stuff sweating.'

'Right. Thanks for that visual.' At least it would distract her from replaying the solicitor's conversation.

'Looks like she'll be a spring scorcher today.'

She pulled an apron from the hook behind the counter. An apron that she might never have had to wear if she'd— no. She couldn't afford those thoughts. Regrets didn't pay bills. 'You planning on seeing any of it?' Rafe came in before her and wouldn't leave until after dark. He claimed that, because the shop was closed on weekends, he had no need of R&R during the week. Possibly his wife thought differently, but Roni rarely saw her; she would appear once or twice a year surrounded by a bubble of excited, noisy children. She seemed to share the friendly, unassuming manner that made Rafe so easy to be around. Rafe didn't ask Roni too many questions, didn't pry, yet held a quiet concern for her welfare. He was a constant fixture and, in a life that had been rife with change and uncertainty, that permanence was remarkable.

She dropped the apron over her head and crossed the waist strap at the back, trying to encourage the loose ends into a knot above her stomach, like the celebrity chefs did on TV.

Rafe waved his knife. 'Keep telling you, Roni, it's not going to reach.'

And it would be less likely to reach by the day. A tingle shot into her fingertips, a fizz of anticipation and excitement curling her lip. 'It won't reach because you're a tightarse. Bet you got a discount on aprons with short straps, right?'

A grin split Rafe's face. 'Yeah, that's it. Entirely my fault. Milk delivery's running late, so stock the fridge soon as it gets here. Bring the old stuff to the front.'

'Really? Old stuff to the front. Hmm. Let's see if I can remember that.' Like she'd not done it a million times. Or at least almost three thousand, but who was counting?

'Morning.' She moved to the till, rang up a daily paper and an iced coffee, handed change to the customer. 'Thanks, have a great day. Rafe, I'm taking lunch at eleven-fifteen, okay?'

'Nice, Roni. You haven't even got your apron tied and you're telling me when you're off?'

'Them's the breaks, my friend. Literally. Hey, don't suppose you know anyone with a rental?'

'Sure I do. How many bedrooms do you want?'

Her heart soared with sudden hope. Two pink stripes and her whole world was looking better. Why hadn't she thought to ask Rafe earlier? Sydney born and bred, he knew about a million people. 'I'll take pretty much anything I can get.'

'How do you fancy three bedrooms, detached, with gardens?'

'Oh, I fancy, all right. Are you offering to quadruple my pay, though?' She couldn't think what came in the sequence beyond quadruple, which would be nowhere near enough.

'No pay rise. Place is going cheap.'

She frowned, her hands busy shifting the baked goods in the warmer, making sure they heated evenly. 'Nothing goes cheap here.'

Rafe tugged sheets of cling wrap off an industrial-sized roll, flipping the sandwiches and tucking the ends of the plastic under. 'Ah, here? You didn't mention you wanted it here. Specificity, Roni. No, this place is in Victoria.'

'So the commute to work would be even worse? Great. You're hilarious.'

'See, that's what I keep trying to tell Tanya. I'm thinking of doing a stand-up night at the pub, what do you reckon?'

'I reckon you'll be shouted off the stage.' She shoved the coffee machine's group handle under the grinder, murdering beans to drown out her boss. Then she relented. With a house full of kids, Tanya wouldn't be able to go along to support Rafe. 'Let me know if you want me to come and fake laugh, though.' Fervently hoping he would refuse her offer, she tempered milk to a creamy smoothness. As a familiar fragrance wafted past her, discernible even over the rich aroma of fresh coffee, she drew a decaf latté, then made eye contact with pinstripe-suit guy. His lip quirked and a five-dollar note slid across the counter.

She didn't bother to accidentally touch his hand.

Greg had been the final lesson, a refresher course her life should have made unnecessary. No man could be trusted. Her and Scritches. And the baby. That's how it would be from now on. And that would be just fine.

Chapter Four

Roni hid one of her scuffed shoes behind her calf and sank deeper into the chair, aware of the odour of deep fryer clinging to her hair and clothes. Not that Derek Prescott had let on. He'd stood as she was ushered into the office, stretching over a gleaming wooden desk to shake her hand and urge her to take a seat.

Had she known she would end up here she could have brought a change of clothes.

Except she wouldn't have. She never needed to pretend anything.

Not since she'd grown up, anyway.

Having requested coffee from the secretary seated in his outer office, Prescott was absorbed in sorting through a sheaf of papers he had retrieved from a leather folder. He shuffled them and tapped the base against the desk, a physical reprimand for daring to slide out of place. 'Now, Ms Gates, I must say, this is a rather unusual case.'

'Case?' He was an actual solicitor, the law-practising variety, the kind that sued people? She surreptitiously wiped her palms on her thighs.

'Yes. Ms Nelson has been a lifelong client. Not only am I much saddened by her passing, but the manner of her bequest will make for some unusual trials.'

'Bequest?' She sounded like a parrot. But he'd said the *trial* word. Surely not in the right context? Or at least, not in the scary context? She tucked her hands under her thighs. 'Mr Prescott, I have no idea why I'm here. I tried to explain that you have the wrong person, but you're convinced otherwise. I don't know any Mary Nelson.'

'Marian,' the solicitor corrected. 'Marian Nelson. Yes, I do realise you are unaware of the tale attached to your inheritance—'

'Inheritance?'

He ignored her interruption. 'Which is no doubt going to make the explanation more difficult. Veronica—may I call you that?'

'Roni,' she replied mechanically. How could she have an inheritance? Unless—the breath caught in her throat. 'Mr Prescott, was Mary—Marian Nelson my mother?' The words tripped over each other as she connected the dots. When she'd been far younger, still compelled to find family, she'd searched for her birth parents. But with her father not listed on her birth certificate she had only her mother's name to go on. And, apparently, Sierra Octavia Simmondsen had never existed, at least not in Australia. Which indicated her mother deliberately hid from her.

Yet . . . an inheritance meant her mother was now revealing herself.

She linked her fingers in her lap, squeezing to stop their excited fluttering. Not at the thought of an inheritance but at the realisation that her mother was belatedly acknowledging and claiming her.

'No.'

Her hands fell limp like dead birds.

'No, Ms Nelson was not your mother. Well, actually, Ms Nelson *is* your mother. But not Ms Marian Nelson. Following my client's death, I am directed to divulge that her sister, Ms Denise Nelson, is your mother. Marian is—was, I mean, do forgive me—your aunt.'

'But . . . Sierra Simmondsen?'

'Ah,' Prescott tapped a fountain pen on the desk. 'Yes, Sierra. It seems that, given enough money, it is not impossible to fabricate an identity in Australia.'

Roni stared at her reflection in the polished wood of the desk as she tried to digest the information. 'Sierra and . . . Denise. They are the same person?'

'Indeed,' Prescott replied sparely, seeming to give her time to process.

'Wait,' she said, jerking upright. 'My mother is alive?'

Mr Prescott heaved a sigh that seemed out of all proportion to her question. He turned the silver pen end over end between his fingers, then looked up as the secretary re-entered. 'Ah, coffee. Excellent, thank you, Robin. Sugar, Ms Gates?'

'No, thank you.' She crossed her arms.

The solicitor stirred his cup and darted a glance at her from beneath bushy eyebrows. Heaved another sigh. Clearly he hoped she would politely let the subject drop.

Prescott tapped his teaspoon three times on the side of his china mug and then laid it on the tray alongside a tiny sugar bowl. Went for a trifecta with the heavy sighs. 'Yes, Ms Gates.' Evidently, he didn't like Roni. 'Your mother is alive.'

'And she wants to see me?' She edged forward on her seat. Even asking the question seemed a betrayal of everything she'd told herself, of her determination not to be needy. A revelation of the desire she'd fought so hard for so many years to subjugate, telling herself that it didn't matter if she was unwanted because she didn't want her parents anyway. But now she needed to know.

'Ah.' He straightened his perfect tie. 'I don't act for Denise Nelson, so I cannot speak on her behalf.' His frown made his reluctance seem somewhat deeper set than a simple lack of authority. 'I'm only authorised to speak with you regarding your aunt's bequest. As you may have deduced from our conversation this morning, she retained a lifelong interest in your welfare. Although constraints were in place preventing her from contacting you, Ms Nelson arranged for small conveniences, such as the driving lessons and the scholarship.'

'The scholarship was real?' Her words came out low, a mournful acknowledgment of lost opportunity.

'Most certainly. Your aunt hoped you would seize the chance to make something of yourself.'

She glared at the solicitor's impassive face. 'I'm doing just fine. I don't need handouts.' Even though no way would she ever have been able to afford her driver's licence without 'winning' the lessons.

Prescott made little patting motions in the air to calm her. 'I do appreciate that, Veronica. As did your aunt. In fact, she took a fair measure of pride in how you've managed over the years. It was the final factor in deciding her bequest.'

The excitement darting through her helped push down the surge of disappointment at finding her mother must know her whereabouts but hadn't sought contact. Years of allowing false hope—before she'd learned better—meant she was practised in focusing on the positive; so what exactly was the bequest? If she had to be called in to a flash office, could it be enough to pay the bond on a new place? Perhaps even a few weeks' rent? She knew that it would be gauche to ask, though. Not to mention needy. She firmed her chin and her mental resolve: if some unknown woman left her a token she would accept it, but she sure as hell didn't *need* it.

Prescott pulled a page from the sheaf of papers. 'Subject to a number of conditions, this property now falls to you, Ms Gates.' He slid an A4 photograph across the desk.

A house.

A bloody house.

No, she couldn't allow such a ridiculous notion. Prescott meant she had inherited the potted plants that stood sentinel either side of the front door in the shade of a bull-nosed verandah running the length of the stone building.

Two windows, evenly spaced on either side of the front door, created a face, the broad steps up to the porch a smiling mouth. Laughing at her wild imagination.

She stared at the photo, searching for a clue. Perhaps the solicitor was testing her greed? Or maybe he meant the wrought-iron outdoor setting was hers? Placed to the right of the door, between the plant pot and an eight-paned window, it looked sturdy. Floral cushions softened the seats of two white lacework chairs and the round table held a single teacup and a vase of drooping, heavy-headed roses.

Roni drew back, crossing her legs and picking at black fraying denim on her knee, trying to feign nonchalance. But her mind whirled. Why show her a photo instead of simply handing over the inheritance? The furniture or plants could have been—surely would have been—sent to her.

So that left the house. Except it couldn't be.

Could it?

As though reading her mind, Prescott nodded. 'The house is old. Over one hundred and thirty years, I believe. But solid. Four bedrooms, although, unfortunately, there is only one bathroom.'

'One bathroom?' She wasn't questioning the number, but trying to buy time while whatever had just exploded inside her head settled down.

'I'm afraid so.'

'But it's a house. My aunt left me a house?' Incredulity forced her voice up to a squeak.

'Oh, no, Veronica.'

No, of course not. She stared at the photo, trying to will the flush of embarrassment to stay beneath her shirt, not to crawl up into her cheeks. What she would give for a hole in the expensively carpeted floor right now.

Prescott tapped the photo. 'Not a house, Veronica. As I said, a *property*.'

Semantics. He could call it whatever he liked as long as he actually meant that this beautiful building was hers. 'Okay, so the house is a property. But you're sure this woman—my aunt—left it to me?'

'No, no, the house isn't a property. The house is *included* with the property. Along with a number of stone outbuildings. Barns and sheds, mostly, I believe. And a smaller cottage.'

The blood thundered in her ears so hard she could barely hear his next words. Which didn't much matter, because they were far beyond her comprehension.

'Set on eight hundred acres.'

Acres. She had no concept of how much an acre was but it was certainly larger than a Sydney backyard. And apparently she now had eight hundred of them. And a mother. She lifted her cup with extreme care and gulped the coffee, scalding her tongue.

Her gaze returned to the photograph. 'This was my aunt's home?'

Prescott steepled his fingers as he looked down at the picture, his voice soft. 'For her entire life.'

'So my mother also lived there?'

37

'I believe that is the case.'

'But she doesn't live there now?' She coughed, trying to cover the sudden note of begging in her voice. Why did it matter where her mother, the woman who'd surrendered her, lived?

'My understanding is that she lives in the district.'

'Then why would my aunt leave the property to me?'

'That's really not my place to say. But she has left you a letter.'

Why did it strike her as odd to receive a letter from someone she had never known existed when she had just been given a house by that same person? Correction, a *property*. 'You said there are conditions attached to the inheritance? Is that . . . normal?'

The solicitor made an odd gurgling noise, which may have been a chuckle. 'Very little about your aunt could have been considered normal. She was a truly remarkable woman.' He turned to his file, flipping pages, and then withdrew an envelope. 'The condition listed here is that you view the property. Not too onerous a task, I would think.' His magnified eyes caught the overhead light as he looked over the top of his wire-framed glasses.

Check out the miracle that would solve all her problems in an instant? 'No, of course it isn't.' The smile twitching the solicitor's thin lips brought her to the edge of her chair. 'Wait—where is this property?'

'Ah, well, that is one of the interesting factors. It's on the edge of the wheat belt in South Australia. Reasonably marginal farming land, I believe, large properties for mediocre return. Though I have the documentation of the yields, I can't pretend the information means much to me. However, Matthew Krueger will be able to assist you with that.'

'Hang on.' Roni half rose, curling one leg on the seat beneath her. 'Wait up. South Australia? But I can't go there—it's two thousand kilometres or something ridiculous, right?' Well out of both her comfort zone and her financial means. 'My job is here. My life is here. And who is Matthew Krueger?'

The solicitor waved the envelope. 'Your aunt left a sum of money, which I am to disburse. She stipulated it was to be used for fares to South Australia and expenses for an extended stay. And Mr Krueger is the farmer who maintains your aunt's property. Well, your property, if all the requirements are met.'

Rafe had set her up. She glanced around for a hidden camera, her gaze sweeping the gleaming black bookcase behind the solicitor's plush leather chair, the framed certificates and hand-blown glass ornaments, artfully spaced, one to each shelf. The ceiling-to-floor window looked across the city to the Opera House, beyond which an airliner skimmed the blue horizon like a child's toy.

Rafe couldn't afford this prank.

So, both her aunt and the solicitor were barking. No way would she give up her apartment, her job, pretty much everything she knew, to trust her existence to an undisclosed sum of money from an unknown person. She hadn't worked so damned hard to take control of her life only to give it up now. 'This is ridiculous.' Her cup screeched across the desk and she made to rise.

Stopped.

Damn. How the hell could she take a stand when she was ankle-deep in quicksand? Single, pregnant and practically homeless, in truth only her minimum-wage job tied her to Sydney. That and a need to remain within her comfort zone. Everything about Sydney was familiar. The sights, the sounds, the smells, the people. The dichotomy of overt consumerism and poverty, the well-heeled and beggars sharing the same streets, the ugliness of the back alleys and beauty of the harbour. That familiarity promised a degree of safety. Yet she was trapped by circumstance and income, forced to consider the solicitor's mad proposal.

That her unknown aunt could so easily control her through the promise of money was infuriating and humiliating, but she couldn't afford pride. Greg was gone, her apartment would soon be gone and, once Rafe heard about the baby, her job would go too. If her aunt wanted to fund her while she arranged to sell the property, she was in no position to argue. Her eyes were now glued to the envelope in the solicitor's hand. It was inconceivable the little packet held enough money to pry her from the security of her routine. To change her life.

It didn't.

Prescott took a silver letter opener from his drawer and slit the package, pouring the contents onto the desk. Several sets of keys on various fobs; a copper initial M, an estate agent's promotional plastic tag, a Toyota key ring. And another envelope, her name written across it in spiky yet elegant lettering.

Prescott pushed it toward her. 'So, Veronica, would you like me to book your airline tickets?'

Chapter Five

Dear Veronica,

I owe you an apology for the manner of our meeting, although I must point out you have the best of the deal; if you're reading this, you're alive and I'm dead.

I can't imagine what it's like to receive a letter from someone who's dead, but there you have it. In fact, I'm not certain even which tense I should use to construct this missive. Do I write in the present, as though I'm speaking with you, or do I adopt a sonorous voice full of wisdom from beyond the grave? Seems there is no instruction manual for this.

Anyway, to our meeting—or lack thereof. Due to circumstances I could not control—and you have no idea how much admitting that such a thing can happen irritates me!—I was unable to be a part of your life while I was alive. I shall endeavour to explain why such circumspection was necessary, although before I do so, I must try to yet again persuade myself it was the right course.

Had I been allowed contact I would have wished to guide you, perhaps provide an additional perspective you might have been missing. In fact, as Derek Prescott, my solicitor and lifelong friend, has no doubt by now explained, I made tiny overtures into your life where I thought I could safely do so without breaching promises I had made. It seems I was never discovered, either by you or by those who forced me to keep the secret. Yet even now, safely dead, if there is such a thing, I'm uncertain how much of the story is mine to tell.

Perhaps I shall invoke the unfairness of my premature passage as my right to share with you what I wish. My disclosure can be the final grand tantrum of a spoilt woman accustomed to getting her way. In truth, you are one of only two things I've been forced to keep hidden in my life, and I rather fear the resentment from harbouring these secrets has broken me. Perhaps now I shall shatter the trust because, though I know it cowardly, the repercussions can no longer affect me. Whether I go up or down, this is one journey on which my sister will not hound me.

My second apology is for the manner in which I explain the circumstances of your inheritance. I'm unsure whether this one-sided storytelling makes the recitation easier, or if I would have welcomed questions to prompt me. However, I did discover long ago that a cup of tea and a lamington ease every disclosure—although the cake tends to have an adverse effect on closure when it comes to one's clothing!

As Derek will eventually inform you of the legalities and financial convolutions, I shall endeavour to supply the hard facts. Except hard is precisely what they are. Hard to relay, even this long after the event.

See, I ramble like an old woman, yet I'm not. I only recently turned sixty-nine, but the doctors threaten I'll be fortunate to see seventy, a possibility that leaves me melancholy as I sit on the verandah, gazing out across this land that I so love. With the bees searching through the lavender bushes and the heads on the roses so full they droop with soporific beauty, it hurts to look beyond at the gum trees bordering the home paddock, wondering if I'll see the delicate pink-and-red ballerina tutus of their spring flowering one more time. It saddens me to imagine that perhaps the lamb in the wooden crate at my feet, his chin damp with dribbled milk, the tip of his tiny pink tongue twitching as though he suckles in his sleep, may be the last one I will ever bottle-raise.

Perhaps I'll survive spring, hazed by the fluffy yellow balls of wattle pollen, and live until summer to smell the air heavy with sweet hay and wild honey. Or, at the most extreme end of my wishes, dare I hope to once more witness the magnificent forty-year flood? The floods actually occur every three-or-so years now, so surely that's not such a big ask? Maybe there is something in

44

all this talk of climate change, though it now seems I shall never find out.

Despite knowing me better than most, even Derek was bemused by my desire to stay on the land after I was diagnosed and advised by doctors to move to the city to seek regular treatment. Treatment for what, I asked? Once cancer has slithered her evil black tentacles into your spirit, twisting and winding through your vital organs, life can be measured in minutes. More for some, less for others. But minutes, nonetheless. So I choose to enjoy those minutes where I feel at peace, instead of being made miserable by chasing extra time that would only be squandered wishing I were at home.

Anyway, I digress and still I've not started on your story. Yes, I'm procrastinating, reluctant to recall the events that led to your birth. But that is foolish, as it is neither your birth nor even your conception that I regret. My remorse is for the manner in which I behaved both before and after the event.

Regardless, I'm going to pause for a moment and brew a cup of tea. Liberate another of the lamingtons Tracey brings me by the dozen each week. That's the sole benefit to this god-awful disease, but one no one likes to mention, as though we can't admit there's actually an upside; there's no longer any point in counting calories, is there? Wonderful as that is, it does make me question the decades of denial, the abstinence that took so many forms. And to what end? Our human commonality, it seems, is that we all must die, regardless of how we have lived our lives.

I'm back. I did consider bringing two lamingtons and pretending one was for you. But though I would happily eat both, Tracey won't bring more until after the CWA meeting on Friday. Rationed! How harsh can this life be?

I have wolfed my cake, licked my fingers clean, and now must put my feet up on the wooden box where the lamb sleeps, or the bull ants will make off with my toes, along with the desiccated coconut they're foraging from the floor.

The lamb's name, by the way, is Goat. I know, graziers should never name their animals. I drive Matt, the sharefarmer, quite mad. Each time I rescue one of the orphaned lambs, I insist he keep it separate from the flock, to be used for wool only, and never mixed with the animals that must be sent to the abattoir or butchered for our own use. Matt keeps telling me that if I live much longer we'll be imbalanced, producing too much wool and not enough meat.

All right, onward. Doubtless it will be an understatement to say you must be wondering why I chose to leave my estate to you.

My parents had only two daughters; in fact, for twenty-three years, they had only one. Then Denise, your mother, came along. Our mother liked to refer to her as a miracle, though that was probably because she didn't care to admit she still had relations with Dad at a quite unseemly age.

I prefer to think of Denise as an accident.

My father—well, no one would ever know what he thought, unless it were about stock or crops. A man of few words, he could nevertheless share his intent with the steeliest of grey glares you could ever fear to witness.

I admit I was glad he had little time for Denise. She was useless to him; a snotty, squalling baby, then a whiny child underfoot. Undeniably a girl, afraid of getting her hands—or feet—dirty, she would rarely be in the farmyard. It would paint a nice picture to say she spent her time with Mum instead, but if I am to be honest—which I have learned, somewhat belatedly, to be the best policy—once she hit fourteen she spent her time chasing anything in trousers.

I, on the other hand, delighted in helping Dad. It suited both my deep love for the property and my avoidance of anything that hinted at that dreaded horizontal tango. Yes, I mean sex. You no doubt use the word comfortably, but I prefer the euphemism—particularly fitting, as I also refused to dance.

With no sons, Dad made it clear, in his largely nonverbal fashion, that he needed someone to run the farm. It has been in our family for one hundred and fifty years and he didn't intend to see the property change hands, much less have the owners' name changed. He settled on leaving the farm to me, to pass to my children, providing I kept the family name.

So eventually, at thirty-seven, and after years of delaying, I accepted a proposal of marriage. Not that I'd been waiting to be swept off my feet by some grand passion, but rather I was hiding from the fear that perhaps I could never love a man. In that regard, I was correct; I could never love a man, not as a husband, though I have many male friends. However, I foolishly believed that by marrying I would learn to fit with a man as a woman should.

I didn't.

But I needed to secure the farm, and Andrew was happy to have a wife who was—barely—young enough to bear children, and who brought money, land and, almost as importantly, a pair of willing hands to work the properties. It has become increasingly difficult to source farm labour as the young men move to the city in search of an easier lifestyle, with an income unaffected by the caprices of our climate. This is why Matt Krueger has become invaluable to me over the years.

Obviously, there were certain problems inherent in my father's stipulation that I should provide the next generation of Nelsons, but it was hardly something I could discuss with him. Despite more than two thousand years of rumours of immaculate conceptions and virgin births, I was wise enough to realise they would be unlikely to apply to me. I would never conceive a child of my own. But I was desperate to continue the heritage of the property, to retain the bloodline that ties the Nelson family to this land.

This is where you enter the story. But although I had planned to share all the family secrets in this letter, I think perhaps that will burden you with too much information, so those details can wait until a later conversation. Instead, we'll skip to the present. Your present, given that I am now the past.

The problem is, although I like to pretend to know you, I don't. Are you someone who will appreciate the gift of this property I have so loved, or will you see it only for the financial benefit it can bring? I realise this shouldn't matter to me, because I will be feeding the worms by the time you inherit. Actually, I'm not sure that's right. How long does it take for insects to crawl into a coffin? Or do they wait for it to decay? Morbid thought.

Anyway, before this inheritance can proceed, I need to know if you have any love for the property. Derek has been directed to provide you fare to travel to Peppertree Crossing. I wish you a safe journey.

Your aunt,

Marian

Chapter Six

The plane lurched in what Roni assumed was a pocket of turbulence. She could only hope that the sedatives that had made Scritches weave around his pet carrier like a drunk meant he wouldn't feel the bumps in the bowels of the aircraft.

The slight crinkle of paper as she squeezed the pocket of her cotton jacket was reassuring. She had reread Marian's letter countless times over the last week, trying to make sense of it. Although the woman's deep affection for the property came through in her writing, Roni kept returning to the same question: why did it matter whether she also loved it? As Marian suspected, she would sell it as quickly as possible to return to Sydney and continue her life.

Such as it was. Rafe said he would hold her job for a while—obviously he also liked familiarity. But she hadn't yet told him about her pregnancy.

Greg had been sorted with a text message, telling him to pick up his Xbox and TV. Of course, getting his physical possessions out of her life didn't truly terminate her involvement with him; at some stage, she would have to let him know about the baby. But she had months to worry about how to do that. With a call to the power company to arrange disconnection, another to the estate agent to let them know the keys would be locked inside the flat, and a stack of books piled near the front door, ready to haul back to the library an armful at a time over the course of the week, her life in Sydney had been erased. Proving she'd never been of any importance.

The plane lurched again and she gasped, gripping the arm rest. The woman alongside patted her hand. 'First time up?'

She nodded, her mouth suddenly dry. Taking off had been bad enough. She wasn't looking forward to landing, but at least the ground was safe and familiar.

'Get yourself a glass of wine,' the woman advised. 'That always does the trick for me. Had a couple before we even took off.'

Great, one of the few times she would actually like a drink, and she couldn't. Wouldn't. Her baby would have every advantage she could provide. The letter had fuelled a dream, a hope that she would be able to provide a future for the baby and for Scritches.

That wasn't the only dream it had awoken, though; the knowledge that she was flying toward her mother was unavoidable, even though she tried not to dwell on it. She drummed her fingertips on her faded jeans, thinking. The letter was bizarre, not only in terms of her unexpected inheritance but Marian's preoccupation with secrets and promises. Roni could only assume that her mother, Denise, had been a teenager when she fell pregnant. Possibly, given Marian's cloak-and-dagger routine, she had also been unmarried. But surely, less than three decades ago, being a single mother hadn't carried much more of a stigma than it did now? A frown creased her forehead and she stroked her belly.

'Queasy?' her companion said with a nod at her hand. 'Here's the trolley now.' She dragged on the headrest of the seat in front to heft herself up so she could catch the cabin crew member's attention. 'Two chardies, please.'

'Oh, not for me. Thanks, though.' Roni glanced up at the flight attendant. 'Do you have the time?' She wasn't game to turn on her phone, even in flight mode. She wasn't going to be responsible for making the plane go down.

'Certainly.' The attendant glanced at her wrist. 'It's two fifty-nine. We've crossed onto Central time, now.' She nodded at the other passenger. 'I'll be back with your chardonnay in a moment, ma'am. Final service for this flight as we'll commence our descent shortly.'

The woman alongside tilted her chin at the envelope Roni tugged from her pocket. 'You made that appear like a magician.'

Right now, that magician had stage fright.

After driving her to the airport—although she wasn't sure whether it was because he suspected she wouldn't go, or to be courteous—Derek Prescott had escorted Roni through the check-in procedure. As her flight was called and he ushered her toward an attendant standing near a ramp, he handed her an envelope. 'Some reading material for the flight,' he'd said. 'I've arranged for a driver to collect you in Adelaide, so you won't need to concern yourself with that end of the journey.'

Now Roni gnawed at her lip, staring at the envelope. She was running out of time to open it, but what if it changed everything? What if it proved the whole thing was a mistake, that Marian had her confused with someone else? She'd been stupid to allow herself to dream, to imagine, even for a few days, that maybe somebody actually cared about her existence.

Like ripping off a bandaid, she tore open the envelope.

My dear Veronica,

If all has gone to plan—and I refuse to countenance that it may not have—you are now on your way to my beloved Peppertree Crossing.

Which means it is time for me to lift my pen and continue your story, before others greedily embellish the fragments they know of secrets that have been kept for decades.

Barely two years after I married, your mother, who was then sixteen, confided in me. She was pregnant. And she wanted to abort you.

I shall try to keep this part of the story to the barest facts because, even now, the retelling causes me pain.

The less I share about your mother, the better. You will form your own opinions, and I would hate to taint them.

No, that's not at all true; I would love to tell you exactly what I think of Denise, of how our relationship degenerated from an early sibling rivalry when she decided that I'd already had my turn at commanding our parents' love and attention. Of how she was jealous of the place I'd earned in our father's heart, and set out to alienate me from our mother. Of how she was determined from a very young age that anything I had should rightfully be hers. But if this letter is intended to be a grand gesture of my 'last words', I should probably maintain some sort of noble decorum. Take the high road, whatever that really means.

Anyway, for all that she was a tramp—there, already I've broken my vow not to malign her—Denise was remarkably unworldly. I told her I would arrange an abortion and she had only to hide the pregnancy until then.

Yet I had instantly, as though guided by something beyond myself, devised a plan, a scheme that would keep the property within my family, the genetics as close to mine as would ever be possible.

Over the months, I secretly wore padding under my clothes, steadily adding to the layers so my belly matched Denise's, and we could both blame the slight weight gain on Mum feeding us too well. Of course, I was paving the way to claim you as my own child, although I did not tell Denise this. At that stage, there was no need for anyone but Andrew and me to know the truth. Denise would ultimately have no choice but to agree with my plan.

Eventually, I took her to the city, ostensibly to have a doctor perform the abortion. When he told her she was too far along for the procedure to be safe, I feigned shock and sympathy. Ever the supportive sister, I told Denise she needn't worry; I would take the baby as my own, and nobody would ever know it was hers.

I returned to tell our parents that Denise had found work in the city and I had arranged for her to stay with one of my close friends. Conveniently, where she would be safely sequestered from the insatiable curiosity of our neighbours.

I don't think Dad ever noticed she'd left, and Mum was thrilled at the opportunity to brag about her daughter's big city job.

With much joy, Andrew and I immediately announced our 'pregnancy'. When Denise was due, we would contrive to be in the city, and would then proudly bring home our 'slightly premature' baby.

As you see, my plan was perfect.

Except I had miscalculated the depth of Denise's animosity toward me. It seems her wits were somewhat sharper than I had anticipated and she was, perhaps, suspicious of my part in delivering her to the clinic too late. Of course, her dislike ran far deeper, for reasons I have not yet decided whether to divulge.

Four months before you were born, we lost our parents—your grandparents—I imagine it feels odd to suddenly have these layers of family? Again, I'm sorry for my part in that. Anyway, your grandparents were killed in a road accident. You will find newspaper cuttings in the office drawer, if you have any interest in the gory details. It was a long time ago, and not something I need dwell on.

Even with them gone, we couldn't admit to Denise's pregnancy. Me, because I would then be unable to go through with the pretence of the child being my own. And Denise because—well, put crudely, what man would ever marry the town bike? We also needed to keep the secret because Denise was underage according to South Australian law, so your father would have been criminally liable.

This is where the story becomes even more tangled, if that were possible. Denise disappeared. A month after you were due, she returned to the farm. Alone.

I removed the padding from beneath my clothes and pretended to be a bereaved mother. A horrible thing to do, stealing a tragedy too many women experience, to support my lies. But the tears weren't hard to come by, all my dreams dashed by—well, being human, I want to say by Denise's selfishness, but in truth, it was all my own fault, wasn't it?

Saddened by these memories of my own foolishness, I will end this letter and allow you to digest the information.

With apologies,

Marian

Roni's chest pounded, though she didn't know whether from shock or due to the plane's steep descent. Or from the odd feeling of elation that swept through her.

She'd been right: her mother hadn't wanted her. But her aunt had. Covering sheet after sheet of lined paper, the spidery longhand script bore testament to that fact, acknowledging the lengths to which her aunt had been prepared to go to claim her.

She blew a pent breath between pursed lips, then smiled distractedly as the woman alongside patted at her hand, evidently trying to reassure her as the tyres touched down on the runway in a screeching welter of melting rubber.

As the plane shuddered toward the gate, Roni faced the thoughts she had pushed aside since she first sat in the expansive confines of Derek Prescott's office. Was the real reason she had agreed to come not because of the cash inducement her aunt offered but because the possibility that someone had actually cared about her had unleashed the dream she had never allowed?

Maybe, now that she had a name and a history, she had a family.

Despite Marian's vitriol, Roni understood her mother. Being near thirty and pregnant was daunting; at sixteen, her mother would have been terrified. She'd been manipulated and used, and surrendering her baby must have seemed for the best. That didn't necessarily mean she wouldn't want to know Roni now, though.

As she followed the other passengers up the ramp to the arrivals lounge, glad to have her feet on solid ground once more, a suited man leaned over the glass barrier, her name written bold in black marker across the board held to his chest.

Relief lengthened her stride. 'Hi, I'm Roni. That is, Veronica.' She gestured at his placard. 'That one. I just have to find my bags. Can you wait?'

'Jim Smithton,' the driver said. 'No need to find your items, Ms Gates. Collection is part of the service. If you'd like to make your way to that cafe,' he indicated an area across the concourse, 'I'll take care of the luggage and then show you to the vehicle.'

Distrust prickled through her. Would this guy run off with her bags? Unlikely. With Scritches? Even less likely. 'If you could get my cases, that'd be great. I'll find out where the animals are unloaded. Meet you back here?'

Jim lowered the sign. 'Ms Nelson-Smythe always waited in the cafe while I took care of the luggage. Said their tea was almost acceptable. Actually, if I recall right, she said it was "dishwater with an interesting twist", but I reckon the fact she regularly drank there proves it's okay.'

Roni had taken several steps toward the escalator but spun around. 'Nelson-Smythe? Do you mean Marian Nelson? You knew her?'

'Sure.' Jim gestured at the insignia on his jacket, though it meant nothing to her. 'I've driven her for years. Only in the city, though. She wasn't keen on traffic, said it reminded her of a bull-ant nest filled with kerosene. I've done the airport run every few months for the last'—he squinted up at the arrivals sign as though that held the figure he sought— 'twenty-odd years. Plus Christmas shopping trips and the Adelaide Cup. The Royal Adelaide Show.'

'You're her chauffeur?'

Jim must have read the incredulity on her face because he held up one hand, spatulate fingers spread open. 'Oh, I didn't drive only for her. It was a shared arrangement.'

Roni sagged in relief. Her sneakers-and-ripped-Kmart-jeans ensemble seemed a little less likely to define her as the impoverished relative. 'Ah, okay. Like a regular-cab kind of thing.'

'Not exactly.' Jim ushered her toward the cafe and gestured at a corner table. 'I drive exclusively for the Nelsons and the Smythes, but it works on a booking system between the family members. Ms Marian was always particular about reserving me well ahead.'

Roni sank in an untidy heap on the chair Jim pulled out. The airline magazine slid from her nerveless hand and slithered across the floor.

Jim retrieved it. 'What would you like to drink?'

'Cappuccino,' she mumbled through lips thinner than year-old insoles.

He didn't disappear long enough for her to catch her scattered thoughts. 'Coffee will be here in a moment. Now,' he pulled a leather-bound notebook from a pocket inside his dark jacket. 'Mr Prescott said four suitcases and one pet carrier, containing a cat, name of Scritches. Right? Great name.'

She nodded. 'Yes. That's all.' Oh. God. Her op-shop suitcases. Prescott said there were funds for her to purchase luggage, or even to move all of her belongings interstate, but she hadn't wanted to tell him that, because her apartment came furnished, all she possessed were her clothes and Scritches. Nope, scratch that last one. Scritches definitely owned her.

The coffee came and she stirred it distractedly, testing the crema on the back of her spoon. Jim drove for 'the family'. She shook her head, blowing out a tense breath. The concept was weird. Surreal. There were people out there who were related to her, who had the same blood flowing through their veins. She glanced around the concourse, as though one of those 'people' would leap forth and identify themselves.

She snorted at her fancifulness and snatched up her phone. She'd burned through her data plan stalking social media, searching both Denise and Marian Nelson, infuriatingly common names that gave her precisely no useful information. But would a farmer's wife with a driver and a double-barrelled surname bring up more results?

She keyed *Marian Nelson-Smythe* into the search engine, then fumbled her phone as links immediately flashed onto her screen. Three pages of results.

Philanthropist.

Supporter of the arts.

Doyen of the South Australian horseracing community.

Board member of the Rural Health Alliance.

Board member of the Rural Women's Coalition.

Roni gulped the coffee like caffeine would be an antidote for the nervous fizz in her chest. Her aunt had not been some countrified nobody. Maybe that went some way to explaining the secrecy surrounding Denise's pregnancy?

Before she had worked through the first page of results, Jim Smithton returned, pushing a trolley that held her bags and a yowling pet carrier. She pressed her hand against the mesh. The sedative had worn off, and the distraught cat was less than impressed with his treatment. 'Shush, Scritch, that's enough now.'

As other travellers glanced their way she stood, addressing Jim. 'I guess we'd better get out of here. Unless you want a drink?' Should she suggest that to an employee? Her hand tightened on her wallet. Maybe her family were some kind of nobs, but she was no one special, and Jim didn't work for her. 'Let me get you a drink, Jim.'

Fingertips rasping invisible stubble, Jim scratched his cheek. 'I, uh—well, thanks, that'd be nice. It's something of a drive, why don't you get a couple of takeaways?'

'Sure thing.' She shot him a smile. 'Maybe you can fill me in on some details while we travel.'

It would need to be a long trip.

Chapter Seven

Despite Scritches' constant serenade, Jim proved a loquacious travelling companion, his demeanour unbuttoning along with the tie he asked permission to loosen. However, after ninety minutes Roni realised she'd learned little about her family other than that Jim, like Derek Prescott, seemed somewhat smitten with her aunt. She did discover a lot about Jim's useless, underemployed sons, saintly wife and two ex-racing greyhounds, though she remained confused as to whether Ella was his wife or a dog. She also found that, with little demand from either the Nelsons or the Smythes for his chauffeuring service, he had a side job driving the community minibus for the district council, ferrying the elderly on shopping trips and to appointments.

Jim lifted a finger from the steering wheel, indicating the road ahead. 'Okay, from the corner here, all the land on the right side is Ms Marian's.'

Roni had refused to take the rear seat in the Land Rover he'd led her to outside the airport. The leather upholstery creaked as she leaned to gaze across him, though she could have looked out of her own window and been treated to the same view. Acres—she assumed—of undulating hills, covered in knee-high lime-coloured grass. The dusty road was bordered by low, sparse trees, the bushfire-blackened trunks stark against bursts of new leaves. Red blooms flared on the occasional eucalypt, and magpies patrolled the verges in gangs, swivelling with bold interest to watch the car.

'You had a fire through here last summer?' she asked.

Jim shook his head. 'Nope. This burned out three years ago. Takes a while to regenerate around here. Hold your breath.' He leaned forward to flick the vent, cutting the flow of air from outside. 'Always a lot of dead 'roos in spring.'

She pinched her nose, trying not to look as they passed a lump of grey fur. Road kill was something she rarely saw in Sydney, only the odd feral cat, or low-flying bird that had lost a game of dare with a car.

Jim glanced over at her. 'I feel kind of guilty.'

She arched a brow. '*You* didn't hit it.'

'Ms Marian always had me stop at any fresh road kill.'

'To clear it off the road?' Roni screwed up her face. 'That one was well clear, anyway. And "fresh" is debatable, considering the smell.'

The car slowed, pulling closer to the trees on the left side. 'To check the pouch for joeys. Thing is, I know Ms Marian's been gone a while, but would you mind if we turned back and I checked that one? It'll only take a minute.'

Roni flapped a hand, waving away the question, though she wasn't as successful with the eye-watering odour. 'Of course.' She couldn't shake the feeling Jim was doing her a favour by driving her out here, and she wasn't about to go all Miss Daisy on him.

Jim executed a three-point turn, the white dust of their passage hanging thick in the air and coating the black duco as he headed a few metres back up the dirt road. He passed the dead kangaroo, made another turn, and drew up just before it. 'May I?' He lifted his chin toward the console in front of Roni.

She nodded uncertainly.

He flipped open the console and drew out a pair of blue surgical gloves. 'Maggots,' he said in response to her unspoken question. 'They love to get in the pouch. I don't mind checking for joeys, but I only had to get maggots under my fingernails once to learn to always carry gloves. Though until the last few years, Ms Marian would jump out herself. She taught me how to detach the joey from the nipple.'

'How to do *what*?' The farther they travelled from the city, the less she understood. 'Don't you just, you know, take it out?' She mimed scooping up a furry bundle and cradling it.

'If the joey's attached, you can't go yanking it off. Their mouths are easily damaged.'

'Then how do you get it out?' She peered at the bedraggled grey mound, the only movement a swarm of blue-black blow-flies that continually lifted and resettled, like waves on a beach. Filthy, disgusting waves, as bad as Barrenjoey Beach.

Jim reached across her again, taking a box cutter from the console. He grimaced. 'Cut the nipple out. Do you want to learn how?'

She shook her head. 'Uh. No. Not this time. Thanks.' And she would make sure there was no opportunity for a next time. There was far too much . . . country . . . out here for her liking. They'd not sighted a house in forever, though the occasional driveway, marked by white-painted tractor tyres standing upright alongside openings in the miles of fences, hinted that people lived out here, somewhere. The only other signs of civilisation were the road and the power poles marching over the hills like an army of triffids linked by wires. Despite the comfortable temperature inside the vehicle, Roni shivered and hugged her elbows.

Jim climbed back in, sliding the gloves and knife into the console. 'You're right, that one was a bit ripe. A small boomer.'

'As in baby boomer?'

'Ha.' The car crunched through the gravel verge and onto the road. 'Oh, wait, you're serious?'

'Uh huh.'

'Boomer. Male kangaroo.'

'Well, that's kind of good. Isn't it?'

'Not so much from his point of view. Now this,' he slowed the car, indicated and turned right, 'is the entrance to Ms Marian's property. You'll have to hold onto your hat as we cross the cattle grid.'

The car crawled between two wooden wagon wheels, painted white to match the three-barred fence that framed the metal grid set in the dirt. Her stomach knotted as the Rover jounced over the bars. She was only moments from the house she was about to inherit. The first real thing she had ever owned.

Parallel to the road they had turned off, a shallow, dry creek bed cut through the paddock, appearing to bisect the property from one distantly invisible boundary to the next. On the edge of the creek, two ten-metre-tall trees bordered the driveway. An umbrella of branches covered with fine, pointy leaves created a shady canopy around the massive gnarled trunks, and Roni almost breathed a sigh of relief. At last, something she recognised. 'Willow trees, right?' She'd seen them in the Chinese Garden in Darling Harbour.

Jim shook his head, his jaw clenching and knuckles tightening on the wheel as the Rover bumped over a narrow crossing of tumbled boulders. 'Peppertrees. See the pink berries? That's what the farm's named for. Peppertree Crossing.'

Of course. She clutched at her armrest as Jim continued. 'Looks like the bridge is taking a beating. I guess there's no need for it to be maintained like it was before, there'll only be the farm vehicles using it now.'

'Bridge? Where I'm from, "bridge" means a kilometre of steel artwork, not a few rocks in a dried-up puddle.'

Jim changed down a gear, easing the car up the creek bank. 'Well, Ms Marian used to keep the bridge in good repair—or have it kept in good repair, I guess—so she could get into town.'

They had not passed a town for kilometres, at least thirty, she reckoned. Not unless you counted a deli sporting a faded Peters Ice Cream logo and flanked by two houses and a cluster of rusted sheds clinging to the crumbled edge of a bitumen road. 'That . . . town . . . we passed a while back, you mean?'

'Bless, you really are a city slicker, aren't you? No. Settlers Bridge is a good size. Farther east.'

'Walking distance?' She'd checked it out on the internet, but the distance shown on the maps seemed to have little relevance to the vastness of the space out here. Isolation wormed beneath Roni's skin. She'd not expected the property to be like this. Blame too much TV, but it should have been like the pictures she'd seen of American estates: a huge, white-painted house surrounded by manicured gardens expanding in a green and gold collage to mowed paddocks bordered by centuries-old deciduous trees. The neighbours' great white mansions should be discreetly secluded but safely reachable—and, most importantly, in distant view at all times.

Lifting one hand from the wheel, Jim jerked a thumb to his left. 'About twenty klicks.'

'And the closest neighbour?'

'Can't say I know offhand. Though Matt Krueger's place would be nearby, seeing as he farms the property for Ms Marian. Farmed, I mean.' Jim nodded toward the undulating paddocks. 'Though they still look like they're being cropped. Now, the house is about a kilometre up here. Long driveway, even for this area.'

'Does my—ah,' her voice pitched high and she coughed to recalibrate it. She wasn't ready to claim her relationship, and didn't even know whether she was still a secret. 'You mentioned you drive for the Nelson family. They live nearby, then?' Though Prescott had said her mother lived in the district, she had no idea what kind of area that covered out here.

Jim slowed the vehicle to navigate a series of potholes deep enough to lead to Middle Earth. 'And for the Smythes. They're over in Murray Bridge, but Ms Denise lives in Settlers. When she's around, that is.'

He knew her mother. She was an actual flesh-and-blood person. The realisation pounded at her temples. 'When she's around?'

'She travels a lot. Makes my job nice and easy.'

Roni nibbled her lips, gazing out of the dusty windshield. Was she ready to meet her mother—or whoever constituted her new family? She'd deliberately repressed any interest in them, refusing to lay herself open to rejection. But now, now they were so close . . .

'Is she away at the moment?'

'Not to my knowledge. But she doesn't always use my services.'

A sudden thought occurred to her and she hauled her bag onto her lap and dug out her phone. Derek Prescott had never actually answered her question about whether her mother knew of her inheritance. She dialled his number. Frowned. Disconnected and dialled again.

Jim glanced at her as he guided the car around a sweeping bend, the left side of the driveway lined with vast stone buildings, the right open to rolling paddocks that climbed lazily to the skyline. He slowed the vehicle to a crawl across a second cattle grid. 'No signal? My service hits a dead zone out here. Ms Marian had a landline, but I'm not sure if it's still connected.'

Roni pushed the heel of her hand against her forehead, forcing back the headache as she stared at her screen. Okay. She didn't need Derek Prescott. In any case, with Sydney a half-hour ahead, it was after business hours. In her normal life she would have locked up the takeaway shop and been on the train, heading home to spend the weekend with Scritches. Sleep in on Saturday, followed by a trip to the laundromat. The afternoon spent with a book. Housework on Sunday, and more reading.

A wave of nostalgia for the familiar, the mundane and safe jagged through her chest. Resolutely, she stiffened her spine. She would view the property per the terms of the will and then get the place on the market. Then she could get back to civilisation, using the money her aunt had left in Prescott's trust to tide her over until the sale. 'There's wi-fi in town, though?' She would rather stalk real-estate agents on the net than approach them directly.

'Sure. I think one of the cafes even has a password they share around.'

She nodded as they passed beneath a solitary, impossibly tall date palm. 'I need to take a quick look around here.

Can you wait, and take me into town after? Drop me at a motel or something.'

'Your wish is my command.' Jim made an embellished wave, then tilted his head toward the window as they passed a screen of peppertrees, the weeping fronds brushing the red earth so that it appeared as though it had been carefully swept clean. 'Here's the homestead. No cars, so I guess you're on your own.'

The concept of aloneness was familiar, which meant she should feel relief, not the twinge of disappointment that prickled in her chest, almost like tears. Not that she would know; she had done with crying long ago. But had she secretly been hoping for a family reunion, a welcoming party so that she wouldn't be the one forced to make overtures to Denise?

If she ever decided to meet her, that was. Could she forgive her mother for never making contact? Or for the fact that she'd continued to ignore Roni's existence years after the stigma of her birth would have worn off?

Roni blinked a couple of times and focused on the homestead. As in the photograph, the long building stood proud on a gentle rise. Spread like a tablecloth before it, a vast paddock of close-mown grass sloped to the row of gums her aunt had described. In perfect symmetry, whitewashed stone sheds bordered the other two sides of the compound, reflecting the late-afternoon shades of lilac and pink.

'It's beautiful.' No. Wrong adjective. Among the fierce starkness of acres of rock and trees and hills, the man-made refuge evoked a defiant sense of security, testament to the labour and sacrifice that had gone into carving a living from the inhospitable landscape. More than beautiful: it was magnificent.

And hers now, surely? She had viewed it, admired it. What other conditions could be attached to the inheritance? As they pulled beneath the shade of a pergola, where clusters of lilac flowers hung like bunches of grapes, Roni's teeth worked around the edge of her thumb, tearing shreds of flesh when she couldn't find any nail.

Jim glanced in the rear-view mirror as Scritches mournfully announced he had woken. 'Sounds like he's eager for out. Mr Prescott directed I give you this upon arrival.' He reached again into the console.

Hopefully not for the box cutter. Despite his affability, their isolation still made Jim prime candidate for the role of serial killer.

He handed her a thick envelope, the P&K logo now familiar. The deeds for the property!

Roni tore the flap.

Not the deeds. A letter.

Dear Ms Gates,

Congratulations on completing the first of the conditions of your inheritance, and upon your safe arrival at Peppertree Crossing.

Lynn Lambert has been in to freshen the house today and stock it with provisions, as your aunt anticipates you taking up immediate residence.

Mr Krueger will call on you tomorrow.

The keys your aunt left you will unlock the house and those of the sheds that are padlocked. In one, you will find your aunt's vehicle, which is at your disposal.

Further correspondence from your aunt awaits you within the house.

Best,

Derek Prescott

It seemed her aunt was intent on ruling her every move from beyond the grave. She crushed the letter in her hand. 'Looks like I won't be needing that ride until tomorrow.'

As Jim carried her cases to the rear of the house, she freed Scritches from his cage and followed, plopping him down in the walled garden sheltering the back door.

After only one tentative scrape in the unfamiliar texture of a dirt patch, the cat stopped, paw held mid-air. Raised with lavender-scented kitty litter, it was clear that soil and prickles did not meet his expectations. 'Join the club, Scritch.' Being marooned out here waiting for some farmer to show up wasn't exactly what she'd anticipated.

She scooped Scritches up and he wriggled onto his back, sniffing the dust coating his paws. Then he gagged. His tongue hanging out, his sides heaved as he convulsed.

Jim dropped the second load of cases. 'He's having a fit! Get him back in the car, I'll run you in to the vet.'

Roni wiped a finger over the cat's lolling tongue. 'He's fine. Pulls this trick whenever he smells something bad. Loves my shoes.' Especially after a long day at work. He would dash over, sniff, retch silently and glare at her accusingly. Then stick his nose back in the shoe. 'It must be like catnip.'

'First I've heard of a cat with a substance-abuse issue.' Jim shook his head, turning a key in the solid wooden door. He stood back. 'After you, love.' It seemed the conversation during their journey now edged their relationship comfortably toward informality.

'Which way?'

'Ah, right you are. Follow me.' Jim threw open the door, turned left and guided her through what appeared to be a sunroom and into the kitchen with a confidence that spoke of familiarity. Though it wasn't yet dark, he flicked on the lights. 'Would you like me to check through the house before I head off?'

The tart, fresh fragrance of mandarins made her mouth water. A blue-and-white china bowl full of the fruit sat at the centre of a scrubbed wooden table, an envelope propped against it, the spidery handwriting instantly familiar. She reached for the envelope, glancing at Jim. 'Uh, no, that's fine, thanks.'

'I'll leave my number with you, just give me a call if you need anything. I'm only in town, so I can get out here pretty quick. As long as I'm not on a job.'

She tore her attention from the envelope, dropping Scritches onto the yellow cushion of one of the half-dozen wooden chairs around the table. 'That's great, thanks.' It was bizarre—and not altogether comfortable—to realise that a two-hour acquaintance with the driver was as close as she came to knowing anyone on this side of the country.

'Maybe don't let Scritches out of the house, he might do a runner. Butter on the paws is supposed to stop them,' Jim advised.

There was precisely zero risk of Scritches running away. He didn't like to be even a room away from her, and had already turned several circles on the cushion and settled, as though his brief experience with real dirt had exhausted him. Head lowered onto crossed paws, he kept one eye slightly open, his purr an unusually low rumble. Clearly he had yet to forgive her for the indignity of his treatment. 'Butter on the paws? So they slip, and can't run away? I don't think that'd work on dirt.'

Jim snorted, apparently taking her seriously. 'I think the idea is that they lick off the scent of their old place, so they settle more easily.'

'Maybe it's more that the butter's a treat, so the cat falls in love with the butter-er, and doesn't leave?' She moved toward the kitchen door as she spoke, trying to edge him out.

'Ah, well, as my paws have not been buttered, I'd say that's my cue,' Jim said.

As he left, Roni nudged the door into the kitchen closed, then lunged for the letter that would hand her the future.

Chapter Eight

My dear Veronica,

As we have previously spoken, I feel we can now be a little more familiar—though I suppose it is hard to be more familiar than sharing the story of your birth.

I trust you had an uneventful trip from Sydney, and that Jim Smithton is still employed by the family, and conveyed you safely to Peppertree Crossing.

Did you study Dorothea Mackellar at school? If you had attended the college I had chosen, you most certainly would have. Regardless, I'm sure you recognise her iconic poetry, particularly "My Country". She describes perfectly the contrast of endless plains and looming mountains, their stark beauty ravaged by both droughts and storms.

We have all of that right here at Peppertree Crossing—well, we do if you're willing to employ a little imagination and consider a decent-sized hill a mountain range! Did you know Dorothea wrote that poem when she was in England, homesick and, I would deduce, heartsick? I can imagine how she felt, because this land evokes such strong feelings in me, longing and love and loss, even though I'm not yet parted from it.

Tell me, what season greeted you? Are the paddocks filled with golden wheat, or do they lie exhausted and grey, waiting for the first rains of autumn? Are there tiny white lambs playing in the stubble of the fallow fields, where tips of green struggle to poke through the ground after the last frost? Is the air filled with bleating angst as the babes lose sight of their mothers for a moment, or are those lambs now fat-tailed teenagers, lying over-full in the sparse shade of the mallee scrub?

Already it seems I miss all these things, though I sit on the verandah with the view spread before me, and when I lie down to sleep, a panorama of memories keeps me company. I suppose it would be more accurate to say "when I rest", because I seldom sleep. It may be an effect of the drugs, or perhaps it's that I achieve so little now, my brain knows I've earned no respite.

I'm clearly feeling a tad maudlin, cataloguing every sight, every nuance of the life I love, as though I can create a memory that will outlast this fragile physical existence. I worry I'll even miss the things I have loathed—because, despite my attempt at waxing poetic, not everything here is beautiful. Some things I should be happy to never again witness, such as the searing heat that has me scanning the sky for signs of bush-fires, praying the north wind doesn't blow fierce and the ominous smudge on the horizon is nothing but dust. Or the droning attack of the blowflies that appear the second I start to prepare a meal that requires any-thing more fragrant than boiled water. I suggest, during summer, you wait until after dark to cook. Lord knows where the flies go, but you'll never see them after dark, or during winter—much to Andrew's disgust, because he liked to fish in the quieter months, and the lack of blowflies meant no maggots to bait his hook.

That leads me to a horrible thought—do the blow-flies migrate to warmer climes? As my imagination leaps to one particular place, reputed to be warmer, I wonder how my actions will be weighed in the balance of things, and hope that any afterlife is not a Hell of never-dormant blowflies.

Not that I'm particularly religious, but as the music box of my life begins to play erratic and fragmented, and I lack the strength to wind the key, I begin to think on What Comes After. It is inconceivable that, so imperfectly alive right now, I shall simply cease to exist. Therefore, I prefer to believe that I shall move on—but whether that place will be better, worse, or simply par-allel to this existence, who can know?

Me, soon, I suspect.

Anyway, enough of my meanderings. My mood is largely due to the sadness of knowing that as you read this you are, finally, where I have wanted you to be for almost three decades. I can't help but wonder, had I reached out sooner, would you have come while I was alive? There are so many things I wish I could have shared with you.

Of course, such rumination is pointless, because for many years I could not have contacted you. I had sworn an oath of absolute silence to protect one for whom I cared deeply. No, not Denise; any promise I made her was under duress, and in her usual narcissistic fashion she simply assumes I will be complicit in her deception.

If I'm completely honest, there did eventually come a time when I could have initiated contact, when my vow was terminated by that great leveller, time. But to what end? You had your life to lead and at that stage I had nothing to offer you, other than the convoluted tale of a dysfunctional family.

In any case, for better or for worse, those decisions are in the past, and we must move forward.

Perhaps now you're sitting in my chair on the verandah. A hint—the one with the embroidered cushion is mine. To be frank, the knots of embroidery thread in the flowers make it a little lumpy. But as my dearest friend, Tracey, stitched it for me, I always use it. She has talent in many of those areas in which I lack.

All right, if you're comfortable, let us rewind our story a tad.

You've probably noticed that when I mention Andrew I use the past tense. He died when I was fifty-nine, shortly after your nineteenth birthday. Had you met

Andrew, I'm certain you would feel his loss. I wonder, is it possible to mourn someone you never met? Perhaps so, as I grieve the absence of the niece I never knew.

Andrew and I assumed Denise placed you for adoption, and I persuaded myself that it was for the best; you would have the security of a forever-family without the tarnish of our mistakes and secrets. However, a few months after she returned, Denise revealed she had placed you in the foster-care system, under an assumed name. Apparently, to surrender you for adoption she needed your father's consent—which would, of course, reveal his identity. Knowing my concern at the impact such a revelation would have on our lives and livelihood, for years she blackmailed me; every argument and demand came with a threat to reveal your father's identity.

Of course, she could simply have claimed that she didn't know who your father was, and placed you for adoption. But the truth was, she wasn't prepared to entirely relinquish you, because that would limit her control over me—control that extended to forbidding Andrew and me to foster you.

So, Andrew and I resolved to do what little we could for you, from a distance. I'm not going to pretend I spent every moment thinking of you. How could I—indeed, why would I, when I had never known you? In all honesty, entire years would pass before I would recall that I had meant to have Derek Prescott check on your wellbeing. So, you see, I would probably have been an appalling mother and perhaps Denise was right to give you up, rather than allow me to practise my ad hoc parenting. Not that I will, for one second, pretend she did so with your best interests at heart.

I did, however, think much on my great love: this property. Denied the capacity to love a husband, all I've ever had are friends, work and my passion for this land. My father left the property to me with the stipulation I make provision for Denise who was, of course, a minor at the time of our parents' death. But who would inherit it after I passed? I had no children, and Andrew had none he could—or rather, would—claim.

He chose to leave his own property to be divided among his siblings, which would seem the logical option to any rational person. But I'm not entirely rational where Peppertree Crossing is concerned. Or perhaps I am too rational? Could I really be expected to leave my property to distant cousins, or to the sister who delighted in taunting me about my childlessness? Her intolerable needling about the fact the farm would one day leave my hands eventually determined my course of action.

Which brings us to where we are now: with you, I hope, sitting in my chair surveying this magnificent property. A property that can be yours. Ah, you notice the caution in my words? Of course, having decided not to leave the property to Denise, I should have willed it to you, and been satisfied with that as the best option.

But, as you will discover, I have become a meddlesome old lady.

Because I don't know you—the fault of which is my own—I don't know the property will fare any better in your care than it would with Denise. She would sell it in a heartbeat (assuming she possesses such an organ!), take the money and move somewhere that has no dirt, no flies, no drought, no hard work—and no soul.

So, to set my mind at ease, and much to Derek Prescott's chagrin, I have devised a way to discover whether you are, or have the capacity to become, the person I imagine you to be. Don't worry, there will be no séances or ouija boards involved. Rather, there is a task—or, actually, several tasks—I wish you to tackle in exchange for immediate transfer of the ownership of Peppertree Crossing.

Now, as Derek cautioned me—he scowled through my whole laying out of what I consider to be a rather ingenious plan—this is a highly unusual manner of bequeathing property. Therefore, I have also provided the option of a more traditional bequest.

If you choose not to attempt the tasks but stay at Peppertree Crossing, you will be entitled to a share of the income generated by the property, with a larger portion paid to Matt Krueger in compensation for his ongoing work. Further, should you take this option, the title will not transfer to your name until a probationary residential period has expired.

This period will extend to ten years and one month.

With love and, I admit, a certain amount of glee, imagining what must now be running through your head, Marian

Chapter Nine

Ten years? She'd probably get less for murder.

She wanted to be grateful for the opportunity she'd been given, but what sort of nightmare inheritance was this? An aunt with a huge estate, money, time to spend supporting this association or that club, who claimed to care—but not enough to make sure her sole heir was safe. An aunt who had left her to be abused, but wanted to play games before handing over an inheritance. An inheritance that would take ten years to claim. Ten years of being stuck in the middle of nowhere, gifted a measly income while some farmer got the bulk of the money from property she should have been free to sell?

She reread the last passages of the letter, hoping she had missed something, but there it was, blue ink on white paper. She either agreed to complete a number of unspecified tasks in return for her immediate inheritance, or she became nothing more than a lodger for the next decade.

Either way, it seemed her aunt planned for her to be stuck out here. And yet she accused Denise of being a blackmailer?

Scritches wound around her ankles and Roni lifted her gaze from the letter clutched in her hand. Evening had drawn close outside the kitchen windows while she had tried to understand the madness of a stranger who would give her a gift and simultaneously punish her. She'd thought this inheritance would solve all of her problems, but instead it had created more.

She rubbed a hand across her forehead. Dusk purpled a small garden beyond the kitchen window. Barely distinguishable shrubs obscured an uneven stone wall, beyond which the rolling fields of soft green crop had turned to seaweed darkness, floating to meet the last sliver of light on the horizon.

Darkness.

And a hell of a lot of it. Not a single pinprick of light.

The isolation trailed icy fingers down her spine. How was it possible to see so far, yet see nothing? She should have taken up Jim's offer to check the rest of the house, had him flick all the lights on so she wouldn't have to wander into darkness. She had been in such a hurry to read her aunt's letter she hadn't even thought to lock the back door behind him, though at home in the city dead-bolting had been a reflex.

She strode into the sunroom, skirting the suitcases Jim had left there, and slid the security chain into place. That she felt safer with multiple doors and locks between her and the outside world was ludicrous, given that the really bad things only ever happened to her indoors, but she bolted nonetheless.

Suppressing a shiver, she gazed through the naked windows into the impenetrable darkness of the back garden—then jerked rigid as she realised she would be spotlighted to anyone standing outside.

Scritches drowsily lifted his head as she raced back into the kitchen and slammed the door, twisting the key that protruded from an ornate lock plate. Her stomach unknotted slightly as the bolt clicked home. If there was a lock on every door, she would be fine for the one night. Tomorrow, when daylight made the unpopulated expanse slightly less terrifying, would be soon enough to explore.

Right before she left.

Because there was no way she would do even ten days of this solitary confinement, never mind ten years. Quickly completing the tasks, whatever they were, was her only option so she could immediately inherit and sell this white elephant. Marian's mad legacy perfectly explained why her mother had hated it here. Manipulated and isolated, she had fled both this property and her history. That had to be why she'd used a fake identity on the birth certificate, and never got in touch with Roni, never claimed her. Maybe Denise just wanted to forget.

She eyed the door on the far side of the kitchen, which presumably led deeper into the house. Rubbed her chilled hands together. 'Okay, Scritch. How about you stay here while I check the place out?' Her voice rang hollow.

She petted the cat until he resettled on the cushion, then she crossed to the door and cracked it open, reaching around the jamb and sliding her hand up and down in search of a switch. She should have done this while it was light, instead of stewing over the terms of the inheritance. Maybe she should call Jim, tell him to come and get her right now. Forget about this whole damn deal and get back to Sydney right away.

Where she had no home, no job, no plan. And, if she left now, no money.

In any case, her phone showed zero reception, so there would be no calling anyone until she found the landline.

Finally locating the light switch, she peered around the door. A hallway stretched to her left, multiple closed doors lining both sides.

She took a cautious step. Long leather coats and jackets hooked onto redgum slabs bolted high on the walls, with boots and shoes neatly ranked on the floorboards beneath, resembled people. Watching her watching them. Creepy as all hell.

High above, white-painted fretwork ceiling partitions sectioned the hall, the stained-glass light shades splashing a jellied mix of red, blue and green onto pale walls.

Unless she'd got herself all turned around, the door to her right should lead into the sunroom. She took five quick steps and twisted the key. Fort Knox. Excellent. That left six doors to tackle.

There was something terrifyingly Alice in Wonderland-ish about the setting, perhaps because the vast hall made her diminutive. Despite the chilling silence, she strained to hear over the refrigerator's constant churn. Where were the voices, the cars, the signs of life?

Sneakers sticking on the varnished timber, she inched across the hall. Her fingers closed around a brass doorknob, worn and dented, but burnished by use to a dull shine. The latch cracked and she reached in, groping through the velvet blanket of darkness.

Buttery yellow light splashed a slice of safety across her toes as she flipped a switch. With three walls hidden by floor-to-ceiling bookcases, the windowless room smelled . . . old. Not unpleasant, but sweet and tranquil. Books overflowed the shelves and were stacked on the floor. A huge lacquered stump, whose thick roots spread across a blue and mauve rug as though the tree grew from the floorboards, supported more books.

Roni edged around a pair of burgundy leather wingbacks. Even in the bookshops that offered buy-a-coffee-read-for-free, where she would pinch a dirty cup from a vacated table, set it before her open book and hide in plain view, there hadn't been this many hardbacks. And none of the muted leather bindings, the cracked gilt lettering on their spines catching the light from goose-necked brass reading lamps. She gazed around in disbelief. She'd stepped into another world, one where a person had both enough money and enough space to devote a room entirely to books. To pleasure.

If she stayed, she would never need to fake-buy coffee again.

Better still, once she sold this place she would be able to buy whatever books she wanted.

Leaving the light on, she backed from the room and shut the door. A Persian runner, worn flat in the centre, the colours flaring jewel-bright toward the untrodden edges, swallowed her footsteps as she crossed to the next room. An open fireplace took up much of one wall, and a wine rack, replete with dark green or almost-black bottles, another. As her gaze drifted up to the fancy-work around the top of the walls and a sculpted flower design in the centre of the high ceiling, she steadied herself with one hand on the back of a chair. The aged leather and timber furniture, made comfortable with throw cushions and rugs, showed the marks of use, yet somehow gave off an aura of wealth. It reminded her of the women she had always been jealous of, those who managed to exude an air of superiority while dressed in jeans and casual shirts.

Thick drapes hid the window and the room held a sweet, lingering perfume, as though a ghost had passed through bearing a fresh-cut bouquet. A bowl filled with faded rose petals fought for space on a spindle-legged table, and Roni ran a finger down the spines of the books stacked there, an eclectic mix with recent editions by Sandie Docker and Cathryn Hein and dog-eared tomes of *The Grass Crown* and *First Man in Rome*, both of which she'd read. Top of the pile lay Peter Luck's photographic homage to 'My Country'. An ancient rotary dial telephone sat alongside the stack, and she lifted the receiver, warily holding it to her ear and starting slightly at the loud buzz.

Again, she left the light on and closed the door.

Her heart pounding each time she grasped a doorknob, Roni was tempted to leave the remaining rooms unexplored. But then she would never sleep.

A cursory inspection revealed four bedrooms, the opposing pairs separated by a bathroom with a green-and-black speckled terrazzo floor and a claw-footed bathtub, and a storage room piled with boxes and suitcases.

At the far end of the hall, the master bedroom boasted wooden robes that could transport her to Narnia and a dresser almost as large as her kitchen back home. The eight-paned window, softly screened with ecru lace, faced . . . more darkness. Roni darted around a four-poster bed to free voluminous burgundy curtains from tasselled tiebacks and drew them along a brass rail, shutting out the night. Though the bed, piled with cushions in shades of white and cream, looked inviting, she wouldn't sleep in here. The bedroom across the hall seemed more likely intended for guests, the Baltic pine bed a fraction smaller.

Large enough to be a tabletop, the wooden door at the end of the hall between the bedrooms must lead outside, onto the verandah she had seen in the photograph. Out there would be her aunt's chair, softened by the uncomfortable cushion stitched by her friend.

Her environs catalogued, Roni strode back to the kitchen, disturbing Scritches as she bent to root through the duck-egg blue cupboards. They were well stocked, but beyond the basics of cereal, canned beans, canned tuna and canned soup, there was little she was familiar with. Especially not the dried . . . What were these things? She read the label. Lentils. The only ones she had encountered had been a stodgy brown colour, encased in the pastry of a vegetarian sausage roll, but there seemed no clear way to turn these bright orange kernels into anything edible.

She checked the fridge, which contained a wealth of vegetables she had no intention of ever trying, and nothing in the way of ready-meals. There was, however, a small, golden-crusted pie. A judicious poke at the hole in the top revealed the filling to be apricot rather than meat, which probably explained the carton of cream also perched on the sparkling clean shelf. 'Soup for dinner, Scritch, then pie as a reward for our restraint, right?'

From the top row of cupboards, native animals etched in frosted glass stared down at her. A koala. A platypus. A kangaroo. An emu. And, incongruously, a palm tree. She retrieved a bowl from the platypus and placed it on the wooden counter that ran the length of the wall beneath the cupboard.

A blue enamel wood stove took up one corner of the kitchen, but the microwave above the adjacent electric range brought a sigh of relief. Cold soup belonged to her youth, when she'd been unable to pay her utilities.

An hour later, her meal bulked out by a couple of slices of crusty bread cut from a loaf she found in a roll-top box, she carried Scritches to the bedroom and plopped him onto the bed. 'Right, that corner is all yours.' She nudged her chin to where she'd piled newspapers in his carry cage. 'But if you can keep all four legs crossed for the night, I'd appreciate it.' She was absolutely not taking him out into the yard until it was full daylight.

She slid into a loose T-shirt, then crawled between lavender-scented sheets, wrinkling her nose at the old-lady smell. A soft thud against the window stopped her heart. She held her breath. Another thud. And another, pounding the window in quick succession. No doubt moths batting against the glass as they tried to reach the light she'd left on. She was used to bugs. Sydney had the giant variety.

But here, who knew what else lurked outside?

Not the least disconcerted and evidently happy wherever she was, Scritches burrowed under the feather quilt and curled against her, his purrs making it difficult to isolate the noises. Probably just as well, with every sound unfamiliar and terrifying. Roni shuddered. Give her drunken neighbours and crazed stoners any day; at least she knew what to expect from them.

Blanket pulled over her head, she huddled close to the cat—all she had left of her past—and tried to steady her breathing so they didn't both asphyxiate in the tent she had created. She needed to discover Marian's tasks and smash them.

There was no way in hell she would stay here longer than necessary. Not one minute.

Chapter Ten

Roni bolted upright as the unearthly scream sliced through her sleep. The hair on the nape of her neck speared up, fear pounding in her chest.

The scream came again, a blood-filled yodel, peaking then trailing away in a choking death gurgle.

Her heart hammered beneath her hand, the bedcovers trembling. The faintest light showed around the edge of the curtain.

The moving edge of the curtain. Framing the window she'd checked was closed last night.

Her blood slowing to the icy dribble of a broken slushie machine, she kicked her legs free of the sheets.

His golden-striped head appearing around the edge of the fabric, Scritches chirruped happily, apparently oblivious to the renewed scream beyond him.

No, the *crowing* beyond him.

Roni sagged back against the pillows, rubbing a palm across her chest. A real, live rooster. Wouldn't be live for too much longer, once she got her hands on it. She drew her feet back under the covers and fumbled for her phone on the bedside table. 'What's the deal, Scritch? It's not even five, normally I have to climb out over you. Come back to bed, you pest.'

Scritches disappeared behind the curtain as a bird carolled.

'Fine.' She closed her eyes. Lay there a couple of minutes. Flipped over. Lay still. Pounded the pillow. Lay still. The tumultuous bird calls filled her head, far more varied than the repetitive chime of the common koel she was accustomed to. Even with the rooster now silent, there was no way she would get back to sleep without the lulling white noise of the motorway.

Toes curling as they met the floor, she crossed the large room, pulled open the curtains and tied them back. Leaned her forearms on the windowsill alongside Scritches as he sat staring out at the world, much as he had from their apartment. Though here, thanks to the elevated position and the open space, he actually had a view.

Tiny birds swooped across the mirror-like surface of a small lake about seventy metres away, halfway down the sloping yard. Nearer the house, galahs swung on the fronds of the massive palm she'd noticed yesterday. They postured and squawked, cackling raucously as they hung upside down and fluttered in a cloud of pink-and-grey feathers, trying to knock each other from the branches.

As a magenta ribbon spread along the horizon, rolling back the purple clouds of night, a family of magpies perched on an electricity wire burst into full-throated song, their rich warble a torrent rushing across rocks and gurgling into a deep pool. The sun rapidly ascended in a fiery ball between the two largest gum trees at the bottom of the yard, fingers of light reaching across the paddocks as though they crept through an opened door.

Caged by the suburbs, she had never had a view to a horizon not cluttered by houses and buildings, never witnessed a sunrise that wasn't imprinted with silhouettes of man-made structures. Arms wrapped across her stomach, she watched, spellbound, until the sun had fully emerged from beyond the distant hills, hanging pendulous in the sky like an overripe apricot.

She swiped a hand across her eyes and sniffed hard. This pregnancy thing had a lot to answer for.

Scritches turned to her and yowled softly.

'Pretty amazing, huh? C'mon, you've got legs, you can walk.' She strode down the hall, clicking off the lights, her night-time fears embarrassing in the daylight. Fortunately she had no one to impress but Scritches.

As she stepped out of the back door, the light barely brushed the rear garden, rendering it soft and lovely—and nothing at all like the fearsome dingo-inhabited wilderness of last night. A low stone wall, like the one she'd spied from the kitchen window, separated the garden, thick and lush with flowering plants, from the farmyard beyond.

A six-foot-high, barbed-wire-topped fence would have been better.

Scritches leaped from her arms to explore the pile of sand he'd scratched up the previous evening, so Roni sank onto a rock alongside a small fishpond. The cat prowled through the greenery and then sat on the moss alongside her, dabbling at the water. As a fish broke the surface, sucking his paw, he sprang back, shooting her a look of astonishment.

Roni clicked her fingers and he stalked sulkily toward her, smoothing against her shins. 'Not the fearsome hunter type, are you? We're a pair of city slickers.' The cat jumped onto her lap, settling to watch the piranhas from a safe distance. 'Don't get too comfortable. We need to head into town and find somewhere to live while we sort out whatever these stupid tasks are. It'll be better there; there'll be traffic and people and noise. More us.'

She started to push the cat off, then froze as a thought hit her: Derek Prescott held the purse strings, and with Marian clearly expecting her to stay right here, he would hardly fork out for a motel. With only a thousand dollars to her name, she wasn't keen on anteing up for it either. So, until she found out what the tasks were, she was stuck. She'd not felt so damn trapped since—*no*. She wouldn't allow the thought. 'C'mon, Scritch, let's go eat our misery.'

Scritches spent a concerned fifteen minutes perched precariously on the side of the enamel tub as Roni showered. Then he inhaled his food at double speed while she laboriously followed the directions on a sachet of porridge. She microwaved the oat–milk blend and nibbled it from the tip of a teaspoon. Not too bad for her first home-cooked breakfast.

Scritches flopped bonelessly as she carried him back to the bedroom and deposited him on the windowsill. 'Okay, puss. I'm headed out there. The great unknown.' She tapped the glass and he pressed his nose against it, scrabbling as he lost his balance. She propped him back up. 'No need for you to escort me, but be good, okay? We're visitors. Well, sort of.' At least until her fantasy of waltzing in here and straight back out with a bucketload of cash was realised. 'Go to sleep, or do something equally non-house-destroying.' The house held a vast amount of furniture, any piece of which the cat might decide needed renovating. She considered locking him in the bedroom rather than letting him roam but decided it would be a brief holiday treat for him to stretch his legs in about fifteen times the space her apartment offered. Make up for the plane ride.

Roni let herself out of the front door, onto the broad verandah. Although the sun shone full on the front of the house, the iron roof curled in a deep arc, shading the brick paving. As she had anticipated, a table and chairs sat to the right of the door, the floral cushion Marian had described on one wrought-iron seat, the other sporting a plain calico pad.

Roni crossed her arms, gripping her elbows. Gooseflesh rippled her skin at the thought that a woman she had never met had sat right there, writing her a letter. She drifted closer and ran her fingers along the back of her aunt's seat.

Then she moved to the opposite chair, edged it from the table and sat, staring at her invisible aunt.

She should nurse her resentment at Marian's manipulation, but it was hard to disregard the note of appeal each letter held. That, and trust.

Not that she wanted anyone's trust. It was one thing she'd learned neither to give nor expect.

The birds' deafening chorus had dulled to muted tweets and calls. Though she couldn't see any sheep in the paddocks, pushed against the wall beneath the table was a wooden crate with a ragged blue blanket in the bottom. The lamb's box. What had Marian called it? Cow, or something equally obscure. No, Goat.

With Marian dead, the farmer had probably turned the sheep into hamburgers, or whatever it was sheep were destined to become.

The throb of a vehicle jerked her attention to where the driveway curled from invisibility on the far side of the stone sheds to meander across the front of the house. Birds darted across the lake, then swooped up to settle on top of a shed as a dusty white ute rattled across the cattle grid rather more quickly than Jim had the previous day.

It had to be the farmer, Matthew Krueger. If he was half as decrepit as his car, he'd be lucky to last out here a day longer than she did.

As the ute pulled alongside the lake, a long-haired collie scrambled from the tray, then the driver unfolded from the vehicle. He heaved a sack from the back, tossed it on one shoulder and crossed to throw open the door of the nearby shed. Chickens flocked from the building, then turned in a feathery wave, following the farmer back in like he was the Pied Piper. A short, piercing whistle sounded, and the black-and-white collie bounded back up onto the tray, racing from side to side of the vehicle, tail wagging like a banner.

A ragged nail hooked a loose thread as Roni scratched the scars on her arm. She had slipped her worn-through sleep shirt back on after her shower, but the deep verandah hid her from view, and surely no one would come knocking this early.

Except— She started from her chair as the farmer re-emerged from the shed and strode up the yard. Toward the house. As she wavered halfway between standing and sitting, wondering at her chances of pretending not to have seen him and ducking inside, his long-legged gait ate the ground between them. Winding between the rose bushes and lavender that hedged the verandah, he ignored the three broad steps and vaulted onto the porch. 'Veronica? Matt Krueger.'

He moved intimidatingly close, his bulk leaving her no room to straighten, putting her at an instant disadvantage. Her muscles tensed, her stomach churning with the memory of powerlessness, and she dropped back into her seat as his callused palm engulfed hers. Scritches yowled at the window, and she jerked her hand free, folding her arms protectively across her chest. 'It's Roni. Krueger? So your dad's the farmer here?'

It was hard to understand his reply with the blood buzzing noisily in her ears, whirling with sounds of alarm. She was alone out here. Alone with him.

But he was only one man, she soothed herself, her fingers plucking nervously at the skin on her forearm. Only one. She'd never been scared of just one man.

Krueger tilted his akubra to the back of his head, eyes hidden behind dark aviators. 'Dad? No. He died a few years back.'

Roni tightened her lips. She'd had a particular image of the farmer in mind—basically a wizened version of Elmer Fudd—and this giant, with his standover tactics, didn't conform. 'You run the place, then?'

'Wouldn't say I run it; Marian definitely wore the pants.' He turned to watch as ducks emerged from the shed and launched themselves onto the lake. 'That is, she was the boss. Guess you're figuring on taking over?'

She took the opportunity to jerk to her feet, longing for the familiar safety of a shop counter between them and Rafe's reassuring presence at her back. Krueger's question had to be loaded. He'd be aware that, per the terms of the will, if she hung around for ten years, he got to leech from the farm income the whole time. But if she completed the tasks and sold the property, he would be instantly out of a job. 'Maybe. Though I'm not sure how the current arrangement works.'

'Sharefarming, you mean?'

'Whatever you call it.'

Krueger swiped a hand inside the collar of his forest-green shirt, then stretched his neck from side to side, apparently weary of her conversation. 'Marian provided the land and I provide the labour. We split any additional expense and income fifty-fifty.'

Equal shares now, but if she chose not to complete Marian's tasks, he would get a larger portion, and she would be dependent on him providing for her. Her fists clenched: her *baby* would be dependent on him. Hell, no. She'd never let that happen. 'You know this area pretty well?'

'Grew up round here, so, yeah, as well as anyone.'

'You'd know the local real-estate agents, then?'

Krueger shoved his hands into the pockets of his jeans, his tone abrupt. 'Sure. You thinking of renting the house out?'

She looked across the yard, fiddling with the edge of her shirt. None of his damn business. 'Haven't decided.' The cat yowled again and she frowned. 'Scritches, shush.'

The farmer glanced toward the marmalade smudge plastered against the glass. 'Handsome cat. Reckon that's about the only animal Marian didn't keep round here. Hungry, or just likes to get in his two cents' worth?'

'Both, always. I got the impression from Marian's letters that you disapproved of her love of animals?'

Krueger lifted a shoulder, a lazy grin inexplicably curling one corner of his mouth. 'I'd be pretty much the last person to disapprove, but she did have a habit of taking in every stray she came across.'

What the hell? Was he having a dig at her? Insinuating she was one of Marian's strays? Instant fury shot through her. Maybe she was overreacting, but it'd been a hell of a week, and she didn't need to be trying to discern his subtext or worrying about his ulterior motives. 'Well, I've loads to get done. So, if you don't mind . . .' She flapped her hands toward the yard, trying to vanquish him from her personal space.

He paused for a moment, but his tone remained steady. 'Sure. Your aunt left a list of what I'd need to show you.'

Her aunt? So much for family secrets. The realisation that he'd probably known Marian was her aunt before she did further fuelled the irritation his attitude had stirred. She jerked her chin at him, her tone as tight as her lips. 'Show me?'

'The yard animals aren't my responsibility. They're Marian's pets, though I've been looking after them since she passed. She said you'd take over. We'll head out now, if you like.'

Nice of Marian to make that assumption. 'I'm going to grab a long-sleeved shirt, then. Sun's already got a bite.' If she had to be walked through these tasks, she needed to put on something with slightly less unplanned ventilation, courtesy of one of Scritches' anxiety attacks.

'Sure thing.' Krueger dropped his hat onto the wrought-iron table with the air of a man who had no intention of going anywhere soon.

She fought to disguise her annoyance. No point getting him offside before she had to. 'Do you want a coffee?'

'Did you find any?' He shoved back a lock of dirty-blond hair as it fell across his sunglasses. 'Marian was a tea fan. Even managed to get me onto the stuff.'

'I've not had a chance to look. You kind of caught me on the hop.' Maybe he'd get the hint he wasn't exactly welcome at this hour. Or any other.

Krueger seemed unperturbed by her tone. 'Ah. I know where her stash is. I'll put the kettle on while you get ready. Wear boots. The browns are out early this year.'

'Browns?' She opened the front door, aware of him directly behind her.

'Brown snakes. Good crop year before last, made for a mouse plague. Means more snakes this year.'

'Are you serious?' She swivelled to point at the screen door that had slammed shut behind him. 'I need boots because they're just running around out there?'

Krueger hooked his sunglasses onto the front of his shirt, revealing ice-blue eyes. 'Not so much of the running,' he smirked. 'Spring, they're looking for mates. They can be a little feisty, but make enough noise and they'll clear out of your way.'

'If I see a snake, I'll be making a noise all right. Wherever you live, you'll hear me.' The removal of his sunglasses had created an uncomfortable intimacy and she quickly headed down the hall, pointing ahead. 'Kitchen's that way.'

'Yeah, I got it. And about seven kays,' Krueger called as she ducked into her bedroom.

'Seven what?' She pulled on her bra and a clean shirt, and dragged a comb through her hair. Then she scooped up Scritches to hide behind as she entered the kitchen.

Krueger had unearthed a china teapot and was measuring loose-leaf tea into it as the kettle came to the boil.

'I live about seven kilometres away. Everything on the opposite side of the main road is mine. Runs parallel to your property.'

Not that she'd wanted to know anything about him, but—her property? He was the first person to call it that, and the thrill was unbelievable. She'd never owned anything larger than a couch, and maybe that didn't even count, given she'd salvaged it from a roadside throw-out.

His hand dwarfing the rose-flowered porcelain, Krueger added two cups to the table and poured water into the pot.

Determined to take charge, she dropped Scritches onto a seat and poured the tea.

Krueger's lips quirked. 'Coffee drinker?'

'Always. How can you tell?'

'You didn't let the tea brew. Or strain it. Marian will be turning in her grave.'

The rare cups of tea sold in Rafe's shop went out with the teabag tag hanging over the edge of the foam beaker. 'Crap. Pour it back in?'

'Don't worry about it. I promise not to tell.'

Roni's fingers locked on the teapot lid; was he inferring that he considered himself the keeper of her family secret?

He pulled out a chair at the head of the table and settled into it. Scritches leaped onto his lap and the farmer rubbed him under the chin, finding a spot that turned the cat into a drooling mess. 'You're a mighty fine fella, aren't you?'

Scritches purred, and Roni tried not to frown. 'Come on, Scritch, down from the table.' She clicked her fingers and pointed to the floor, cringing as she realised her error: he never obeyed. 'You said Marian left a list?'

The farmer unbuttoned the pocket of his shirt and pulled out a fold of paper. 'Yup. Fairly basic. Pretty much feeding and watering, for now.' The brief warmth had left his tone.

'For now?'

Shoulders hunched, though he still crowded the kitchen, Krueger observed her over the fragile rim of his teacup. 'You've only got a few kinds of fowl at the moment. Chickens, bantams, ducks, a peacock and his harem. And Goat, of course. But you've missed the brunt of lambing season, so no bottle-raising.' Careful not to dislodge Scritches, he eased an envelope from the back pocket of his jeans. She immediately saw her name written across it in the now-familiar, spidery script. 'It seems Marian has other plans for you.' He sounded almost apologetic, as though he knew there was worse to come.

In which case, yet again, he knew more than she did.

Chapter Eleven

Dearest Veronica,

I am going to assume you have accepted my challenge and intend to tackle the tasks that will see Peppertree Crossing become yours—though if I have schemed well, this transfer will be more meaningful than a simple change of name on a deed. We shall see.

Did I mention that Enid Blyton is my all-time favourite author? You'll find a complete collection of her works in the library, if you've not already done so. One of the stories is the tale of a child set a number of tasks. Unbeknown to him, his reward for completing each chore is hidden within the task. For example, he's told to clean the chickens' layer boxes. Had he completed the job properly he would have discovered his shilling—or penny, or whatever it was—beneath the straw. However, the lazy child threw fresh straw on top of the dirty, so never found his payment.

This story always appealed immensely to me. Your ultimate payment, obviously, is Peppertree Crossing itself, but rather than revealing hidden incentives, each task I set will provide a reward of a different, perhaps less tangible kind. A treasure trail to self-awareness and emancipation, I hope. While you may well roll your eyes, I assure you that devising this has given me hours of pleasure.

Evidently, you've met Matt Krueger. He's quite lovely, isn't he? If ever a man would have been able to sway me from my preferences . . . Well, add to that impossibility the fact that he's around forty years younger than me and you'll know I joke—though not about him being lovely. 'Salt of the earth' is how Andrew quite rightly described him.

Anyway, now you've already crossed off two tasks—travelling to Peppertree Crossing and meeting Matt—you see how simple they are? Let us move on.

Part of my rationale for marrying was because I feared I would be unable to manage the farm alone. The secrets I kept, both for myself and for others, re-inforced this feeling of inadequacy. Guilt and secrets are heavy burdens, Veronica, and I believe they contributed to Andrew's death. I never expected him to become a frail old man, unable to handle the farm, but shame and remorse make life hollow, and eventually unten-able. As Andrew failed, I was forced to discover that not only was I capable of managing the property but that I was damn good at it.

I've only had twenty years of being confident in my own abilities, and I want so much more than that for you. I realise you were independent in the city, but here, life requires an entirely different set of skills. I want you to become self-sufficient, but not in today's manner, not by working and paying rent. I want you to be able to provide for yourself on a sustainable level and to learn that success is a result of hard work, forethought and a little luck—even I will admit you cannot be held responsible for bushfire, flood and drought.

The basics of life, for the body at least, are bread, meat, milk, vegetables and fruit, although Matt would doubtless argue some of those. To this end, he has been given instructions regarding what I expect from you, and how he is to assist. I'm not going to pretend he was thrilled with either the concept or the planned execution but, fortunately, neither he nor Derek will deny a dying woman her last wishes. As you see, I've used my regrettable circumstance to the very best advantage, and my good friends will see my requirements fulfilled. However, I shall allow Matt a little fun in disclosing the details as he sees fit.

Lynn Lambert has stocked the cupboards, but the supplies will last only a week or two. You'll find my sourdough starter in the cellar. The culture is more than eighty years old and I'll dare proclaim it 'the staff of life'—though it's probably best you don't repeat that gem among the stauncher Lutherans in the area. The chill of the cellar will have kept the starter alive, and

Lynn has been instructed to feed it in my absence. Ha, that makes it sound as though I intend to return. Don't worry, I don't plan to haunt you—though it's a shame I couldn't put myself in that cold room, Walt Disney style! See, although I make preparations, I am still far from being ready to go . . .

The instructions for making your bread are alongside the crock. And so, I have set you on the path to complete your next task. When you have your first slice of hot, buttery, fresh bread, spare a thought for me, Veronica. It is truly one of the simplest, yet most exquisite pleasures life has to offer.

With love,

Marian

Chapter Twelve

Roni waved the letter at Krueger, who had sipped tea while she scanned it, his attention ostensibly on Scritches. 'You know what this says?'

His gaze flicked to hers, then back down to the cat, but not before she caught the glint of laughter in his eyes. 'Pretty much. The guts of it, anyway.'

'Bread? What the hell?' Perhaps Krueger could also shed light on Marian's long aside about the inexplicable guilt borne by a man Roni had never met—could never meet—but she immediately bristled at the thought of asking him for either favours or information.

'Marian did make the best loaf this side of the Mount Lofty Ranges,' Krueger said, his fingers raking long furrows through Scritches' ginger fur.

'Well, go Marian. I didn't fly across the country to take a cooking course in some damn cellar.' She shuddered; a room full of darkness that she hadn't checked last night.

'It's actually a cottage, not a cellar.' Krueger placed Scritches on the floor.

'Why call it a cellar, then? And what's this starter stuff?'

Scritches swung around at her sharp tone, and Krueger stood. He stared at her, rubbing his chin. The long, awkward pause effectively killed the brief conversation, and she fiddled uncomfortably with her cup. 'I'll show you,' he said eventually.

She pushed her cup aside and followed him out the back door, across the walled garden and through a rusted wrought-iron gate to where a tiny stone cottage nestled into the hillside, partially hidden behind a screen of ivy.

Krueger slid a timber plank free of two iron channels and pushed open the door, faded paint flaking his hands like dried blood. 'This was the original homestead. Marian called it the cellar because the thick walls make for good cold storage. Most homesteads around here started out like this, only a couple of rooms, but over the years they've either been extended or ripped down to repurpose the stone.'

She tried not to gawk in surprise at his sudden garrulousness. 'Doesn't look like there's a shortage of stone around here.' She waved a hand toward the sheds. No lack of dirt, either.

'Makes working the ground up tough.'

And there he was, back to short replies again. It was as though he caught himself and pulled back. Like he didn't trust her enough to share the full thought.

The feeling was mutual.

He gestured at the opening. 'After you.'

She stepped timidly into the darkness, wrinkling her nose at the earthy, sweet scent. Did snakes like the dark? His caution about wearing boots had been pointless, given she only owned sneakers and the work lace-ups she'd abandoned in Sydney. 'No power?'

One hand on the lintel, Krueger ducked inside. 'Give it a second, your eyes will adjust.'

There'd be a whole lot more light if he had the brains to move his bulk out of the doorway. Roni edged forward, the temperature noticeably cooler, her sneakers gritting against the dirt, hands outstretched as she gradually discerned a slab bench along one wall, with tiers of shelves above it.

Krueger hustled past and took a jar from the bench. 'This what you're looking for?'

'Are there instructions?'

He picked up a plastic folder. 'Maybe take it outside.'

She rolled her eyes in the darkness. 'No kidding.'

Rocks jabbed her back as she leaned against the wall outside, folding the instructions and then tucking them into her jeans pocket. A yellow crust covered the top layer of a jar two-thirds full of grey goop. She screwed up her face. 'This does *not* look like anything edible. Hang on, I'll Google it.'

'Don't reckon you will. Marian couldn't get internet, and the only phone signal is either up the back paddock or down the yard. You'll have to put in a satellite dish.'

'I doubt that'll be necessary.' She wouldn't be staying that long.

Krueger tugged his phone from his jeans. 'I'll take a picture and ask Mum if she knows anything about it.'

Short of magic, Roni couldn't see how this glob would ever turn into bread. But it had to, because she couldn't afford to fail the task. She needed this house, for her, for Scritches, and for the baby. Or, more correctly, she needed the money this house would bring. 'Yeah, that'd be great, thanks.'

Krueger snapped a couple of pictures, then carried the jar back into the cottage, sliding the bar into place across the door as he returned. 'Give me your number and I'll text Mum's answer. We'd better get a move on if you want that crash course in self-sufficiency. I have to head to church in about an hour.'

'Oh. Right.' She pulled her number up and passed him her phone. 'That's the Lutheran church? Marian mentioned something in her letter. Do they have a Saturday service?'

'Yes. And no.' He focused on her screen, his tone suddenly tight, as though she'd trespassed on his privacy. 'Special occasion. I go occasionally to keep the old lady happy.'

'Old lady?'

'Mum. You don't use that expression?'

'Not for any of my parents.'

A crease appeared between his eyes. 'Come again?'

'My fosters preferred first names.'

'Ah. Yeah.' He made a business of pocketing his phone, then jerked a thumb toward the garden gate.

Conversation clearly wasn't his thing. At least, not with her. Well, tough, because she wanted details, and Krueger

112

seemed ideally placed to provide them. 'You knew my family well?'

Krueger speared her with his gaze, as though gauging her right to the information. Then he squared up to her, his hands jammed into his pockets. 'Your uncle, not so well. He was a man who liked to keep to himself, seemed to have a lot on his shoulders. Didn't believe in hanging out at the stockyards just to shoot the breeze. He was all about business. A straight talker, didn't say much, but when he did it was exactly what he thought. No lies, no muddying the waters. It was almost like it was a point of honour with him.' He scowled, and she got the feeling he was judging her somewhat less positively. 'Marian, though, she was like a second mum to me.' A fleeting grimace, almost as though he was in pain, flashed across his face. He shoved his sunglasses back on and turned away, striding ahead. His voice dropped so low she had to break into a jog to stay close enough to hear. 'Always had faith in me. Encouraged everything I wanted to do.'

She glared at his shoulder. So, her aunt had found someone to unofficially adopt. And now he strutted around the place like he owned it, made himself at home in the kitchen. Her kitchen. Maybe the prospect of turfing him out on his butt wasn't all bad. 'And my parents? You know them?'

The planes of his face shifted, his jaw tightening. 'I know your mother.' They passed beneath the vine-covered arbour on the side of the house, where Jim had parked the previous night. As they reached the front verandah, Krueger vaulted up and grabbed his hat from the wrought-iron table.

Standing above her, legs spread like he was an explorer flagging a claim, he indicated the lake. 'Fowl go in that shed alongside the dam. Their grain's in bins, I'll show you how much of each they get. Marian was adamant they have organic feed, though they free-range all day. You need to make sure they're locked away by late afternoon, and don't let them out before first light.'

Roni snatched at a strand of hair the cool morning breeze blew across her face, tucking it behind her ear. Her irritation turned to anger as he spouted off instructions as though his knowledge would prove his superiority. Screw this. Now, more than ever before, she had no reason to take orders. Especially from someone who'd been closer to her aunt than she could ever be, someone who—Roni froze, trying to keep her expression neutral as her thoughts whirred. Marian had put Krueger in control of handing out her tasks, making certain he knew what she 'expected' Roni to achieve. And she had charged him with seeing that her wishes were fulfilled.

The air left Roni's lungs in a gasp as the realisation hit: not only was there no logical reason for Matt to help her but Marian had set him up as the judge of her success—even though he would profit from her failure.

She stared up at him. 'I'm sure I can figure it out.' Except, with the unfamiliar terms he threw around, she felt nowhere near as confident as she forced herself to sound. But she couldn't risk showing weakness. She knew where trusting the wrong person led.

'I'm sure you can.' He sounded faintly amused and she didn't appreciate that his change in humour seemed to be at her expense.

Krueger dropped from the verandah and marched down the yard, skirted the lake—dam—and made for the chicken shed leaving her to chase after him yet again. 'Pretty much all you need do for this week is take care of the poultry. The orchard is on the far side of the house, and you'll eventually have to check the irrigation system as we head into the summer. Goat's in there at the moment, keeping the grass down, but he's a greedy bugger, so he'll need penning as the stone fruit comes on. The nearest veggie patch has been manured and fallow for months, but you need to dig it over before you plant.'

She lagged behind so Krueger would be forced to slow to her pace to spew his orders.

'You've lost your berries to the rabbits. They're always a problem when there are no dogs or cats around the yard, but Scritches might be able to help you out there. Once you've fenced the plot, I'll bring you some fresh runners. Let's see, what else?' He rubbed at his chin again and she realised it was his go-to when thinking. 'Market day's Thursday, I'll swing work so I can pick up your poddy then.'

'Whoa.' She planted her feet. 'Didn't that start out as "All you need to do is feed the chickens"?' What the hell was a poddy? Or fallow? The only part of his monologue she understood was the accusation that she was somehow responsible for the dead plants.

Krueger pushed open a door into the wire-fronted stone shed. 'Actually, that started out with poultry, not just chickens. Marian liked the idea of giving you one task at a time, so you could earn the next. But I figure maybe you'd like to know them up-front, so you can get your head around what you need to do.'

'Uh huh. Or so I run away screaming?'

He took off his sunglasses in the gloom but didn't look toward her. 'Could go that way, I guess. Your call.'

Like that wasn't what he intended. A steel feed bin clanged as he kicked it, which was exactly what she felt like doing. She would show him just how much he had underestimated her.

'The birds all have different requirements,' he went on stiffly, 'but, as you said, I'm sure you can work it out. Just keep the wet birds and dry birds separate. Scoop is in each bin. I've written on the inside of the lid how much they get. Remember to pen them up on time.'

'I got that,' she grated out. Did he expect a salute? Marian could have written directions instead of allowing this cowboy-wannabe to get his rocks off by lecturing her like he was running a world-class research facility.

Stubble rasped as Krueger drew a hand across his chin, his eyes as blue as a glacier. And about as inviting. 'Right then. I'll be back at the end of the week with the poddy.'

She waved the phone she still clutched. 'Yup.' She wouldn't ask what a poddy was. She'd Google it.

Shit, no, she wouldn't.

He gestured for her to precede him out of the shed. 'And one more thing. The bridge at the end of the driveway is looking pretty crook. I told Marian I'd take care of it but she was adamant you needed to. Said to tell you that learning to build bridges is important. Guess you know how she liked to talk in riddles.'

She knew nothing about her aunt, riddles or otherwise. 'Seems it doesn't need much of a bridge. There's no water.'

'It's a winter creek.'

'Not a problem, then.' With summer still weeks distant, she would be well clear before winter.

'If we get a downpour, it'll be impassable. You need to collect the rocks that've rolled off the crossing and toss them back up.' He bent to pat a fluffy chicken as it pecked each imprint his boot left in the dust. His rigidity seemed to ease a little and he shot a glance at her. 'Tell you what, give me a call when you want to tackle it, I'll come lend some muscle. We'll smash it out in a morning.'

So he would have an opportunity to make her feel guilty about selling the farm that represented his livelihood? Or because he thought her incapable? Neither option was palatable. 'I can handle it.'

As the border collie leaped from the back of the ute Krueger clicked his fingers and pointed at the tray. The dog jumped straight back up. Krueger opened the car door. 'Fine. I'll be back Friday.'

Friday? She was expected to stay here alone for the next five days?

The ancient vehicle revved hard then drew out of the yard, disappearing behind the stone sheds before eventually reappearing to crawl along the driveway that stretched emptily before it. Much as the week stretched before her.

Chapter Thirteen

She spent the morning investigating the house and exploring the stone sheds. From towering erections two storeys high to squat hobbit holes, they held what had to be several lifetimes of . . . stuff. Gargantuan pieces of farm machinery, which wouldn't have looked out of place on a mining site, sacks of grain, bales of hay, mountains of old corrugated-iron sheets, dented washing machines, the frames of rusted bikes and other assorted rubbish filled the barns.

In a smaller shed, protected by a sliding door that swung precariously from two flywheels balanced on a top rail, she discovered a silver late-model Toyota Camry, powdered with dust.

Locating the key among the bunch she had pocketed, Roni slid behind the wheel. Goosebumps rippled down her arms as tweedy perfume created an almost tangible presence. Afficionado of too many horror movies, she checked the back seat through the rear-view mirror. Of course, there was no one there. Wouldn't be until she installed a baby seat. Anticipation rippled through her and, grinning, she started the car and opened the windows a crack. Then she turned it off and scrambled out. With plenty of food in the house and enough biscuits for even Scritches to get by, she wouldn't need the car for a day or two, and by then the ghostly fragrance would have dissipated.

Her phone vibrated and she yanked it from her pocket, immediately trying to swipe into the internet. Nothing but an unmoving progress bar. Evidently, texts didn't require as strong a connection though.

Mum didn't know anything about sourdough, so I Googled. Looks the same as yours, so I guess you're good. Matt

Not particularly useful, but at least he'd followed through. *Thanks.*

Without waiting to see if the reply sent, she shoved the phone in her pocket and stepped out of the shed, surveying the sun-drenched farmyard. Home was kept familiar by the sounds of life: people yelling, children crying, traffic horns, the soothing buzz of the highway. But here, there was nothing.

No, that wasn't true. Muted groans came from behind the house, as though a zombie horde staggered up the hill. The odd bleat indicated the noise might be from a flock of belly-aching sheep, but the dirge made her skin crawl.

She kept one eye on the hill—just in case—as she ducked between the strands of wire that separated the orchard from the farmyard. Dozens of trees wore buzzing dresses of pink and white, and she stretched to steal a blossom from the bees. The earth trembled beneath her feet, vibrating through her legs for mere seconds before a bolt of lightning struck the small of her back, slamming her to her knees.

A demonic yellow eye, the pupil a vertical black slit, blinked at her.

The eyeball snorted wetly in her face. Or rather, the elongated grey-white, fuzz-covered snout immediately below the eyeball snorted. Pink lips stretched to nibble at the hand she'd thrust out to ward it off. Then a wool-covered head ducked beneath her arm, demanding a pat.

'Goat?' She clambered up. The size of a mobility scooter, his grey coat full of burrs and stuff she didn't really want to put a name to, the animal looked nothing like the snow-white, frisky-tailed lambs of storybooks. The beast gurgled deep in his throat and her heart thumped in crazy response. Had anyone ever been murdered by a sheep?

As her hand jerked back he crowded in, sharp hooves trampling her sneakers as he butted at her hand. 'Ouch! Back off a bit.' Okay, so maybe he was after affection. She tousled the top of his head, between his ears.

The sheep leaned against her, snorting as he half-closed his eyes.

'Ugh, what is that?' She sniffed her hand. Woollen jumpers in a damp winter. 'Hate to be the one to break the news but any kind of cute you might have is obliterated by your need for a bath.'

The sheep groaned and shook his head.

'Speak people, do you? At least I won't be all alone out here, then. Come on, out of the way.' She pushed the sheep with her knees as she advanced toward two raised beds bordered by railway sleepers. Like a laden shopping trolley shoved sideways, Goat shifted reluctantly.

'Are these supposed to be vegetable gardens?' One plot buried beneath a jungle of weeds, the other had been invaded by the thick stems of a single species. She snapped a knee-high, purple-blotched shoot and watched rank green juice dribble onto her hands. 'Does everything out here have to reek?' she muttered, wiping her hands on her jeans. 'No offence, Goat. Just saying.'

The sheep jumped onto one of the beds, head down and snorting a challenge. Feet close together, he turned a couple of circles, then leaped directly into the air. Landed, and watched her intently.

She would almost swear he was grinning.

Great. One morning in solitary confinement and she'd already lost her marbles.

She moved away, but he darted to cut her off. Roni hesitated, then changed direction. Again, Goat lunged, then froze, studying her. Turned a couple of circles on the spot. Grounded his feet and stared, like a puppy waiting to snatch at a stick he was being teased with.

'You're playing?' She'd never realised that sheep were just like dogs. Roni feinted left, but then corrected and darted toward him. Goat reared on his hind legs, tossed his head, and then thundered away across the yard. He pulled to a dusty halt. Snorted. Stomped the ground. Then charged toward her wild-eyed, his nostrils flaring.

Hell, his behaviour wasn't playful, it was an exercise in domination. The ground shook and she squealed, throwing up an arm to fend off the ton of woolly lamb chops barrelling toward her.

The sheep halted centimetres short of crushing her and stretched his neck, velvet lips kissing at the inch of skin exposed above the waistband of her jeans.

Heart fluttering wildly, Roni risked a peek from beneath her arm. 'It's definitely a game, right?' She shakily fondled his head, then tugged on his ears, the way Scritches liked. Goat leaned in with a trembling snicker of his lips, practically purring at the contact. 'Aw, you poor thing. Are you lonely, with Marian gone?'

He pushed closer, positively vibrating with happiness, and she snatched her hand back. 'Oh no, don't you go getting too attached, pal. I'm only passing through.'

With a farewell pat, she darted toward the gate set between the orchard and the walled kitchen garden, Goat's breath panting hard against her back. She fiddled with the latch and scurried out, dragging the gate closed. Goat reared up, resting his front hooves on the mesh so he was level with her face. He bleated piteously.

She pulled the shirt from her chest, trying to billow cool air down her front. Without a filtering layer of smog, the clear blue sky—and a dose of fear—had her soaked with sweat. 'Sorry, Goat. I've got stuff to do. You can help me in the veggie patch later.' Shame the sheep hadn't taken it upon himself to clear out the weeds, like he'd mowed the rest of the orchard. She would need to get some plants in if she was to earn her escape from here in a week or so.

Week. There. She had allowed herself to think it. There was no way she could accomplish Marian's tasks in a couple of days, particularly with Krueger overseeing and judging them. Walking back to the house, she keyed a list into her phone and jiggled it around until she was happy with the order.

Make bread
Weed veg garden/fence/plant
Check irrigation
Feed chickens
Poddy???

Tick those five boxes and Marian's little odyssey into self-sufficiency would be near enough complete. Then Roni could sell up and find a place for her, Scritches and the baby.

The cat thundered down the hall as she wandered into the kitchen. She opened a can of tuna and fed him a chunk, then threw herself together a tuna sandwich and sat to re-read the growing collection of Marian's missives.

Her aunt claimed to have desperately wanted her yet hadn't cared enough to rescue her, back when she'd needed rescuing. But at least it seemed Marian was determined to do right by her now. Mostly to spite Denise, but the reason didn't matter. Much.

She passed another chunk of tuna to Scritches, enthroned on the yellow-cushioned chair he had claimed as his own. 'You all right there, buddy? Mumma's got to go and earn us some money.'

Mumma. She liked the sound of that. One hand strayed to her belly, as it had frequently over the past few days. With the sale of this property, almost all her fears would be erased. She would have money to raise her child, the safety to provide all the love she had been denied. To cherish and protect it.

Especially protect.

She used her foot to fend Scritches from the back door as she headed outside. 'Not yet, Scritch. I'll take you for a walk tonight. You can come and meet the crazy goat-sheep thing.'

The fish schooled at the top of the pond as her shadow swept the water. Did they need feeding, like everything else she suddenly had responsibility for? She grinned; it would be ironic to discover Krueger had forgotten to give her instructions.

The contents of the glass jar she collected from the outdoor cellar didn't look any less toxic than earlier, the occasional bubble oozing through the festering primordial swamp. Hot, buttery fresh bread, huh? As both her task-master and judge, maybe Krueger should be forced to eat what she created. Then again, maybe not: she needed him alive to vouch that she had fulfilled her tasks.

Back in the kitchen, Scritches jumped onto the bench as she set the jar down. He sniffed at it, tip of his tail twitching, then made a leap for his chair but misjudged the distance and had to claw his way up.

'Smart move, Scritch. Even Rafe wouldn't serve this up.'

She flattened the instructions on the countertop with a sigh. Nothing like a three-step packet-cake mix, which was about the limit of her culinary ability. Apparently, she was supposed to 'feed' the starter and leave it a day before she made bread, but that couldn't happen. She had to stick to her plan of accomplishing one of the tasks each day or she'd be stuck here forever.

With the fabric top removed from the jar, the starter looked even less appealing. She scooped out the worst of the growth, the rancid disk splattering in the sink, and then stirred flour and water into the remaining mixture. Pretty much how she'd made glue when she was a kid, but already the batter looked better.

She elbowed Scritches away from the recipe. 'Move, you. Cat hair's not going to improve this.' She mumbled parts of the recipe aloud, just to kill the silence. 'Place flour in bowl. Create a well. Add a palmful of starter and water. Bring together.'

Dough caked her fingers, hanging in great globs, and she grunted, then laughed at Scritches' expression. He had a knack of raising eyebrows he didn't possess. 'Next, tip onto a floured board and knead ten minutes.'

Knead? Without the help of Google, maybe she could channel the baking she'd seen on TV.

She tentatively squeezed the sticky goop a couple of times, but then stopped; she had every research resource she could need, right here in this house.

Hands scraped and washed, she crossed the hall, the vast cavern far less terrifying in daylight. The library shelves

126

lacked any obvious organisation, but she eventually found a row dedicated to gardening advice, cookbooks and small-animal husbandry. Huddled on the floor she pulled out books, unable to resist the wealth of choice, the mountain alongside her growing higher. It was impossible not to be distracted from her search for basic directions by the photographs of braided breads and knotty rolls. Maybe someday she would try something like that.

Someday soon, that was. She'd better be a quick learner.

Armed with information gleaned from a yellow-paged, dog-eared book that looked like it had seen a lot of love, she headed back into the kitchen. She tipped more flour onto the board, squeezed the gummy mixture together and punched her fist into the centre. As the dough spread out, she formed it back into a ball. Punch. Tug. Fold. Punch.

Her knuckles smacked the board, and her bicep ached. She swapped arms. This was getting old quickly. Surely five minutes would do? No, better make it seven; she had to pass the test. Serving pies and sausage rolls out of Rafe's warmer was a darn sight easier than this. Her wrists and shoulders jarred with each impact, the dough slowly yielding, homogenising from a lumpy, floury mass to a smooth, elastic ball that stretched silkily between her hands. It smelled better now, warm and yeasty instead of like the week-old dregs of Greg's beer. Still, she would go gluten-free for life rather than repeat this workout.

Cover with damp towel and leave in warm place to rise. Six hours min.

'Six hours?' She looked at Scritches. 'Misprint?' Did no one out here realise that bread was only ninety-nine cents a loaf at Woolies? Even calculated at Rafe's minimum-wage hourly rate, this loaf cost well over that.

Scritches wandered into the sunroom behind her, eyeing the towel-covered bowl she balanced on the windowsill. She waggled a finger at him. 'Don't you touch it. I'm not repeating all that messing around, so we've only got one go at impressing Krueger. You want to get out of here, right?'

She gave the cat a stroke, then slipped out the back door.

Like bread-making, weeding took forever, the novelty of the activity soon wearing off. Maybe it wasn't so much that time moved slower in the country as everything took longer. And a darn sight more effort. The sun had disappeared over the hill behind the house by the time she'd yanked what had to be at least an acre of weeds. Not that she knew how much an acre was, but the more her back ached, and the more the wiry strands of grass wrapped around her hands, slicing her knuckles open, the larger the veggie patch grew. She'd have to look up just how much exercise was healthy for the baby. That and what she should be eating, whether she should buy some vitamins.

She sat back on her heels, her gaze ranging the farmyard. Ominous puddles of darkness gathered beneath trees that had seemed to offer a shady oasis during the afternoon, and the zip of nervous adrenaline chased away her fatigue. The chickens crowded the closed barn door and she groaned. Krueger would be all over her if she forgot to pen them, inking a gleeful black mark on his score sheet.

As she reached the coop, the fowls crowded her feet, squawking and squabbling. Some were kind of cute, especially the fluffy white one who had dogged Krueger's footsteps. She ushered them through the door and threw scoops of feed into the musty-smelling gloom. It didn't look much for the number of birds who flocked inside, so she added a few extra. And a few more.

Mixed with something that smelled inexplicably like honey, the pungent fragrance of eucalyptus intensified as both the temperature and the sun dropped. The chirping of wild birds filled the air, and a kookaburra whooped in the nearby wilderness. She shivered. Just her and critters out here. The sky behind the house coloured in great pastel swoops, the unfamiliarity of a sunset chased her up the yard. This time she would make sure she had the curtains closed and lights on before the dark crept in.

She shucked her shoes at the back door, wincing as thorns embedded in the soles gouged her hands. When she saw that the towel over the bowl of dough had tented into a mountain, she grinned smugly. Then scowled at the instructions: *Punch the dough back to its original size.*

Somewhat counter-intuitive, she felt, but the next step was even more ridiculous. *Cover until doubled in size (6–8 hours).*

Seriously? No wonder Jesus or Moses or whichever biblical character it'd been made a couple of loaves go so far—he hadn't time to make more. But, damn, she couldn't afford to get this wrong so, although it meant she didn't get to tick the task off her list, tomorrow would be soon enough to bake the bread.

She yawned, and Scritches lifted his head to squint at her. She probably couldn't stay awake long enough to bake tonight, anyway. All that fresh-country-air crap had exhausted her.

Or pregnancy had.

The now-familiar bubble of excitement fizzed inside. She would skip dinner, tuck the three of them into bed, and have hot bread for breakfast. 'Okay, Scritch. Shower. You coming?'

The cat reluctantly plopped off the chair.

With one hand on the deep green floral border of the cream wall tiles, Roni groaned as she clambered over the high side of the elegant tub. 'Are you getting in, then?'

Scritches eyed the water swirling in the base of the bath but stayed on his ledge as Roni slowly caressed a soapy hand over her belly.

Now she had her plan firmly in place, everything was moving swiftly. She would have her baby's security assured in no time.

Financial security, anyway.

Emotional, though? She knew what it was to grow up with no history. How she had invented parents and siblings when the other kids drew family portraits in primary school. How she lied to doctors about family medical history, because admitting she didn't know made her feel incomplete.

But now, thanks to Marian, she could provide so much more for her baby. Even if she decided against meeting her mother, she had her name; she needed only her father's to create a history for this baby, a sense of belonging and continuity that she had never known.

She caressed her belly again. 'You *will* have a family,' she whispered.

Chapter Fourteen

Stomach temporarily full after breakfast, Scritches settled onto his cushion as Roni retrieved the bowl of dough from the sunroom. She frowned. Unlike last night, it lay grey and heavy, landing on the board with a solid *thunk*. Following the instructions, she patted it into a disappointingly flat loaf on a metal tray she found inside the antique Aga. At least she didn't have to cut wood to feed that monster, she thought as she shoved the loaf into the surprisingly modern electric oven, then rubbed her floury hands on her grey T-shirt.

The chickens evacuated the coop in a flurry of feathers, squawks and honks as she pushed open the door to check for eggs. 'What the hell?' Last night the shed had been dry and dusty, maybe a tad organic-smelling, but nothing too repulsive. Now, however, the floor was awash with . . . she didn't really want to think about the 'what' part. No wonder the chickens were in a hurry to escape. Surely the extra grain she'd tossed them couldn't have caused this? She swallowed convulsively, her sneakers slipping in the slime as she picked across to the layer boxes. According to Krueger, the local CWA collected the excess eggs for their fundraising. Well, they could have the lot of these organic monstrosities. She would stick with spotless, uniformly sized eggs presented in a pristine carton decorated with pictures of cute, clean birds.

She folded the bottom of her flour-covered shirt to create a pouch and carefully loaded the eggs. One slipped from her hand and plopped into the mud-that-wasn't-mud. It didn't break, but if the CWA wanted that one, they could come and dig.

She blew out a terse breath. This had to be the most ridiculous path to inheritance ever, but she had to keep her eyes on the prize. Surely the property was worth enough that she would be able to buy somewhere small? Not in Sydney, no one could afford that, but somewhere she could pick up work at a supermarket or deli, and put down roots for her little family. If collecting shit-smeared eggs and pretending to fathom some life lessons her aunt imparted was the price of her financial freedom, she was in. For a week.

As she stepped from the shed she froze, clutching the eggs tighter. Across the dam filled with noisy ducks sat three kangaroos. Kangaroos in her yard. The tallest rocked back on his haunches, ears twitching as he kept watch, while two smaller ones lapped at the muddy water. No, wait; there were four animals. A joey tumbled from its mother's pouch and pushed its nose in the water. Then it scrambled back in a tangle of ludicrously long legs and tail, as the mother patiently waited for it to rearrange its limbs.

Other than Jim's bundle of road-kill fur, the only kangaroos Roni had seen were mangy, lethargic specimens in a tourist park. But these animals, with their thick silver-and-grey pelts glistening with crystalline dew-droplet reflections of the rising sun, seemed alert but unafraid. Though she had petted the drab, captive beasts, she would not dare approach these muscular creatures. Instead, she stood still, watching them as the chickens fluffed and rolled at her feet, scratching cascades of dust over their backs.

Eventually, the kangaroos bounded away, clearing the wire fences without breaking stride, then disappearing through the fields of crop into the smudge of scrub blurring the skyline.

Roni made her way back to the house, unable to shake the feeling she had witnessed something unique, unspoiled and glorious. As she entered the walled garden, her mouth salivated madly at the scent of hot bread. She tumbled the eggs into a pot plant near the back door, then headed to the kitchen. The disappointment of her screwed-up face reflected in the oven window: the loaf still resembled a blob. But perhaps there was magic in the fifteen minutes remaining on the timer.

She scrubbed her hands in the kitchen sink, watching soil and ... stuff ... swirl down the drain as she planned the rest of the day. After she finished the weeding, she'd take a look at the fences. By mid-afternoon she would head into town and buy some seedlings, rather than wait on

Krueger's condescending promise to provide plants after she had obeyed his instructions. She assumed he would report her successes back to Derek Prescott, and a photograph of a fully established vegetable garden would have to tick the box on their task sheet.

She shook her hands as if she could flick away the surge of nerves along with the drops of water. Because there was that other thing in town: the one she had been trying not to think about.

For years she'd sublimated the desire to know her parents, using the hurt of their desertion to cauterise her yearning for connection. But could she ignore her mother's existence when she was only kilometres away? Her lips trembled as she blew a breath out. 'She should come to us, right, Scritch? If she knows we're here, that is.'

She was being a coward, but what point was there in seeking rejection? Except now . . . she rubbed her belly. Now she had a responsibility to her baby, a duty to provide, at the very least, a history. Names, stories, maybe even photos.

Forcing the decision aside, she wiped her phone against her jeans to remove a smear of dirt from the screen—she hoped it was dirt—and pulled up her job list. Feed chickens: big tick. She snorted. Wait ten years and one month to inherit, or complete her aunt's tasks? She had this in the bag.

As she sat, a tiny breeze stirred the floral curtain decorating the top third of the kitchen window. Along with not needing to lock the door each time she passed through, working windows were a novelty. Scritches took instant advantage of her position, settling as much of his bulk as he could fit on her lap, but untidily spilling over like a jellyfish stranded at low tide. 'Okay, Scritch, T minus five minutes. Let's watch this bread rise. More fun than slicing it for Rafe's sandwiches, huh?' Rafe was right, she would end up a crazy old cat lady. The cat lounged against her stomach and she grinned; soon enough her conversations wouldn't be limited to Scritches, and there would be no room for him on her knee.

No, not no room; she'd always make space for him. Just less room. Because both her lap and her life would be full. When her phone timer sounded, the dough still hadn't transformed into a high-topped crusty loaf. Following Marian's instructions, she inverted the bread and rapped the base with her knuckles to check that it sounded hollow. Then she took two small, flowered plates from the emu cupboard and a serrated knife from the drawer. She sliced a thick wedge from the end of the small cob, her stomach growling as fragrant steam rose from the bread.

Scritches managed to get a searching paw on the plate. 'Shoo, Scritch. That one's for Aunt Marian.' She sawed off another slice, spread both with instantly melted butter and smeared them thickly with jam labelled 'Tracey's Apricots 2018'. She carried them to the front verandah, nudging the screen door open with her backside, and placed one plate on the table in Marian's spot, then sat opposite and lifted her bread in salute. 'To you, Marian. Your whole task thing is crazy, but I admit, this is not all bad.' She fanned the hot bread and bit into it.

Then slapped a hand across her mouth.

What the hell? Despite the nectar of the apricot jam, the dense bread lay rank on her tongue.

She jumped up, spitting the bitter mouthful onto the dirt below the verandah. Krueger had assured her the starter was okay, but she'd known that nothing that looked like grey vomit could be healthy.

She frisbee'd the slices of bread toward the farmyard. The chickens scurried up, the smallest—bantams, Krueger had said—like chubby little old ladies with their skirts hiked up around their knees, all a fluster as they bustled toward her.

Toward the bread.

The potentially lethal bread.

Arms windmilling, she rushed down the steps and darted toward the birds. Forcing the bantams to retreat, she whirled about, only to find the peacock and his drab hens had circled in behind her and were tearing apart the bread like the law on a highwayman.

'No!' She lunged, and the birds fled in jewelled-blue, squawking disarray as a flash of candy-apple red from beyond the trees at the bottom of the yard caught her eye. A car. Crap. The last thing she needed was a visitor, not unless it was Derek Prescott come to tell her this whole thing was a joke. Well, not the whole thing, she still needed the inheritance. Just the ridiculous tasks, assessed by a guy who had a clear interest in her failure.

She tightened her ponytail, ran her hands over her hair, and tugged her shirt straight as the car disappeared behind the sheds. As she watched the cattle-grid warily, waiting for it to reappear, the knot in her stomach grew.

Her features obscured by a nimbus of curls, a woman peered over the steering wheel as the car cruised past to draw up beneath the vine-covered pergola on the far side of the house.

Roni moved toward the vehicle, but her steps faltered and she stopped, rooted to the dirt.

Mum?

Chapter Fifteen

As the woman scrambled from the car and dashed toward her, Roni couldn't move. But she wasn't prepared to analyse exactly why she suddenly felt her legs stiffen, her throat tighten, her stomach churn—because that would mean admitting to a chink in her armour, admitting the depth of her lie of the last twenty-nine years, when she'd repeatedly sworn that she had no interest in her parents.

Her mother should be mid-forties, but the woman hurrying toward her had clearly had a hard life; she looked a good fifteen years older. Could regret do that to a person?

'Veronica!' Gossamer purple and pink webs of layered fabric floated around the woman, her blonde halo untamed by the bright pink ribbon threaded through the curls.

A bubble of hysteria climbed Roni's throat; add a few feathers and her mother would look like one of the matronly bantams. Soft and warm. Vastly different than Marian had depicted.

'Yes?' She scanned the woman's face. No similarities. It would have been nice to find a little of herself, a sense of belonging, a notion of beginning and continuing.

The diminutive woman flung her arms around Roni, no hint of reserve in the floral-scented embrace. But her desertion remained an unequivocal fact. One she would have to explain. Roni broke her mother's grasp and retreated.

The woman allowed her hands to slide down Roni's forearms but snatched at her wrists. 'I saw Matt at the clinic today and he told me you'd arrived. I couldn't even wait long enough to bake you something, so I'm afraid these aren't today's, but Marian did always say they tasted better the next day, anyway.' Rapid-fire dialogue thrown over her shoulder, she dashed to the car, then back to Roni, bearing a Tupperware container. 'Lamingtons.' She held the box toward Roni like a tribute.

Roni stared from the container to the woman. Lamingtons? 'Oh, you're not . . . I mean, you're . . .' The name was on the tip of her tongue.

'Oh, silly me,' the woman fluttered. 'Just because I feel I've known you forever, I forget that you don't know me. Tracey.' She nodded, as though the name would explain all Roni needed to know.

'Tracey?' Slowly the pieces slid into place in her mind. She angled one hand toward the verandah. 'Tracey of the cushion?'

Tracey clutched a fistful of the beads clattering around her neck, her voice tremulous. 'Oh, my. Did Marian tell you about that? She loves—loved—that silly little cushion so much. Never let anyone else take that chair.'

Roni looked down again at the Tupperware. The sponge squares, chocolate-iced and dusted with desiccated coconut, were probably a good enough reason to pretend cushion-love.

Tracey caught her glance. 'Shall we go in and pop the kettle on? We can have a nice cuppa and get to know each other better.' Not waiting for agreement, she led the way beneath the arbour, toward the back door. 'Oh, I do so love when the wisteria blooms.' She brushed a hand over a grape-like bunch of the purple flowers hanging from the trellis. 'I was afraid I'd miss seeing it this year if you didn't arrive soon. And the fragrance! Reminds me of so many wonderful spring afternoons spent here.'

Tracey deposited the lamingtons on the kitchen counter as Roni filled the kettle. 'This is your first try?' she asked as she poked the bread with a seashell-pink fingernail. 'Well, it has to be, doesn't it, since you've only just arrived.' She sniffed at the misshapen lump. 'Have you made bread before?'

'No, and I don't plan to try again.' Except, she'd have to.

Tracey picked a minute crumb from the loaf and popped it in her mouth. 'Not a bad first go at all,' she said, as though she'd not heard. 'There's quite a knack to breadmaking.'

'I followed the instructions exactly. I can't see how something can be less than perfect if the rules are fol-lowed.' Another lie, because she'd always followed the rules, yet nothing in her life turned out perfect. She'd loved her first foster parents, yet they'd abandoned her. She'd worked hard at school, yet she didn't have a career. She'd stayed quiet when ordered, had tried so hard not to cry, yet still it had hurt.

'Did Marian leave you her recipe?' Tracey's blue eyes turned liquid as Roni pointed at the handwritten page still lying on the countertop. She ran a finger along the lines, as though she caressed the words. Or the memory of the writer. 'I'll bet she didn't tell you the secret ingredient, did she?'

'Secret? Seems there's a few of those around this place.'

'Oh, we'll see what we can do about that. But first, the bread. The secret is . . . love.'

Lucky Roni hadn't swallowed the bread earlier or that predictable, hackneyed line would bring it right back up. She tried to conceal her eye roll. 'Hard to be loving on that jar of grey muck.'

Tracey's trill of laughter sounded genuine. 'No, not love of the bread. Love of what you're doing. Marian never found the time to devote to "hobbies", you won't find any scrapbooks or photograph albums here, but she did love to bake bread. She said the kneading worked out some of her angst and anger, and she appreciated that she could produce something that would nurture her friends.' Tracey cut a slice from the loaf. 'Bread is the perfect representation of her. An indispensable, fundamental, strong foundation.' She sounded like she was quoting something she'd been taught. 'Nourishing and—oh.' She'd bitten into the slice. 'Well, I suppose looks can be a little deceiving.'

'Right?' Roni sighed. 'I honestly thought I'd made a decent job of it. Well, other than the fact that it looks like a lump of clay. But I figured it had to taste better than it looks.'

'Never mind. You'll have to try your hand at another loaf. It can only get better, right?'

'I'm not so sure about that. I could burn it next time.'

'The trick is in the kneading. Marian used strong flour, and she said it had to be well kneaded to release the gluten. That way you'll end up with something lighter than . . .' Tracey dropped her slice with a resounding clunk. 'This.'

'It's not only the weight. It tastes so bitter.'

Tracey nibbled another crumb, her forehead creased. 'Bitter? Like sourdough, you mean?'

'Yes—no, wait. You mean it's supposed to taste that way?'

Tracey smiled. 'There's nothing wrong with the taste of your bread, love, only the texture. Yes, it's supposed to be sour. That's what makes it so perfect with jam. Come on, I'll help you throw together another loaf. Then we'll have our cuppa.'

With Tracey guiding her technique, Roni stretched the far edge of the dough, folded it over the bulk, and pressed down with the heels of her hands, working in a circular fashion until the mix was thoroughly kneaded.

Tracey dusted the flour off the breadboard into the sink. 'There, we'll see how that one turns out tomorrow. Marian and I always worked well as a team, too. I guess you could say she was the bread to my jam in many ways.' As Roni picked up the jar of starter and headed toward the door, Tracey put out her hand. 'Oh, that can stay in here now, love. Just top it up with flour and water like Marian's recipe says, and it can feed on the airborne spores.'

Roni stared. 'Sounds like we're growing fungus.'

'That's pretty much what the starter is. Wild yeast, picked up from the spores floating around us.' Tracey spun in a circle, fingers trailing in the air like she could catch fairy dust. 'Amazing thought, isn't it? This enchantment in the air.'

Roni had wondered whether Marian and Tracey had had a thing going on, but that hippie observation made it a decisive no. Though her aunt's dry humour was evident on the page, Roni was pretty certain the woman had been the stern, forceful type, not given to flights of fancy.

Or to the gathering of fairy-dust spores in her kitchen.

Tracey rummaged in the emu cupboard as Roni poured boiling water into the teapot, determined to let it sit a while this time. 'Ah, found my cup.' The older woman retrieved a delicate teacup decorated with a border of small yellow roses intertwined with a blue ribbon. 'Funny how we cling to familiar things, isn't it?'

That Roni understood. And Scritches was the only familiar thing in this alien existence. The cat lifted a sleepy head from his yellow cushion, as though she'd silently communicated her thoughts to him.

Tracey took another cup from the shelf, her lips trembling as her finger traced a single bold burgundy rose on one side. 'This was your aunt's.' Roni recognised the cup from the photograph of the house Prescott had shown her. She had examined the picture so closely she'd had to hold her breath to avoid dampening the paper. 'And how about this one for you?' Tracey held up a cup with a tracery of tiny blue flowers around the rim, scrollwork lettering beneath forming the words 'Forget Me Not'. Evidently she didn't recognise the irony.

Tracey popped a lamington onto each saucer. 'I don't think anyone really uses saucers with their teacups anymore, do you? But they do look so elegant as a pair.' Between them they carried the morning tea out to the verandah.

They both stood, staring at the chairs.

'I'm sure Marian would've wanted you to take her seat,' Roni offered.

'Do you think?' Tracey's eyes threatened to overflow.

How the hell would she know? Still, no harm in trying to alleviate Tracey's obvious pain. 'I'm certain. She mentioned you very fondly in her letters.'

Tracey sat carefully on the embroidered cushion. 'That's lovely to hear. It's funny, you can know someone so intimately, yet still you don't know how they portray you to others.'

Intimately? Roni was back to wondering exactly what the two women had shared. Regardless, it seemed Tracey was her best source of family information.

'You and my aunt were very close?'

Tracey gently chased a bee from the table with the edge of her hand. 'You know all the bees are dying? Terrible thing.'

'Sure.' But she had more important problems than that.

Tracey seemed to remember the question. 'Yes, Marian and I were closer than sisters. Though, given Marian's relationship with her sister, that wouldn't be too hard, would it?' She flashed Roni a grin. 'Go on, I know you're dying to ask me all kinds of things. Go right ahead.'

Roni flinched at her directness. 'I, uh, to be honest, I have so many questions, I don't know where to start.'

'How about I start for you, then? I know you've met Matt. Isn't he lovely?'

Not at all where she wanted to go. 'For a jailer, I guess.'

'Jailer?' Tracey frowned. 'What do you mean?'

Roni traced a finger around the rim of her teacup. 'You know about the tasks Marian set?'

Tracey nodded.

'It seems my inheritance hangs on hoping Krueg— Matt—won't fail me just because he's pissed.'

'Why would he be angry?'

Roni kept her eyes on her cup. 'He has no guarantee what I'll do with the property when I inherit it, so it's logical he has an agenda.'

'Oh, you needn't worry. Matt's not that kind of person. He'll give you a fair go, love. More than fair, if I know anything.'

She swallowed her snort of disbelief; in her experience, that wasn't the way life worked. Tracey's simplistic view didn't allow for either greed or necessity. 'The way it's set up, he gets an extra ten years' income if I fail. Hardly incentive for him to play fair.'

'Matt has other strings to his bow. In fact, I think he works the farm mostly as a favour to your aunt. They were very close.'

'Yeah, I got that.' She broke an edge off the rich brown-and-white-speckled cake to reveal a fluffy interior. 'Oh, I've never seen a lamington that yellow.'

'I use Marian's duck eggs.'

'They're edible?'

'Well, I wouldn't fancy eating one straight up, but they're perfect for baking. We'll get stuck into some practice as soon as you're settled.'

'Practice?'

'Oh,' Tracey flapped a dismissive hand, 'I'm such a scatterbrain. I've muddled everything in the wrong order.' She broke off as the rooster decided the sun had just risen for the fourth time that day. 'Your timing is perfect, though. You just missed the Royal Adelaide Show, so everyone tends to be a tad baked out, and many take a break until the Christmas fundraisers begin. You won't have too much competition, just the diehards who like to make sure their name's in the newsletter each month. But don't worry, we'll do some trial runs before then.'

Roni raised her eyebrows questioningly. The roiling sensation deep in the pit of her belly suggested that whatever she had missed wasn't going to be something good.

'Oh, I'm sorry, love,' Tracey said. 'Marian would lecture me on having my ducks in a row and being organised before I speak. Not that it ever did her any good.' She took a sip of tea and tapped the table. 'Now, let me see. First, back to Matt. He's not the only one with tasks for you. Marian gave me a list as well.'

'No.' Roni's heart plummeted into the black chaos of her stomach. Would she never escape this place? 'More tasks?'

'Don't look so worried, love. I wouldn't even really call these tasks. Marian was eager you get to know the community, and she decided either the CWA or the church would be the best avenue. You can get some funny old biddies at the church. Not that the association's immune, mind. You'll want to steer clear of Christine Albright. Anyway, Marian was of the impression you've not been brought up religious, so she thought baking might be a better fit.'

She'd done enough pleading with God to decide he was non-existent. 'I have to bake something for your club?' God, don't let it be bread. And how was the Country Women's Association even still a thing?

'Well, no, you don't have to.'

Okay, so maybe God did exist.

'There are plenty of options, you don't have to bake at all. Do you prefer knitting or sewing? There's an ongoing quilting competition, and a group that knit beanies year-round for the premmies at the Women's and Children's. Or even a group sewing teddy bears for the Flying Docs to give their young patients. I thought the baking competition would be a great starting point because I'll be able to help you with it, but it's completely up to you what you do.' Tracey slung her beads excitedly from side to side.

Yeah, sure. If it was truly up to her, she and Scritches would be on a plane back to Sydney.

Roni rubbed her forehead, gazing out over the yard and beyond, the kilometres of undulating green-grassed paddocks stretching to the far-distant horizon. No, she wouldn't be going back to Sydney, because there was nothing there for her. Nothing but Greg, who still had to be told about his baby. Told so he could ignore it, like his other children.

She closed her eyes. 'Baking it is, then. Do I have to make something specific?' Like, packet-cake mix would be really good. Surely she had improved since her last attempt?

'The lamington drive's one of our Christmas fundraisers, but the competition to decide whose recipe will be used is judged next month. Mind, everyone still bakes to their own recipe, regardless of the winner. Who's to know once the lamingtons are all packed up? But we never have any complaints.'

'Lamingtons. Like these?' She took a bite, the chocolate coating dissolving on her tongue. 'This is incredible.' Screw love, they were made with a touch of heaven.

Tracey looked pleased, nibbling her own cake. 'Promise not to tell anyone, but I add a drop of orange essence to the sponge. Makes all the difference. It's not so much that you can taste it but it freshens the cake and adds a tartness to counteract the chocolate dip. Anyway, once you've mastered the sponge, lamingtons are really not hard to make. Just a tad messy.'

Roni nodded, her mouth full. She knew all about messy. Messy summed up her life. 'You tasted my bread yet you really think I can make these?'

'Your aunt used to say anything's possible if you make a plan. No, wait, that's not right.' Tracey held up a finger, bottle-blonde ringlets juddering as she shook her head, trying to work a memory free. 'Wait, I have it. What she actually said is that an idea without a plan is no more than a dream. That's what she'd tell your mum whenever she turned up here, wanting money to pursue one of her fantasies, which always revolved around chasing after some wealthy man.'

The fork fell from Roni's nerveless fingers. 'You know Denise?'

'Small town, love. Of course I do.'

Chapter Sixteen

Scarred by her experiences with borrowed families, she'd long ago buried any dream of finding her parents, but since she'd spoken with Derek Prescott, the possibility of really belonging had dared to resurface.

Each day, the need to discover where she had come from had grown—like the child inside her, who would at least now know of its grandparents. She pressed a hand to her belly, as much to calm the baby she couldn't yet feel as to settle her fluttering nerves.

'I take it Denise hasn't lobbed up here yet, then?' Tracey quartered her lamington with the edge of a fork.

Roni glanced guiltily at her own plate, where only scattered shreds of coconut evidenced her greed. 'No. Do you think she will?'

'Unfortunately, yes.'

Roni watched Tracey carefully. 'Why unfortunately?'

'Knowing Marian, I doubt she held anything back in her letters. You know she and Denise were never close? And she told you about your father?'

Roni nodded, though her head jerked as the final sentence registered. All she knew of her father was that his identity seemed to be an even greater secret than her birth.

'I must say, Marian saw more in that man than I ever did. Of course, she didn't tell me the truth of the story for many years, but how she forgave him after what he did—' Tracey sat up straighter and shook herself a little, like a disturbed bantam. 'Anyway, water under the bridge, isn't it, love? The fact is, she did forgive him. Denise, however, is an entirely different kettle of fish. She's never taken any blame. Though, to be fair, a child can't be held responsible for that kind of promiscuity. But you see, she never changed.'

Roni thrust up her hand. 'Wait. Marian forgave who for what?'

Tracey waved her fork in circles, as though rewinding the conversation. 'Forgave your father.'

Roni lifted one shoulder. 'What was to forgive? He knocked my mum up. Shit happens.' She sure knew that. 'How was it any of Marian's business?'

'Oh. Oh, no,' Tracey flustered, half rising. 'Oh, I didn't realise you didn't know. Marian said she intended to tell you all the secrets.'

All the secrets? God, how many could there be?

'Oh, I wonder . . .' Tracey's fingertips drummed agitatedly on her lips. 'The letter . . . I have a letter for you from Marian, but I can't remember when I was supposed to give it to you . . .' She cast around the verandah as though either the letter or perhaps Marian would appear to exonerate her. 'It's at home.'

'It's okay. You can give me the letter later.' She was torn between wanting the letter now and terror at the thought of what it might contain. 'Maybe just tell me the secrets?'

Tracey shook her head adamantly, her cheeks flushed, though she sat back down. 'Oh, no, I can't tell you, it's Marian's secret. Well, hers and Denise's and . . . Anyway, it's not mine to share.'

'Tell me more about my mother, then,' Roni said. 'Why do you say "unfortunately" she'll visit?'

Tracey relaxed back into her seat. 'Oh, yes, I can tell you about her. The way she and your aunt fought! Like oil and water, those two, you'd not think they shared the same parents. Though they didn't so much share, from what I understand, as battle for them. Eventually, Marian accepted that Denise was their mother's favourite and she gave up trying to find approval. She'd always been closer to her father, in any case. But that wasn't enough for Denise. It seemed she wanted anything Marian had.'

Tracey traced a fingertip around the delicate rim of her teacup, shaking her head. 'Truth to tell, they both had their faults. They were practically a generation apart, and Marian should have known better than to allow Denise's constant taunts that she would live to take the property from Marian's dead hands to get under her skin.'

'No! She didn't actually say that?'

'I assure you, she said that and so much more. That's why she'll turn up here,' Tracey rapped the tabletop, 'like the proverbial bad penny. There was no love lost between those two. But you mustn't blame Marian for that. Despite their differences, she would have been a sister to Denise if Denise had only let her. But Denise was determined to thwart Marian in every way she could, from—well, from things you'll discover, to hiding you away, to trying to claim Peppertree Crossing, both then and now.'

Okay, maybe Denise did sound every bit as bad as Marian had made her out to be. Perhaps Roni needed to reassess her desire to provide her child with grandparents. 'She's contesting the will?' That wasn't going to make for any kind of happy family reunion.

'I'm sure Marian has it tied up so carefully, Denise won't have a leg to stand on. Not a sober one, anyway.' Tracey dropped her gaze to her lamington, as though she feared she'd said too much.

Roni leaned forward. 'Then why would she come here?'

'Well, you *are* her daughter, so it would be nice to think that may have a little bearing on it.' Tracey flashed faded blue eyes up to Roni, regarded her solidly for a moment, then grasped her hands. 'But promise me you won't fall for her tricks. You're her only child, but you also stand to be an exceedingly wealthy child. Wealthy enough to stir maternal affection within her frozen heart, I'll warrant.'

Roni withdrew her hands. 'It's okay, I don't fall easy.' Or ever. 'Tell me more about this CWA thing. When's the meeting?'

Tracey clapped, her pink fingernails flashing in the sunlight creeping beneath the curved iron sheets. 'Wonderful! There's one Friday week. I'll come by to get you so you can meet the girls. Well, most are old ducks, really, but there are a couple around your age. Taylor and Fiona. It'll be nice for you to have some friends here.'

She wasn't planning on sticking around long enough to need friends. In fact, twenty-nine years hadn't been long enough for her to require anyone but Greg. And she had been a long way from needing him.

∾

Tracey's revelations stayed with her, along with the promise to deliver the missing letter within the next few days. While she processed what she had learned, she turned her energies to clearing the remaining garden, tugging out tall, juicy weeds attached to odd-shaped, dark purple, lumpy roots.

Hands on hips, she surveyed the freshly churned earth. With the weeds pulled, the dark rectangles looked inviting—for a vegetable, anyway. Fencing the beds would be the perfect finishing touch and, thanks to her earlier reconnaissance, she had an idea of how to do it.

She dragged pallets from the sheds, hauled them up the yard, then spent the rest of the day trying to build an enclosure. It proved far harder than it had in her imagination, and Goat insisted on helping, either leaning against each pallet until it toppled or leaping on them to prove the instability of her structure.

Exhausted, she eventually gave up. It was probably safe, early in pregnancy, to work hard, but she didn't want to take chances. Propping the pallets on one another, she would wire them together later. She headed back into the house, pretending not to hear the domino cracks as Goat destroyed her hard work.

The next morning she baked the loaf Tracey had helped her prepare. Hard, heavy and dry, it obviously was not feeling the love she had tried to direct toward it. Maybe because, busy in the yard, she'd let the dough rise for too long? She mixed another batch, left it on the windowsill, fed the starter and carried the failed loaf down to the chickens. Having survived their first experience of her cooking, they greeted her enthusiastically. Goat bleated piteously, leaning over the orchard fence to watch, so she retrieved a few chunks of bread from the ground and took them to him. He nuzzled into her hand, searching for more, and she took a little comfort in knowing she had plenty of mouths to hide her culinary disasters.

In the afternoon she cleaned the house and unpacked her three suitcases, hesitating only a moment before hanging her clothes in one of the massive closets.

Early in the evening she took a book from the library and curled under the light doona with Scritches. Her body ached, but it was a good ache, a sense of achievement, of physical labour that actually produced a result. She read for hours and slept better than she could have imagined.

By Thursday the fowl house haul was more mud than egg, and Roni knew she would have to do something about the coop. She'd not moved beyond the yard for five days, though, and first she wanted to explore a little further afield.

She picked her way across the cattle grid nearest the house, balancing carefully on each rung. Squeezing between the strands of the fence might have been easier, but she didn't like the look of the barbed top-wire. Crows cawed raucously, strutting along the edge of the paddock as she followed the great sweep of driveway which circled the outer perimeter of the sheds. Solid stone, with neither doors nor windows on this side, the ten-metre high fortresses looked invincible, the labour required to erect them unimaginable.

As she reached the last shed, she pinched at her lips with one hand, shooing tiny flies with the other. She could strike out through the long, green crop toward one of the belts of scrub, but there was the risk of the snakes Krueger had mentioned. The driveway offered greater safety and less chance of getting lost, though it was a damn sight longer than it had seemed in the car; by the time she reached the dry creek bed parallel to the main road she was huffing.

She scaled the white-painted fence rail and straddled it, gazing back at the property. Her property. The crop willowed like an inland sea in the slight breeze, the hill behind the house dotted with dirty grey sheep. Sheep that Goat refused to acknowledge, never looking up at their strident calls.

A hawk keened above, and she tipped her head back to watch it spiral against the achingly blue sky. An inexplicable melancholy gripped her. What would her life be if she'd grown up in this freedom? What would it have been like to spend her childhood here? To gaze across endless paddocks, not another house in sight? To breathe deeply of air that hadn't already been circulated through a million lungs?

As a child she would have explored the deep, tangled scrub the birds darted through, would have spent hours walking without facing the cold accusation of shop windows, embarrassed by the lack of money in her pocket. She would have had pets, every kind of animal she could name. And she would never have been inside a dark lounge room, with a TV throwing monsters onto the walls.

She dropped from the rail and wandered back over to the rock levy across the creek. Hands shoved into the pockets of her jeans, she frowned at the boulders that had rolled from the track and scattered across the sand. Another of her tasks. She sighed. Though Marian's scheme made no sense, she couldn't help but think of the whole not-looking-a-gift-horse-in-the-mouth thing. Plus, her anger would be better directed at the parents who'd dumped her. The mother she should want nothing to do with. Yet she had wandered the house, looking for photographs. Tracey had told the truth, though; Marian didn't keep photos of people, only of animals. There was nothing in the house to tie Roni to her past, and nothing to help create her baby's future.

So it was up to her to take care of that herself.

She raked her hair back into a ponytail, securing it with a band from around her wrist, then clambered down into the creek bed. Here she could see that cement drainpipes pierced the rocks on several levels, from one side of the bridge to the other.

She selected one of the smaller rocks and lifted it using a combination of a dead jerk to her knees, precariously balancing it there, then rolling it up her thighs. Then she stood like a gorilla, staring up at the bridge. It hadn't seemed particularly high two minutes ago, but from here it was well over two metres. There was no way she could lift the rock, the only way to get it up there was to somehow scramble up the side of the creek carrying it. Maybe she shouldn't have shut Krueger down when he offered to help. His height, not to mention muscle, would have been a godsend. But why had he offered? If he had half a brain he could give her an instant fail on the task.

Cursing, she thanked the state care system for her extracurricular education in profanity. She needed all those forbidden words right now. She staggered a few steps, then lowered the rock onto the sandy bank. Hefted it and staggered a few more. Her knees jelly, her sneakers slid on the treacherous slope. Maybe if she put the rock down and shoved it up the side?

The rock ploughed into the sand, then refused to budge.

Sweat poured down her face, pooling between her breasts by the time she got the boulder to the path and placed it among the others. Swiping aside the wisps of hair stuck across her cheeks, she surveyed her achievement.

The bridge looked no different than it had a litre of sweat ago—but her hands did. Her already short nails were scratched and splintered, the base of her thumb grazed. She frowned at the rocks in the creek bed. Dozens of them.

Maybe hundreds. Marian's tasks weren't only mad, they were impossible.

Still, with the rain months away, maybe Krueger would forget about the bridge. In the meantime, she needed to head home and concentrate on the jobs that were actually achievable.

No, not home. This property was nothing but a meal ticket.

❧

Lunch and a cup of tea made everything seem a little better. She pushed her plate aside as Scritches, who had long since finished his food, sat staring at her with all the wide-eyed pathos he could muster.

'Okay, Scritch, how about some Vitamin D?' The tasks could wait. She had no rent to pay, no bills to fund, so why rush? With no trains, no buses and no work, her deadlines were self-imposed.

Actually, there was plenty of work. But, with a tangible outcome—feeding the chickens to collect eggs for the CWA, pulling weeds so she could plant vegetables—the chores were more . . . fulfilling than working in the takeaway shop. She nodded decisively. She would damn well tackle that bridge again, to prove it couldn't beat her. But maybe only a rock or two a day, though, so the baby would be safe.

She refused to do the math on how many days that added up to.

Scritches rushed to the pond as she took her seat nearby. He sniffed around, then patted a timid paw at the water to see if the fish were better behaved today. It didn't take him long to decide that exploring the small courtyard was exhausting, and he curled in the sunshine near her feet.

He looked so content, and he'd been denied freedom for so long. For his whole life, in fact, much like her.

Careful not to disturb him, she went inside to retrieve her book. What did it matter if she spent an hour reading in the sun? Completing her tasks would take a little longer than the schedule she'd set, but still not ten years' worth of long.

An hour became several, and she was halfway through the book before Scritches yawned and stretched to his full sixty centimetres, from crooked tail-tip to banged-up nose.

'About time you woke.' Roni also stretched, her backside numb from her perch on the rock, though she'd been too absorbed to notice. 'Time for you to go safely inside and for me to earn our keep.'

For nearly a decade 'our' had meant her and Scritches, and she had never wanted more than that. Now she pulled up her shirt and ran her fingertips over her belly. Unsurprisingly, Marian's library hadn't yielded any books on pregnancy. Not human pregnancy, anyway, though if she were about to lamb, she was pretty up there with all the info. Tomorrow, finally, she would head into town, where among other errands she would find a public library and borrow some books. Something with pictures, although she could already imagine her baby, tinier than the Polly Pocket doll she'd had when she was five, curled safely within her.

She would also pick up seedlings for the garden and, though she'd not fancied the vegetables in the fridge, some fresh fruit, something healthy for the baby—who needed a name, she couldn't keep thinking 'the baby' about the child safe inside her.

The thought brought to mind a memory of the baby kangaroo she'd seen at the dam, scrambling back into the safety of its mother's pouch. *Roo.* That would do nicely. From now on it was her, Scritches and Roo.

Roni dropped the cat onto his yellow-cushioned chair in the kitchen, rooted through the pantry, pocketed a couple of dried apricots and headed toward the orchard.

'Go-oat,' she sang out at the gate, immediately rewarded by his drumming footsteps. Animals were more dependable than people. Scritches, Goat, even the fowls always raced to see her. Unlike her mother. 'Whoa, there.' The animal barrelled into the gate, trusting the mesh to halt his advance. Gentle lips nibbled the fruit from her hand, then nuzzled all around, looking for more. 'C'mon, let's go see what havoc you've wreaked on our veggie garden.' Roni pushed into the orchard, resting a hand on the sheep's back as they walked side by side around the corner.

'What the *hell*?'

She had steeled herself for Goat's devastation of her makeshift fencing—but this wasn't what she had anticipated.

The roll of wire she had carted up from the sheds was nowhere to be seen, but both beds were neatly fenced, metal poles supporting the pallets, a picket gate providing access.

Roni's fists clenched. Krueger. Interfering as though she couldn't manage. But when had he done it? Prowling around her place as though he had a right to be there, like some kind of stalker. Anger surged, and she slapped at the mosquito on her arm harder than she needed to. If the mozzies were out, it was later in the afternoon than she'd realised. She needed to get today's loaf in the oven and clean the coop before she locked up the fowl.

Casting another furious glance at the fence, she headed inside, washed the greasy lanolin traces of Goat from her hands, then prepped the dough, muttering about Krueger as she viciously sliced the mound to allow the steam to vent. This time, the mix actually resembled a loaf. Excitement dissipated her anger and she bounced on her toes: the bread would work.

She set the timer on her phone and left by the back door, jogging the seventy metres down to the fowl house. In one of the sheds, she loaded a wheelbarrow with a rake, shovel and anything else that looked vaguely useful, then parked it against the side of the coop. Rake in hand, she sized up the job.

Enormous.

Start at the start, then.

Fifteen minutes later she had raked a ton of foul-smelling excrement into a mound in the centre of the shed. It should be impossible for anything this wet and slimy to be airborne, yet it clogged her nostrils and coated her hair and clothes. She snorted with sudden amusement; cleaning the grease-trap at Rafe's had seemed bad enough but she'd never expected to become a farmer. Her chuckle died as an unfamiliar sound intruded.

Any noise that wasn't sheep or birds stuck out around here.

A car.

Her mind leaped to the one place she had forbidden it, again betraying her secret hope. Her stomach clenched. God, this couldn't be her mother, not when she was covered with shit and sweat.

She shoved the barrow inside the chicken shed. Perhaps if she hid, her mother wouldn't find her.

But Krueger would. His ute drew up alongside the coop and he sauntered in. 'G'day. Saw the tools, figured you must be in here.'

She swallowed a tart reply. 'Yup.'

His collie raced in after him, and Krueger whistled, a sharp burst of air between his teeth rather than through pursed lips. The dog cocked a furry black ear, glanced at the farmer, then dashed back to the ute, sitting on the tray and panting so hard it looked like it was grinning.

Krueger nodded at her mountain. 'That's a load of manure.'

She raised an eyebrow rather than acknowledge his talent for stating the obvious.

'Have you been separating the wet fowl from the dry?'

'Sep—' Shit. He had said something about that, hadn't he? 'How am I supposed to tell which are wet? Cuddle them before I put them to bed?'

Krueger grunted, though it may have been a stifled laugh. 'Whatever floats your boat. But I meant separate the water-dwelling birds from the others. As in, the ducks and geese from the chickens. The wet birds go next door. It's cemented, so you can hose the muck out. Chickens are bad enough, but ducks make an unimaginable amount of mess.' He pointed at her manure. 'Well, not unimaginable now. But your eggs will be unusable if you keep them together.'

Shovel in hand, she turned her back to Krueger on the pretext of checking out the adjoining shed and closed her eyes. So damn confident this manual labour was a no-brainer, she'd paid little attention, and now he had a black mark to add to her score sheet. If he noticed the plant pot full of crap-covered eggs near the back door she was screwed.

She startled as his callused hand closed over hers on the wooden shaft of the shovel. 'Here. You finish raking, I'll shovel.'

About to refuse, she glanced out at the encroaching dusk. Without any streetlights, it was time to get inside, with the doors locked. She picked up the rake.

Krueger made short work of the pile and passed her the shovel as he took the handles of the laden barrow. 'This is too fresh to go on your veggie patch; it'll burn the plants. Do you want to start a compost pile near there?'

Though she was not a gardener, still she knew compost took a while to rot down. She wouldn't be here long enough to benefit from it, so he could heap his shit anywhere he wanted. 'Sure.'

She paced alongside him as he crossed the yard swiftly, despite the weight of the barrow. He pushed it through the orchard gate and tipped the contents near the fence. As he took the tools from her, piling them in the tub, the veggie patch caught her eye. 'Hey, did you take away the wire I was using to fence this?'

'Yup.'

'I didn't need your help.' She knew too well that if you asked for anything, even five bucks for a school excursion, it came with a price. 'I was going to get to it tomorrow.'

He paused, his hands on the shovel handle. Glanced up at her, a slight frown between his eyes. 'I'm sure you had it under control. I found myself with some time on my hands, thought I'd ride over and see how you were doing. The house was all locked up and quiet, so I entertained myself.'

'I was home,' she said defiantly. 'I like to lock up early.'

'Fair enough.'

Back to few words, he was impossible to read. She knew the tactic, had employed it herself. But that was because she had things to hide. What was his excuse? 'Well, thanks anyway.'

'No worries.' He didn't seem to notice the begrudging tone in her voice. 'Guess you're not a fan of spuds?'

'Potatoes? Sure.' Mostly in fried form, though. 'Why?'

Krueger jerked a thumb over his shoulder, at her mound of weeds. 'You pulled them all out.'

She snorted at his ignorance. 'They're not potatoes. It's some gross purple weed.'

'Spuds,' he repeated, striding over to unearth one of the knobbly purple roots from the pile of weeds and snapping it in half; it bled purple on his tanned hands. 'Potato tubers. Marian's friend brought them from South Africa. Unusual variety, but they make a mean mash.'

Her stomach plummeted to her toes then bounced back up into her throat. She grabbed at the root. 'Are they dead?'

'Don't sweat it.' Krueger covered her hand, both of them holding the tuber as though it were a trophy. 'We'll let them grow some eyes, then replant them. It's just set you back a season.'

She snatched her hand back and rubbed her face. Krueger grinned at god-alone knew what. Nothing about this was funny. In the space of a few days she had poisoned Marian's chickens, killed a prized crop and repeatedly failed at bread-making. 'Hell, the bread! Goat, get out of the way.' She shoved the sheep who was leaning against her thighs, but he took the nudge as a caress and refused to shift.

'Seems he's taken a liking to you. Goat, c'mere.' Krueger clicked his fingers and the sheep obediently stepped toward him.

'It's not mutual,' she lied. The sheep was as daft as Scritches, seeming to instantly bond with the farmer. 'I have to get the bread out of the oven.'

She quickly learned this apparently was farmer-speak for 'Please, do come inside. Make yourself at home,' Krueger easily striding alongside her as she raced from the orchard and into the house. He swept off his hat and ducked through the doorway, though he'd probably have cleared it by a centimetre.

She locked the back door behind them and he flicked a hand toward the latch. 'You're locking me in?'

'City habit. Lock as you enter.'

'You lived by yourself?'

At least Marian had left something out of his information pack. 'Since I left state care.'

'Must've been tough going it alone in the city.'

'Not really. Better to be on my own than—' Than in a darkened room with a group of men. Three. Always three. No other number scared her, rarely gave her pause for thought. But put her in a room with three men and she'd lose it. She wheeled abruptly and slammed into the kitchen.

Krueger's stomach rumbled behind her. 'Sorry, busy day. I had to skip lunch. And it smells really good in here.'

With a thin-knit jersey shirt tucked into faded Levi's, he looked mighty tidy for someone who'd been working all day. She put on her sweetest smile. Partly because the loaf she took from the oven looked damn good, and partly because, in light of her failures, she needed to win him over. 'Fancy a slice? By the time I brew'—she stressed the word to prove she'd learned—'tea, the bread will have cooled enough to cut.'

'No way I'd refuse that offer. Looks like you'd give Marian a run for her money. I'll go wash up, if you don't mind.'

'Sure. You know where the bathroom is?' Of course he did, probably knew every inch of the house far better than she did. Shit, had she left her knickers hanging over the side of the tub?

Krueger returned and dropped onto a vacant chair. Scritches looked up, blinked sleepily, and then erupted into purrs as he registered the company and dragged himself onto the farmer's lap.

'G'day, Scritches. How're you liking the country life? Making yourself as useful as your mum?'

He remembered the cat's name? Okay, so maybe Matt Krueger had a redeeming feature. 'Kettle's on, I'll go wash up.'

She crossed to the bathroom. No stray knickers, thank God. As she turned on the tap, she glanced at the mirror above the pedestal basin.

Shit. Literally.

No wonder Krueger laughed at her in the orchard. Her face smudged brown with dust and manure, she'd accidentally finger-painted purple potato-juice stripes across her cheek.

The taps turned to full, she ripped off her clothes and ducked under the shower. With no clean clothes in the room, she dragged back on her filthy jeans and T-shirt, but left off the sweaty bra and prickle-infested socks. She ran her fingers through wet hair; that would have to do. She needed to impress Krueger with her achievements, not her looks.

Krueger looked up from pouring water into the teapot. 'Never met a woman who could shower and dress that quick.'

'Know a lot about women's bathing habits, do you?' she snapped as she took out a knife. She'd liked Krueger better when he was condescending instead of amused. Using a tea towel, she clamped down and started to slice the hot loaf. 'We'll take this out on the verandah. Oh—!' The bread was soggy in the middle. Loaf number god-only-knew-what and she'd forgotten to tap the base to check for the hollow thud that meant it was cooked through. What now?

Disguise. Lots of butter and Tracey's jam.

She spread the slices thickly, arranged them on two plates, and poured the tea. 'Milk, sugar?'

'Black, straight, thanks.'

'You take the tea, I'll bring the bread.' The less opportunity he had to look at it, the better.

The screen door snagged her heel as she followed him out.

Krueger sat, his legs stretched halfway across the verandah, gazing into the twilight. She paused for a moment, watching him. He looked lost in his own thoughts, but she had no idea what they were.

She slid the plates onto the table. 'I didn't hear you come over last night.'

'Rode.'

She sipped more tea than she wanted, casting about for something to say.

Apparently unperturbed by the awkward silence, Krueger regarded her solidly, again seeming to assess her. 'I went to the market today but decided against the poddy,' he said finally, before taking a mouthful of bread; she hoped his wince was at the heat. 'This is really good. I reckon I could pick Tracey's jam anywhere. But hot bread is the perfect vehicle for it.'

She tried not to snigger at his choice of words. Maybe he watched *My Kitchen Rules*, too. He wolfed down his two slices, and she edged her plate toward him.

'Are you sure?'

'Yeah,' she encouraged, 'I had bread at lunch. Don't really want any more.'

'Excellent.' He scooped up her slice.

'So why no poddy?' She carefully phrased the question to hide her ignorance.

Krueger's gaze slid away, a hand running over his chin as he focused on a clump of bushes down the yard. The sound of birds settling for the evening filled the pause. 'I thought taking in a little one might be too close to home.'

Her blood chilled. 'You mean I have to foster?'

Fine lines etched the tanned skin around Krueger's eyes and she found it absurdly hard to pull her gaze away. 'Sort of. You hand rear the orphan poddy until she's old enough to be inseminated, then presto, you have a milk cow. But it's kind of full-on for you to handle right now.'

A calf. Though relief released her shoulders, her lips tightened. What right did Krueger have to judge her ability to raise a baby? Of any kind. 'Is that your call?' she snapped.

He regarded her for a long moment, his eyes reflecting the sudden iciness of her words. 'Not at all. Completely up to you. Just let me know what you want to do.' His tone

171

held a cautionary chill, and he drained his cup and set it back on the table. 'I'd better shift it or I'll be in trouble at home. Thanks again. I'll duck back in a couple of days, see how you're getting on.' He rammed the akubra on his head, though dusk had thickened around them. 'Want me to hang around while you lock up?'

'No, I'm fine.' Yet she couldn't hide the twinge of regret that she had altered the dynamic, driven him away just when he seemed a little more tolerable.

He stood, reaching into his breast pocket. 'Tracey asked me to give you this.'

Her fingernails dug into her palms as he dropped an envelope on the table. Please don't let there be any new tasks. She couldn't take any more failures.

❧

She was midway through tidying the kitchen, Marian's unopened letter lying on the table like a summons, when she heard the vehicle. Drying her hands on a towel, she made for the back door, looking through the sunroom windows.

Even in the dim light of the moth-covered bulb above the back door, she knew her mother instantly. The hereditary similarities were striking. Same chin, the nose she was accustomed to seeing in the mirror. Her mother's hair was blonde and straight, though, instead of her own pale-brown waves.

Her hand trembled as it moved to the chain on the door. How did she greet the woman who had deserted her? Who, perhaps more importantly, now stood on her doorstep?

Twenty-nine years of pretending she hadn't wanted to know her mother, hadn't needed her parents, hadn't been lonely and unwanted, coalesced in this moment. Her mother stood before her, and maybe, just maybe, Marian had misjudged her. Perhaps Denise had come to apologise, to explain that she had been forced to give Roni up and longed to make amends.

'Veronica,' her mother smiled. 'Welcome home.'

And, just like that, she had a family.

She licked her dry lips. 'You must be . . . Denise.' She couldn't call her Mum. Not yet.

The woman was taller than her. Leaner, too. Perfectly made up and elegant in jeans and a simple collared blouse.

Denise touched her own nose. 'My goodness, you see the resemblance? How amazing.' She peered at Roni. 'You favour your father, you know.' She laughed, a throaty chuckle. 'Funnily enough, I can see some of Marian in you. That would have pleased her.'

Roni stood back. 'Come in.'

Denise tapped a manicured nail against her lip for a moment. 'Are you sure? I mean, I don't want to pressure you . . . but I do so very much want to talk with you.' She lifted one shoulder, the gesture apologetic and disarming.

'Of course,' Roni said, although her mind screamed at the bizarre situation.

Denise's high-heeled boots tapped on the floor behind Roni. She glanced around as they entered the kitchen. 'Can't say the place has changed in the last few years.'

'You haven't been here since . . . ?'

'Not for a long time. Oh, I came out here regularly, to see how Marian was faring, but she was predisposed toward greeting me on the verandah. Kept me outside like I was a Jehovah's Witness come knocking. No matter.' Denise dismissed the memory with a flick of her wrist. 'She probably thought she had just cause. Past is past, though, isn't it?'

Roni's heart thumped erratically. Was this how reunions normally went? Stilted conversation built around the pretence that nothing untoward had occurred in their relationship? She had so many questions, but her brain refused to form coherent phrases. 'I resemble my father? He's still . . . ?' Around? Wants to meet me? Most importantly, who is he?

Again, the flick of the wrist. 'Oh, he's long dead. I thought Marian would have told you. Sad, but not unexpected.'

Disappointment pierced Roni as her new family instantly halved. 'But you'd stayed in contact with him?'

Denise raised her eyebrows as she took a seat at the table. 'Oh, yes. I made certain we stayed very close. I'm surprised Marian didn't mention our . . . relationship. I would've thought, having decided to disrupt your life and share our secrets, she'd divulge all. Still, I suppose it wasn't a bond she could understand. I assume you know about her and Tracey . . .' She trailed off delicately.

'Sort of. Best friends, weren't they?'

'Well, rather more than that. At least my sister found love somewhere.' Denise flinched as Scritches uncurled from his cushion and stretched. He eyed her, then sat again, as though he were a participant in the conversation. 'I imagine there's so much you want to know. What exactly did Marian tell you? Naturally, it's bound to be somewhat biased, as will be my own account. But I have no doubt you're intelligent enough to form your own opinions.'

Roni pinched at her lip. Would she betray her aunt by speaking with her mother? The woman was, despite Marian's accusations and Tracey's caution, apparently reasonable and balanced. But was there a risk she was allowing her perception to be moulded by her desire to know her mother? 'She didn't tell me much. Only that you were pregnant with me when you were very young and single.' Her cheeks flamed, and she checked the instinctive move of her hand to her own belly. 'And that she wanted to keep me but you placed me for fostering.' Her sanitised synopsis laid no blame, didn't evidence a trace of the desertion she had felt for so many years. But it invited her mother's explanation.

Denise nodded, her painted lips twisting into an appreciative bow. 'Somewhat lacking in detail, but the basics are true enough. Yet still, I imagine it was horribly hard for you to hear.' She sighed and looked down at her hand for a moment, as though pondering what to share. 'Of course, Marian's reason for wanting to keep you was somewhat more convoluted than simply pretending she cared what became of you. In any case, I decided you'd have a better life elsewhere. This town is . . . inbred. Parochial and archaic, rife with rumours and secrets and lies. I was certain Sydney would provide you with far better opportunities.'

Denise sounded so hopeful, something shifted in Roni's core; her mother had done what she felt was right. She couldn't have predicted how that would turn out, couldn't know Roni would be abused and unloved. Denise had made a decision with her baby's best interests at heart, exactly as Roni would do. 'It did,' she lied to alleviate her mother's concern.

Denise nodded, her shoulders easing. 'Excellent. Now, what do you have planned while you're here? I want us to spend a lot of time together. We have so much to talk about.'

The unusual sensation of tears thickened her throat. She never cried. But she was damn close. 'Actually, I've a list of jobs to complete. But I'll make time,' she added hastily, in case Denise thought she was being rejected.

Denise arched a perfect eyebrow. 'Aren't you going to put this place on the market? To be honest, although I'm thrilled, I'm surprised to see you here. I was planning to find you in Sydney once all this had been settled.'

Why wait until then? The words hovered on Roni's lips, but she dismissed them as petulant; Denise was here, now. Doing her best. 'It's complicated. The sharefarmer has a list of tasks I have to complete before the title passes to me.'

'Matthew Krueger?' Denise hesitated, drawing her fingertips across the tabletop, her tone reluctant. 'I don't want to interfere, Veronica, but a word of caution. Watch out for him. Your aunt was . . . *unhealthily* close to him.'

'Close, like, how?'

Denise's cheeks tinged pink, and she looked down at her lap shyly. 'I'm probably the last person who should throw stones, particularly in that direction, but suffice to say I was surprised by his influence here. Given your aunt's . . . tendencies . . . I expected her to be immune to his charm.'

Roni's fist clenched. It was bizarre, but she realised she hadn't wanted to be right about Matt being after the farm, by whatever means.

Before she could ask for details, the slim black fitness tracker on Denise's wrist vibrated against the table and she glanced at it, sucking an annoyed breath between her teeth. 'Oh, I have to go,' Denise said. 'I'm so sorry. To be honest, I hadn't even intended to come tonight, I wanted to let you settle in before I descended on you. But then I was passing by and couldn't resist. I'll tell you what,' she rummaged in her leather handbag. 'I'll leave you my number, and you call when you can make time to catch up with me.'

Roni nodded, following her to the door, trying to ignore the notion that her mother was being ripped from her life again. Ridiculous. She'd promised herself never to allow those kinds of emotions, that level of need.

Denise pressed a cool palm to Roni's cheek. 'I know I'm asking a lot, Veronica. I don't deserve your time, that's why I'll leave it up to you to make contact. I hope you can forgive me for doing what I thought best for you.'

Roni locked the door and leaned her back against it. Held in the tears.

Chapter Seventeen

Dearest Veronica,

Have you found your feet in my little piece of paradise? I know you've now met the dearest of my friends (and, of course, baker of the most excellent lamingtons!). I'm also aware she has—or should have, depending on how scatterbrained she was—unveiled your most recent task.

Yes, I know. The CWA brings to mind a roomful of lavender-scented old biddies cackling over the deafening click of their knitting needles. And, truthfully, this is sometimes an apt description. However, there seems to be something of a trend of younger folk joining the association, so you shouldn't be entirely at the mercy of the crones. In any case, age is irrelevant. I want you to get to know your neighbours but, more importantly, I want you to realise that, while independence is valuable, we all sometimes need to lean on other people.

Although I craved isolation and the lack of judgment that only seclusion can bring, my friends have become dear to me. Faithful despite my tantrums, regardless of my idiosyncrasies, and immune to my occasionally haughty demeanour—occasional being an entirely relative term—my friends, among whom I count your father, persevered. It was they who created true joy in my life.

But friendship, I have discovered, is something of a balancing act. The relationship must be rooted in equality; therefore, it is imperative to not only offer assistance but to accept help. Difficult, I know, when pride is both one's greatest asset and greatest handicap.

I wish I'd recognised this double-edged sword earlier in my life. My pride insisted I keep secrets when, if I had replaced it with courage, perhaps things would have been different for both of us. Only with risk comes reward.

Still, I didn't, and they're not, so that brings us to now.

How is my lovely Goat faring? Though I bottle-raised many sheep, pasturing them into their old age, he is by far my favourite. Such a character. When you find your way to the town, he does love breakfast biscuits. Don't let him eat too many, though. He'll happily scoff the entire box, then lie around all day, belching and bloated.

Are the chickens laying? Every year I swear I'll cull the numbers, but once the hens go broody I can't bear to steal their eggs. There's nothing quite like the sight of tiny yellow or black chicks following their mother all over the farmyard. And ducklings! They are the sweetest thing ever. Do keep watch for hawks, though. They float on thermals, so high you can barely spy them, then stoop and take a chick in the blink of an eye.

Has Matt shown you around the property? He knows everything you could possibly want to learn about the stock and the crop yields and will help you find your way through your tasks. Likewise, Tracey will take you under her wing. She has no children of her own—one of the many things over which we bonded—and is quite thrilled with the idea of teaching you to cook—assuming you chose that option, rather than quilting or sewing? She's very much hoping you will though, as you can see, she's as skilled with a sewing needle as she is with a wooden spoon. If you learn to bake with Tracey's skill it's as well I'm no longer there, or I would become a rather portly old lady.

As you see, when I put pen to paper to talk with you, I'm loathe to stop. Perhaps because I hope these conversations draw us closer, belatedly forging the connection I should have created so many years ago. Or maybe it's because I procrastinate, avoiding sharing another secret. One I promised my husband never to reveal—yet I must, because this secret truly belongs to you.

You may have noticed I mention my husband and your father frequently, almost interchangeably? That is because they are one and the same.

I'd not been married to Andrew for two years when he evidently decided that was too long for a man to go without sex. I could have lived with that. The town is not far away, I'm certain he could have procured a prostitute. Or even a girlfriend. A fine-looking man, Andrew was accustomed to female attention, and I imagine that made my own lack of interest harder to bear.

Remember I told you I regret the secrets I have kept? That was another of them: I should have been honest with Andrew before we married, told him I would have no issue with him seeking his physical pleasure elsewhere, as long as we maintained the property.

However, your mother saw no reason for him to look elsewhere. It's important you understand that I don't blame her for this: although she was, shall we say, experienced, still she was legally a minor, and Andrew an adult. He confessed to me immediately. For all his dalliance with Denise, he remained an intrinsically good man who paid for his mistake by spending the next nineteen years crippled by regret and fearing revelation. Which neither excuses nor absolves his behaviour, but it is what it is.

After admitting their affair, Andrew barely spoke to Denise. It seemed he couldn't face her, couldn't face what he had done. How he had betrayed me, his wife, but also betrayed her, a teenager in our house. Anyway, she was furious. Perhaps she truly thought he loved her. Whatever her reason, it was this anger that saw her spitefully place you in the foster system.

Suffocated by my own disappointment, I never once spared a thought for Andrew. Because of my inability to tell him my truth before we married, he had been robbed not once but twice of his chance to have a child of his own. Still, I truly believe that we could have brought you home if it weren't for the depth of Andrew's shame and his fear of retribution. Had he admitted his paternity we could perhaps have had you removed from the foster system. However I suspect not only was Andrew afraid he would be tried by both the legal system and our peers but, as the years passed, he simply could not face the thought of seeing you, the proof of his infidelity, each day. It would have been different if we had raised you since birth; our pretence would have grown alongside you until it became organic, the truth of your origins nothing more than a vague recollection clouded in the haze of a long-forgotten summer, the sharp edges softened by love and shared memories. But to bring a teenager into our house, a young woman who would have every right to question where she came from? That was not something Andrew could live with. Your heritage was, in fact, a secret he took to the grave; only I knew the truth of his remorse, and Denise knew of his guilt. A weapon she has wielded, as I told you, for many years.

But, while Andrew had his reasons, I had my own fears. Cowardice that prevented me from arguing my case. Your case. I was incapacitated by the suspicion that if I betrayed Andrew's trust, or didn't surrender to Denise's continual petty blackmails, Andrew would leave me. Although I did not love him as a wife, I did love the man; yet it wasn't any form of love that factored into my reasoning. I had no wish to lose the advantages being married brought, not least of which was the disguising of my own sexual identity. But, more importantly, I believed that if Andrew left, I would not be able to manage; I would be forced to sell my beloved Peppertree Crossing.

So you see, Veronica, while my husband and sister— your father and mother—bear their own guilt, the greatest shame is mine. I traded you for Peppertree Crossing.

Now I seek to make reparation.

With love,

Marian

Chapter Eighteen

Roni's hands trembled as she put aside the letter. So briefly she'd had it all. A family history, a mother who cared, a property to inherit. Then, in the space of a few paragraphs, her existence had become the stuff of a sordid read featured on the lurid cover of a weekly magazine. 'Man impregnates gay wife's teenage sister.'

She felt empty, as though a prize had been snatched away right as she finally committed to reaching out to grasp it. But, as she tried to grapple with the fact that her uncle and father were the same person, that her mother had stolen her own brother-in-law, resentment crept in. Even if her parents had been in love, the inescapable truth was that neither of them had cared about her. And Marian, who now lectured her on the importance of taking risks, of being self-sufficient and emancipated, had done nothing but lie to obtain the security she craved.

Was that, though, the intent of her letter? Did Marian admit to her own failings as a lesson? Yet what could a woman, brought up with the wealth and privilege that allowed her to play with people like they were chess pieces, understand of real life?

Roni rubbed her temples, folded the letter and slid it with the others behind a breadboard on the kitchen counter. She wouldn't cry, nor would she confuse desires with needs. Neither family nor friends were necessary.

∽

Her back against the chicken coop, legs stretched along the ground, Roni encouraged the friendliest of the fowl to take feed from her outstretched palm, grinning as she managed to smooth a hand across the burnished feathers of the rooster. The sun rose between the gums, fundamentally the same sight every day, yet still it was fresh and new, a daily miracle that awakened a feeling of anticipation, as though life held promise. She took a deep breath, feeling the tension that had kept her rigid and miserable all night finally ease. She had survived far worse than this. So her family were all kinds of messed up: did that really change anything? With food, shelter and security for Roo and Scritches, life right now was better than she'd ever had it.

The magpies warbled their morning chorus, and from a distant scrub, a kookaburra joined in. Miss Fuzzypants, who appeared to be covered in white dandelion fluff rather than feathers, waddled into her lap, head cocked inquisitively to one side. Roni cracked a grain between her teeth, feeding the crumbs to the bantam. The serenity seemed to seep into her pores, imbuing her with a sense of hope. Perhaps taking the tasks a little slower, staying here a while longer, wouldn't be the worst thing in the world. She'd wanted to rush back to the familiarity of Sydney, but realistically, she could never create a home there for Roo. She needed a new plan. But first, she must secure her inheritance.

As she'd not driven since high school, she took a couple of practice runs up and down the corrugated driveway before tackling the bridge, which seemed narrower than when Jim had driven across. If she stayed too long she would have to widen it for her own access.

She turned right at the end of the drive, praying that, with spotty reception on her phone, the town was either signposted or easy to find.

It turned out to be both. The road wound through straggling scrub, then dropped down a steep hill and opened without warning to river flats studded with fat black-and-white cows. The flats continued on her left, but the right side of the road became a town, the street bordered by large blocks hosting substantial stone houses. A grin curved her lip. On a whim, she'd flicked through Enid Blyton's *The Magic Faraway Tree* in Marian's library. The two very different views, suburban and country, with the road dividing them, reminded her of the tree, growing different fruit in layers, revealing a surprise every few feet.

She slowed as she passed the town-limit sign. Settlers Bridge. The gardens on the right sprouted a mix of spectacularly flowering rose bushes and recycled lounge chairs, positioned to gaze toward the distant glint of a grey river hedged by trees that she was quite certain, this time, were willows. Either that or folk round here really liked to watch cows. She buzzed down her window for a better view and her eyes watered. Wow. Maybe the residents didn't use those lounges all that often. The aroma was . . . organic.

After three blocks, the arterial road came to a T-junction, the left turn leading to a bridge over the river, the right threading between two double-storey pubs that appeared to be gatekeepers to the main drag. The four lanes were bisected by a brick-paved centre strip planted out with industrial-sized wine barrels of purple and orange bougainvillea, rocketing skyward like fireworks. Along the street, faded iron verandahs created lazy eyelids over dusty glass windows crowded with clothes or bric-a-brac that could have been stock from the fifties. Further down the street the two big banks, both low, ornate stone buildings, faced off with each other. It seemed the town planners had decreed each shop must be mirrored on the opposite side of the road.

Selecting a space that wouldn't require her to exercise long-forgotten parallel-parking skills—though it seemed unlikely there would ever be a need to drive around the block to find the perfect spot—Roni pulled beneath a red-flowered gum on the kerb near the IGA. The small store directly opposite, almost invisible behind the 'Australia Post Outlet' sign that covered most of the grimy window, boasted a white-flowered gum. Mistake, or a rebellious council employee?

She followed the short cement ramp up to the door, batted through the orange plastic fly strips that hung there and took a trolley.

She shopped slowly, toting up the items in her head, making sure she would have enough cash when she reached the register. A woman strolled past, matching her pace to the curly-haired toddler grasping her hand. The child stared up at Roni with huge eyes.

Soon she would be that woman, her child's tiny fingers firmly encased in her grip, a life forever meshed with her own. Dependent on her.

She couldn't wait.

The bakery stand was loaded with bread. And lamingtons. A possible fallback for the CWA contest? She chewed at her thumbnail. No. Marian asked for relatively little in exchange for the property and, despite her aunt's manipulations, she couldn't cheat. Besides, Roo deserved a mum who knew how to cook—and, in any case, she needed the money for Goat's Weet-Bix. In the next aisle she added a large bottle of multivitamins to her basket. Expensive, but they'd make up for any shortfall in her diet.

'You're new here, lovey.' The burgundy-haired cashier made it a friendly statement.

'Yes. I'm staying at my—out at Peppertree Crossing.'

'Oh, you'll be Marian's niece, then.' The woman huffed as she hauled a watermelon onto the scales.

Evidently, Marian had gone out with a bang, making up for years of silence. Roni nodded.

'South Australia doesn't do plastic bags, lovey. You'll have to take a box. Unless you brought a carry bag?'

'Sorry, no. I didn't realise there was a bag rule.'

The cashier flattened the sunny-yellow apron over the comfortable lumpiness of her stomach. 'No problem, just letting you know for next time. No, no,' she waved away Roni's cash. 'Marian's groceries go on her tab; her accountant squares it at the end of the month. She said same goes for you. Just sign the docket here.'

Roni scrawled her name on the bottom of the printout. If she'd known she didn't have to hand over cash she would have splurged on the packet of Tim Tams she'd picked up and put down twice. But, then, that would be taking advantage of Marian's generosity. In fact, Roni would rather pay for her own groceries, but insisting seemed likely to encourage a conversation of more depth and length than she felt prepared for.

'You found the house all tidy and the cupboards stocked, then?' the woman continued. 'I didn't know whether you'd prefer an apple pie or apricot, but I always feel that apricot has just that bit more flavour to it. Hubs doesn't agree. He insists that apple is a classic. But you know men; creatures of habit.'

'Oh, you're . . .' Roni trailed off, trying to remember the name Derek had given. The woman's nametag had slid down one pendulous bosom and Roni tipped her neck to make it out. Lynn. 'You're Marian's housekeeper, right?'

Lynn smiled. 'I used to pop out there to help her out. I don't suppose you'll be needing me now, though?'

She sounded hopeful, but all Roni could think of was the expense. 'I guess not. But I'll see you in a couple of weeks when I've worked my way through this lot.' She hefted the grocery box.

'Oh, sooner than that, lovey,' Lynn said. 'Tracey said you're coming along to the meeting next week.' She tucked the signed docket in the till. 'You're doing lamingtons, right? I'm more into quilting, myself. I try to avoid the cooking fundraisers, because I'd eat all the profits.' She slapped her stomach and grinned. 'Oops, sorry, love, rush hour.' An elderly gentleman had shuffled up behind Roni, shunting his groceries down the conveyor-less counter, and Lynn smiled at him. 'Hello there, Young Eric. What can I do you for today?' She fluttered her fingers at Roni. 'See you then, lovey.'

As Roni turned away, Lynn whispered loud enough for an apparently hard-of-hearing Young Eric to catch, 'That pretty little thing is Marian's niece. You know, that one. Down from the big smoke.'

Her cheeks burned, and she exited quickly. So, she was *that one*. Just how much of her story had Marian shared? And how angry was Denise about the revelation? She hadn't seemed upset yesterday, more dryly amused. Mind, she also hadn't seemed like a woman who would steal her sister's husband and dump her own bastard in another state.

Roni slammed the car door and took out her phone.

Tracey answered on the second ring. 'Hello, love, where are you? Standing in the middle of a paddock? Marian always said she had to stump halfway up the hill to get a signal, unless she used the landline. Or are you running away from a bowl of dough that's taken on a life of its own?'

Roni smiled despite herself. She would win the battle with that damn bread if it was the last thing she achieved here. 'Actually, I'm in town. I was wondering . . .' She rubbed at a worn patch on her jeans. Never in her life had she dropped in on someone.

'In town? Pop over for a cuppa then, love. I've just pulled a batch of pumpkin scones out of the oven.'

It only took a couple of minutes to find the house Tracey described: solid stone trimmed in Brunswick Green with a matching green picket fence and red-painted verandah. Rose bushes bloomed in the front garden and a cast-iron setting, much like Marian's, graced the porch, overlooking a broad, tree-lined street.

'It's open,' Tracey called from the depths of the house.

As Roni hesitantly opened the flywire door, Tracey appeared at the end of a short hallway, rubbing floury hands on a chequered apron. 'Don't be a stranger, love, door's always open. Come on in. I've got to get this batch in the oven. Bear doesn't bite.' She disappeared again.

Roni wiped the dirt from the pavement on the doormat, then made her way along the hall, trying not to stare too obviously at the photographs lining the walls. A medium-sized grey dog, fluffier than a pompom, barrelled into the hall and sat at her feet, a friendly smile on his face.

Tracey popped her head around the door jamb. 'Did you spot your aunt in the pictures?'

'I've no idea what she looks like.'

'Oh. Oh, of course you haven't, you poor thing.' Bangles jangling, Tracey embraced Roni in a one-armed hug and led her back to the front door. 'Well, you will now. Though Marian wasn't one for albums and scrapbooks, I certainly am. Look. Here. And here.' She pointed to a pair of framed eight-by-tens, two laughing women sitting astride an elephant, their faces obscured by sunglasses and hats.

'You rode elephants?' The only reins she'd imagined Marian holding were those of the farm.

'Oh, yes. That would be, what, twenty years ago, I think. Before Andrew got sick. Bali, of course. What Aussie doesn't make a Bali pilgrimage?'

Maybe one who'd never been able to afford to leave Sydney.

'And look, this is a lovely photo. Adelaide Cup Day, 2008. Doesn't she look beautiful?' Tracey clasped her hands, lips thinning as she pressed them together.

A handsome woman raised her champagne glass toward the photographer. Roni's heart tripped. Clear-cut features, an aquiline nose much like her own—and Denise's—but steel-grey hair in a pixie crop rather than a brown-streaked mane. But her eyes. So familiar.

Roni had spent more time wondering about Marian than about Denise, probably because they were linked by the letters. To discover they shared so many features rocked her, the sense of homecoming, of finding where she belonged, hitting her with an unexpected, almost physical force. She staggered, fingertips pressed to the wall.

'Are you all right, love?' Tracey bubbled with instant concern.

'Yeah, sure. It's just I've never . . . never had a face to put to the name. Well, I guess until a couple of weeks ago I didn't even have a name. Are there—do you have any pictures of . . . of . . .' Her mouth wouldn't form the words. Denise's visit had been too short, almost dreamlike, and she needed tangible evidence to piece her family together.

'Your parents?' Tracey said gently. 'I've none of Denise, but there'd be some of Andrew in my albums, somewhere or other. I'll dig them out for you later. Oh. My.' A horrified look crossed her face. 'You did read the letter? You know now?'

'I know. And I met Denise. She came around. Briefly.'

Tracey paused, hand in the small of Roni's back. 'How did that go?'

Roni lifted one shoulder. 'Fine, I guess.'

Tracey waited for a beat, then pointed along the hallway. 'Come into the kitchen and sit down, I've a cuppa brewing. It must have been a shock for you, discovering you have family over here.'

'That's an understatement.' She pulled her phone out of her back pocket and placed it on the table. As she sat, the dog—Bear—rested his head on her knee, looking up with soulful eyes.

Tracey slid a deep-blue mug with a large hand-painted sunflower on one side across the table and added a plate of split, buttered scones. 'Try a scone, love, they're best when they're hot. Marian said she'd discovered you ended up in state care rather than being adopted?'

'I was fostered.' Why, even now, with all her experience, did that still sound better than admitting to state care? As though, at least briefly, someone had wanted her to be part of their family.

Just not in any acceptable way.

Tracey's fair eyebrows rose. 'Why didn't you stay with your foster family, then?'

The scone turned to a lump of lead in Roni's mouth and she swallowed painfully. Why? Because she couldn't take the fear and humiliation any longer. It had required every ounce of courage she had to inform the authorities of what had been going on. Only to have them lock her in care like it was a juvie, like she was the one who'd done something wrong. 'It just didn't work out too great.' She choked the words out and washed them away with hot tea.

'It's such a shame you couldn't have come here, then.'

Roni's trembling fingers crumbled the scone into tiny pieces on her plate.

'Marian would have loved it. I know she would have loved you.'

Yeah, well, shame Marian hadn't sent for her before state care became a necessity. Before the nightmare. Before she was broken. She shoved her hands under her thighs, where Bear immediately tried to snuffle them out. 'Seems there was a whole lot of loving going on in my family. You know, with my uncle being my father.' A father who'd married

194

so he could have children but had been too ashamed to claim her.

Tracey shook her head and tutted. 'Yes, well that was messy. Bear, enough,' she chided the dog, though her tone was fond.

'Denise said she stayed close with him?' Why was she picking at the scab, reinforcing that, despite their supposed antipathy toward one another, she was the only one who had been excluded from the family?

Tracey snorted. 'Stayed close? Oh, she tried. Not that Andrew would have a bar of her. That woman never knows when enough is enough, it's like she has something to prove. And she was particularly bad with Andrew. Of course, none of us knew about them, but there was plenty of gossip. She revelled in your father's guilt but especially loved to taunt Marian that she'd had Andrew once, and could again.' She handed Roni a paper serviette. 'The ridiculous thing is, if she'd known her sister better, Denise would have realised Marian was immune to that particular threat.'

'That *is* messy.' Roni pressed a palm over her mobile, hoping Denise wouldn't pick this moment to reply to the text Roni had impulsively sent on the way into town. After vacillating all night, she finally decided that, regardless of their history, for Roo's sake she should get to know her mother. Now she wasn't so sure. 'Seriously, is your dog actually smiling at me?'

Tracey chortled. 'He's a keeshond. They're known as the smiling Dutchman. Knows the way to any woman's heart, that one. Though he has Matt wrapped around his paw, too.'

'Speaking of Krueg—Matt. He said something about a cow sale. Do you know if it's held every week?'

'Cow sale? The stock market, you mean? Yes, every Thursday, end of Maurice Road.' Tracey waved a hand as though the direction would mean something to Roni. 'But why on earth do you want to know about that?'

'M-Matt'—using his first name sounded odd—'was going to pick up a poddy for me, but he's been busy.' A creative mix of truth and extrapolation.

'Really? I wouldn't have expected him to go there. Most of that stock is headed to the abattoir.'

Roni lifted an eyebrow but Tracey nudged her chin at the plate of scones. 'What do you think of them then, love? Flo Bjelke-Petersen's recipe. Oh, she'd be before your time, wouldn't she? I don't know that she was ever in the CWA, but I'll tell you, we do love her recipes. Good homestyle food, none of your fancy cooking-in-a-plastic-bag rubbish. I was thinking, we might even start you off with her scones.' She shook her head. 'I don't know what Marian was thinking, insisting you try bread first.'

'Apparently something to do with self-sufficiency. So Matt can judge whether I'm good enough.' She hid the sour words in strawberry jam. 'Though he did say the loaf was nice yesterday. It wasn't.'

Tracey snorted into her cup. 'Matt would say it's nice because he's nice. He suggested I drop by regularly to make sure you're not alone too much. As though he needed to ask!' Her halo trembled in mild annoyance. 'And the poor boy probably hasn't had any home cooking, good or otherwise, since Marian passed.'

'His mum doesn't cook?'

'Elayne? I suppose she does. She's not in the CWA, though.'

Clearly, the CWA was the measure of all women.

Over a little more discussion about baking and the people she would meet at the CWA, Roni finished her cup of tea. 'Okay then, I'd better be off. Oh, is there a library in town?' Her heart raced, not solely because of the sugar hit. Within minutes she would be able to see exactly how her baby looked right now, at almost ten weeks.

'Of course there is, love.' Tracey seemed miffed that Roni would question the likelihood. 'Open every Thursday, because that's pension day. It's in the council office. I'll write down the address. Better yet, pop past here on Thursday and I'll take you down and introduce you to Sid. Just make sure you leave plenty of time, because he loves a good chat about everything you're reading.'

Thursday only? And a librarian who got his nose in her business? She would have to think her way around that one, but for now she would make do with bookmarking some pages on her phone to read through later. As she pulled from the kerb, pressing a palm to the horn in response to Tracey's enthusiastic farewell wave, her mind flicked to Greg. She neither wanted nor expected anything from him, and experience proved she'd get even less. But he had rights. At some stage she would have to tell him about the baby. But not yet. For now, Roo was her secret, one to nurse closely, revelling in the thrill that came with every thought of the life growing within her. So much to dream about. So much hope and potential for a future, things she'd not have dared imagine being possible only a fortnight earlier. And undeniably, all thanks to a woman she had never met.

She shook her head, as though she could erase the confusion. Even in their absence her family seemed determined to tear her apart. She felt both anger and gratitude toward Marian, and loathing and . . . something she chose not to label, something unbearably hopeful, toward Denise.

The hardware store was easy to find in the small town, and, with unexpected cash in her wallet as a result of not paying for groceries, she loaded her cart with seedlings. The lush greenery she could imagine filling the vegetable beds would impress Matt Krueger when he came by. Which was supposed to be today, and now she realised with a jolt of confusion that a tiny part of her regretted she would miss his visit.

Pushing the thought away, she grabbed a punnet of each variety. Then doubled up. Never mind self-sufficiency, she would produce enough to feed the town. Show Matt how it should be done.

She paused among the fruit trees, fingering the labels. Nectarines, apricots, almonds, oranges, some with buds furled tight, waiting to burst open. Should she expand the orchard? It would prove her commitment to Marian's self-sufficiency ideals.

And then maybe she should stay to see the trees fruit? A buzz of excitement tingled through her at the thought, but she quickly tamped it down. It was clear that remaining longer than necessary would see her dragged into the community. She knew it was safer to stay comfortably numb, encased in her own existence, than to open herself to hurt and disillusionment. She had made that mistake as a kid and then stupidly ignored the lesson, allowing herself to trust Greg.

No one would slip past her defences again.

Her phone chimed and Denise's name flashed onscreen. Defying her determination to stay numb, her heart smacked painfully against her ribs and she angrily opened the text.

Fantastic! Let's do coffee tomorrow morning! Soooo looking forward to it! Ring me on your way in, I'll give you my addy. Bout ten?

Roni pressed her fingertips to her lips. She wouldn't count the exclamation points. She mustn't. They didn't mean anything.

Did they?

Chapter Nineteen

Roni stared at the message, disappointment heavy in her chest.

Sorry, tiny problem's come up. I'll have to cancel today. Mum xxx

Lucky she had checked her phone as she crossed the cattle grid, before driving all the way into town for the second day in a row. She carefully slid her thumb across the screen, making certain the message saved. Mum xxx. From now on, would there be birthday and Christmas cards with the same valediction? *Shame. Anything I can help with?*

The reply came instantly. *No. Thanks, though. I'm just really sad not to see you xxx*

She hugged the phone to her chest for a moment, then took a deep breath. *I'm in town on Thursday, would that work?* A simple suggestion was not the same as being needy.

Oh, it might! I was hoping to make it before then, though. Will let you know for sure later xxx

Roni sent back a smiley face, then spent fifteen minutes repeatedly checking her phone. Had her response been too offhand? Maybe she should have ended the message with a kiss?

No. She wasn't ready to go there, yet.

She started the engine and turned the car around. With plants to get in the ground and work to do, she couldn't park on the edge of the drive all day, waiting for contact that might never come.

Still, she took a break every hour, walking up the hill behind the house to get a signal and check her messages.

Hours later, after getting all the plants in and locking the chickens away, she made her final foray for the day.

Sorry, Veronica. I planned to come out and surprise you tomorrow, because I really don't want to wait almost a week to see you again. We've a lot of time to make up for! But my car's broken down, so I'm kind of stuck. Spent all day running around, trying to get a decent quote on repairs xxx

This was the sort of normal Roni had always secretly longed for, a to-and-fro of the mundanities of life. The message had only been sent eight minutes earlier, and she told herself she shouldn't reply immediately. It would look needy. Except . . . *Did you manage to get anything sorted?*

Gazing out over the paddocks, she stood on the side of the hill waiting for a reply, until dusk made it difficult to pick her way back to the house.

It was another three days before the flash of Denise's name on the screen made Roni's heart leap as though she'd been waiting for a lover's message.

No luck. Turning into a drama of major proportions. Would be an easy fix but I've lost my credit card, so had to lock my accounts. No money = no fix. Blah xxx

The garage won't extend credit? She'd have expected a country town to be easygoing.

They're weird about it round here. Not a problem, just takes a few days for the new card to arrive. No biggie, it'll sort itself, I'm just stuck for a while xxx

Roni headed back down to the house where she busied herself feeding Scritches his second breakfast and Goat a handful of Weet-Bix before watering the vegetable garden, lush and green in the early-morning sun, then mucking out the chicken coop. After lunch, she strode up the back paddock again. *I can come in today if you need running somewhere?*

No, that's fine. I'll work it out. Just have to wait until Thursday. Hard, though! xxx

Disappointed at the rejection, she spent the remainder of the day reading in the back garden, Scritches curled on her lap. But she couldn't concentrate. What else could she have said that would show Denise she was prepared to at least explore their relationship?

Wednesday morning she walked down the yard, holding her phone until she found a spot with signal. Tracey's name flicked up on the notifications, but she opened the text from Denise first.

Good morning! xxx

She turned her back to the sun climbing between the trees at the bottom of the yard so she could see the screen more clearly. *Morning! x* There, she'd done it. And it felt . . . good. There was no weakness in appending that one tiny letter.

Had a thought. Can you get in today? Soooo looking forward to catching up, can't wait. We could make it lunch and settle in for a nice long afternoon xxx

Roni rubbed a palm against her chest, trying to calm the nerves that kicked in like she'd been asked on a first date. *Sure, sounds great! Address? x*

There's a cafe on Main. Ploughs and Pies. See you there at noon xxx

Still smiling, Roni opened Tracey's message. *Hi love, are we still on for tomorrow? Did you want me to show you where the library is? I've popped together a Tupperware of lamingtons and a few other bits—from what Matt tells me, I'm worried you're working too hard to feed yourself properly.*

Roni tutted, sending a quick note to say she wouldn't be available. She couldn't go in to town today, tomorrow and then again on Friday for the CWA meeting.

With her mother's elegance in mind, she took a white collarless blouse embroidered with tiny wildflowers from the wardrobe and pressed it. Teamed with the black three-quarter pants she'd picked up at the Salvos—and never had anywhere to wear—it was a little thin for the chilly breeze that whispered around her ankles but the nicest one she owned. And it meant she could wear her cheap, strappy sandals instead of the sneakers that were taking a beating in the yard.

Had it not been for the cartoonish rendition of farm machinery and a steaming pie painted on the window, she could have confused the cafe with the sandwich bar directly opposite. Denise wasn't there, so Roni took a seat.

'Be right with you,' a woman rearranging the cake cabinet trilled. A job Roni had done hundreds of times, though the cellophane-wrapped commercial desserts Rafe stocked didn't look as tempting as the cream-filled concoctions lining these shelves. Despite the familiarity of the setting, she didn't feel the least homesick.

The middle-aged woman bustled over, holding up a palm before Roni could speak. 'Even if strangers weren't unusual around here, I'd have noticed you. Marian's niece, right? Such a striking similarity.'

Odd everyone associated her with Marian rather than her mother. 'Roni,' she offered.

'Samantha. How do you like our corner of the world? Finding your way around?'

'It's been . . . interesting. And yes, it's not too hard to navigate.'

The woman settled into the chair opposite, her elbows on the red-chequered plastic tablecloth. 'I suppose you're used to the city. Marian said you were in Sydney for years.'

Not only had Marian shared the secret of her existence but her details as well? 'My whole life, actually. First time away.'

'Oh, goodness, this must be exciting, then. Are you alone, or did you bring your significant other?'

She must have looked surprised because Samantha laughed, slapping a hand onto the table. 'Oh, don't mind me being nosey! Anything that isn't a secret in this town is up for gossip. Well, not that secrets are exempt. Tracey tells me you're joining the CWA?'

'Not so much joining as checking it out.'

'You'll love it. We have tons of fun. Did she tell you we have bingo at the end of next month? Rebecca from the butcher provides a meat tray prize. Just in time for the summer barbies, so it always gets a good turnout. Then there's the Christmas raffle—oh, listen to me, rattling on like a road train, and you're probably dying for a drink. What can I get you? First one on the house, a little welcome to town.'

'That's really lovely.' Rafe could take a few customer-service notes here. 'But I'm meeting my m-mother for lunch.'

Samantha's smile tightened. 'Oh. Denise? She doesn't usually bring her business here.' She jerked her chin at the sandwich bar across the street. 'Did Tractors and Tarts cut her off?'

They both looked toward the door as the bell jangled. Samantha rose. 'I'll see you at the meeting on Friday, Roni.' She pointedly ignored Denise, who didn't seem to notice as she wound between the empty tables.

Roni half-stood and Denise wrapped her in an expensively perfumed, one-armed hug. Her other arm clutched a bundle of white fluff. 'Veronica. Thank you so much for coming in. Sorry I'm late. I forgot I'd have to walk here.' She winced as she pulled out her chair.

'You should've called, I'd have picked you up.'

Denise sat slowly, free hand pressed to the small of her back, the other wrapped around the white Maltese terrier she placed on her lap. 'It's fine. I'm sure it's good for me to walk, despite what the doctor thinks.'

'Doctor?'

Denise waved a hand at the dog. 'This is Bonnie. I know, I know. It's a little odd carrying her around with me. But really, she's my baby. All I have. At least, until now.'

Denise stood again, flinching and closing her eyes for a second before smiling at Roni. 'We need to order from the counter. Samantha's funny like that. Any idea what you want? I'll go.'

'Whatever you have is fine.'

'Would you watch Bonnie?' She lowered the dog onto Roni's lap, patting it as it settled. Scritch was not going to love that smell.

Roni chewed on her lip as her mother made her way across the cafe. Denise's impeccable make-up didn't disguise her pallor, lines of pain etched from the corners of her eyes down to her lips.

'Croissants and coffee. We shall pretend to be in Paris, no?' Denise affected an accent and dropped the 's' in Paris as she scooped up the dog and resumed her seat. 'Have you been overseas?'

'Only if a ferry across the harbour counts.'

'Well, you're still young, plenty of time. Oh! I've just had the best idea!' Denise leaned forward, her free hand covering Roni's on the table. 'I'm headed to Europe next month. Why don't we go together?'

'I don't—' She used the interruption of Samantha sliding the coffees onto the table to collect her whirling thoughts. Not that she could think logically. The hope and joy threatening to explode within her at the whirlwind ride of the past few days—going from no family to talking of travelling the world with her mother—battled with her innate wariness, her years of experience. She couldn't afford to take her mother's words to heart, not yet. She deserved some answers first. 'That sounds great. But I wouldn't be able to go for a while.' She would have no funds until the property settled.

Denise tapped a packet of stevia into her cappuccino. 'Well, how about I push it back a few weeks? I'll lose some money on my reservations, but the chance to spend time with you, at long last, is something that can't be counted in dollars.'

Roni wanted to leap from her chair, to make promises, to rush to the travel agent right away. But she had to be cautious. According to Marian, this woman had deserted her—although, the more she spoke with Denise, the less credible Marian's story seemed. Roni knew what it was to be manipulated by those who should care; whoever Denise had been at sixteen, whatever mistakes or choices she had made, she now seemed a warm, compassionate woman.

Denise pulled out her phone. 'Let me make a note to call my agent when I get home. I don't have her number on me. Or the itinerary, but I'm sure I can remember most of it—it was always the trip of my dreams. Except now, oh, I can't believe this, Veronica. Now it'll be simply perfect.'

Her voice throbbed with emotion and she pressed her fingertips beneath her eyes. 'I'll tell you what I remember and you let me know if there's anywhere you've ever desperately wanted to go. I'll have the agent create an entire new itinerary, especially for the two of us.'

By the time the flaky, golden croissants arrived ten minutes later they were still in France together, Denise waxing lyrical about the wineries in Bordeaux, where they would spend a week before heading to Spain, and making careful notes in her phone of anywhere Roni mentioned. Which really wasn't many places, as she'd never allowed her imagination to wander overseas. But now . . . there would only be a short window to travel before Roo arrived, and she would have to check with the doctor that it was safe, yet it would be so wonderful for her child to have her grandmother already a mainstay in her life.

Roni had finished eating, although Denise had only crumbled pastry onto her plate, feeding it to the puppy on her lap, and they had ordered a second coffee before she realised that, swept up in the fantasy Denise wove, she had learned nothing about her mother's life. Contagious though Denise's enthusiasm was, Roni still needed answers. As Denise finished an animated tale regarding the somewhat inebriated patriarch of a family she'd been seated alongside on a flight to South Africa, Roni seized her opportunity. 'Marian mentioned my father died nearly ten years ago.'

Denise arched an eyebrow. 'Oh? I thought she hadn't told you anything about Andrew?'

'She left me letters.'

'Really?' Denise clapped her hands lightly. 'Such a practical idea, so very Marian. You know all the family secrets, then?'

Roni shrugged. 'I've no idea. I'm hoping you'll fill me in.'

'Of course. Anything you want to know. You'll find I don't believe in keeping secrets.' She bent her face close to the dog's, who licked at her eagerly.

The tension drained from Roni's shoulders and she leaned her elbows on the table, cradling her coffee between her hands. Could Denise really be such an open book, so forgiving of the sister who had planned to use her as a brood mare to provide an heir for Peppertree Crossing? Roni closed her eyes, releasing a sigh on the pretext of blowing her already cool drink; their future relationship could so easily have been destroyed had Roni only considered Marian's side of the story.

Thanks to Marian's letters—or maybe because of them—there was one detail she needed to hear directly from Denise. 'Was there a reason you had me fostered out? I mean, I know you couldn't raise me, and I understand the circumstances of my conception must have been awkward, but why fostering?'

'You mean as opposed to adoption?' Denise gazed at her, a tiny frown between her brows. 'Oh, believe me, I considered both options. I had counselling, you know, before I could place you. So even though I was terribly young, I tried to weigh up what was best for you.'

'Wouldn't "best" have been adoption, so I'd spend my life with one family?' Instead, by the time she was nine she'd been terrified of harsh words within her foster family, worried they would divorce like the first set, or that she would make a mistake, break a rule, disappoint her foster parents, and be kicked out of the family. Again.

Although, eventually that had been the preferable option.

Tears starred Denise's eyes and she bit at her lower lip until her even teeth left indents. She hid her distress in Bonnie's fluff, her voice muffled. 'Oh, Veronica. I wanted to keep you so very badly. If I was given one wish it would be that you never know the pain of being punished for a tiny mistake by having to give up something you love more than life itself.'

Roni's hand instinctively dropped to her flat belly.

'But there was no way I could keep you.' Denise straightened, meeting her gaze unblinkingly. 'So I decided on fostering. I knew if I allowed you to be adopted, there was no chance I could ever claim you back.'

Roni's heart thumped so painfully, she shifted her hand to her chest. This story was similar to Marian's, yet so very different. In the most important way possible. 'Claim me?'

Denise nodded earnestly. 'Fostering is only until the birth family can take the child back. So I thought that was the best chance for me—for us, Veronica.' The dog twisted to lick at her hands as she slid her fingers into the fur, her nails glittering like rubies in snow. 'I figured I would finish high school and then go to university so I could get a decent job. Provide for us both. But when your grandparents died, Marian took control of—well, that detail doesn't matter. There's no point laying blame now, is there?'

She knew what her mother had been going to say: *Marian took control of the money.* Her aunt had made no secret of that fact.

Denise continued quickly, minimising Marian's betrayal. 'It's just, without the funds for education, I could never hope for a career where I would earn enough to be able to raise you properly. I knew you'd be better off with the stability of both a mother and a father.' Her voice broke and she took a deep breath to steady it before she continued. 'You know I never married, Veronica? That's because I never found a man I believed was good enough to be your father. Oh,' she waved a dismissive hand, 'plenty of them would have been fine as husbands. But I wanted more for you. For us.'

Roni nodded, biting her lips together. A tiny part of her wanted to push a little more, to ask why her mother hadn't searched her out more recently. But there would be time enough for that in the future. Denise's final sentences were all she needed, an instant balm soothing the pain she had held inside for nearly thirty years.

Chapter Twenty

Thursday, she headed back into town to find the stock market. She'd intended to save the fuel, but the desire to tick off the tasks burned within her: free of Marian, and therefore Matt Krueger's oversight, she could focus on her relationship with Denise.

On the drive, her fingers kept straying to the phone on the seat beside her. She was tempted to call Denise but, departing with a hug and kiss despite Samantha's glowering presence, her mother had promised she would be in touch as soon as her travel agent sent through the new itinerary.

Roni felt a twinge of guilt at the thought of using Marian's money to build a relationship with a woman her aunt had clearly despised—and yet, hadn't Marian sought to harm that relationship to suit herself?

As long as she met Marian's demands in regards to the tasks, which were little enough to ask in return for the inheritance, surely she was free to decide whether she should communicate with her own mother? Maybe, whatever was between Marian, Denise and Andrew was not her business. That was their history. She would build her own story.

The market was a vast, open-sided shed filled with pens of bleating, lowing animals of every description, the air tangy with manure and fear. She instinctively wanted to flee but steeled herself as she approached a short, weather-beaten man who, judging by the broken veins in his nose and reddened cheeks, might be a farmer.

He seemed confused by her request. 'Hobby farm, is it? So what is it yer wanting? To keep the grass down, then? You don't really need a poddy, a bobby calf will suit you.'

'Uh, yeah.' She'd been proud to use 'poddy' correctly, and the new term threw her. 'Okay, I guess so. Problem is, I need it delivered to Peppertree Crossing.'

The farmer pushed a filthy towelling hat further back on his head, assessing her from the toes of her sneakers up to her breasts. No further. 'Name's Stan. Can let yer have one of me own bobbies, if that's the case. I'll drop it round termorrer morning, okay?'

'Okay,' she agreed uncertainly. They hadn't discussed price, and maybe she should have left it to Matt: after all, he had said he'd get the poddy—but he'd clearly been unwilling, and she didn't want to owe him any thanks.

'You'll be wanting to head over to Daish's and pick yourself up some calf-raiser and tits.'

'I still need to bottle feed it, then?'

'Sure do. Unless you have a better idea.' He leered suggestively at her breasts, and she crossed her arms over her chest.

'Bottles it is. See you tomorrow.'

Finding the thick black rubber teats—not tits, as Stan called them—on a dusty shelf in Daish's Farm Supplies, alongside the calf milk replacement mix, she was spared the humiliation of asking for them. The long-haired guy behind a counter covered with grubby-looking bits of equipment took her money with a marked lack of interest. She stashed the teats in her bag, glancing hopefully up and down the street as she stepped out into the sunshine. Running into Denise in the town wouldn't be needy, simply coincidental.

Daish's was on a backstreet, and there was nothing to be seen except for a dog on the tray of a ute parked opposite. After she'd dropped the sack of calf-raiser into the boot of the car, she strolled along the street, taking in her surrounds as she drank in the soft warmth and air, which seemed fresh despite the bitumen and cement surfaces. Tracey had given her directions to the library, but realistically, she could have driven around for five minutes and found it. Sited in a valley, the town was laid out in a grid pattern, one end bordered by the river, the other by a steep, tree-studded hill. Main Street was the heart of the town, a secondary street on either side boasting miscellaneous shops, many of which edged toward being light industry. Daish's Farm Supplies, electrical and refrigerator repairs, pump supplies, hardware, a second-hand shop, print and ink supplies, a doctor's office. It seemed that despite the size of the town, almost anything she could need would be available.

And, housed in a beautiful stone building with a high-peaked roof and elegant bow-fronted mullioned windows, the Settlers Bridge Regional Council Chambers. A small timber sign hung from the larger colourful board listing the council contact numbers and hours. *Library—Open*.

Although she had not explored far, she knew that beyond the business centre the roads widened, radiating out like a geometric spiderweb to connect a surprising number of houses. It was clear there wouldn't be enough employment in the town for the population—though, judging by the main street today, it seemed a large proportion of the residents were retired. Perhaps because it was pension day, as Tracey had mentioned, but whatever the reason, the town had come to life. There were about twenty people scattered along the shaded pavement between the cafes and the banks. Parking in front of the pubs at the far end of the street seemed to be a premium. Toting shopping bags or making a halting beeline toward Ploughs and Pies—no one seemed interested in Tractors and Tarts—the shoppers clustered in small groups to chat. One couple pored over the yellowed posters in the IGA window. Much pointing and nodding made it seem as though the discounts promised by the fly-spotted pages were the most exciting thing they'd seen in a fortnight.

No Denise, though. Roni puffed out a disappointed breath and headed back to the car. Dare she swing past the library? It looked intimidatingly small, and Tracey had already warned her about the librarian. There would be no keeping her secret if she borrowed a book from there.

Worrying at one of the many scratches her arms had accumulated over the past two weeks, she pondered her options. She wouldn't go to the library yet; she would tell her mother first. Roo represented a new start for both of them.

∞

She was cleaning out the coops when the calf arrived the next day. Stan lifted the gangly-legged, rusty-brown beast over the orchard fence, where it mooed piteously. 'This what yer after, then?'

What she was after? God, yes. She fell instantly in love with the lustrous brown eyes beseeching her from behind ridiculously long lashes, as a rough and incredibly long tongue curled out to suckle on her fingers. She didn't even care if Stan planned to fleece her on the price. 'Perfect. How much?'

'She's right. Just fix me up with my share come autumn and we'll call it square.'

She quirked an eyebrow at his odd accounting system. 'Sounds good. Okay, then. I'll see you round.' He needed to leave so she could try bottle-feeding the calf, because just the thought of it had all her maternal instincts kicked into overdrive.

As Stan's ute and trailer rattled across the cattle grid, Goat raced up, either drawn by the sad cries of the calf or, more likely, because he was insatiably nosy. He gently butted the calf's side, and the calf staggered and snorted, licking at its wet nose.

'Okay, Goat, play nice while I go make baby's bottle.' Baby. Like the dancer in the old eighties' movie with Patrick Swayze, the name seemed to fit the long-legged calf. She felt a pang of concern; Baby, her first deliberate addition to her growing family, would be a damn sight harder to pack in a carry cage and move to a new home than Scritches. And Goat? Well, Goat wasn't truly her problem, he belonged to the property. But she would have to make sure the new owners knew of his passion for cereal biscuits.

Following the instructions on the bag of calf-raiser, she mixed the formula and tested the temperature on her wrist. Scritches rubbed around her legs, certain anything she devoted so much time to must be intended for him. She poured a little in a saucer and popped it on the floor.

Scenting the warm milk before she had reached the orchard, Baby pushed so hard against the bottle, Roni had to brace herself on the gate. The milk disappeared within seconds, the calf butting her hip, trying to find more. 'Sorry, Baby, but I'm not overfeeding you as well.' The chickens had been lesson enough.

Mid-afternoon, Tracey fluffed by to collect her for the CWA meeting, shopping bags hanging from her arms. She dumped them on the table and enfolded Roni in a hug. 'Hello, love, it's been forever. I thought we'd throw together some scones to take to the meeting.'

Roni extricated herself from the embrace. 'If my bread's any measure, the CWA will be wiped out like the plague's gone through.' Actually, yesterday's loaf had been the best yet. She chewed at her thumbnail, unable to shake the notion she owed Tracey an admission. 'I saw Denise again the other day.'

Tracey didn't skip a beat, unpacking a Tupperware of lamingtons and several other containers from the bag. 'Samantha mentioned it. A couple of casseroles and a soup for you, love. It must be exhausting trying to handle this place all by yourself, and we don't want you getting run down.'

Roni lurched back. No one had made her a home-cooked meal since . . . since her first foster parents. 'I—' She should refuse the food, because accepting intimated acceptance of so much more. And she couldn't go there.

Tracey stacked the meals and popped them into the freezer. 'I cooked a lot of Marian's meals. She could look after herself, but preparing something nice and tasty or taking the time to think about what she put in her mouth were well down her list of priorities. I'm willing to bet you're much the same. I swear you've faded away in the last week. Too much running around, not enough sitting, and no decent meals, I daresay. I've mixed the veg in with the casserole, in case you don't like them.'

Her jeans had become so loose she'd dug out a belt to keep them up, which left her a little concerned. Shouldn't she be starting to show by now? As soon as she'd told Denise the news, she would need to organise a GP. And now, for the first time, she'd be able to share her family medical history with a health professional. She smiled at Tracey. 'That's so nice of you.'

'Nonsense. It's what friends do. Now, you get out the mixing bowls and we'll whip up these scones and shuffle off to the meeting.'

∽

Entering the clubroom, which was festooned with football and netball team banners, was no different from starting a new school. That initial moment of silence as everyone checked her out—making her wish she hadn't worn her Best & Less yoga pants, though at least her T-shirt had a nicely scalloped neckline—then a flurry of whispered conversations, hands hiding mouths as eyes darted in her direction. Obviously, few of her secrets had escaped the rumour mill.

Tracey ushered her in, introducing her to women she would immediately forget. She could never be more than an outsider among these people who had known each other for generations.

Amid the predictable questions about how she liked the countryside and whether she was married—to which the women no doubt already knew the answers, courtesy of Samantha—Tracey guided her to one of the formica tables.

Nodding as though fascinated by the tea-lubricated conversation regarding the merits of adding lemonade to scone dough, Roni thumbed her phone. One of the gardening books at home had her considering a plan for a potato patch, and she was eager to research the feasibility while she had internet access.

'Is Matthew playing for Imperials this year, Veronica?' A stout woman's fingers dexterously wound a needle through a quilt large enough to cover a room.

'Sorry. Is who what?'

'Matthew Krueger is still farming Marian's property, isn't he?' The flashing needle paused, the woman's chest swelling as she drew a deep breath. She leaned forward, raising her voice to make eavesdropping easier for the elderly. 'Well, it's not like she'd ever let the poor man go elsewhere, is it? I just wondered, without dear Marian cracking the whip, if Matt would find time for the football club this year?' She jabbed a finger at the gold and purple logo on the wall.

'I've no idea.' The snide remark about Marian shocked her. Everyone she'd spoken with so far seemed to hold her aunt in high regard.

'We've missed him the last few seasons. Dean Squires does a fair job of captaining, but Regals won't see another premiership until they get Matt back.'

'He was the captain?'

'Was, until that unfortunate business a couple of years back. Between sorting that out and Marian running him ragged, he's not had time.'

Her ears pricked. 'Unfortunate business?' It seemed she wasn't the only one with secrets in this town.

'You must've heard about it, given that your mother contrived to be the centre of it.'

Seated alongside Roni, Tracey tugged the woman's quilt toward her, examining the stitching. 'Now, Christine. That's all rumour.'

Christine snatched her fabric back. 'If everyone knows about it, I'd say that makes it fact, not rumour.'

'That makes it gossip, not fact.' Tracey lowered her voice. 'Even Fiona never confirmed anything, and you know as well as I do that if Fiona stays quiet, there's a jolly good reason.'

Heads snapped back and forth at the verbal ping-pong and Christine drew herself upright, playing to her audience. 'Reason would be that Fiona's quite happy with how things have turned out, thank you very much. Denise did her something of a favour, by my reckoning.' She lifted her chin to include Roni. 'You'd know the truth of it, though. Your mum's not one to play her cards close.'

Denise had hinted at something between herself and Matt, and it seemed that Christine—and therefore the rest of the town—were aware of it. Yet, no matter what she thought—had thought—of her mother, no one else had any right to judge her. Roni shoved her hands under her thighs. 'Even if she'd shared, I'm not into gossip.' Something of a lie, because she would kill to find out what the story was.

Christine snorted. 'Well, I'm sure we all have our secrets. Though your mum's have clearly come back to haunt her.'

The woman was really itching for a fight. In the space of minutes she'd managed to have a go at Marian, Denise, Matt and the unknown Fiona. 'Not haunting. Just passing through.'

Tracey flipped the quilt back, deliberately covering Christine's needle. 'So, are you brave enough to go up against Veronica in the lamington challenge, Christine? As I recall, you had issues with your chocolate sauce last year.'

The needle jabbed at the fabric. 'It was over forty degrees that day.'

'Yes, I remember. Unseasonably hot. Of course, it was the same temperature for all the entries.'

Christine ignored Tracey's barb. 'You bake, Veronica?'

'I'm honing my skills.'

'You said you were just passing through, though? You'll be gone before the contest.'

Roni folded her arms. No one got to tell her what to do. Not anymore. 'No. I'll still be here.' Whenever the competition was.

Christine's grey helmet of hair barely shifted as she cocked her head. 'No plans to get the farm on the market? I'm sure Matt would like to see a price on it.'

The ten-year clause on the inheritance was one secret this woman didn't know, then.

Tracey snapped her glasses case shut. 'Why on earth would he want that, Christine?'

'That place is an albatross around his neck. Marian sure had her head screwed on right, had us all fooled into thinking she was doing right by him when really she was laying the groundwork to make sure she had years of labour lined up. Rest of us can't find a decent worker for love nor money, but she's had Matt at her beck and call for a decade.'

Roni pushed herself from the table. 'Matt seems to think fifty–fifty is a fair split.'

Tracey also stood, patting at Roni's forearm. 'Anyone who knew Marian well'—she shot a venomous glance at

Christine—'would never dream of accusing her of being anything less than fair.'

No matter how conflicted she felt at her aunt's attempted manipulation of her own relationship with her mother, Marian didn't deserve Christine's nasty insinuations, but before Roni could formulate a reply, a flurry of conversation near the clubroom doors drew her attention.

'Oh, look, Taylor's here. I thought she might not make it in today.' Tracey snatched her appliquéd bag from the table, thumping it against her hip. 'She often only pops in at the end of the meeting. Of course, she doesn't have time to waste on gossip. Christine.' Her hair echoed her curt nod, and she fluttered across the room in a billow of purple chiffon to hug a woman with dark, braided hair.

Tracey waved her over. 'Taylor, this is Veronica, Marian's niece.'

'Roni,' she corrected as she smiled at the woman who appeared to be about her age. Unlike most of the other women present, she wore neat black trousers and a white blouse, looking as though she'd come from an office.

Taylor lifted a hand in greeting. 'Hey, Roni. You look like you were dragged here against your will. First time my gran brought me I spent the meeting posting pictures of pubs as camouflage.'

'Sounds entirely reasonable.'

'Veronica's having a go at the lamington drive,' Tracey bubbled happily.

'Lamingtons? You're brave.' Taylor made her eyes huge, but then relented with a grin. 'Though if you have the guru helping, you'll be okay. Do you remember my first attempt, Tracey?'

'You're saying that you're better now?' Tracey teased. 'That reminds me, I'd better lodge our forms.' She darted across the room, pausing to chat with different groups like a sparrow bobbing from one crumb to the next.

A dimple appeared in Taylor's cheek. 'Ouch. But she's right, mine never improved.'

'I'm screwed then.'

'No, don't let me scare you off, I'm pretty useless at that kind of stuff. I'm more inclined to fundraise by buying everyone else's produce. Plus, that way my husband doesn't have to prove his undying devotion by pretending my cooking's edible.'

Taylor's humour eased the acid of Christine's malice, though Roni made sure to keep her back to the older woman. 'Wish I had that option. I've been baking bread for the last fortnight, and I'm sure I'm going to kill Marian's chickens by using them to hide my failures.'

They had moved toward the small kitchen, separated from the main hall by a long, waist-high laminate counter. Taylor flicked on an electric jug. 'Kudos to you for even trying. Luke's given up on me learning the finer points of being a farmer's wife.'

'If you don't find this stuff second nature, there's no hope for me.'

'Ha. I checked, but sadly, there's no hereditary homemaker gene. When I moved here Gran tried to teach me the basic skills, but I can still burn water.'

'Moved here? Aren't you a local?'

Taylor spooned coffee into mugs. 'Don't let this lot hear you call me that. I'll be tarred and feathered and run out of town.'

'I doubt it. Seems they all like you.' Taylor's entrance had garnered more interest than her own.

'There's a big difference between acceptance and being considered a local. Like, about a seventy-year difference, I'd say.' Despite her words, Taylor acknowledged the waved greeting of another woman with a nod and a smile, a casual confidence that could only come from knowing that she belonged.

Roni winced at her stab of envy. 'So where are you from?'

'Sydney. I came over to see my grands ten years ago and re-met my husband.'

'Re-met? Is that like a B&S hook-up? Or a dating service?'

Colour bloomed in Taylor's cheeks and she concentrated on filling the mugs. 'No. Long story. Speaking of long'— she indicated the women immersed in recipe swapping, sewing and gossiping—'how many hours of this have you survived?'

'Too many. Is it really on every month?'

Taylor handed Roni a cup and pointed at a tray. 'Milk and sugar. Hate to be the bearer of bad news, but it's every three weeks. But I generally only come to the committee meeting, to make sure there's a quorum.'

Steam wafted a memory of Rafe's shop, suddenly an immeasurable distance away, a lifetime ago. 'Kill me now.'

Taylor sipped at her coffee, slitting her unusual slate-grey eyes. 'How long are you staying?'

'At Peppertree Crossing?' Roni stared into her cup, realising she didn't honestly know the answer anymore. 'Not long. Short version is I have to prove to the farm manager that I'm capable of running the property.'

'Matt Krueger? You'll have no problem there. He's easygoing.'

'So I hear.' She kept the sarcasm from her tone. So far, it seemed only she, Denise and Christine didn't adore Matt. In fairness, though, Christine hadn't a good word to say about anyone. But it was irrelevant; she wasn't about to allow mainstream opinion to seduce her into liking the farmer.

'He's Luke's cousin, so I know him pretty well.'

Roni choked in surprise and tried to cover it by blowing on her coffee. 'He's probably mentioned this stuff, then. I mean, it's out there, isn't it?"

'Not said a word. But Matt keeps pretty much to himself nowadays.'

Roni's ears pricked up. So his often-taciturn nature wasn't the norm?

Taylor glanced over at a burst of laughter from a nearby table. 'How does the CWA fit into the story?'

'Some convoluted scheme Marian came up with. About making fr—contacts.'

A grin flashed across Taylor's face and she indicated the hall, echoing with women's voices and the rattle of teacups. 'You plan to spend all your downtime with this lot? Tell you what, before harvest season gets crazy, Luke and I usually

226

throw a barbecue. Why don't you come, meet a few people who are a little less'—she lowered her voice—'vintage.'

She would rather stay home with Scritches. But friend-making was on Marian's list, and ticking it off would get her closer to . . . where?

She'd accepted that Sydney no longer meant home, because she needed somewhere to settle with Roo. But with Denise in their lives, perhaps there could be new options.

Chapter Twenty-one

Sunday afternoon, Roni was turning the last few forkfuls of soil in the potato patch she'd marked out when she heard the rumble of Matt's ute. As she pulled off her gloves, wincing as her blisters caught on canvas, and shoved her hair into place, she tried to pretend to herself that the flutter of anticipation in her chest was irritation at the interruption.

'Hey.' Matt tipped his akubra back as he loped toward her.

'Hey,' she replied, slightly disappointed to find he was back to monosyllables after his almost-chattiness a week earlier.

Scritches dashed over and wove around Matt's feet. 'Hey there, dude.' As he bent to scratch the cat's head, the sheep stampeded up, ramming Roni in the back of her knees.

Matt's hand flashed out to steady her. 'Easy there, Goat, you'll knock your mum over. I take it he's not loving the competition, now Scritches is out and about?'

'You wouldn't believe I've just spent two hours in the

orchard with him. Though the three of them do seem to play together.'

'Three?' Matt's eyebrow lifted.

She wiped her palms on her filthy jeans, took a quick, nervous breath, then jerked her chin over his shoulder, toward where Baby, timider than the other animals, stood in the shade of a hibiscus tree overhanging the fence. The calf lowed softly, then licked its nose.

Matt glanced at the cow, then back at Roni. A smile twitched the corner of his lips and she softened with relief. Why was she always so quick to expect the worst from him? Surely Rafe had proved to her that all men weren't the same.

'So, you got yourself a calf, huh?' Matt moved toward the animal, and Baby kicked up her heels, dashing to meet him halfway.

Roni couldn't help herself. 'Isn't she beautiful?'

'Certainly a fine-looking beast.' Matt rubbed a hand across his mouth. 'Be an interesting proposition to milk, though.'

'Why? Is she the wrong kind?' She moved in protectively.

'No, nice jersey, they're generally good milkers. The thing is . . . who sold it to you?'

'Stan somebody-or-other.' Her heart squeezed into her throat. Did Stan produce defective cows?

'Ah. Well, it seems Stan landed you with a bobby.' Matt ran large hands along the cow's back and down her legs.

'Yeah, he said that.' She twiddled a blade of grass between her fingers. 'Her name's Baby.'

'Hmm.' Sun-worn lines crinkled around Matt's eyes. 'Well, I suggest you be real careful with that milking, because he may not take too kindly to it.'

'But you said jerseys are good—wait! *He?*' She stared at Matt in appalled silence.

Matt nodded. 'Yup. You've bought yourself a little bull. What did Stan charge you?'

At least she hadn't paid for Baby. Like hell Stan would get his full price now. 'Nothing. He said we'll work it out later.'

'Work it out—or take a share?'

'Probably the share thing. Why?'

The calf sucked lustily on the side of Matt's hand. 'Because a share means a steak. E and an A, not s-t-a-k-e. As far as Stan's concerned, he provided the calf, your part of the bargain is to fatten it. In a month you'll be eating veal. Or give it a few months, beef.'

'No!' She flung an arm over Baby's warm neck. His flanks quivered, and he snorted wet breath onto her. 'No way. Baby's not anyone's dinner.' So much for proving how capable she was. Roni's cheeks burned with mortification. 'I'll turn vego before I do that.'

Matt slapped dust from the calf's rump. 'Join the club. I see there's some of Marian in you.'

'She was a vegetarian?'

'Nope. That's me. Kind of goes with the job. I meant when you arc up, you remind me of her.'

'I always expect vegetarians to be, like, anaemic little fairies.' Her cheeks flared as the words escaped.

Matt snorted. 'I think gorillas disproved that before me.' He rubbed the hard ridge on Baby's forehead. Then he huffed out a heavy breath, his words slow. 'Look, if you plan to stick around, I'll geld the calf. He'll never be any use and will cost you a fortune to feed when there's no graze. But he'll probably stay docile. And off the plate. Just a larger version of Goat, I guess.'

'You can do that?'

'Sure. Looks like he's got the scours.' Matt pointed at Baby's filthy hind legs. 'It's not too bad, but I'll give you some electrolytes to mix in his milk. Remind me before I leave, I've probably got some in my bag.'

'You carry a cow first-aid kit?' Still too embarrassed to meet his gaze, she concentrated on picking at her blisters.

'Looks like he's not the only one needing first aid.' Matt's strong fingers wrapped around her wrist. She flinched and he released her immediately. 'Are those from digging?'

She lifted her chin toward the new garden. 'I read up on potatoes, and there doesn't seem to be any reason to grow them in a raised bed. In fact, I'll probably get a better crop this way, because I can layer manure and dirt as the plant grows.'

Matt surveyed the plot, nodding slowly as she sucked on her palm. 'Impressive.'

It was stupid to feel so proud of dirt, but the patch had been damn hard work. And Matt's acknowledgment made her achievement that much sweeter. Only because it meant he'd tick off her task, she assured herself.

'If you'd yelled out, I would have given you a hand.'

'I didn't need help.'

'I got that. But not needing it doesn't mean you can't take it.' He looked at her searchingly for a long moment. 'We all help out our mates around here.'

Why was a tiny part of her disappointed that he inferred she was one of his mates? She shook her head, dispelling the question. 'Cuppa?' she blurted.

Matt glanced toward the ute, as though he would rather make a run for it. 'Yeah. Okay, I guess so.'

She pointed to the verandah. 'Take a seat. I'll get it.' That was the way to do it; stake her claim, keep him out of her house.

As she carried out the laden tray, Matt leaped up to hold open the screen door. 'I'll put a soft-close on that for you.'

'It's fine,' she started, although it was a lie; every time she stepped out, the aluminium frame bit her heels. She paused. Marian had made mention of accepting help, and Matt had chipped her for failing to do so, only minutes ago. She forced a smile. 'But if you have some spare time, that'd be great.' She passed him a plated scone. 'I promise it's better than the bread.'

'I liked the bread. Was kind of hoping you'd made more.' As he bit into the scone, she held her breath. He scrutinised the morsel in his hand. 'So, there *is* an issue.'

Her shoulders slumped, and she poked her own scone. 'What's wrong with it?'

Matt popped the remainder into his mouth and swallowed. Hands splayed, he indicated his empty plate and assumed a mournful expression. 'The issue's your portion control.'

'I'll get you another.' Flustered, she made to get to her feet.

Matt waved her back down. 'Joking. Well, not really; if you've got any left, I'll raid the kitchen before I leave.' He rubbed at his jaw as his gaze left hers, wandering to the peacock perched on the fence at the bottom of the yard, his jewelled plumage spread wide. 'Look, I, uh, don't need to clear out just yet. If you wanted to take a cruise around the property, I'll show you where your boundaries are, that kind of stuff.'

She stared at him. Why offer a tour of a property he considered practically his?

'Roni?'

'Sure. I guess my farming knowledge could use a little tweaking.' She pulled a wry expression and hiked a thumb toward the orchard, where Baby lowed desolately.

'I'm sure the mistake's been made before.'

'Really?'

'Nope.' He looked different when his grin erased the taut lines of assessment from his face. 'I guess this whole deal'—he encompassed the farm with a wave—'must seem strange to you.'

'Actually,' she frowned as she weighed her words, wondering where the truth behind them had suddenly come from. 'It doesn't feel as odd as it should. Like, yeah, it's different. But it doesn't feel wrong.' She shrugged. 'Anyway, finish your tea, and let's hit the road.'

The cup grated against the lacework of the table as Matt pushed it away. 'Not so fast. If we're going to be stuck in a confined space, I'd like to know that you're not an axe murderer. Marian's character assessment wasn't always that flash. Evidence: one pseudo-farmer.' He made a pistol with forefinger and thumb, aiming at his chest.

'Pseudo-farmer?'

'I asked first. Tell me about yourself, Veronica Nelson.'

'Gates.'

'Not Nelson?'

'My first fosters gave me their name.'

'First? You had more than one family?'

'Sure.' He didn't have to make it sound weird. Few people wanted their own pre-teen daughter; even fewer were prepared to take on someone else's cast-off. In her experience, those that did were after the Centrelink payment. Or something else.

'How many?'

'Too many.' Nobody needed that much family.

Matt's fingers toyed with his hat on the table between them, his forearms dark against the white metal. 'I'm sorry. I imagine that would've been hard.'

The trap cinched around her chest and her words came out tight. 'You get used to it.'

'Bullshit.'

She almost dropped her cup. 'What?'

His icy eyes drilled into her. 'You might have built up your armour against the hurt. But that's not the same as getting used to it.'

234

'How the hell would you know?'

He held her gaze for a long moment. 'Because I know how it hurts to lose people.' The stark anguish in his tone shocked her. Although he'd claimed to be close to Marian, she'd not realised how genuine his loss was. He didn't try to hide his hurt, instead he leaned closer. 'Yet you're trying to persuade me that something as soul-destroying as being shunted from one family to another got easier?'

'I'm not trying to *persuade* you of any damn thing,' she snarled, trying to cauterise the pain of being unwanted. 'I get what you're saying, you miss Marian. But I don't, because I never knew her. And it's the same with fosters; I made sure not to get to know them.' Except those she'd known intimately, in ways she didn't want to remember. She wrapped her arms across her chest, gripping her elbows. Squeezed to control the shudder.

'That's no way to live.'

'That's your opinion.' Raised with the privilege of family and friends and history and prospects, how could someone like Matt ever understand that sometimes, walling off your heart was the only way to survive?

Matt rubbed at his chin, then spoke low. 'You're right, I miss Marian every bloody day.' His voice broke, and he clenched his jaw for a second. 'But that doesn't mean I avoid getting to know people for fear they'll leave me.'

'Then I guess we're very different people, aren't we?' She bit out the words. Damn it, for a few minutes there he'd actually seemed likable.

Matt sighed heavily, his words slow and reluctant. 'Marian taught me something.' He gave a short, mirthless laugh. 'Actually, she taught me plenty, though some of it was too late. But there was one thing in particular. She said it takes courage to allow a dream, but true bravery comes in learning how to chase it.'

Roni scowled, instantly jealous. 'So, you have a dream?' No doubt funded by her aunt.

'Living it.' Yet his tone was bitter and she noticed the thinning of his lips and the whitening of his knuckles. Her chest clenched with sudden understanding: he wasn't only mourning, he hid something dark and painful.

He spread one hand open in question. 'But what about you? Is there more to life than accepting whatever it throws at you?'

Despite her curiosity, she was immediately on guard; was this a trap, finding out if she planned to sell the property from under him? 'I'm not into fantasies.' Except for the dream she now had for her little family.

'There's nothing you want to do with your life?' A frown appeared between the blue eyes, so intent on hers.

'Life's not about what I want to do. Only what I need to do.' She refused to look away, to be intimidated by his assessment or censure.

He paused for a long beat. 'That's pretty sad.'

'Again, your opinion.' And he was far too free with it. She folded her arms across her chest, signifying she was done with his third degree.

'Fair call.' Matt thrust to his feet. 'Sorry, Roni. I didn't mean to ruffle your feathers. I guess, with everything else going on, I forget how lucky I was that Marian encouraged my dream.'

He was determined to rub in his relationship with her aunt, but it didn't matter. As long as his dream wasn't realised by getting his hands on her property, she would only be a bit jealous.

Maybe more than a bit. What would it have been like to have someone to share her fears, hopes and desires?

She dug her broken nails into her palm, forcing the weakness away. Roo would have all that and more, but she was well past needing it for herself.

Yet a small voice inside her refused to be silenced; dare she allow the dream that perhaps Denise would finally embrace that role?

A fluster of noise from a shed on the northern side of the yard drew her attention, the rustle of wings combined with a mournful hoot, and she seized the excuse to change the topic. 'That's one confused owl. It's practically the middle of the day.'

Matt piled the plates, his grin now genuine. And suddenly, she didn't even care that his amusement was at her expense. Though he'd trespassed on her privacy, the torment in his eyes as he spoke of his dream told the truth; despite the unfair advantages of his life, Matt was broken. He knew what it was to hurt.

Unaware of her discovery, he chuckled. 'Lucky you're a great cook because you'll never make it as an ornithologist.

That's a pigeon.' To prove him right, a flock of the birds evacuated the shed. 'Is Scritches over there?'

Why did something as simple as his use of the cat's name soothe her jagged edges? 'He wouldn't know what to do with a bird if he caught it. No point calling him, though, he has selective hearing.' With the farmyard to roam, Scritches was well and truly over his separation anxiety and now disappeared for hours at a time. When he was done exploring, he would charge through the yard, yowling as though she had been the one to desert him. 'Guess we'd better hit this border-patrol stuff.'

Matt loomed over the table. 'Sounds like we need to arm ourselves.'

Maybe she did. Because Matt intrigued her. There was something magnetic about him, both attracting and repelling her in almost the same instant.

And, without ever having experienced it before, she instinctively knew the feeling was beyond dangerous.

Chapter Twenty-two

Given how tidy he presented, Matt's ute was surprisingly dusty inside. He swept an armload of stuff from the passenger seat, tipping it into the footwell at her feet. She eyeballed the paperwork and—according to the wrappers— field dressings. Odd combination. Not a half-eaten burger or empty stubby in sight. Definitely not the car to be stuck in during the apocalypse.

'I'll take you round the perimeter first, give you an idea of how far the property extends.' They jostled over the bridge at the bottom of the driveway. His outburst and her new understanding seemed to have cleared the air, removed a little of the unspoken tension between them.

'Don't forget to give me a yell when you want to work on this,' he added, obviously not noticing her one-rock repair.

'You don't think maybe that task was metaphoric?' Please let it be a metaphor. Metaphors weighed a darn sight less than boulders.

'For what?'

'You know, building relationships, becoming part of the community.'

Matt shrugged. 'Metaphor or not, the job needs doing.'

'Sure.' Despite his prosaic statement, she was in no rush to tackle the bridge again.

Elbow on the open window frame, Matt steered with one hand, his penetrating gaze hidden behind aviators. Good. He could keep his ice-blue probing for unsuspecting aliens. He changed gears and lifted his chin toward the opposite side of the main road. 'Everything you can see beyond that fence line is mine.'

'Same acreage as Marian's?'

'Smaller, fortunately.'

'Fortunately? I thought size was important?' she said, then winced as a slow grin tipped his mouth.

'Some of us are confident enough to rely on less tangible assets.'

'So, you sharefarm whatever land you can get hold of, instead of owning it?' she hurried on.

'Nope.'

'You don't farm other properties? Or you're not trying to get hold of land?'

'Yup.'

She swallowed a sigh. She couldn't articulate what it was about Matt that got under her skin. Right now, though, that particular irritant was his attitude. He changed from hot to cold quicker than the shower in her apartment. And with as little reason. 'You don't like farming?'

'I don't dislike it. It's just not what I planned to do.'

'That's where those dreams of yours come in?'

'Yup.'

'But you said Marian supported your dreams? How'd you end up farming for her if it's not what you want to do?'

He paused a long moment, but she was coming to expect that. 'I owed it to her.'

She clutched the seatbelt as they jostled over a section of road ridged into waves. Matt had no interest in the property? Was that credible? In her experience, no one helped anyone for nothing. What weapon did Marian have that saw Matt put his dreams on ice to work for her? Christine Albright had alluded to something, and maybe that tied in to Matt's secret torment. Yet he adored Marian.

She waved at the paddock, where the crop had started to turn golden. 'If you don't want to farm, why have all this land?'

'Belongs to family. My father, then my brother.'

'Why doesn't your brother do the farming, then?' If she'd had a sibling, everything would have been easier. Every pain halved, every joy doubled.

'He's dead.'

She stared straight ahead. There was nothing to say; she dealt with her emptiness alone and expected others to do the same.

'Ten.'

'Huh? Ten what?' She shot a glance at Matt as he pulled the car to the side of the road.

'You had your ten questions. Reckon it's my turn now.'

'Sorry, but I don't have ten interesting answers in me.'

He turned the ignition off, but the click of the engine continued, counting the seconds he watched her. 'I doubt that's true. But I'll give you a choice. Ten questions, or you come walk that paddock with me.' He indicated a field of yellow outside her window. 'I need to check the stock trough on the far side. Sheep will be moved up there after we've taken the wool off.'

'You shave them, then shift them?'

'Shave them? Yeah, that's it,' Matt grinned.

She groaned. 'It's not shave, is it? I knew that sounded wrong . . .'

'We generally go with shear round here. But I can see an argument for using shave. A good, close clip brings in more money.'

'Okay, fine, feel free to make fun of me.' She followed him from the ute. 'My broad shoulders can take it.'

Matt placed his boot on a fence wire, then heaved the top strand up. 'Scoot through. I wouldn't call those shoulders broad. But you're doing okay. No way I could up stumps, move states and handle it like you are.'

An almost-compliment? As she crawled awkwardly between the wires, her knuckles brushed Matt's thigh. She scrambled clear, scrubbing her hand against her jeans, trying to erase the ridiculous frisson that shot through her.

She had no time for that kind of crap. Matt might not be the enemy she'd suspected, but he was still a man, still unnecessary, and still in her personal space.

He glanced down as he strode through the crop. 'You didn't find any boots to fit? Sneakers aren't much good out here.'

'Marian's are too big for me,' she panted.

Matt grunted with laughter at her unintended double entendre, but she was too busy trying to match his stride to take offence. The spiky grass reached above her knees, growing in channels designed to trip her. Regardless of whether she took a short or long step, her feet fell wrong each time, either sliding from the crumbling ridge of dirt or tangling in stems.

Matt slowed. 'Follow the furrow to the edge of the paddock, then go along the fence line. You'll find it easier.'

'I'm fine. Just do what you have to do.'

'Fair warning: it involves spiders.'

'Must be big spiders if you need that.' She nodded at the metal pole he carried.

His grin altered his entire persona and, as he legged it over another fence, she ducked through without waiting for him to hold the wires. Better a gouge from barbed wire than risk touching him.

'Right you are.' He gave a slight shake of his head and released the wire he'd held for her. Using the pole, he levered up the cement hood that covered a third of a water trough. As it lifted, he dropped the pole and grasped the lid, flipping it to balance across the trough. Redback spiders tunnelled urgently into the thick white webs that covered the underside of the dome.

'Ew. Are you going to kill them?'

243

'Nope.' He used a grass stalk to push the spiders toward the centre of their nest. 'They're not causing any trouble. But I don't want to grab a handful when I lift this back on.'

Spiders rearranged, he fiddled with a floating ball in the scum-covered water, depressing it so the pump hissed and filled the trough. 'All good. I'll just cover her back up.'

She stooped to take an end of the lid.

'Don't touch it!' Matt barked and she jumped back. He pointed. 'You nearly got a handful of that redback. In any case, the lid's too heavy for you.'

'It's fine.' He didn't need to think her useless.

He grunted, hefting the cover and sliding it into place. By himself. 'I reckon the fact you didn't scream at the red-backs covers you for five questions.'

She liked this Matt. Removed from the house, concentrating on physical work, he seemed freer, more relaxed. 'Hey, the walk was worth ten, remember? And I grew up east; redbacks are nothing once you've found a funnel-web in your shoe.'

'Fair enough.'

The conversation lapsed as Matt fiddled with a valve on the outside of the trough. She plucked a piece of grass. The crop growing along the fence was different to that in the paddock, the gossamer hollow heads on delicate stalks eddying like fairy wings in the slight breeze. 'It's amazing they can turn this stuff into cornflakes.'

Matt pushed his sunglasses to the top of his head and surveyed her for a long moment. 'Need a fair bit of GM to make that happen.'

'GM?'

'Genetic modification.'

She swept a hand, encompassing the panoramic patchwork of green and gold spread below the hill they stood upon. 'But this is corn or something, isn't it?'

'Mostly wheat, lupins, some barley. But that's not corn.' Matt nodded at her piece of dead grass.

'What is it, then?' She twirled the stem between her fingers.

He rubbed at his chin.

Her fingers tightened on the stalk.

His tone was deadpan. 'That'd be my wild oats you're handling.'

'What? Gross.' Damn. She didn't need his humour, dry or otherwise, because funny was . . . undeniably attractive.

He turned, indicating below them. 'Your house is in that valley there. You can just make out the top of the palm tree.' He shifted to point into the distance. 'See that line of darker green? That's the river. Runs along the far boundary of my land. That way, east, is Settlers Bridge. Behind us is Adelaide.'

Roni spun slowly, getting her bearings. 'Sydney is . . . that way?'

Matt took her hand, altering the trajectory of her finger. 'About there. Why, you intend on making a run for it?'

'Maybe not.' The significance of speaking her tenuous decision aloud dragged her hand down.

'Might be as well, given all your dependants.'

'What?' She almost choked.

'Goat seems to have taken to you. Then there's Baby. And of course, Scritches may not be too keen on going back to the city after a few weeks here.'

'Oh,' she muttered, instantly relieved he hadn't discovered her secret. 'Scritches can stretch his legs for a bit longer. Tracey's entered me in some CWA lamington challenge.'

Matt stood still, staring over the paddocks for a long moment. Then he nodded, as though concluding an internal monologue. 'That's great.'

Great she was staying, or great she was baking?

Matt kept his eyes on the furrows as they picked their way back across the paddock. 'If you need someone to test-drive those lamingtons, you've got my number.'

Unfamiliar emotions she didn't care to name bubbled inside her, clear and sparkling like the early summer air. 'Aren't you supposed to judge my cooking, not inhale it?'

'Judge it?' Matt pressed on the lower fence wire with his boot but didn't lift the top strand. 'I'm not exactly CWA material.'

'No, for Marian's tasks.'

His strong hands closed around the top wire. 'You've lost me. What does judging have to do with the tasks?'

The muscle strained in his thigh as his foot controlled the taut wire. She really shouldn't be close enough to notice that. 'You're supposed to decide whether I'm worthy of my inheritance.'

He released the fence with a twang and stepped back. 'Why? That's none of my business.'

'Well, you *are* managing the property.'

The breeze sang against the wires and Matt pushed up his glasses again, as though the intense eye contact would help him understand. She wished she had her scratched sunnies; his gaze threw her off balance. He shook his head. 'You've got it all wrong, Roni. I'm not keeping score. I just have a list of stuff Marian wanted you to get a handle on. Some of it, like the bridge, I said would be safer if I was around to help you.' He lifted his huge shoulders in a shrug of bemusement. 'That's the extent of my involvement.'

'But then why are you . . . I mean, you're putting so much time into this—' She gestured at the paddocks, then at herself, trying to mask her confusion. 'Why would Marian saddle you with the job?'

'Not gonna lie,' he said with a grunt of amusement, 'I did wonder that myself. But I figured Marian had her reasons. She always did. Sometimes—most of the time— it was easier to go along with her schemes than to try to fathom the rationale.'

'She said Derek Prescott would be assessing me.' Except . . . was that actually what Marian had said, or what Roni had concluded? Shit. She needed to reread the letters. And quickly.

Matt lifted the wire again. 'Her solicitor? Well, I can't say I know anything about—wait up—' He untangled her hair from a barb, then flipped the ponytail over her shoulder. 'Okay. Go. I don't know anything about Derek. Your aunt could be a complex woman and, much as I loved her, I'm not going to pretend I always knew what was going on in her head.'

'She would have discussed the whole inheritance thing with you, though? The ten-year deal?'

He opened the ute door for her, an oddly chivalrous gesture on the side of a dusty road. The collie leaned forward from the tray, and Matt fondled the dog's ears. 'Good girl, Tess.' He turned back to face Roni. 'About the only thing I know is that when the shit with your mother blew up a couple of years ago, Marian became adamant the property would never pass to her.'

If Matt didn't know there existed an option for him to continue farming the property, he couldn't be trying to screw her out of her inheritance. Roni fisted her hands to contain her sudden relief. 'Tracey said that Denise wanted to run off with some rich guy. That's the shit you mean?'

'He wasn't bloody rich.' Matt dropped heavily into his seat, his tone harsh as he slammed the door. 'And Denise drained the life from him. Literally.'

∞

Matt's mention of her mother changed the mood in the ute. She didn't want to hear anything against Denise, yet somewhere deep inside, his words reawakened her caution. She wanted to build a relationship with Denise, and she knew that Marian had manipulated the situation—and most likely the story—to suit her own ends. But was it realistic to believe that everyone who spoke ill of Denise could be wrong? Roni had yet to meet a person who didn't harbour some degree of animosity toward the woman. Though hell, it wasn't like Denise had dumped them on state care's doorstep. They needed to take a ticket and wait in line.

She winced, refusing to rehash the old hurt. She was mature enough to recognise the dilemma her mother had faced and she was the only person in a position to appreciate the reasons Denise had given for her decisions.

The tour of the property became a site inspection, a discussion of facts and data pertaining to crops and sheep. Whatever memory had stirred in Matt threw up a wall between them, and there were no more exchanges of personal questions, no further banter.

Even so, she paid careful attention as he trotted out statistics on the paddocks of sheep they passed. She multiplied the flock numbers by the average fleece weight, converting it to a dollar amount based on the latest sales figures he divulged. When he nodded approval as she came up with estimates for the next season's wool tally she tried not to smile too broadly, inexplicably hungry for his praise.

Life experiences had made her wary, but this was a whole new world. Maybe she didn't need to bring forward her prejudices and fears. Perhaps Marian was right; only with risk came reward.

'Okay, that's probably enough information to spin your head for today, yeah?' Matt said as they bounced over the second cattle grid and into the yard. 'Took longer than I expected. I need to shoot off now, I'm running late. Got another pretty full-on week, so I'll stay out of your way for a while—'

'A dingo!'

Matt glanced across the farmyard, following her pointed finger, then slammed his foot on the accelerator. The ute hurtled toward the chicken coop. He smashed the brake and flung himself from the cab almost before the vehicle stopped rolling.

A small red dingo raced away from the shed, its tail streaming like a banner. Tess leaped from the back of the ute and gave chase.

'Dammit!' Matt thrust an arm across the coop doorway, preventing Roni's entry as she dashed up behind him. 'Don't come in here. It's a mess. Bloody foxes don't usually come during the day. She must have cubs nearby.'

'A fox?' The word iced her veins. Even girls from the city knew what foxes did to chickens. And now she could see the feathers, sticking to Matt's worn RM Williams boots. Fluffy white feathers. 'No! Where's Miss Fuzzypants?' She shoved past Matt, though he barely moved to allow her access.

He grabbed her arm. 'No, Roni. Don't. I'll clean up.'

Ignoring him, she dropped to her knees alongside a forlorn bundle of blood-streaked feathers. 'Is she dead?' The trembling words scarcely made it past the lump in her throat.

Matt hunkered alongside her. 'Yeah, she is. It would have been quick, though. Look, the blood isn't even hers, it looks like the rooster put up a fight. Miss, ah, Miss Fuzzypants' heart would've given out.'

She could feel Matt watching her. No doubt expecting her to cry. Well, that wouldn't happen anytime soon. With one finger, she stroked the downy feathers. She couldn't bring herself to check the rest of the shed, though, keeping her gaze on the bantam's limp body as she struggled for control. 'So much for my growing dependants, huh? I guess it's just as well you're not grading me, because this'd be a monumental fail. Allowing Marian's prize chickens to be murdered.' Worse than failing Aunt Marian, though, was the knowledge the funny little chicken had depended on her for both sustenance and safety, and she'd screwed up.

'It's not a fail, Roni,' Matt said gently. 'It's part of life out here. We always have trouble with foxes. You'll have to keep the remaining birds locked in for a while, now. Once foxes have marked the location, they keep coming back. Trust me, Marian lost plenty of poultry herself.'

'But not Miss Fuzzypants.' Her chest heaved and she bit down on her lip.

'No.' Matt's hand stilled hers on top of the soft, warm down. 'Not Miss Fuzzypants. I'm sorry, Roni. If we'd been around the yard, the fox wouldn't have come in.'

'You'll kill it?'

'No.'

'Why not?'

'Because the damage is already done. She's trying to feed her cubs the only way she knows how. I'm not going to kill an animal for trying to take care of its own.'

She dashed a hand across her nose. 'But Miss Fuzzypants didn't do anything wrong; she didn't deserve to be hurt.' Not that pain was meted out on a merit basis. Wrong time, wrong place, whether it was a chicken coop or a darkened lounge room, was all the justification required.

'Neither does the fox.'

'I thought farmers were supposed to hate foxes?'

'Told you, I'm not great farmer material.' Matt's knees cracked as he pushed himself from the dirt and extended a hand to tug her up.

'So, what now? You feed the carcasses to your dog or something?' She had to talk tough, pretend it didn't hurt.

'How about I grab the spade and you pick a place to bury Miss Fuzzypants?'

She didn't dare look up at him or the tears would spill. 'It's just a dumb bird. You said you're running late; I'll take care of it.'

'Not late for anything important, and I know you like to be in the house before dark.'

Matt strode across the yard, returning minutes later with a spade and two feed sacks. He gently placed Miss Fuzzypants on the sack, then wrapped the fabric around her and passed the bundle to Roni as though he handled a baby. 'You take her, I'll dig. Did you decide where?'

She shrugged, feigning indifference.

'How about under the peppertrees, then?' Matt pointed to a row of lime-green trees, the soft, swooping foliage brushing the red dirt. 'She loved to fossick around under there, didn't she?'

He dug two graves: a large one for the chickens she still hadn't brought herself to look at, and a smaller one for

Miss Fuzzypants. Dug them deep, too. Not a token scrape in the earth, even though it was baked hard and full of chips of shale and flint.

By the time he'd built a cairn over Miss Fuzzypants' plot, darkness had fallen and the collie had returned, nosing against him. Matt tugged the dog's ears, but his attention was on Roni. 'Are you okay?'

She willed steel into her voice. 'Of course. Just pissed. It's still a fail and you know it.'

'You only fail if you give up.'

She forced a wobbly smile. 'I'm sure I read that on a fridge magnet somewhere.'

'I thought it was a meme. But my blatant plagiarism doesn't change the fact. Roni?' He waited until she glanced up at him. She prayed like hell her eyes weren't red. 'Don't give up, okay? You're doing just fine here, and the last thing Marian would want would be for you to quit over a chicken.'

'No chickening out, huh?'

Matt grinned, but again the smile didn't reach his eyes. She knew that move so well, that act so no one knew how you were feeling inside. He jerked his head toward the house. 'C'mon, I'll shut the rest of the birds in and then see you inside.'

She wanted to stay outside, where the gathering dusk could hide the emotions burgeoning inside her, but she needed to get inside—to lock herself away from this man who stirred unfamiliar thoughts and desires.

She couldn't afford to allow any deviation from the path she had set herself. Her, Scritches and Roo. No room for anyone else.

Allowing even a chicken into her heart had been a mistake.

Chapter Twenty-three

No rooster to wake her this morning. No Miss Fuzzypants waiting to greet her. No need to rush to let the chickens out; the survivors had to stay locked in for a few days.

She rolled over and tried to go back to sleep.

Couldn't.

Instead, Matt kept creeping into her thoughts. He was so unpredictable, one moment fun, maybe even bordering on flirtatious, the next taciturn and withdrawn, monosyllabic to the extreme. What the hell was his deal? She was now fairly certain he held no intent toward the property, but then why did he keep shutting her out? What was in his past that left him so ... so ... She jerked upright in bed, upsetting Scritches from his perch on her belly.

So like her. Wary.

She fluffed the quilt, pounding at imagined lumps. Wary enough that he'd said he wouldn't be back again this week, and that left days stretching ahead of her. She had plenty to do but no real incentive to get anything done, now she didn't need to impress him.

No, that was wrong. She'd been trying to earn her inheritance, not impress him.

Hadn't she?

So why was she sitting here thinking about him?

She threw herself from the bed and stalked to the bathroom.

As she stepped from the shower a few minutes later and wrapped herself in a towel, she froze. Had she heard something?

Scritches was ahead of her, racing to the back door before a knock even sounded. He chirruped and rubbed himself against the wooden frame.

'Who is it?' Roni twisted the damp towel tighter.

'Hey, Roni, only me.'

Matt. Why did her heart rate increase? Because she looked forward to a good, though undeclared, battle of wills? 'Hang on, I'll be there in a minute.' She raced back to the bedroom and dragged on cheap yoga pants and a long T-shirt, tousled her wet hair. Hell, twenty past five, barely dawn. What kind of hours did this guy keep?

There was no one outside the back door as she unlocked it, but a barnyard chorus drew her to the orchard.

His head pressed against the calf's flank, whose front hoof was clenched between his knees, Matt glanced up. 'Realised last night I forgot to leave the medication for Baby, and I wanted to check him for footrot, too. Stan's mad as a cut snake, tends to keep his weaners in a wet barn.'

'Thanks. I thought you had a full-on week, though? It could've waited.'

'Footrot waits for no man,' Matt intoned sonorously, then shot her a glance. 'I kind of wanted to swing by and check on you, too. Yeah, I know—you've got it all under control, right?'

She crossed her arms as a breeze stirred the air. 'Not much left for me to have under control, is there?'

'Reckon Goat and Baby here would think different.' Matt dropped the calf's hoof and stood, dusting off his jeans. 'I noticed yesterday you made inroads on the veggie garden. Some interesting choices there. You really eat all that stuff?'

'I can't pronounce half of it, never mind eat it. Looks like I've already managed to murder some, though.' She nodded at the wilted leaves.

Matt pushed Goat out of the way with his knee and crossed to the bed. 'Guessing you bought the seedlings from the hardware shop? Their stuff's greenhouse raised, so you don't have much chance once you put them outdoors. And the plants aren't seasonal.' He lifted a floppy, yellowing stem. 'Brussels sprouts. Disgusting, and a winter veg.'

'Why would they sell plants that are unsuitable?'

'Money. The universal motivator.' The humour dropped from his voice. 'Bottom line for why anyone does anything, isn't it?' He pinched off the top of the plant and crushed it in his hand.

'That's hardcore cynical.'

'Or realistic.'

She frowned at the vegetable patch and spoke slowly, unaccustomed to putting her private thoughts into words. 'Maybe it's possible to start out pursuing money but then realise there are more important things in life. Like a sense of accomplishment.'

Why did her pulse ramp up as Matt assessed her for a long moment? Hell, she should be used to it by now. Eventually he nodded. 'Maybe. Anyway, I'd better head. I'll catch you next week.'

Again the invisible wall slammed into place, as though he mistrusted her intent. Not surprising, given she was no longer certain of it herself.

More irritating than the wall, though, was her resentment of it. She should appreciate that he backed the hell off and left her to do her own thing. Yet she felt . . . deserted. Damn, what was it about this man that made her feel such a need to be seen?

She turned on her heel, throwing the words over her shoulder. 'No worries. I'll see you whenever.'

It was wrong that 'whenever' seemed to stretch interminably before her.

❧

During the week she discovered berry-covered bushes growing in the shelter of the sheds at the bottom of the yard. Birds flitted in and out, making nests among the protective thorns. The trees were blackberry, or raspberry, or something. Should she dare try to impress Matt by cultivating the wild berries instead of waiting for his plants? Perhaps Tracey would teach her to make a pie?

She tried a couple of berries, screwing up her face at the astringent taste that dried out her tongue. Easily fixed, though: each day she'd bucket water across from the coop. Add sunshine, of which there was now plenty, and she would have a bumper crop.

Scritches shadowed her footsteps as she roamed the farm, poking his nose into everything and flopping into bed exhausted and dusty each night—much like her. If the prospect of raising Roo in the city hadn't been deterrent enough, how could she consider taking the cat back there, restricting him indoors after three weeks of blissful freedom?

Why would she?

She didn't have a single valid motive for returning to Sydney but a growing number of reasons for staying here. Despite the threat of the fox stealing her remaining chickens, she liked country life. There was a sense of security with the stone walls of the farmhouse wrapped around her, soothing solitude in being able to walk kilometres without encountering traffic and crowds, peace in the silence that was never actually silent but filled with the whisperings of tiny creatures, the songs of the birds and the poetry of the breeze lilting across the ripening crops and through the trees. Here was better for Scritches. Better for Roo. And maybe better for her.

It was almost a full week before the text she'd been waiting for arrived. She had been continually tempted to message her mother, hoping for news, but had limited herself to one text a day, never enquiring whether the travel agent had prepared the new itinerary. She refused to appear needy.

This time, Denise was waiting for her inside Ploughs and Pies.

Samantha greeted her cheerily from behind the counter. 'Hello, Roni. Had a go at those lamingtons yet?'

Keeping her head down at the CWA meeting, she'd not noticed Samantha there, but obviously Samantha had heard all about her. 'Not yet. Can't say I'm in any hurry. Baking's never been my thing.' She nodded toward the well-stocked cabinet. 'I guess you'll be doing it, though?'

'Oh, no.' Samantha swiped a cloth over the top of the glass display. 'I'm more into plating and presentation than baking. These cakes all come from McCue's Bakery, over in Murray Bridge. I recommend the Napoleon cake or the honey Swiss roll. Or, if you're not a sweet tooth, the savoury slice is to die for.'

'You've persuaded me. Has Mu—Denise ordered yet?'

Samantha's plump features hardened. 'Not yet. Likes taking up real estate but not paying for it, that one.'

Roni blinked at the harsh words. 'Ah. Okay. I'll see what she wants.'

Denise clutched Bonnie close as she stood to press her cheek to Roni's. 'I'm afraid I was awfully early, Samantha's probably had enough of me sitting here. I had to get a lift with a friend because my car's still off the road. Gosh, the last few days have taken forever! I kept picking up my phone to chat, but I didn't want it to seem like I'm elbowing in on your life.' She lifted one shoulder, a note of entreaty in her tone. 'I know it's going to take a long time for you to forgive me. And that's entirely fair.'

Roni slowly shook her head. 'No. No it won't.' She cleared her throat to remove the wonder from her voice. 'You made a hard decision, and you made it with the best of intentions. What more could a kid ask?' Behind her back, she curled her fingers into a fist, digging her nails into her palm. She refused to revisit the harm her mother's choice had caused. Clinging to those negative emotions and memories couldn't be healthy for Roo. 'Anyway,' she continued, not wanting to linger on uncomfortable topics. 'What are you eating?'

'Like you said last week, I'll have whatever you're having,' Denise smiled, lowering herself onto the steel-framed chair, her free hand pressed to the small of her back.

Roni made a quick trip to the counter, ordering savoury slices and cappuccinos. As she returned, she played with fragments of sentences in her head, wondering how to reopen the conversation about the holiday so that she could share her news.

She didn't need to.

'So, have you thought of anywhere else you want to add to our itinerary?' Denise asked brightly. 'The travel agent will have the quote back to me today and we can move forward with finalising everything. Is your passport current?'

Roni frowned. 'No. I've never travelled . . .'

'Oh, yes, of course.' Denise glanced at her watch. 'I forgot.'

The admission disconcerted Roni: she could remember every word of their two conversations. 'That's fine. You probably have a lot on your mind. Which reminds me, I've been meaning to ask all week, what kind of job did you end up in? You know, after uni didn't work out for you.'

'Oh, some of this and some of that. Jack of all trades, master of none, you know how it is.' Denise's rings flashed as she reached for the coffee Samantha delivered. She winced, holding her breath for a moment. 'To be honest, my back problem makes it somewhat difficult to pursue a career for any length of time.'

Delivering flat pastry rectangles, the tops crusted with melted cheese and crispy bacon bits, Samantha snorted. 'Damn flies,' she said, shooing an invisible insect as she pushed a plate—which seemed to contain far less salad than Roni's—toward Denise.

Denise arched an eyebrow but picked up her fork and angled it to slice a corner from the centimetre-thick pastry. 'I must say, I'm glad you buy these in, Samantha. May as well pay for the best rather than try to pass off sorry imitations.'

Samantha frowned as though she wasn't sure whether she'd been slighted or praised. As the bell over the door jangled, she turned to it with a speed that gave away her relief.

'Try your savoury slice, Roni,' Denise said. 'They're really very good. A regional specialty.'

Following her mother's lead, Roni sliced the pastry with her fork, although using the knife provided would undoubtedly have been easier. A rich layer of mince and onion in thick gravy was sandwiched by two slices of pastry, one shortcrust and one flaky. And Denise was right, it was delicious.

As they ate and chatted, Denise suggesting they extend the holiday to add more countries, anticipation grew in Roni until she was almost breathless. She had to share her secret with the one person who wouldn't judge her.

'Well,' she said, when Denise paused, 'the thing is, I'm not sure how long I'll be able to travel.'

'Oh, wait.' Denise picked up her phone, although Roni hadn't heard it. 'Oh, no. This is really too bad.' She frowned at the screen.

Roni looked around the cafe as Denise jabbed at keys.

'Oh, no, no. Not good enough,' Denise muttered, her monologue seeming to invite questions.

'What is it?'

Denise blew an exasperated breath between pursed lips. 'The travel agent just got back to me. Apparently, the fee to change my booking is nearly a thousand dollars. Completely unacceptable, considering the business I've given them over the years. Still, never mind.' She smiled reassuringly. 'I can't wait to explore Europe with you, make up for lost time. The problem is . . . oh, no. Don't worry about it.' She shook her head and thrust the phone into the leather handbag that swung from a clasp hooked to the table. Not looking at Roni, she toyed with the red ribbon Bonnie sported. 'You were saying you don't know how long you can vacation for?'

'No, that's all right, go back to this problem.' Roni's gut churned uneasily.

'It's nothing. Simply that ridiculous credit card issue I told you about last week. I'll need to get a new card before I can pay the travel agent. It'll be a bit tight, time-wise, but we'll just have to hope they hold the bookings.'

'I see.' Doubt oozed like poisoned syrup through her veins, the crushing weight pooling in her chest. You didn't grow up in the foster system without learning to question everything. Everyone.

Denise waited a beat, then grimaced, massaging her back. 'Sorry, I'm not wonderful company when I'm in this much pain. I honestly don't know how women tolerate being pregnant more than once in their life.'

Roni closed her eyes for a second, focusing on her own pain. Did it hurt more that her mother thought her an idiot or that she was trying to con her? 'If I paid the cancellation fee, we'd be able to travel together?'

'Obviously I wouldn't ask you to do that. But,' Denise kissed the dog's nose, apparently immune to the ice in Roni's tone, 'if you lend me the money until my card's sorted, we can make sure we don't lose our reservations.'

'May as well round it up. I'll lend you money for the car, too?'

Eagerness curing thirty years of backache, Denise sat

straighter. 'Oh, that'd be just wonderful, Veronica. If you're sure you don't mind.'

'The problem is, I don't have any money.'

A deep line fought the botox between Denise's eyebrows. 'Surely Marian left you funds? She always had cash on hand. Have you searched the house?'

'She's paying the bills, but there's no cash involved.' Her mother's greed dashed Roni's last doubt. Her last hope.

'Derek Prescott could advance you a little something. Or I know a broker who'll give you cash against Marian's car.'

Roni stood, regret and anger vying for dominance. And disappointment. Not at Denise; she had no reason to expect any better from her. But at herself. She knew better than to trust anyone, especially the woman she had been warned against, the woman who had already deserted her. 'You think I want to buy your undying maternal affection? Think again, Mother.'

Denise thrust to her feet. 'Oh, Veronica, I'm so sorry. You've construed this quite the wrong way. I knew we should've gone for counselling before we tried to build our bridges. But it's all right, I do understand. It must be quite overwhelming to discover there is one person in the world who only wants the best for you. It's natural for you to be mistrustful.' She unhooked her bag from the table, smiling gently at Roni. 'Don't give it a moment's thought, I'll sort it and we'll talk later in the week.' She blew a kiss from the flat of her hand and swept from the cafe, leaving her coffee undrunk. And the account unpaid.

Her cheeks burning, Roni took out her wallet and made her way to the register.

'That's the lot, then?' Samantha's voice sounded falsely bright, hiding pity.

266

Chapter Twenty-four

Not wanting Tracey to hear the gossip on what was clearly a very effective grapevine, Roni had gone straight there after the cafe. Tracey made tea and listened to her admission of how she'd been foolish enough to entertain a childish dream of a relationship with her mother.

'She's an odd one, that woman,' Tracey said. 'No explaining what she does. Marian would have been the first to tell you that both she and Denise were manipulative, but Denise is just plain bloody selfish. She just doesn't care for anyone's feelings.'

Tracey cut a large wedge from a cake topped with glistening caramel-covered apple slices. 'Here, love, try a slice of apple upside-down cake. I'm trying to decide whether it needs cinnamon in the topping. Tell me what you think.' She slid the slice onto Roni's plate. 'You know, you can't change people. You can only learn to live with them. Or consider whether it's better to learn to live without them.'

She was right. The fantasy of a relationship with her mother had only existed for a few days of her entire life; before that she'd been too smart to be seduced by hope. Now she would pretend it had never happened.

She left Tracey's a kilo heavier, but her heart a little lighter, her plan firm: her best revenge against her mother would be to succeed in what Marian wanted her to achieve.

And, coincidentally, that's what would be best for her family, too. Her real family.

∾

'Door's open, love,' Tracey responded to her knock a week later. 'Kettle's on.'

Tracey's house had become familiar, each visit during the week highlighted by cake and tea, each departure seeing her plied with more casseroles than she could ever eat.

As Roni wandered toward the kitchen, pausing to fondle Bear's ears and silently greet her aunt in the photos on the wall, Tracey continued to chatter. 'It's going to be another warm one today, so I whipped up the sponge cake last night, while it was cooler. You can have a go at dipping the lamingtons, then take them home with you. You never know who might pop by on the weekend.' Her hair bounced enthusiastically over her arched brows. She'd not missed one opportunity to check how frequently Matt came by.

Never. That was how frequently. Roni hadn't seen him

for nearly two weeks. 'Well, I guess I can guarantee it won't be Denise.'

'Try not to take it personally, love,' Tracey tutted. 'If it makes you feel any better, Jim Smithton tells me he took her to the airport yesterday. She's off to Brissy.'

Despite her nonchalant façade, perfected over so many years, Roni had lain awake at night, second-guessing her actions. Was it possible that, hypersensitive to being manipulated—thanks to Marian—she had misjudged her mother? Her gut instinct screamed no, but her brain desperately wanted to make excuses. Her mother had been raised with certain expectations and privileges, so was it possible she saw nothing wrong in asking to borrow money? Maybe she truly intended to pay it back?

Yet Denise had said she would be in touch, and this new desertion was final proof of her mother's indifference. 'Kind of hard not to take it personally when your own mother can't bear to be within several hundred kilometres of you.'

'Like Marian said,' Tracey paused, one floury hand in the air, gaze on the ceiling as she searched for the exact memory. '"Blood isn't thicker than water. It just stains worse." You don't need someone simply because they share your genetics, Veronica. You choose who you let into your life.' She tapped the top of the yellow sponge resting on a cooling rack. 'I'll pop around early next week, and you can do a couple of practice runs at making your own cake before the meeting.'

'Couldn't we do scones? I've got them down pat.'

'Dipped in chocolate sauce and coconut? Maybe not. Here, have a cuppa first. Lady Grey helps everything. Did I tell you it was Marian who got me onto tea drinking?'

Roni smiled; only like a dozen times. And tea was something else she'd need to ask a doctor about.

Tracey patted her lap as she sat and Bear put his front paws up, leaning his head on her shoulder and gazing adoringly at her as she spoke. 'After China, we swapped to green tea for a while. But the green tea here is nothing like the blend they use overseas.'

'You went to China?'

'Oh, yes. We travelled all over the world. Andrew never minded. I think, deep down, he knew how Marian was. And, really, he wanted to see her happy. I guess he owed her that much.'

'After the inconvenience of my birth, you mean.' Roni kept her gaze on the pot of chocolate sauce simmering on the stove.

'Well, I wouldn't have put it quite like that. And now it seems your birth may have been quite convenient. It certainly provided Marian with somewhere to settle her assets, and an opportunity to stick it right up Denise.' Tracey flushed and stood. 'Sorry. You started me off thinking about her again, and that always makes me snappy. It's just that she's never improved. After what she did to Marian and Andrew, you'd think she'd have learned her lesson. But then the Kruegers . . . The woman has no limits.'

The spoon Roni had picked up clattered into the pot of chocolate. 'Kruegers? You mean Matt?'

'Oh, yes. Matt. Well, not really Matt. But never you mind about that.' Tracey flapped a hand at her own face. 'My, it *is* warm, isn't it? Let's get these cakes done before they go stale. Now, first you need to shave off a thin sliver, all the way around the sponge. A lot of people cheat on this step, don't want to waste the cake, but how would you feel if you got the lamington with a crust? Plus, the sponge won't soak up the sauce properly unless you open it up. In any case, I freeze all the offcuts to use in rum balls or trifle. I have some rum balls in the freezer somewhere, remind me to send them home with you.'

No matter how Roni tried to steer the conversation back to Matt and Denise, Tracey resisted her attempts. Three hours later she left with a tub of rum balls, a Tupperware of lamingtons, sticky arms, a chocolate and coconut covered shirt, Tracey's foolproof recipe for sponge cake—and more questions than when she arrived.

∽

Despite her fridge full of treats, Matt didn't show up on the weekend. Roni tried making the no-fail sponge cake, then fed it to the chickens.

Monday, when Tracey hadn't turned up by mid-afternoon, she had another go. Slightly better, but still not fluffy and light. Her mind distracted, she tried to calm it by cleaning out the mixing bowl, then separating the duck eggs, beating the yolks until thick and creamy before adding sugar and flour. She whipped the whites and folded them through the mixture, all the time wondering where Tracey could be.

It was new, this feeling of expectation, of having someone to wonder about.

She climbed the hill a couple of times, checking for messages. Nothing. Which was reasonable, because Tracey owed her nothing, neither friendship nor explanation. Though she had said she would come, she had every right to change her mind. She could disappear. Just like Denise.

She scrubbed a fist across her chest, scowling. Why did the thought of Tracey deserting her hurt more than Denise's actual desertion? Must be pregnancy hormones.

As the second cake sat cooling, she glanced at the clock, chewing on her thumbnail. Night had fallen, Tracey wouldn't come now. But what if, with miles of dirt road between town and the farm, she'd had a flat? Or hit a roo? Or run off the dirt verge, where the dust lay thick and slippery?

She grabbed her phone, nudging Scritches away from the back door. 'No night hikes for you, buddy. Not safe.'

For the fourth time that day, she moved quickly beneath the soughing branches of the ancient pine trees lining the track up the hill. She wouldn't call Tracey, but would it be intruding to send her a message, just checking that she was okay? A low, mournful hoot close by speared through her, and the cicadas and small creatures rustling through the undergrowth instantly stilled at the warning.

Her footsteps pattered against the shale, speeding up to match her heartbeat as she kept her gaze confined to the miserable puddle of light from her torch. She tripped, but caught herself before she fell. Sucked in a deep breath.

Told herself to get a grip, that no one out here dogged her footsteps, no threat lurked around a corner.

It had never been darkness that caused her pain.

She switched off her torch and tipped her head back, waiting for her eyes to adjust and her heart rate to slow, gazing at an infinite sea of sparkling diamonds appliquéd onto the dark velvet cloak of night.

Her phone found range, blipping twice. Two messages. Seeing they were from Tracey, she didn't pause to read them but pressed call back. The phone rang out. The second time she dialled, Tracey answered, her hoarse, exhausted voice almost unrecognisable. 'Veronica, love, did you get my messages?'

'Are you okay?'

'Just a touch of flu. Thought it best I don't give it to you.' Tracey coughed fitfully.

Roni blew out a long breath, relief easing her chest. 'You sound awful.'

'Feel it, too. Slept right through today. I'll let you know when I'm up to scratch. I have to kick this bug so we can get onto the lamingtons.'

'Don't worry about that. I've got it all under control.'

'Ah, I knew you'd—' Tracey broke off, coughing. 'Sorry, love, can't really talk. I'll call you later in the week.'

Roni made her way back to the house, her mind buzzing. For the sake of her baby she should stay away from someone with flu, but Tracey needed her.

In the kitchen, she pulled open a recalcitrant drawer, over-stuffed with pamphlets and handwritten notes. Despite

Tracey's bottomless freezer, perhaps she'd like something fresh. She scoured recipes, comparing ingredients with what she had on hand. Intending to try her hand at Flo Bjelke-Petersen's scones, she'd bought a large pumpkin the previous week.

Soup it would be, then.

She worked methodically, roasting the pumpkin first, because the recipe promised that would enhance the flavour, carefully softening the onions without allowing them to colour, tasting the stock before adding salt.

Three hours later, she stirred boiled rice through to thicken the soup.

Done.

She stretched, cracking her neck from side to side and rolling her shoulders, then pushed the pot into the fridge. It was past midnight, the latest she had been to bed for weeks. Tomorrow she would pick up lemonade and something nice at the shop, in case the soup didn't taste as good as it smelled.

It was odd but rewarding to have someone other than Scritches to care for.

∼

By Friday, Tracey was still ill. Her own memories of having been coddled non-existent, Roni had hauled the television from the lounge into the bedroom and spent each afternoon fussing around Tracey, making cups of tea and nagging her to stay hydrated, wincing at every throat-raking cough. In the twilight she would head home, then stay up late to make a fresh soup or casserole, though Tracey had little appetite.

Her hair sweat-straggled to her head, Tracey feebly tried to push herself up in the bed.

Roni dashed forward to place a pillow behind her. 'Please let me take you to the doctor. You don't seem to be getting any better.'

Tracey's chest rattled as the breath scraped through her throat. 'No, it's just a touch of the flu. Takes a while longer to get over it each year, that's all.' Dark circles ringed her eyes and she gasped like she couldn't find the energy to inhale. 'I do have something to ask you, though, love.'

Roni sat on the edge of the bed. 'Shoot.'

'I worry about Bear. You know, in the future. He's too old to start over with a family he doesn't know. And I can't bear to think of him closed up in kennels.'

The dog pushed his greying muzzle into Roni's hand, as though adding his own plea. 'Bear will always have a home with me.' The words were out of her mouth before she'd thought. But no amount of consideration would change her intention, anyway. 'But you're going to be just fine. At least, you will be if you'd eat something.'

'No need to eat when I'm just lying around, love. And it's not like I can't stand to lose a few pounds off these batwings.' Tracey lifted one arm, the floral nightie hanging loose at the shoulders, her dehydrated skin crepey and pale, like a long-dead flower petal. 'Now, we need to make plans for our world domination of the CWA this afternoon.'

'You're not well enough to cook.' Roni swirled Scrabble tiles around the purple box balanced on the lap-table.

'No, but I *am* well enough to direct you to take a tray of sponge cake out of my freezer. I feel terrible I didn't have time to run through making the lamingtons again, but between us we'll still be able to pull off this year's title.'

'Are we allowed to do that?'

Tracey huffed, then broke into a coughing fit, her shoulders bowed and arms clenched across her ribs, as though to stop her bones from shaking loose. 'Of course we are. There's nothing in the rules to say we can't enter as a team. I baked the sponge, you're in charge of the dipping and rolling.'

'Not just the competition. The tasks. It was important to Marian I learn to bake the lamingtons. I swear I've tried every day this week, but the chooks are about to explode. They're laying fairy cakes instead of eggs. Though I'm a little concerned about what they're using as icing.'

As Tracey wheezed with laughter, Roni held a straw to her lips. 'Here, the lemonade's flat, the way you like it.'

Tracey's fingers clawed at her hand, clinging with surprising strength. 'Love, Marian wanted to test your willingness, not your ability. If she'd seen the way you've tootled in here every day looking after me, I know she'd be more than sold. And don't think I don't appreciate it, either. But now we have to make sure you get to that meeting. You remember where the clubroom is?'

Nobody had ever said they appreciated her. She rushed to fill the silence with unnecessary words. 'Sure. Cocoa, icing sugar and coconut in the pantry? It won't take the sponge long to defrost in this heat.'

She *would* make this work.

She painstakingly trimmed the sponge and cut it into squares, then dipped each in chocolate sauce and rolled them in coconut, resisting the urge to lick her fingers as she placed them on a wire rack to dry. By the time she finished, sweat trickled between her shoulder blades, though roller blinds blocked the sun that beat mercilessly against the window.

After tidying the kitchen, the dishes washed and returned to their cupboards and coconut and crumbs swept from the floor to deter the marauding sugar ants, she tiptoed into Tracey's room and sat alongside the bed for a few minutes, listening to her stentorian breathing.

Tracey looked older, frailer than she had little more than a month ago. Bear lay alongside the bed, head on his paws. He wouldn't move until she came to let him out tomorrow. Roni turned the ceiling fan low, packed away the Scrabble board, replaced the flat lemonade and added a glass of water, then quietly left the house.

The reflection from a dozen silver-foil windscreen protectors blinded her as she pulled into the carpark bordered by purple-flowered jacaranda trees.

Like the previous meeting, the clubroom was filled with women bent over crafts, their grey heads nodding as gossip travelled. A younger woman in tight blue jeans and a black button-through shirt leaned against the canteen counter, raking her up and down with an intense stare. Then she spoke to her neighbour, her chin nudging in Roni's direction.

Roni squared her shoulders. Tupperware wedged on her hip, she marched toward the counter, but pulled to a halt as a chair squealed and Christine Albright rose like a behemoth in front of her. 'Veronica, we were beginning to think you'd decided not to enter.' Her eyes narrowed on Roni's container. 'Are those yours? They're very evenly sized.'

'Mine and Tracey's. We're entering as a team.'

'A team? I'm not sure that's allowed.'

The IGA cashier, Lynn, circled in behind Christine. 'Of course it's allowed. Specially if Tracey says so. Who'd know the rules better than her?'

'Well, as she and Marian were always in cahoots making them . . .' Christine ran a thumb under the narrow belt valiantly trying to cinch the waist of her floral print dress. 'Never known a pair thicker than those two. It's a wonder poor Andrew even considered himself married.' She flicked a fingernail against her buckle. 'Though I don't suppose he did for much of the time, did he?'

Definitely no secrets left in this community.

'Hush, Christine. You'll frighten poor Veronica off. We need new blood, remember?' Lynn made it sound as though she might be sacrificed to a cult. The cashier leaned closer, an eye-watering waft of sweet perfume failing to overpower nicotine. 'Tracey not with you, Veronica?'

'She's ill.'

'Not again! She's never really picked up since your aunt died, the poor thing. And she does tend to overdo things.

She needs to remember she's not so young anymore.' Lynn seemed sublimely unaware of her own liver-spotted hands.

'It's just the flu.'

Christine nodded sagely. 'That's how Marian's started. Months of feeling ill with "just a flu", wasn't it, Lynn? Then all of a sudden, the diagnosis comes out of nowhere.'

Roni clutched the container as fear squeezed her heart. 'She said it's a bug.'

She startled as Taylor stepped up alongside her, tapping the Tupperware. 'If you don't hurry and lodge these, I'm going to steal them and enter them under my name. They look divine.'

'Do you think you'd fool us?' Lynn waggled a finger.

'Can only hope,' Taylor grinned. 'Paperwork's on the canteen bench, Roni.'

'Lucky for Luke your gran stays fit enough to keep your pantry full.' Christine's lips pursed tighter than a cat's bum as Taylor steered Roni from the group.

'Absolutely,' Taylor called back, then lowered her voice. 'I dropped past Tracey's to check on her and she asked me to rescue you. Some of this lot can be a bit full-on once the baking gauntlet is thrown down.'

'Christine sure is.'

'Oh, she doesn't even need to get a whiff of competition.' Taylor directed her toward the women who'd whispered at her entry. 'Fiona, Nancy, this is Marian Nelson's niece, Roni.'

Always Marian's niece, not Denise's daughter.

The attractive blonde bared perfect teeth. 'Roni. So, you're the city slicker everyone's talking about.'

'I don't know that there's much to talk about.'

'Don't you bet on it. Small town, we're desperate for goss.'

The other woman, Nancy, shot a quick grin at Fiona. 'You do a fair job of providing that, Fi.'

Eyes locked onto Roni in unblinking, reptilian assessment, Fiona ignored her companion. 'You won't be hanging around long, though? No one in their right mind stays here if they don't have to.'

So much for country welcome. These women were worse than cliquey high school seniors. Roni thumped the tub of cakes down on the counter, then sent up a quick prayer that she hadn't damaged the perfect cubes. 'Actually, the longer I'm here, the more I like it.'

'But you'll head back home soon?'

She stared at Fiona for a few tense seconds. 'I haven't decided where home is.'

Fiona turned away, belatedly including Nancy in the conversation. 'That'd be the genetic factor. Some people don't make choices. They simply take everything, with no regard who it rightfully belongs to.'

'What—' Roni's protest squeaked out on a surprised breath.

'Fix up the entry forms, Roni,' Taylor interrupted. 'And we'll go down to the pub for that drink.'

As they exited the building into the soul-sucking heat minutes later, Taylor fanned herself with one hand. 'Sorry. You might've been better off if I'd left you to Christine. I forgot Fiona has a history with your mum.'

'Her and half the town, it seems. What's her gripe?'

A purple blanket of petals muffled their footsteps as they crossed to the vehicles in the shade of a jacaranda. Taylor searched her bag, eventually producing car keys. 'I can't really share that. Hey, remember I mentioned a barbecue at my place? Harvest will start early, on account of the heat, so we're doing it tomorrow evening. BYO drinks, I'll lay on everything else. And I promise, no Christine or Fiona.' She beeped the lock on a dove-grey Pajero. 'Though maybe I should brave them to go back in and pinch your lamingtons.'

Disappointment suddenly swirled in Roni's stomach as she realised that Taylor's mention of the pub had been nothing more than a ruse for them to escape the meeting, then annoyance at herself for presuming it would be anything else. 'I've another sponge at home. Mine, not Tracey's, though. So, you know, consume at own risk.' Actually, her latest effort didn't look too bad. Although she'd found fresh bags of feed delivered to the coop, it seemed likely Matt would be a no-show for the twentieth day in a row—not that she was counting—so the cake may as well go somewhere other than the chickens.

'Awesome. If you save me from hiding the Sara Lee boxes, you may be my new BFF. The property's a bit off the beaten track, so I'll get Matt to pick you up.'

Her palms clammy, Roni's fingers turned to ice. How was it possible to both hate and love that plan at the same time?

Chapter Twenty-five

Jittery with nerves, given their awkward conversation last time she'd seen him, Roni contrived to be near the coop watering when Matt arrived the next day.

He parked the ute alongside the house, then strolled down to her, his face hidden by his aviators and akubra. 'Hey, sorry I didn't get around last week. Busy season.'

Last week? More like three. 'Has it been that long? I know what you mean about busy.' She hefted a pair of buckets, hoping she wouldn't look too duck-like as she waddled with them.

'Here, let me.' Matt took the buckets. 'Where to?'

She'd had plenty of time to prepare off-the-cuff witty responses, yet now she was practically tongue-tied. His reserve and her inability to read him threw her off stride. She pointed to her precious bushes, which had responded well to regular watering.

Matt put the buckets down and pushed up his aviators. The corner of his lips twitched.

Shit. She knew that reaction.

'These bushes?' He pointed.

'Yeah.'

'These boxthorn bushes?'

'Berries.' Boxthorn did not sound promising.

'Whatever you say, boss.' Water slopped onto his dusty boots as he took up the buckets again.

She closed her eyes for a second. 'They're not edible, are they?'

'Well,' he drew the word out, 'I believe technically they are. But African boxthorn is a declared pest plant. Farmers are supposed to eradicate them. Not, ah, encourage them.'

'The birds really like them,' she defended as tiny brown and grey sparrows darted into the jewelled foliage.

'They make a great protective screen. Bet you've had no problems with prowling lions.' His smile finally broke through.

'Okay, I get it,' she huffed. 'Just don't bloody water them, then.'

Matt upended the buckets onto the plants. 'Hey, Scritch. What've you done to your nose, mate?'

As usual, the cat rubbed up against the farmer's legs, splitting the air with his purrs. 'His nose is always banged-up, he uses it to root around in stuff.'

'Must be part echidna. Poor fella, I've got some cream that'll help heal that.'

283

Great, one nice word for the cat and her own prickles smoothed right down. But, to be fair, it wasn't like Matt had taken a shot at her for watering the weeds. Nor even really laughed at her stupidity.

Matt straightened and rubbed a hand around the back of his neck. He glanced at her, then made a chore of stacking the buckets. 'You look good.'

She'd thrown on an asymmetrical blouse with her jeans—and then spent thirty minutes in front of the mirror, trying to decide whether her left or right shoulder looked better revealed.

'Thanks.' She bent to stroke Scritches. Not that he deserved it, but her face needed a moment to cool down.

'How're the other kids doing?'

Her neck cracked as her head whipped around. 'What?'

'Baby and Goat?'

'Oh. Good. Baby was limping for a few days, but I put on the cream and he seems fine now.'

'I came early a few mornings and checked him. Mind if I take another look now?'

'Course not.' No matter how furious she was—mostly with herself—at the way his presence unsettled her comfortable new familiar, she liked the way he engaged with her animals.

'I was thinking,' Matt said, matching her pace as they crossed to the orchard. 'Now that you've got Baby, you might not want a milk cow? I could arrange a goat. As in, a real goat, not a Goat goat. Only if you promise not to call it Sheep, though, because these names are doing my head in.'

'You can milk goats?'

'Sure. If you can handle milking a cow, a goat's easier, based on the size alone.'

'My experience with milking is limited to fighting the screw top on the carton.' That one earned her a faint smile.

'I've a cow with a calf at heel. You could come by, have a go at milking her. That is, if you're thinking of sticking around long enough to make adding to your family worthwhile.' Matt adjusted his hat and rubbed at his chin, watching the sheep and cow thundering toward them.

She would be adding, all right. 'I can't see any reason not to stay. For a while, anyway.'

'Excellent.' Matt kept his gaze on the livestock. 'That should make Scritches happy.'

Only Scritches? The silence between them was heavy and stretched on until she pointed toward the house. 'I'll grab the lamingtons while you do Baby?'

'You baked?' Matt smiled. 'Awesome. Don't suppose there's one left that couldn't fit in the container?'

Her voice hooked a little crazily on the reply, sudden butterflies getting down and dirty in her throat. 'I think there might be a couple. I'll put the kettle on.'

A few minutes later she settled into the chair opposite Matt. 'I never imagined this would be my life. Sitting on a verandah, drinking tea and eating cake like a pair of oldies.' She spluttered as she realised that she might have just verbally coupled the two of them. 'I mean the whole tree change thing, that kind of stuff.'

Matt reached for a lamington. 'Sounds cool to me.'

Which bit? She tensed as a sudden desire to know, a longing for something undefined, surged through her.

'Did you really bake these? They're as good as Tracey's.'

No, they weren't. They were heavy and a little dry. Yet Matt sounded as though he meant the compliment. And her heart was beating way too fast.

The unnerving blue eyes settled on her as he leaned toward her over the wrought-iron table. 'Actually, I've a favour to ask, Roni.'

Her heart calcified into a tight knot, crushing the emerging butterflies. Greg's favours were always of the can-you-spot-me-some-cash-for-weed variety. She'd known this was coming. *Them.* Greg. Denise. Now Matt. Her only value was to provide for others.

And what she didn't willingly provide, they took by force. Hands bunched in her lap, she was unable to drag her gaze from Matt's.

Matt's voice lowered, as if he were making sure no one could overhear their dealing. 'If you've a couple spare, I'd really like them for during the week.'

A couple of what? Joints? Hits? 'You mean you want . . . the lamingtons?'

'Hell, yeah. Don't take them all to Luke's. He won't appreciate them the way I will.'

Relief bubbled in her laugh. 'You could've been eating test runs all week. The animals are over being my garbage disposal.'

He pulled a disappointed face. 'I knew I'd miss out if I stayed away.'

He wanted free cake: she had to take his words at face value, not wish more into them. She glanced at her wrist, though she never wore a watch.

Matt nodded. 'Yeah, we'd better shift it. Not sure what time the game starts.'

It took them twenty minutes to reach Taylor's place. Much like Roni's, it was set in a valley and surrounded by stone sheds. 'These places seem to be built to a formula.'

Matt used two fingers to steer, his left hand lying on his knee. 'Guess the German settlers recreated what they knew. My farm's much the same.' He pulled up alongside four other vehicles, three of them utes, one a motorbike. 'If you want to hide those lamingtons at the back of Tay's fridge, I'll make sure they don't get forgotten. I'll grab the drinks.'

Roni watched in the rear-view mirror as he unlatched a small fridge on the tray of the ute, transferring the contents to an esky. She'd brought apple juice, hoping her abstinence wouldn't cause questions.

The guy who opened the front door matched Matt for height, his eyes an unusual shade, almost violet. 'Mate, good to see you. It's been like, forever.' He shook hands with Matt, clapping him on the shoulder. 'I was beginning to think you'd lost your way.'

'Sorry, got side-tracked. This is your new neighbour, Veronica. Roni, Luke Hartmann.'

Luke lifted a hand. 'Hey, Roni. Chins will really start wagging once the old biddies find out you've persuaded Matty to take time off. Speaking of work, Tay's been held up, so you'll be the token female for a half-hour or so. Come on in.'

She forced herself to smile. She didn't do social events at the best of times—now she'd be alone?

'The guys are down here.' Luke led them along a central hallway and ushered them into a lounge room.

A room with two men already in it.

The walls splashed with lurid colours as the TV volume cranked up.

Her chest tight, her hands curled into fists as she fought the flashback. She wasn't fourteen anymore.

Taylor would be here in a moment. And there would be four men with Luke and Matt. Four was fine.

Luke made the introductions. 'Steve, Jake, meet Roni. Grab a pew, I'll get some chips. Want me to take your esky, Matt?'

Roni returned the greetings and dropped onto the couch. The cushions sank, trapping her.

No. She wouldn't think that.

Except, right now, there were three men in the room.

Steve and Jake messed around with the remotes, angling the TV, and then sat either side of her. Why had she given in to her shaky legs and taken the first seat she'd spied, instead of the single chair Matt now occupied?

Luke returned, flipping off the overhead light as he entered. 'You're in pole position, Roni. Makes you the designated chip holder.' Illuminated by the flickering TV, he placed a plastic tub of Doritos on her lap. 'There's dip and stuff, too, but I'll let Tay sort that out when she gets back or I'll be in trouble.'

Steve's chuckle vibrated through her. 'Last year you screwed up the dip with whipped cream, so you can't really blame her, mate.'

Four men now. She was fine.

She tightened her grasp on the Doritos as Steve reached for a handful.

Matt stood again. 'I'll grab our drinks. You guys want anything while I'm up?'

No! No, four men minus one would be . . . She wanted to tell him not to leave, but fear glued her tongue to the roof of her mouth.

Jake reached a hand through the gloom, toward her thigh.

No, not her thigh. The chips, just the chips. She had to cut this out, to refuse the memories and fears. It had been years ago, half a lifetime.

Luke turned the TV up and the guys settled further back on the lounge. Alongside her. So close she could feel their pulses, hear their too-rapid heartbeats. Smell their sweaty excitement.

Darkness fringed her vision. The bowl slipped in her grasp. Her toes curled, cramping against the straps of her sandals. Her stomach turned to rock.

If she moved, tried to stand, to escape, they would shove her face-down on the lounge. Bury her screams in the cushions as they turned up the TV. She knew how it went.

No. There was no need for this. No reason to let the memories in.

Except she could taste the blood in her mouth, she could hear the screams.

Her screams.

Heart racing, she couldn't breathe. The hands came faster. Pretending they were reaching for snacks, but reaching for her. Threatening to brush her legs. Her thighs.

Closer.

Closer.

Any second now the touching would start.

Her breath sobbed in her throat. Her jaw ached as the first scream clawed for escape. Chips avalanched over the edge of the bowl.

'Roni?' Matt stood in front of her, holding out a drink. Though he blocked the TV screen, shut off the glaring images that triggered her brain, she couldn't speak. Could only stare at him as she dragged at the air for oxygen that didn't exist.

He set the glass on the coffee table with a crack that should have snapped her out of the miasma of terror. It didn't. Nothing could. She was trapped, just like she'd been all those years ago. Nothing had changed, nothing was better. A kid again, she was unable to protect herself. Unable to fight back. Unable to speak out. Panic oozed in, as thick as tar, crushing her chest.

She knew how to combat it. Breathe and count.

But the numbers wouldn't come. Nothing would come, except the memories; blinding flashes of light in the dark room, scars from her past ripping apart her future.

Eyes locked to hers, Matt extended his hand. 'Hey, I meant to show you how Taylor netted her fig tree. Might work in your orchard. Come and have a look now, while it's still light out.'

'Smooth, mate,' Luke laughed. 'That line's right up there with, "Come to my room and see my etchings".'

She prised her fingers from the bowl, willing her hand not to tremble as she snatched at the lifeline Matt offered.

'Hey, no buggering off with the chips, you two.' Steve took the bowl from her lap, and she leaped up so quickly he tumbled sideways into the depression she left.

If she'd been a second slower, he would have fallen onto her. Into her.

Dizziness swept in and her legs faltered, darkness thundering in her ears and pressing on her brain. Matt's arm around her waist half-dragged her from the room.

A thigh-high rail ran the length of the verandah, and Matt led her to it, his support firm until she'd planted her hands on the wood.

Chest hollow, she curled her shoulders in. Fighting for breath. Fighting not to cry.

Like a tide, the fear slowly receded.

She had known it would. It always did, but knowing never made the panic attacks easier to face. Matt stood silent, close but not touching, as she struggled for control. Struggled to pretend she was normal again.

As her panted breaths slowed, her fingers unclenching from where her nails gouged the wood, she felt the tension seep from his stance. 'Sorry.' She laughed unsteadily. 'Just been one of those weeks, you know. Well, turning into one of those years, really.'

She caught the shake of Matt's head, though she couldn't bring herself to look at him. 'There's more to it than that, isn't there?' he said. 'Did someone say something? Do something?'

How dare he probe? 'Nothing. It doesn't matter. Not anymore.'

'Yes, it does,' he insisted. 'Something in that room triggered you.'

'Armchair psychologist.'

He grunted, probably relief at the realisation she wasn't going to break down into full-blown hysterics. 'Sometimes I catch Dr Phil during lunch.'

Trying to hide her shuddering breath, she waved at the yard. 'Where's this orchard you're showing me?' Damn. Her voice trembled, and tears sprang to her eyes. Not tears of fear but of mortification at how close she had come to revealing her secret.

'Near the creek. Bit of a walk.' The dust from a Pajero jolting up the driveway thickened the encroaching dusk. 'Ah, here's Tay.' Matt sounded like he'd been granted a stay of execution. He vaulted from the deck, greeted Taylor and hauled her groceries into the kitchen. Roni trailed him like a lost puppy, useless and underfoot. Matt put the carry bags on the table, gave her a nod without meeting her gaze, then ducked back to the safety of the lounge room, fig trees forgotten. Clearly putting as much distance between them as possible.

Fine. That suited her perfectly.

'Sorry I got held up.' Taylor unpacked the bags onto the counter. 'Did the guys feed themselves?'

'Yeah, they have beer and chips.'

'You managed to drag Matt away from such bounty? Props for that. Nice guy, isn't he?'

'That seems to be the consensus.'

Taylor caught a packet of spaghetti sliding toward the tiled floor. 'Everyone's happy to see him opening up again.'

'What—'

A bellow from the lounge room interrupted and Taylor smiled. 'I can never work out whether they're louder when they're winning or losing. Want to tip these salads into bowls for me? Maybe I'll be able to fool them into thinking I cooked.'

'Don't do that, babe.' Luke entered the kitchen and grabbed Taylor by the hips, spinning her to face him. 'They might not eat.' He took the sting from the words with a kiss.

God, how long did Taylor say they'd been married? Because they kissed like they'd just hooked up. Roni looked away, fiddling with bowls instead of staring.

Except she *was* staring.

Because suddenly she wanted someone to kiss her like that, kiss her like she was the only thing of importance in his life, like she was the only person in the room. Kiss her with absolute intention, as though he would protect her forever.

She grabbed a knife and stabbed the bag of salad leaves, slicing it open.

'Anyway,' Luke continued, as though he hadn't just spent two minutes making out with his wife. 'Guys don't eat green stuff, you know that. Feed the man meat.' He plucked up a couple of leaves and tossed them in his mouth, then pulled a face.

Taylor took out another bowl. 'Except Matt. Remember? Some mate you are.'

'Oh, yeah. Maybe you can work on him, Roni? He's letting the team down.'

Roni squirmed. Hell, it wasn't like they were an item. 'Hardly my business.' Technically, she was his boss. Who had just humiliated herself in front of an employee who didn't have the decency to pretend he hadn't noticed. 'In any case, I'm thinking of turning vegetarian myself. I accidentally bought a bull calf and I don't want to have to eat him.'

Luke chuckled, dropping to a kitchen stool and pulling his wife onto his lap. 'How do you accidentally buy a bull?'

'I went to the market to get a poddy and came away with a bobby. Similar letters. How's a girl to know?'

'See, it's not just me.' Taylor slapped her husband's shoulder, then turned to Roni. 'Luke gives me shit when I screw up. Like when I don't know a reaper from a fertiliser spreader, or can't tell the difference between his crops.'

Almost giddy with the adrenaline surge that followed a panic attack, Roni didn't feel such an outsider. 'I bet at least you don't get accused of manhandling his wild oats.'

'I wish.' Luke nuzzled Taylor's neck. 'If my wife would work a little less, maybe I'd get the chance to do some accusing.'

Taylor wrestled from his grip. 'Scram, you. Go heat up the barbecue, seeing as you're clearly not into the game.'

'I just found more interesting things to heat up,' Luke grumbled. 'See, Roni, this is what happens when you're old and married. Don't say I didn't warn you.'

Taylor's tea towel caught him a smart crack across his backside as he left the kitchen. 'Sorry about him,' she said, though she smiled fondly at his back. 'He's getting kind of antsy to have kids.'

'You don't have any?'

'I don't want to rush things.'

'Didn't you say you've been together ten years?'

'Yeah.' Two shallow lines furrowed between Taylor's eyes. 'Doesn't feel that long, though. We've plenty of time. I hope.' Her expression turned melancholy, but then she forced a smile. 'Who knows how life will turn out? That's why I say grab onto whatever's offered, and enjoy it while you can. Taxes can be avoided if you've got a great accountant, but death sure as heck can't. You want to take those bowls? The barbie's out the back.' She nodded toward the hallway. 'Just follow Luke's whistling. I swear, I'd be able to find him from a thousand miles away. Well, technically, I did.'

What was the story Taylor hinted at with her half-mentioned tales, the reminiscences that drifted off with a wistful smile? How could Roni even ask about such a thing? Socialising was something she had never before felt the need or desire to participate in. It seemed awkward and unnatural, and she had no idea where the boundaries lay. Her own were the only ones she had ever been interested in.

And she needed to focus on keeping them intact.

Chapter Twenty-six

Armageddon came on Tuesday. At least, that's what it looked like when she woke. The horizon to the north was a dull, surreal red, the air hung thick and ominous. By the time she'd fed the chickens, the thermometer near the back door read thirty-nine degrees. The atmosphere seemed muffled and soundless; a superheated vacuum filled with menacing portent.

With it too hot to work outdoors, she cleaned the house and then changed into shorts and a T-shirt to head into town. She would spend some time with Tracey, having skipped going in yesterday. Without company the day had dragged long and oddly empty.

By the time she reached her car in the shed opposite the chicken coop, the red pall in the distance had gusted in. Airborne dust and sand hid the sun and tainted her now-familiar world with the shades of hell.

In town, she pulled up and ran to Tracey's door, rapping with her knuckles as she let herself in, then used her backside to wedge the door shut against the hot wind.

'Down here, love.' Tracey's call came from deeper in the house, not the bedroom, and Roni grinned. If Tracey was back in the kitchen it meant there was a chance of something delicious for lunch and, more importantly, her friend was feeling better.

'So,' Tracey chirped, a gauzy robe of multitudinous pastels swirling around her. 'Guess who came to visit me yesterday?'

'You want to clue me in?'

Tracey slid a plate onto the table and the aroma of a toasted ham, cheese and tomato sandwich, rock-salt diamonds glittering in the golden-fried butter crust, wafted to Roni's nose. Her mouth watered.

'Dig in, love. From what I hear, you need feeding up. Sounds like you've been doing a lot of work out at Marian's.'

'Oh.' Why did her heart suddenly beat erratic at the possibility Matt had been talking about her? Especially as they had been politely distant on the drive back from Taylor's, and they'd not spoken since.

Tracey passed her a cup of tea and lowered herself into a chair, picking around the edges of her own sandwich. 'Matt tells me I have serious competition in the lamington stakes. Sounds like you should have put your own in the contest.'

'Oh, he's exaggerating.' Roni spread her empty hands wide. 'See, I was too embarrassed to bring one for you to try.'

'Embarrassed, or did Matt clean you out?' Tracey teased. 'I imagine that man would need a lot to fill him up.'

'He probably took them to feed his chickens. God knows, mine are stuffed fit for Christmas.'

Tracey patted her hand. 'Learn to take a compliment, love. He likes your cooking. That's a good thing, right?'

'I guess.' It would have been a good thing when she believed he was assessing her. Now it was kind of . . . heart-warming?

No! The tea shivered over the edge of her cup. Matt was her sharefarmer, nothing more. Neither of them wanted him to be anything more. Her presence often rendered him reticent, while his left her confused and challenged and . . . thrilled?

Shit. No. Not thrilled.

Since *those three*, she had never felt any interest toward a man, not even Greg, despite trying to persuade herself that their relationship was more than a need for the safety of familiarity.

Yet the thought of Matt had her stomach doing weird things.

Her belly, where another man's baby resided. Why the hell was she letting her imagination run away with her? She licked her fingers, dabbing up the last salt crystals. 'Where's that Scrabble board? As you're clearly back on form, I'm not giving any free passes today.'

Playing against a real person was vastly different to playing on her phone, and concentrating on the game took her mind off Matt well into the afternoon. Finally winning the game by adding 'y' to 'harp' on a triple-word square, she swept the tiles together and stood. 'Okay, having proved I'm not a pushover—'

'I'd say Matt hopes differently.'

'I don't imagine he hopes one way or the other,' she snapped. A wounded look flashed across Tracey's face, and Roni closed her eyes for a moment and deliberately softened her tone. 'You don't understand, Tracey. There are . . . complications.'

Tracey tossed the last ivory tile into the box. 'Love, life is a complication. A glorious, messy and, if you're lucky, long complication. One that is always resolved, and generally far too soon.'

Roni chewed on the inside of her cheek, once again tempted to confide in Tracey. But if she shared one secret, would she be able to stop? She needed to hold tight to both her reserve and her independence. Only by remaining alone could she keep the secrets of both her past and her future. 'Well, on that incredibly profound note, and having proved I'm a more-than-able Scrabble adversary, I shall take my leave. Undefeated.'

'But I defeated you all those other times.'

'Today marks a new dawn. We're only counting from now.' She leaned down to press a kiss to Tracey's cheek, startling herself with the impulsive action. 'I'm so glad you're feeling better.'

Tracey's eyes filled, and she pressed her hand to her cheek as though she could hold the kiss in place. 'And I'm so glad you're feeling as though you fit in around here, love. Oh, that reminds me, I'm due to give you another of

Marian's letters. Come on, I'll see you to the door. It's on the hallstand.'

Roni took the envelope, running her thumb over the familiar handwriting, anticipation warm inside her. 'Tell me it doesn't say I have to breed cocker spaniels, or open a boarding house.'

'Marian didn't like cocker spaniels,' Tracey grinned. 'Go on, off with you, love.' She opened the front door, then staggered back as though she'd cracked the entrance to a furnace. The sky roiled with clouds of red dust, fine particles obscuring the picket fence at the end of the garden. 'Oh! Maybe you'd better not go.'

Roni threw up a hand to protect her face from the blasting sand as she stepped outside. 'I have to. The animals are alone. I'll see you tomorrow.'

She clutched the letter against her stomach and tucked her chin to her chest as the wind shrieked, throwing grit into her eyes. Her skin melted to her bones. Leaves skittered along the road, snagging on her legs. She dragged at the car door then dropped into her seat, cranking the air conditioner as soon as she'd turned the ignition.

Though she had automatically buckled her belt, she had to unclip it to wriggle to the edge of the seat, so she could peer through the filthy windscreen. The wipers ground from side to side, barely shifting the sand. Dust coated the superheated dash. She coughed, checked the air vents were closed, and pulled slowly from the kerb.

With little visibility, she inched through deserted streets. Gusts of scorching wind buffeted the car sideways and her fingers clawed on the melting steering wheel, her arms aching with the strain of holding the vehicle true. She squinted, trying to find the white centre line, away from the wild swaying of the power lines strung each side of the road.

She reached the speed sign marking the edge of town, the car crawling up the hill between the wildly whipping trees. Her eyes burned as she peered into the murk.

Her thighs sweated, her knee trembling as she stomped the brakes, then edged around a fallen tree.

And another.

She should turn back.

Tracey's place was closer. It would be safer.

But she had to make sure Baby and Goat had found shelter.

The change in vibration signalled she had left the bitumen and moved onto the dirt road. The temperature inside the car spiked. The air conditioner failed. Sweat poured down her back. The heat stole the oxygen. Her chest burned as she gasped for air, each searing breath raking through her dry throat.

She cracked a window to equalise the pressure as the front swept across the land. It made no difference. Any second now, her eardrums would explode.

With a boom like the world split in half, the invisible heavens cracked open. The dust on the windscreen became an instant avalanche of mud. The wipers lost traction, skimming the slime. The temperature plummeted and goose-bumps peppered her arms but, her knuckles tiny white mountains, she didn't dare release her grip on the wheel to turn the heater on.

Pounded by the downpour, each bedraggled tree was unfamiliar. Every slight bend in the slippery road was new. The car lurched and splashed into previously unnoticed potholes. Slowing even more, she used one hand to swipe the steamed windscreen, then opened the window further, flinching as the rain stung her face.

She couldn't see half a metre beyond the bonnet. Couldn't hear a thing above the rain pounding the windscreen so hard the glass should shatter. Her headlights reflected in a cascade of splintered crystal drops. As she lightened her tread on the accelerator the car slewed, grinding to a near halt each time she ran into the gravel mounded either side of the track.

The tempest ended as instantaneously as it had begun, the dark clouds rolling back to reveal a rain-washed sky. Birds burst into song, as though a new day had dawned in the late afternoon. If they had managed to find somewhere to hide, surely Goat and Baby would also be all right?

Roni heaved out a shuddering breath, trying to ease the tension that gripped her middle, and unlock her cramped fingers from the wheel. Framed by the pewter sky and the raggedy, wind-lashed branches of the peppertrees, the white-painted entry fence to Peppertree Crossing lay only a hundred metres ahead. She'd made it home.

Home.

She had never wanted to be anywhere more in her life. Tears trembled on her lashes. Scritches would be curled on his yellow cushion in the comforting safety of the over-stuffed and oversized homestead. The ninth book she'd taken from Marian's library waited on her bedside table. The loaf of bread she'd baked early, in case Matt showed up, sat beneath a towel on the kitchen counter.

Goat and Baby would poke their noses out of their lean-to shelter in the orchard, Baby probably wondering at his first experience of rain. The poultry would crowd the door of the coop, looking for dinner and wanting to come out to scratch at the damp, soft earth.

All of those things were now, in the most irrevocable and definitive way, home.

She pulled the car onto the cattle grid, then slammed the brakes, gaping at the sight before her. Water thundered along the creek, every bit as spectacular as Marian had promised. It lapped at the bridge, tiny whitecaps breaking on the rocks that thrust free of the surface.

'Wow.' Phone in hand, she leaned from the window. The battery died after she'd snapped only a few photos, and she grunted, tossing it onto the passenger seat.

Though the torrent rushed through the gully, the water lapping over the bridge wasn't as deep as the puddles she'd driven through. She wound up the window, put the car into drive and eased forward, crawling onto the rocks.

No problem. The tyres gripped, unaffected by the water flow. They passed the midpoint of the bridge.

Rocks shifted under the left front tyre. The vehicle lurched.

She gasped, instinctively hitting the brakes. No! She

should keep moving. Get the hell off the damn bridge, before it washed away.

The bridge she hadn't fixed.

She tentatively pressed the accelerator. The car inched forward.

The back end slid, tyres spinning as they lost traction. The vehicle canted crazily to the left, throwing her sideways, the only view through the passenger window of dirty, swirling water.

She slammed into reverse and gunned the engine.

Nothing.

Into drive again.

Nothing. No, worse, something—the car tipped further to the left. Any second now it would roll, trapping her.

Yanking her door handle, she scrambled from the vehicle, reflexively slamming the door, and stumbled across the remaining few metres of bridge. The cold water tried to pull her from the crossing but was shallower than she'd expected.

She snatched at the trailing branches of the overhanging peppertree and hauled herself to safety, her heart pounding as she turned to look back at the car.

She had overreacted. From here it didn't seem too bad. Definitely leaning to the left, but the situation didn't look nearly as precarious as it had felt. In fact, her panic seemed kind of stupid now. Should she go back and try to move the car? She nibbled on her lip. She was in no hurry to feel that rush of fear again. Better to leave the car until the floodwaters had died down. Then she could build the bridge wider, give the tyres something to grip.

Like she should have done before, when Matt had warned her about the summer flash floods.

She crossed her arms, shivering. It had started to drizzle again, and she faced a long walk home. Still, it was pretty, the rain lending a new aspect to scenery that had become familiar. The golden stalks of wheat drooped damp and forlorn, and she frowned. Taylor had said reaping was done while the crops were dry; would rain affect the harvest? Would that negatively impact Matt's income? And hers. At least that would be something she could safely ask Matt about when she next saw him.

The drizzle turned to sharp slivers and she picked up her pace, relieved when she rounded the sweeping bend, bringing the solid reassurance of the homestead into view. A hot shower was definitely in order, and her stomach insisted lunch had been a long time ago. With her phone in the car—and dead, anyway—and the sun again hidden by lowering clouds, it was impossible to guess the time, but it felt as though night encroached.

As the rain started to bucket down she cut across a paddock and through the lower fence of the home yard, stopping to feed the chickens. Then she dashed to the orchard. Goat snickered at her and Baby lowed, but neither were coming out from the shelter they stood safely inside, munching on baled hay.

At the back door, she stripped her sodden clothes, dropping them in the sunroom as she let herself into the womb-like security of the house.

Scritches yowled, his fur plastering to her wet legs.

'It's pretty horrible out, Scritch. Are you sure you want to go?' He was sure, standing on his hind legs to nudge at her hand for only a second before dashing out the door. 'Okay, well don't be long. It's definitely getting dark.'

No point locking the door, he'd want back in soon enough.

She squelched toward the bathroom, flicking the light switch. Frowning, she stepped back into the hall and tried another switch. No power. That meant a quick shower, because showering in the dark was definitely an invitation to axe murderers, no matter how nice your location.

The hot water peppered her chilled skin with tiny needles, the pain giving way to pleasure as she closed her eyes and luxuriated in the warmth.

Eventually, she glanced at the high window. Dark, both inside and out. She groped for a towel and wrapped the fabric tightly around her chest. Scritches needed to come in.

Eyes closed, she trailed her fingertips along the cool abrasiveness of the long passageway wall, her feet cushioned by the Persian runner. She counted the doorways, stopping in just the right spot to open the door into the sunroom without smacking into it. A bedraggled Scritches meowed plaintively at the external door.

'You nut. It's not like there aren't about a thousand places under cover where you could have waited.' She cuddled the cat, who rubbed his wet, tousled head under her chin. 'C'mon, you can come help me find my clothes.'

She had no idea where to look for candles or a torch, but she knew the kitchen well and, thanks to Rafe, could make sandwiches with her eyes shut. For Roo's sake, she would dig through the fridge to find some salad.

A long-sleeved jersey halfway over her head, she jumped as a fusillade of banging thundered up the hall.

She'd not heard a vehicle, but fists urgently pounded on wood as she tiptoed along the hall, keeping close to one wall. Scritches' nails clicked as he ran ahead of her, silhouetted by the blue, moonlit sunroom. He rubbed himself against the back door. He only did that for one person.

'Matt?'

'Roni, are you there?'

His tone was urgent, making her heart speed faster. Tracey? She unlatched the door and pulled it open.

Matt was covered from shoulders to mid-calf in a dripping Driza-Bone, unrecognisable but for the anger in his tone. 'Christ, Roni, I was worried about you.'

She squinted as he played a flashlight up and down her body. 'Me?'

His hand closed around her upper arm. 'You're okay?'

'Ouch. Except for that arm. Why wouldn't I be?'

He glanced down at the grip whitening on her arm, then released her and slumped against the doorframe, huffing out a long breath. 'Tracey called. Said you would've been driving when the weather hit. Fuck, Roni, when I saw your car stranded I thought you'd gone into the creek.' He closed his eyes and dragged a hand down his dripping face. A muscle in his jaw jerked. 'I couldn't get to the vehicle; the bridge is under about a half-metre of water.'

'But the rain's lighter now.'

'Flash floods come from higher up the system, not the rain that's falling here.'

His tone suggested that this was something she should have known. She crossed her arms over her chest, silently daring him to lecture her. 'If the water's that high, how'd you get here?'

'Rode.'

'A motorbike?' Her disbelief obvious, she stepped back, reflexively waving him inside.

He dropped his hat onto the window seat, the light from his torch swinging crazily around the room as he ran a hand through hair darkened by the rain. 'Bike? No. Horse. The creek's narrower higher up, and he's a good jumper. Damn it, Roni, if something had happened to you, Marian would've come back to haunt me.'

Hence the anger. 'No need to worry about me. I can take care of myself.'

'I know that. I like that. But still.'

Oh. She'd turned toward the hall but stumbled as his words hit her. Quickly, she moved into the house, where it was darker. 'I'll grab you a towel.'

He shook his head, drops splattering her. 'Amigo's still in the rain. Thing is'—he pulled at his chin—'when the power went out in town, I thought yours might be out too.

So I picked up some food. I was driving over here when Tracey called.'

With the moon behind him, it was hard to tell where he was looking, but it seemed to be anywhere but at her. 'You were going to ask me to dinner?'

He rubbed a hand across the back of his neck. Bent to stroke Scritches. Cleared his throat. 'Kind of depends, now.'

'Depends?'

'On what your answer would've been.'

She bit her lip. Looked at Scritches, as though he'd reply. 'Well, that kind of depends.'

'Depends?'

'On what food you brought. I don't do vegies.' Only for Roo.

A grin flashed across his face and he shoved the hat back on, reaching for the door handle behind him. 'Something Mum used to feed us when we were kids. I'll give Amigo a quick rubdown and be back in a few.'

Roni shook her tingling hands and blew out an unsteady breath. He hadn't been angry, but concerned. And maybe not only because Marian had engineered a situation where she was sort of his responsibility.

She flew up the hall and squinted at the bedroom mirror in the faint light from the window. She wore the thin jersey and old trackpants she'd managed to find under her pillow in the dark, but if she couldn't see, maybe neither could Matt. She couldn't even fix her hair because, semi-dry, it was a mane of unmanageable curls that would only get worse if confronted with a comb.

The knock on the back door sounded softer this time. 'Come in, it's open.' The echo of Tracey in her words brought a grin to her lips. At least she hadn't ended with 'love'.

Matt was in the kitchen, sans hat and Driza-Bone. She handed him the towel she'd blindly grabbed from the linen cupboard. 'Do you want to take a shower? Water's still hot.'

'No, I'll be right.' Matt ran the towel over his face and head, leaving his blond hair standing in spikes. 'It's Amigo who got well soaked. But he's tucked into the stable nice and warm now, chowing down on fresh hay.'

She knew; Matt smelled sweet, like the bales in the lower shed.

He swung a backpack onto the table. 'I'd planned to pick up some extra stuff from home, but when I saw your car, I just grabbed my pack and the horse. So, we'll have to make do.'

Planned? He'd actually thought about this? Her hand tightened on the back of the chair as he laid the torch on the table and unloaded the contents of his pack into the beam of light: a small sausage-shaped tube, a couple of tomatoes, a packet of chips and a carton of crackers. He waved the crackers. 'I'm hoping you have some of your awesome bread, but these'll do otherwise.'

'Baked this morning.' She couldn't keep the pride from her voice as she moved across the darkened kitchen to where the bread sat under a tea towel, but she miscalculated and her hip banged the table. 'Ouch!'

Matt snatched up the torch and flashed it toward her. 'You okay?'

'Well padded.'

The beam of light rested on her hip for a long moment. 'You didn't find candles?'

'Didn't look.'

'I'll grab them.' He headed toward the sunroom, leaving her in the dark. Though she was probably throwing off a glow from her flushed cheeks. Had she imagined that . . . moment? When he'd looked at her and his voice dropped lower, had somehow vibrated through her?

Within seconds he returned, carrying candles and a box of matches. 'Marian always liked to be prepared.'

'Yeah, I guess I should've been, too.'

In the flare of a match, he glanced across the table at her, a tiny frown between his eyes. 'You're doing just fine.'

Okay, so, despite the rain, it definitely wasn't cold in here. In fact, she was feeling rather too warm.

The fragrance of burning wood and paraffin filled the room as he flicked out the match. 'So, where do you want this feast? Kitchen table doesn't quite cut it for a picnic.'

'Would the library work?' Her favourite room, cloistered by the shelves of books, made cosy by the smell of leather and old paper.

He nodded. 'We'll need pepper, butter and your bread.' He left a lit candle on the table and carried his pack and the food across the hall to the library, moving with the easy grace of a large cat. 'Oh, and a couple of glasses,' he called.

She grabbed the items, along with the candle.

He'd pulled a rug from a chair and spread it on the

floor. The food was laid out on it, and candles glowed on the side tables. 'Got to have a picnic rug, right?'

'So I've heard. Can't say I've ever picnicked.' She sat as far from him as she could on the small blanket. 'Unless the local takeaway counts.'

Matt rocked back on his haunches. 'I'm sorry.'

'What for?' Instant aggression, her armour, prickled in her tone. She'd never needed pity.

'From the bits you share, it seems your childhood wasn't much chop.'

'Not everyone needs to have the same experience,' she flared. Comparisons always made her feel . . . less. Less than the kid with a family, less than the woman with a career. Less than the farmer who could claim an idyllic picnic-filled upbringing, despite the pain that now simmered beneath his surface. 'My first foster parents had divorced by the time I was nine, so picnicking wasn't high on their agenda.'

'Nine? Hell, Roni—'

She pointed at the plastic sausage, heading off the trite phrases of commiseration she knew would come next. 'What is that stuff?'

He held it up. 'My secret weapon. Liverwurst.'

'Liver?' She grimaced.

'Nope. Liverwurst. Totally different.'

'I thought you were vegetarian.'

He leaned to one side to pull a knife from his belt. 'Only mostly. For some things, I'm happy to break the rules.' His brows briefly contracted, as though the words led him elsewhere. Then he hacked a couple of pieces from her loaf, spread them liberally with butter and the liverwurst paste. Sliced tomato went on next, then pepper, and finally a small handful of potato chips.

She looked dubiously at the slice he handed her.

'Don't knock it till you try it.'

'But then the knocking's okay?'

He nodded. 'Then I give you permission to bring it. I'm never entirely decided whether I like this stuff or it's just the childhood association.'

She nibbled at the edge of her bread, looking up through her lashes as Matt moved to a more comfortable position then practically inhaled half his slice. Okay, so it wasn't poisonous. She took a bite, snatching at the chips that fell from the wedge.

Salty and peppery, the different textures of the spread, tomato, and chips all combined perfectly with the crusty softness of the bread.

'Okay?' Matt raised an eyebrow.

She held up one finger to stop him speaking. Finished the entire slice before she replied. 'It was okay. I mean, you know, if you're stuck in the dark in the middle of a storm, I guess it'll suffice.'

Matt prepared another two slices, handing her one without asking. 'Oh, wait.' He pulled a bottle from his bag.

She carefully laid down her slice of bread. 'I don't drink.' Hadn't since they forced it on her, except for the few times with Greg, when she'd needed to numb herself. The familiar bubbles of remembered fear fluttered in her throat. 'I'll grab water.'

Matt turned the bottle so she could read the label. Appletiser. 'You took juice to the barbecue, so I thought this might work.'

'Oh. Well, no need for you to miss out. Marian has a huge wine collection in the other room.'

'I don't drink either.'

'You don't?' Her voice pitched high in surprise. 'I've never known a guy who doesn't drink.'

Matt concentrated on unscrewing the bottle. 'Well, I guess I did back in the day, but not for the last ten years.' He rubbed at his chin. The go-to move when he seemed uncertain. 'My old man died of cirrhosis.' As he poured the juice, she caught the play of muscle in his jaw, like he ground his teeth.

Was this the secret he hid, the one that caused the flashes of torment in his eyes?

He blew out a long breath. 'Watching your dad change, from being the man who taught you to ride a horse, into a mean old bastard who'd whip the animal for no reason, kind of makes you think about doing things differently yourself.' His gaze flicked to hers, blue chips of ice catching the candlelight. 'Then my brother died with a full bottle of Jack in him. Enough reason to stick to my guns.'

Roni sat very still. When he'd mentioned deaths, she'd figured he was trying to ingratiate himself, talking up his devastation at Marian's passing, but the stark expression on his face made a lie of any pretence. 'I'm sorry. I don't really know what to say.'

He lifted a shoulder. 'Not their fault. I guess we all get addicted to whatever we find takes away the pain.'

'Like solitude.' She'd purged her life of the complications brought by allowing people into her personal space. It had become a compulsion, an addiction to rejection.

'What do you mean?' Shifting to his knees, Matt leaned closer, as though he was truly interested.

She realised she'd said too much, yet now she felt an urge to draw a parallel between their lives, their loss. 'Did you—' She bit at her lip. Hell, she shouldn't say anything. 'You said you knew my uncle?'

'Andrew? Sure.'

'He was my dad.'

Matt nodded slowly. 'That explains a lot. He seemed a decent guy. Never complained about Marian putting me through school.'

'You went to a private school?' Jealousy flared instantly. She'd shared a secret, yet all she got in return was more proof that Marian truly had loved Matt.

'No. I went to the local high school. But Marian put me through the Bachelor of Science and then Vet Medicine at Adelaide Uni.'

'You mean'—she screwed up her forehead, the conclusion dragging reluctantly from the depths of her brain—'you're a vet?'

Matt wiped his hand on his jeans, then held it out to her. 'Dr Matthew Krueger, at your service.'

She took his hand reflexively, his grip warm and dry, his palm callused. 'But you're a farmer?'

'Sideline. I'm a vet during business hours. That's why I haven't been here as much as I would've . . . liked to be.' He relinquished her hand and pushed to his feet. 'I guess we'd better clean this lot up, so you don't get mice. Or is Scritches a decent mouser?'

She snorted. 'For some reason he has to put literally everything in his mouth, but I'm not sure he'd ever actually be able to catch anything.'

'Sounds like he has pica. Was he a rescue?'

'Yeah. Some kids were tormenting him in a carpark when I found him.'

'I hope he appreciates how lucky he is that you came into his life, then.'

She refused to search his words for hidden import. Instead, she gestured toward the library door as Scritches pushed his way in. Bless the cat. 'Ask him yourself. He's pretty talkative.' And she wasn't about to be. She had no room in her head for the conflicting emotions this man woke in her.

'Hey there, Scritch.' Matt went for the spot behind his ear that Scritches loved so much. 'You look after your mumma, okay, buddy?' She flinched at the title, her hand moving to her belly. Matt straightened. 'It's late, I'd better make tracks.'

'It's still pouring.' She pointed at the ceiling. Though it wasn't cold, the noise of the rain drumming on the iron roof gave a feeling of winter. 'Why don't you stay? There's a spare room.' What was she doing? After years of carefully making it almost impossible for her boyfriend to sleep over, she impulsively invited some random guy?

And, God, what if Matt didn't realise she was only being neighbourly?

He rubbed at his chin. 'Are you sure? I'd prefer not to drag Amigo out again in this. And if I stay, I'll be able to give you a hand getting the car off the bridge first thing in the morning. If you want me to, that is?'

If she wanted him to which bit? She was so flustered, his words weren't making sense. 'Sure. Whatever. I'll get you some fresh sheets.'

'Wait.' He laid a hand on her arm as she scrambled up. 'I'm going to come clean with you here.'

Shit. He wasn't thinking neighbourly at all. How did she retract the offer?

'I'm always up for some dessert.'

No. Hell, no. He could call it what he liked, but she wasn't up for it.

He angled his head toward the kitchen. 'Don't suppose you have any lamingtons left?'

Why did disappointment flash through her? 'No lamingtons.'

Matt looked appealingly crestfallen.

'But I tried a carrot cake early this morning.' And not a packet one, either.

'You're having me on. Serious? Carrot cake's my favourite. Least, it was until I had your lamingtons.'

'I'll grab you a slice then get your linen.'

He ate his cake standing over the kitchen sink while she went to the bathroom. As she exited, she almost ran into him in the hall. They stepped to opposite sides of the runner, as far from each other as they could possibly get.

'Awesome cake. Thanks.'

'No worries. Well, goodnight.' It wasn't like it was a date—not that she'd ever been on one—so why did she hesitate, her heart pounding, waiting to see if he might kiss her goodnight?

He gave a nod and turned into his bedroom, and she scurried up the hall. Closed her door and quietly turned the key. Then she crawled into bed, her arms around Scritches.

Sleep didn't come quickly. Instead her mind turned over and over. What the hell was she going to do? She needed to provide a safe future for Roo and Scritches. And Goat and Baby, and perhaps eventually Bear.

But a growing awareness whispered that maybe she also wanted a home for her heart.

Chapter Twenty-seven

Although she was an early riser, by the time she and Scritches left their bedroom, Matt was nowhere in sight. His bedroom door was open, his bed neatly made.

Goat and Baby were damp and miserable-looking. No sign out there of the farmer. Vet. Whichever role he played today.

She fed the fowls, then wandered across the yard. A handsome horse, a million feet tall, snorted sweet breath at her, his whiskers tickling her arm. So Matt was still somewhere about the farm, and she should probably throw together some breakfast. Vegetarian, and not involving carrot cake. Though it seemed he wouldn't complain no matter what she gave him. A tingle buzzed down the centre of her chest at the thought and she rubbed it away. He would get toast, eggs and some of the slightly wrinkled mushrooms from the bottom of the fridge. Definitely no sweetness.

Over the sizzle of mushrooms turning golden in butter, she didn't hear Matt enter the room. He gestured at the table set for two. 'Hey, I didn't expect you to lay on breakfast. That smells so good. I'm used to a bowl of cornflakes, if I'm lucky. More likely a protein bar in the car on the way to work. Speaking of cars, yours is all good now. It's in the shed.'

'You got it unstuck already? You're not even wet.'

'Water's all gone. Give it another hour and you'll swear the creek never flowed.'

She slid two eggs onto his toast, one onto hers.

Matt held up mud-covered hands. 'Do I have time to wash up?'

'You'd better. I'm not sure if Scritches will let you have the bathroom to yourself, though, he always has to perch on the bath when I'm in there.'

She thought she heard him murmur 'understandable' as he headed across the hallway, but she pretended not to hear. She had no space in either her head or her heart for this man. For any man.

∞

She spent the day dragging fallen branches to create a huge bonfire near the dam, brushing out Baby's mud-streaked coat, and guarding the chickens as she let them peck at the rain-softened ground. Everything took far longer than it should have, and by mid-afternoon she'd had enough of work, her skin turning clammy and sweaty by turns, her head aching and her throat swollen. She sighed and dragged herself up to the back paddock while she still had a little energy, so she could look up the number for the local medical practice and make an appointment for the next morning. She was definitely coming down with something, but she also felt a flutter of excitement at the thought of making the first of her baby visits. She stroked a hand over her belly, flatter than it had ever been thanks to all this physical labour. Roo was her future and her only way to fix—or at least move on from—the past.

As she clambered into the car the next day, she found the letter Tracey had given her sitting on the dash, forgotten in the stress of the storm. Now she was running slightly late for her appointment, so Marian's latest chat would have to wait. She tucked it into her bag. The anticipation bubbling within her almost pushed back the feverish headache that had kept her awake all night. In a few minutes she would hear her baby's heartbeat. See pictures, even. Maybe count tiny fingers and toes.

The receptionist in the small cottage that had been refurbished as consulting rooms looked down at her ledger, though a computer sat on the desk. 'I have you in with Dr Hartmann. Take a seat in the waiting room, it won't be long.'

The waiting room consisted of five chairs pushed against the corridor wall, three of them empty. Roni smiled at an elderly woman there, then closed her eyes as a wave of dizziness swept her. Maybe morning sickness was finally catching up.

'Roni, hi. Come on in.'

The voice sounded familiar. Too familiar. She prised her heavy lids open to see a white lab coat swinging loosely over Taylor's black pants and pinstriped blouse. The receptionist had said Dr Hartmann. God, why hadn't the name clicked?

Her brain too slow and foggy for full-fledged panic, she followed Taylor into a consulting room.

Taylor sat in a swivel chair, gesturing to a straight-backed one. 'Take a seat. How'd you fare in the storm? Our power was out for the entire night. Had to bring out some old kerosene lanterns that were in the house when Luke renovated it.'

'Mine was out, too. Luckily Matt came over and knew where to find Marian's stash of candles.'

Taylor opened up a screen on her computer. 'Matt, huh? For some reason, that doesn't surprise me as much as it probably should, given he's been such a hermit the past few months. Did the creek flood? It runs through our bottom paddock, but I didn't get down there to check.'

'Yeah, it was spectacularly impassable.'

'So Matt was stuck at yours?'

'He rode over, so the creek made no difference.' She liked Taylor, but there was no reason to set tongues wagging. Well, no more than she was about to, anyway. 'I had no idea you're a doctor.'

Taylor tapped at the keyboard. 'After I moved over from the east, I decided to go to medical school. It seemed important I follow a dream.' The infuriatingly secretive smile ghosted her lips, the look she got whenever she spoke of her past. 'Two dreams, I guess; meeting Luke and becoming a doctor. Anyway, what can I do for you?'

'I think I'm coming down with something. Maybe Tracey's flu.' Chicken shit. She bit her lip then blurted, 'And I'm concerned because I'm nearly four months' pregnant.'

To her credit, Taylor only blinked at the revelation. 'Okay, well, we'll take some blood, check you out for the flu. Have you had the scheduled prenatal tests done?'

Guiltily, Roni shook her head. 'No. I kind of . . . ran out of time with coming over here.'

'Not a problem. While I'm doing the vampire bit, I'll draw extra blood for those.' She took Roni's temperature. 'That's well up. I'll write you a script for some symptom relief that's safe.' She cuffed Roni's arm, took her blood pressure, swabbed, and inserted a syringe. 'Your first pregnancy?'

'Uh huh.'

'And it's going well? Any problems?'

She wanted to brag about how amazing Roo was. 'Going so well I keep forgetting I'm pregnant. No fatigue. No morning sickness. Not until this morning, anyway.'

'Four months, did you say?' Taylor made notes, switching between an index card and the screen.

'Fifteen-and-a-half weeks.'

'So, no movement yet.'

'No. It's too early, isn't it?'

'Very unlikely you'd feel anything yet. Give it another three weeks.' She smiled. 'And a couple of months after that you'll be in here complaining about not being able to sleep because of the kicking.'

Anticipation fizzed and bubbled through Roni, and she couldn't stop herself grinning back. She was discussing her baby with someone who was almost a friend.

After this, she was going straight over to tell Tracey about Roo. She had a feeling—no, she knew—the older woman would be thrilled. Why on earth had she feared judgment for something that was so wonderful? She caressed her belly. The life growing inside her.

'Okay, pop up onto the bed, unzip your jeans, and I'll have a feel.' Taylor rubbed her hands together to warm them, then gently ran them over Roni's belly. Slowly, her smile faded. 'This is a confirmed pregnancy? And you're sure on the dates?'

'Positive and positive.' Sudden fear sat heavy on her chest. 'It was a home pregnancy test, but I read they're just as accurate . . .'

'Yes, they are,' Taylor reassured, still palpating her stomach. 'I'm just going to get the ultrasound; it'll be easier to see on the screen.'

Roni shoved up on her elbows. 'Is there something wrong?' Her voice caught on the words. There couldn't be anything wrong. This was her entire future.

Taylor squeezed her shoulder. 'No, I was only feeling for your uterus but you're very small. We'll get a heartbeat on the monitor for you, though. Lie there and relax while I grab the equipment from the other office.'

Relax? Her stomach cramped with sudden fear. She grasped the metal sides of the narrow bed, determined to shut off the panic. Roo was simply a small baby, hiding deep and safe in her womb. The ultrasound would find her.

Taylor wheeled in the machine and applied gel to what looked like a massager. 'I'm afraid the transducer will be cold.' She squirted gel onto Roni's stomach, then rolled the handpiece across as she watched the small television screen on the machine. Her smile faltered.

A shudder rippled through Roni as she tried to contain the black fear blossoming in her chest.

Taylor's smile turned to a frown.

Roni tried to wet her lips with a dry tongue. 'What's wrong?' She couldn't make out anything on the screen, but that meant nothing; X-rays never made sense, either.

Taylor looked back at Roni's belly, shifted the transducer, turned back to the screen, then shook her head. 'Roni, I'm just going to get Doctor Clarke in here. He has more experience in obstetrics than I have. I could be doing something wrong.' The deep crease between her eyebrows said it was more than that.

'No, just tell me. Is there something wrong with Roo—with my baby?'

Taylor exhaled between her teeth, scowling at the screen. 'It's just—I can't find anything.'

Oh God. The walls of the room closed in on her. 'There's no heartbeat?'

'It's more than that. At fifteen weeks I should be able to see the baby. There's—nothing. You're positive about the dates?'

She nodded, the plastic cover on the hard pillow crinkling against her ear. 'Sixteen weeks on Saturday.'

Taylor turned to the phone. Pressed a few buttons, spoke quietly, and less than a minute later a man in a white coat entered.

'Roni, this is Doctor Clarke.'

She tried to breathe. To force oxygen to the baby growing inside her.

Dr Clarke took the transducer and went through the same motions as Taylor had just performed. He shook his head. 'Gestational sac, no embryo.' He clicked off the machine. 'Roni, did you have any blood loss early in the pregnancy? Any cramping?'

'No.' She spoke through clenched teeth.

'How many weeks did you think you were when you took the test?'

She didn't think. She knew. 'Nine.'

'And you've not tested since?'

She shook her head. There had been no need. She'd felt the connection with Roo.

'No pregnancy symptoms? Nausea, fatigue, cravings?'

She shook her head again. No, because Roo was the perfect baby.

Dr Clarke glanced at Taylor, who moved to the opposite side of the bed, taking Roni's hand as the senior doctor sat on a chair alongside. 'Roni, I'm sorry. What you have is a blighted ovum.'

She was broken, faulty. 'Will I be able to carry my baby safely to term?'

He pinched at the bridge of his nose. 'There is no baby. A blighted ovum is when the gestational sac forms but it's empty. You may have all the symptoms of pregnancy but there's no baby in there.'

'No.' She shoved herself upright on the bed, her feet knocking against the doctor's knees. 'No, that's not right. I know there's a baby. There has to be.'

Clarke looked across to Taylor. 'I'll source some brochures, Doctor Hartmann.'

He left the room abruptly, and Roni turned to Taylor. 'He's wrong, isn't he?'

Taylor's eyes were liquid, but she shook her head. 'No, Roni, he isn't. I'm so sorry. Usually the sac spontaneously aborts before now. You'll find you miscarry within a few weeks, though I can organise a D&C at Murray Bridge hospital immediately, if you prefer?'

Have her baby ripped out of her? No way.

Taylor was still speaking, but Roni couldn't hear her over the blood rushing in her ears. She zipped her jeans, snatching the pamphlets Dr Clarke thrust at her as she ran from the clinic.

Fumbled her car door open. Drove too fast through the town, then slowed down; driving carefully, keeping Roo safe.

Her hand moved to caress her baby. Touched her flat belly. Her empty belly. Her barren, useless belly.

She shook her head, bit her lip until she tasted blood. No, the doctors were mistaken. They had to be wrong.

Because without Roo she had nothing.

With no recollection of the journey home, she stripped off her clothes, her belly still smeared with gel, and crawled into bed.

It was the flu, that was all. She was sick, in bed, and her fevered mind was playing tricks. She had been aware of every moment of Roo's existence. The baby was part of her, part of her plan for the future. Her, Scritches and Roo, their life together was only just beginning.

Wracking chills seized her, and she shivered and trembled beneath the quilt, clutching Scritches for warmth. Her disjointed dreams were filled with babies and nurseries and happy families playing in parks as she drifted in and out of consciousness.

She opened her eyes to find it dark and realised she'd been woken by insistent knocking on the front door.

Taylor's voice muffled as though she pressed her mouth to the crack of the door. 'Roni? I brought some flu meds. Your tests came back positive. I'm going to leave the medicine here at the door, okay? I'll come by again in the morning.'

The pregnancy test was positive?

She smiled. She'd known they were wrong.

Then fear clutched her heart, twisting it in an icy grip; Taylor had only tested for flu.

She squeezed her eyelids tight and rolled over, her back to the door. She needed to go back to her dreams, to where she did everything right, where she kept Roo safe.

She slept fitfully, waking each time to find her face wet with either tears or sweat, the bed crumpled and soaked.

In the darkest, loneliest hours of the night, Roo slid from inside her.

She staggered dizzily to the bathroom, mopping at the dark blood that flowed painlessly down her thighs.

The only pain was in her heart.

❧

Knocking on the door again. She couldn't get up, even if she wanted to.

She pulled her knees tightly to her chest. No concern about squashing Roo now. Never again.

Taylor's voice. 'Roni? I'm really worried about you. Please let me in.'

What the hell for? She didn't need anyone. Or anything. She should have stayed in Sydney, where it was her and Scritches against the world.

Like it had always been.

She closed her eyes.

❧

Hammering on the door this time. The back door.

Scritches jumped from the bed with his little meow-purr of joy and bolted down the hall.

There was only one other person he would run to.

'Roni? If you don't answer I'll bloody well break the door down.'

Matt. God, no. She couldn't see him. Couldn't let him see her.

She forced herself up, aware of more clots, more of Roo's short life sliding from her as she stood. She made her way down the hall, ricocheting like a pinball from one wall to the other. 'Matt? I'm fine, but you can't come in. I have the flu.'

'Taylor said she's worried about you.'

Apprehension squeezed her chest. What had Taylor told him?

'She said she dropped off flu meds for you yesterday, but they're still at the door. Roni, open up, let me at least make you a cuppa and give you the meds.'

She slumped against the wall. There was no medicine for her pain. Her emptiness. 'No. Just leave the stuff at the back door, I'll get it later. I don't want you to catch anything.' Don't want you to catch me.

'Listen, I'll take care of the animals. Just get yourself back to bed, okay?' Matt was still talking, but the grey fog cloaked her brain again and she wandered to the bedroom, crawled back into her cocoon.

∽

Scritches yowled and nudged her with a wet nose, batting a paw against her closed eyes to let her know he was in danger of starving. The harsh waft of ammonia burned her throat.

Crumbs of kitty litter dug into her feet as she dragged herself out of bed and staggered to the kitchen. She shook the cat's biscuit box, upended it uselessly. Poked around in the cupboard where she kept his food, an arm folded across her cramping stomach, as though she needed to protect it. As though she could hold Roo in there, when even the dream of her baby had now slipped away.

She had meant to buy more cat food when she went into town but had forgotten. Scritches was right, he would starve.

She would let him die. It was all her fault.

Her knees gave out and she slumped on a chair, elbows on the table, head in her hands. Her chest heaved as though she would throw up, her heart squeezing and lungs contracting. The sobs worked their way free from her womb. Dry, wrenching spasms at first, ripping her apart and tearing from her throat.

Finally, the tears came. Tears she hadn't allowed since she was fourteen, when she'd proven the uselessness of crying. Tears that now would never stop. Tears that held no catharsis, because there was no way to wash away such pain.

She sobbed.

Minutes passed. Maybe hours.

Finally exhausted, with tears still streaming down her face, she opened a can of tuna and offered it to Scritches.

He sniffed and stared balefully at her.

She opened a can of Spam, but he wouldn't even sniff at it.

Instead, he jumped onto her lap, pressing a wet nose into the side of her neck, a warm body against her broken heart.

Telling her that he depended on her.

Bacon. He liked that, but only cooked. She dragged herself to the freezer. Wiped the back of her hand over her eyes and scrubbed at her nose.

She had to pull herself together. She couldn't fail Scritches like she had Roo. He was all she had left in the world.

Chapter Twenty-eight

My dearest Veronica,

Did you wonder how you came to be called that? I suppose it was the only thing this family ever gave you, until now. You see, your mother knew from childhood it was the name I would choose for my daughter, in the unlikely event I should have one. In fact, in the smaller guest bedroom you will find a tatty, worn teddy bear, whose name is Veronica.

It would be nice to think your mother named you for me, but I know better: she did it to spite me. The funny thing, though, is that it makes it even easier for me to now pretend you are my daughter. How angry Denise would be to learn she had unwittingly done me a favour!

No angrier than she currently is, I suspect, having her secret known to the town. You probably wonder why I used my last weeks to tell everyone at least part of the story of your conception, after so many years of silence. The fact is, I didn't want it to be a subject for rumour and innuendo when you arrived. Far better the tale was thrust into the open and the initial excitement died down while I was still alive.

I will also admit an unattractive part of me wanted to witness Denise suffer a little for all the years of misery she caused me, along with the harm she caused the Krueger family. To some extent, I blame myself for that tragedy. I should have curbed Denise's tendencies when she seduced Andrew. I should have banished her from the family, if such a thing is possible. Most certainly, I should not have kept topping up her funds, which can only have encouraged her to stay close to me—close to them. Physically, not emotionally, you understand.

So, you see, although I'm your benefactor, I am far from selfless. Another of my flaws.

Don't be like me, Veronica, don't waste time. I learned, too late, to stop being a paradox. I wanted to be happy, yet I allowed negative people in my life. I wanted things to change, yet I did nothing to effect the change.

You must take control. Decide what you want from life, and go and get it. Always remember, Veronica, you can't reach for anything if your hands are full of the past.

Fine words for a woman disclosing the less-than-salubrious tale of her own past, aren't they? But you see, having to lay down your story has given me greater

335

clarity than ever before. Along with my joys, I see my shortcomings and mistakes so clearly now.

But this is a moment to focus on the joys. As you have this letter it means you've completed all of my tasks. Ah, you're surprised? You still have so much to do? No, you see, my plan wasn't to measure your success but to challenge your willingness to try in the face of uncertainty, not knowing how much more would be thrown at you. Above all, I wanted you to learn trust, compassion and self-love. These were qualities I lacked for many years.

Knowing that you now possess far greater attributes than my own, I pass to you both your inheritance and my wisdom—I'm choosing to call it such because no one can argue with me at this point! I can rest easy leaving Peppertree Crossing in your care. Of course, I have no intention of resting but of stirring up merry hell wherever I have been sent!

Veronica, my love, without ever having truly known you, I miss you. I can't bear to think this could be our final communication so, hopefully over many years, you will find odd notes and missives from me tucked away around the property. This way, we can get to know one another better, and I shall feel I'm still involved.

But the sad fact is, I'm not.

Now, what will be, will be, and I can only seek to influence the outcome, not endeavour to change it.

As time, particularly mine, is fleeting, my advice would be to make the best of life, Veronica. Don't be afraid to take chances that may lead to mistakes—when death draws close, you'll find yourself wishing you'd made far more. Don't stand on the edge of the cliff, fearing the impact. Instead, anticipate the flight. Leap.

However this venture ends, Veronica, don't ever forget that it was more than simply an experience.

It was a life.

All my love,

Marian

Chapter Twenty-nine

She should have been elated to discover that the property was hers. At least Scritches would be safe.

But that's not what she felt.

Instead, now she also mourned Marian. Another person she had never fully known stolen from her.

Without realising it, she had come to enjoy the one-sided chats with her aunt, overcoming her mistrust and appreciating the growing sense of knowing where she had come from, of recognising shared character traits with the woman she could never meet. Briefly, there had been a family bond. But now it was ripped from her, like pages from a book.

Like Roo.

She set the letter on the quilt and picked up the brochures the doctor had thrust at her as she ran from the surgery.

They were wrong. They said Roo had never really existed. It was a lie. Roo had been real, because the loss of a dream couldn't hurt this badly.

She rolled over in the cold bed and closed her eyes.

This time she heard the car before the rap on the door. No point pretending she wasn't there, it seemed the entire district knew where to find her.

Tracey shifted from one foot to the other just beyond the screen, an agitated sparrow. 'Love, you look dreadful! I'm so sorry you caught my flu.'

'Don't come close, I'm contagious.' Roni tried to back away, but Tracey thrust the door open and threw tight arms around her.

'Don't be daft, love, I can't get it again.'

The softness of the embrace threatened to start her tears anew. Did her body intend to make up for years of drought? She sniffed hard, refusing to let them spill, though her surroundings blurred.

'Oh, love, you must be feeling really terrible. Come on, into the kitchen with you, I'll put the kettle on. And I've brought chicken soup.'

Roni sank into a chair. 'How did you hear I caught the bug?' There was no need for anyone else to know about Roo. The baby would forever be her secret, untainted by others' opinions or their unnecessary words.

'Matt, of course. He rang days ago but, truth to tell, I still wasn't on top form myself.' She placed a steaming mug in front of Roni. 'Here, start on that while I heat the soup. It tastes much nicer done on the stovetop, rather than in a microwave.' She turned back to the hotplate, still speaking. 'Then he called again this morning, saying you were basically incoherent the first couple of times he came by yesterday, then you shouted at him to go away last night.'

She didn't remember that.

'And he's tried calling on the landline but you've not been picking up. I told him that's entirely understandable; I could barely drag myself from the bed. Don't know what I would have done without your help.'

She did vaguely recall hearing the discordant, unfamiliar ring.

Tracey shook her head. 'You've got him awfully worried, you know.'

'He's a good neighbour.' Roni held the mug close, letting the steam clear her head. She would never allow him to be more than that. She was broken.

'Hmmph,' Tracey snorted. 'Didn't notice him being quite such a good neighbour when it was me laid up. He's a fine man, that one, you have to admit. I mean, he's not my type, obviously, but that doesn't mean I'm blind.' The soup ladle dripped as Tracey turned, eyebrows raised, waiting expectantly.

Roni shook her head, too exhausted to think clearly. 'Not interested. Told you, I don't need any more complications.'

'I'd have thought he'd be an asset, not a complication.'

'I don't need a guy to bail me out.' Her own dream destroyed, she owed it to Marian to keep hers alive. Follow in her footsteps. Maintain the farm single-handed and alone. At least that way she could protect Scritches and care for the other orphaned and unwanted animals she had collected.

Tracey set a bowl in front of her. 'Of course you don't. As Marian expected, you're perfectly capable.' She bent to the soup. Salty and good. Her shoulders relaxed a little, though her head pounded. Yet, as sick as she felt, it wasn't fair to snap and snarl at Tracey. She heaved in a breath, though the effort took all her strength. 'Matt's a nice guy, I'm not arguing that. But like you said, Marian trusted me to be capable, to run this place like she did.'

'How does that exclude Matt? He's been here for years.'

'Yeah, but he only worked here. If I let him stay, he'd have to run the place because I don't know what I'm doing. I have to let him go so that I learn. Marian managed alone, so I will too.'

'Oh no, Veronica, you've got it all wrong.' Tracey's fluffy hair trembled like a windblown dandelion clock as she plopped onto a chair. 'Marian was a strong woman, but she certainly wasn't alone. Sure, she directed every move Andrew and Matt made—that was typical Marian—but it's not like she drove the header or carted the grain to the silos. She was the manager, but Peppertree Crossing flourished as a result of teamwork.' She sat forward, patting Roni's hand. 'See, she didn't only have Peppertree Crossing to love. She also loved Andrew and she loved Matt. She loved me, too. Love doesn't mean losing your dreams.'

Roni shook her head, trying to hold back the sob. 'I didn't say anything about love.' Or about dreams. Both were ephemeral notions, a playground for fools and hopeless romantics.

Neither had been enough to keep Roo alive.

❧

She let Tracey in each day, but every time Scritches let her know Matt was at the door, she pretended to be asleep. She needed more time to process her emotions. She couldn't risk letting anyone else get close to her while she was vulnerable, while anything she felt might be nothing more than her grasping for comfort.

Eventually, she opened the door to him, forcing a smile. 'Hey. Not sure whether I'm still infectious, so you might not want to come in.'

'I don't care about that.' His glare pierced her like an ice spear. He was mad because she'd ignored him.

He gestured jerkily, requesting her permission to enter.

She stood back unwillingly. 'Your risk.'

His fists unclenched. 'I'll take it.'

In awkward silence they made their way to the kitchen, Scritches tying them together by winding figure eights around their feet.

'Sit down, I'll put the kettle on.' Matt waved a hand toward the table. 'You're as pale as milk.'

'I'm fine,' she replied, pushing away the memories of the blood loss. So much blood. 'Shouldn't you be at work?'

He looked at her quizzically. 'It's Sunday.'

She stared back at him. 'Ugh, I've had the flu for four days?'

'Four days? Try eleven. I've never seen the flu knock anyone around that bad. Taylor wanted you in hospital, but she said you refused.'

She had no recollection of discussing it with Taylor.

'In any case, I'm on holidays. At least, from being a vet. It's reaping season. Did you take the meds Taylor left?'

'Sure.'

'And you've been eating?'

Again, it was concern that made him seem angry. What was it about this place that made people care? Tracey, Taylor, now Matt. 'You know I have. You sicced Tracey onto me.' She scowled. 'Have you ever been force-fed chicken soup?'

The tension seeped from his shoulders and he sank onto a chair. 'Wouldn't that be like waterboarding for vegetarians?' Scritches jumped onto his lap but then moved back to hers, kneading and purring but watching Matt, as though he couldn't decide which knee he preferred.

'Yeah, well, maybe I should tie you down and try it. I reckon I'm about nine-tenths liquid now. I probably slosh when I walk.' She dragged her fingernail along a groove in the tabletop, avoiding looking at him. 'Hey, thanks for taking care of the animals. I don't think I could've staggered that far.'

'No worries. We—they—all missed you, though. Goat comes to the gate to let me pet him, but I'm wise to it; he's just using me to lean on so he can see across the garden, waiting for you to come.'

'It's cereal love. As in the breakfast variety. I bribe him.'

'Is that so? I was feeling kind of second-rate. I'll stuff my pockets with cereal when I see him today, then.'

'Nu-uh. That's my trick. You're forbidden. He has to l-love me best. Actually, I'll go feed him now,' she finished hurriedly. She didn't want to sit around talking anymore. 'Then you can see who's the favourite.'

'Not a fair contest unless we have equal quantities of cereal.' He pushed to his feet and flipped the kettle off.

'You're on.'

She snatched at the back of a chair as she stood, and his hand snaked to the small of her back. 'Sure you're up to it?'

'Yeah. Of course. Just been sitting around for too long.' She grabbed a handful of Weet-Bix from the pantry and strode from the room, determined to show him just how okay she was.

She didn't recall the orchard being so far away. Scritches accompanied them part way, then darted off down the yard. Roni shaded her eyes with one hand, squinting after him. 'Poor thing hasn't been out for a few days. Guess he needs to go check everything's in order.'

'Man of the house,' Matt agreed.

Goat nuzzled hard into her hand, then leaned as far as he could over the gate, sniffing and blowing at the pocket of her light windcheater and butting his head against her chest.

'Hey, dude, take it easy with your mumma. She's a bit fragile.'

Mumma. She never wanted to hear that word again. 'Hardly. It was probably only a cold, not even the flu. Tracey had it far worse than I did.'

'I was more concerned about you.'

She refused to look at him, focusing intently on Goat.

He raised an empty hand in defeat. 'You're right. Goat likes you better.'

'Of course. But it'd be a fairer contest if you weren't hiding the biscuits behind your back.'

The corners of Matt's eyes crinkled. 'Just testing his smarts.'

'I'm not sure there's a whole lot to test. He's probably stomach-driven, like Scritch.'

'Well, I might have to make Baby my best mate, then. Mind, once I castrate him, he might not act so friendly toward me.'

'Would you blame him?'

'Can't say that I would.'

Eyes closed for a moment, she allowed the fresh breeze to wash clean over her body. She felt like one giant, aching bruise, the pain both inside and out.

'Okay?' Matt asked quietly.

'Sure.' She forced a smile and pushed herself from the gate. 'I'd better look in on the chickens. I'd been letting them run around for an hour or so outside since the fox, so they'll be going crazy penned up for this long.'

'Out? How do you round them up to get them back in before night?'

'Yelling. Running. Extra food. Maybe a little cursing.'

Matt grinned, though his eyes held far too much concern. 'This I've got to see.'

'I don't think I fancy that much exercise today; I'll stick with feeding them in the coop.'

'Why don't you head back to the house? I'll take care of them.'

'I'm fine.' Damn. She'd never be able to follow Marian's advice, never be able to trust. The moment anyone intimated they cared, all her defences rose, prickly as an echidna's spines. Because she knew where fake concern led. Despite the summer warmth, she shivered.

Matt cast her a sideways glance and she forced herself to drop her arms from where she'd crossed them over her chest as they walked down the yard.

He pointed toward the coop, where Scritches hunched over something. 'So much for him not being the great ginger hunter. Looks like he's caught you a present.'

'I'm not sure I want anything he's scrounged.'

'Probably a good call.' Matt narrowed his gaze on the cat. 'What you got there, mate?' Then his voice rang out like a gunshot. 'Shit!' He broke into a run, covering the twenty metres in seconds. 'Hell, no! Scritch, drop it!'

A grin quirked Roni's lip at the thought of the fun Matt would have trying to get hold of whatever disgusting thing the cat had picked up; she'd lost plenty of socks to play fighting. Whatever it was, Scritches had trouble carrying it. He was dragging his hindquarters, using only his front legs. He looked toward her and yowled.

She frowned in surprise at the odd noise and tried to hasten her step.

Matt snatched at something and pulled the cat in the opposite direction. Instead of fighting back, Scritches dropped to one side and lay still.

Wobbly with fatigue, Roni rested one hand on the hot steel of the coop as she reached them. Matt booted Scritches' prey further aside, and it coiled into itself, bloodied guts hanging from one glistening loop.

Coiled.

Her breath stopped.

A snake.

Fear paralysed her and she glanced from the twitching copper scales to Scritches. He lay on his side, rib cage heaving, hindquarters jerking spasmodically.

'No.' The word trembled on her lips.

'No!' This time it ripped from her as she flung herself to her knees. 'No, Scritch, no!'

'Listen, Roni.'

She shook her head, trying to push Matt aside as she reached for Scritches, who convulsed, his great golden eyes glazed and unfocused.

Matt seized her shoulders, forcing her to look at him. 'Roni, listen! You've got to sit with him. Keep him still, okay?'

Her lips numb, the words were barely intelligible. 'Is it poisonous?'

Matt's jaw hardened. 'Yes. Try to stop Scritches from struggling. But if he stops moving, just let him be, don't try to rouse him. You hear me, Roni?' He shook her by the shoulders and then, at her jerky nod, he raced up the yard.

She ran her hand over Scritches' soft fur, pressed a finger to his wet nose. His breathing laboured, he didn't even look at her.

For the first time ever, he didn't purr at her touch.

'No, Scritches,' she whispered. 'No, not you. You mean

more to me than anything. You're the only thing that's real in my life. Don't go. Please don't go.'

The golden tiger stripes quivered as Scritches struggled for breath. His limbs spasmed, then stiffened. She wanted to cradle him, to cuddle his warm body in her lap. But Matt had said not to move him, so she lay beside him in the dirt, her face close to his, one hand on his trembling flank, the other on his head. Willing him to look at her.

Slowly, his eyes closed. A shudder rippled through his body and then he lay completely still, his side no longer rising. No longer fighting.

'No.' Tears rolled sideways across her face, the dust beneath her turning to mud.

Matt dropped next to her, IV needle in hand. 'Okay, buddy, let's get this into you.'

'Is he—'

'Not yet. Quicker he gets this, the more chance he has.' He inserted the needle. 'That's why I keep antivenom in the ute.' He depressed the plunger, then withdrew the needle, his face pinched.

She pushed upright and grabbed Matt's arm. 'Please make him be okay. Please. I've never loved anything, never had anything love me like he does. He's all I've got.'

Matt winced and looked away from her to the motion-less bundle of dust-covered fur. 'I'm going to grab a drip. Though I think we might not need it.'

They were too late. She couldn't live without Scritches. She'd have no one, nothing. She concentrated on the cat, willing him alive.

Not that it had worked for Roo.

She ran her fingertips over the soft fur. Though she didn't look up, she heard Matt's heavy tread as he ran, felt the rush of air as he skidded to a halt alongside her. He moved a stethoscope bell across the cat's motionless chest. She held her breath, wishing her own heartbeats into Scritches' immobile body.

Matt's hand covered hers. He squeezed gently, then repositioned her hand and pressed her palm down. 'Here. You can feel his heartbeat.' His fingers lingered on hers.

'I can't feel anything,' she whispered desperately.

Matt shifted the stethoscope, put the earpieces in her ears. 'Listen.'

There was nothing but the pounding of her own blood. She shook her head, her hands trembling as she clutched the cold metal tubes. 'I can't!' What if Scritches' life relied on her believing in it? Was that how she'd failed Roo, had she lacked faith?

Matt cupped one hand against the side of her face, stilling her agitated movement. 'It's okay, Roni. *I* can. I've got him for you.'

Scritches' legs kicked spasmodically, and Roni's hand flew to cover her mouth. Was that an involuntary reflex? Or was it how rigor mortis set in? How the hell would she know?

'Good lad.' Matt moved the stethoscope, angling his head to one side and squinting as he listened intently. 'Knew you'd be one tough dude.' His eyes caught Roni's. 'I reckon he'll be fine. Cats are pretty resilient to snake bite, and the antivenom intervention was immediate. Plus, the bite was here.' He indicated Scritches' hind leg. 'Well away from his organs.'

He pointed to the dead reptile. 'See his belly? Well, not the chunk Scritches ripped out of the poor bugger. Above that. The bulge? That'd be a rat or something, ingested within the last few hours. He'd used a good portion of his venom on that, so Scritch didn't get a full dose.'

'Poor snake be damned,' she hiccoughed. 'He could've killed Scritch.' Relief overwhelming her, the tears she'd hidden for so many years rolled free.

'Ah, Roni, it's okay now.' On his knees still, Matt tossed his stethoscope in the dirt and pulled her against his chest, strong arms wrapped around her as though he could shield her from . . . from what? Nothing threatened her, she didn't need his protection.

But for a second, a tantalising, safe second, she allowed the embrace. Then she shoved him away. Swiped a hand over her eyes, as though she could somehow stop the tears. 'Fuck. I'm sorry. I'm being stupid. It's fine. I'm fine.'

Matt allowed her to move away a little. 'Take a minute, Roni.'

'I don't need a minute.' She wanted to thrust to her feet, to demand they return to the safety of her house, but her chin quivered so hard she knew her legs would do the same.

Matt's voice dropped low, almost indiscernible over the warble of magpies. 'Roni, you don't have to be so tough all the time. Crying doesn't mean you're weak. It can mean you've had to be strong for too long.'

'What the hell would you know? You know nothing about me, about my life.' She snatched at anger, hoping to keep fear and exhaustion at bay.

He watched her for a long moment, absolutely still, completely silent. 'You're right. I don't know enough about you. What I do know, though, is that vulnerability isn't a flaw.'

She mashed her lips together. She had no right to attack the man who had just saved Scritches' life, but she couldn't afford to expose herself to any more pain. She had worked so hard to insulate herself from the world, she dared not let anyone in. Matt had to be kept at a safe distance. 'Sorry. I shouldn't have said that.'

'Rationality and emotion aren't exactly close bedfellows.' He pushed to his feet and extended his hand, pulling her up and steadying her. 'Right. Let's get our patient home. And, by the looks of it, I need to get you home, too. I'm going to give Taylor a call and ask her to drop by, okay?'

Exhaustion washed over her in waves. She didn't have the energy to refuse.

Chapter Thirty

Matt had mentioned he would be on the reaper for long hours for the next few days, but still she found herself listening for the noise of his ute each morning. He had checked that the landline worked, promising her he would only be minutes away if she called.

She didn't need his support or reassurance. But that didn't mean she didn't want it.

Tracey came early on Tuesday, enormously pleased to share that Matt had tasked her with visiting. 'Stone-fruit season's starting upriver, so I whipped up a peach crumble for you. Oh, and Samantha called with the inside news. Not official until the meeting, but guess whose lamingtons took first place?' Her hair vibrated with excitement. 'Our recipe will be used for the fundraiser.'

'That'd be your recipe, Tracey.' Still, it was an achievement she could never have dreamed of.

'Nonsense. It's now our recipe.' Tracey ladled out a generous serve of crumble and covered it with thick cream. 'Now, get that into you. You're wasting away, no wonder Matt's concerned. I'll teach you how to make this next, if you like.' She smiled slyly. 'I'll bet Matt would like it. Oh, and I saw Taylor in the supermarket. She said she'll drop by again tomorrow evening, and to warn you she'll be able to tell at a glance whether you took your antibiotics. You know you had to take the full ten-day course?'

In a town riddled with secrets, few seemed to be tightly held. Roni could only hope hers was among them.

With Scritches remarkably none the worse for wear, though he had spent the previous couple of days acting the invalid, lying around until his saucer of milk was pushed close enough for him to lap without strenuous effort, Roni felt better. Still, fatigue hit her at the oddest moments. Like halfway through the delicious crumble. She pushed the bowl away, staring at it morosely.

'Don't like it, love? I'll get some apricots tomorrow, make you turnovers if you prefer.'

'Oh, no, it was amazing. Honestly, I've never in my life had anything like your baking.'

Tracey fluttered closer, patted at her hand, then pulled up a chair. 'That's because when I bake for you, I add an extra dose of love.'

Roni bit at her lip. Such a corny line. Tracey was joking, and she sure as hell wasn't going to cry again.

Dammit, yes she was.

'Oh, there, love, it's all right.' Tracey's arm went around her shoulders. 'Leaves you terribly ragged, this virus, doesn't it?'

That, among other things.

'Don't worry, you'll be fine. Taylor will see you right.' Another squeeze, then Tracey let go.

Instinctively, Roni leaned toward the other woman. She wanted those arms wrapped around her again, she wanted the comfort of that maternal embrace, but she snapped her back straight. 'Oh, it's nothing, I pick up plenty of bugs on Sydney's snot-factory public transport. I was terrified when you were so sick, though.'

She sucked in a quick breath, like she could vacuum the words back. Tracey was neither young, nor seemed particularly healthy; caring about her was an invitation to hurt. But what choice did she have? She could continue to hoard her isolation, clutching her loneliness like a miser's treasure, in the hope of remaining immune to the certainty of pain. Or she could accept this fragment of joy, made even more precious by its transitory nature. Much as Marian had done.

Tracey tutted, finger-pecking at crumbs on the wooden table. 'Lordy, I'm a tough old bird. I get that darn flu every year, but I tell you, I've no intention of dropping off the perch anytime soon. Marian would never forgive me if I did, now I have you to look after.'

'I wouldn't forgive you, either.' There should be a thunderclap, or a chorus of trumpeting angels, something cataclysmic and spectacular to acknowledge her epiphany. Instead, swallows swooped past the kitchen window, dipping water from the pond. Farm machinery chuntered in the distance and Baby lowed in the orchard. Scritches stretched and groaned on his yellow cushion. All good, safe, homely sounds.

'Marian was right about you all along. She knew this was your home.' Tracey sighed tremulously, excavating the edge of the crumble with a spoon. 'I miss her terribly, but at least she sent you to me.' She pushed the plate back in front of Roni. 'Which means that I'm in charge, and I get to say that you need to eat a little more of this, and then I'm packing you back off to bed. You look about done in, love.'

Did Tracey really believe a few days of flu had knocked her about worse than it had a sixty-year-old woman? Or did she suspect there was more to her story? Roni scrubbed a hand across her face, the thought of bed suddenly irresistible. Did it truly matter what anyone thought when they seemed willing to accept her regardless?

She allowed herself to be herded back to bed.

Tracey drew the curtains, allowing the room to rest in soft twilight.

Safe and secure. Like a womb.

Except for her womb.

The tears trickled across her face, dampening the pillow until Scritches padded in and curled close, his rough tongue licking at the back of the hand she used to stifle her sobs.

Thanks to Matt, she still had Scritches. The pain would get better.

It had to.

ॐ

Though she was asleep, the change in air pressure alerted her to another presence in the darkened room a moment before the hand touched her face.

She knew how this went, the hand over her mouth stifling her cries, even as they tried to make her cry harder. She kicked her legs free of the covers, rearing upright before the words reached her sleep-dazed brain.

'It's okay, Roni. Tracey let me in as she was leaving. I wanted to check your temperature, make sure the fever has definitely cleared.'

It took her a moment to place Taylor's soft voice. She sank back into the pillow, the brief reaction exhausting her. 'Sorry. Nightmare.'

The doctor's cool hand pressed against her forehead again. 'Now you're awake, we can do this the more professional way, but it feels like you're okay. I need to speak with you about that D&C, though. There's a risk of infection if we don't—'

'It's all right. She's gone.' Roni couldn't mask the hollowness in her voice any more than she could bring herself to look at Taylor.

The mattress dipped as Taylor sat on the edge of the bed. 'I'm so sorry. I can't pretend to know how hard this is.'

'It's not hard.' She kept her lips tight, so the sobs that welled in her chest couldn't escape. 'I'm being ridiculous, making a fuss about something that was never even there.' Nothing except Roo, that was. Roo and her future.

'That's not true. A blighted ovum is a loss, not a phantom. Two weeks ago you believed you were carrying a healthy baby. You're entitled to absolutely any emotion you choose.'

'Any emotion?' Her chin dimpled and wobbled uncontrollably. 'How about guilt, then? Because not only did I fail my baby, but you know what? Maybe a tiny part of me is relieved. Actually bloody relieved. This way I'll never have to face my ex, never have to hear how much I've messed up his life, how little he wants us. Never have to argue over rights or access or money.' She shoved upright in the bed. 'And you know what the worst thing is? Maybe my baby knew how scared I really was. How—no matter how hard I tried, how much I told myself everything would be perfect—I was afraid I wouldn't be able to look after her. That I wouldn't be able to keep her safe. Maybe she could sense all that, and that's why she never grew.' Her voice cracked as the emotions she'd not even dared allow to become thoughts poured out of her, a torrent of fear and shame. 'See, I'd have been a crap mother.'

'Sounds like you'd be a perfectly normal mother.' Taylor frowned at the quilt, then glanced at Roni before focusing again on the fabric. 'I'll tell you something. The thought of having a baby terrifies me. That's why I've been putting it off, even though Luke's keen.'

Roni stared at her, nonplussed. 'Why would it worry you? You've got everything so together. You've a job, a husband . . .' And no memories that made her scared to move beyond the safety of what had become familiar.

Taylor pinched at her lip, her brow furrowed. 'I think I fear the unknown. There's never any guarantee how a pregnancy will go . . . something could happen to the baby, or to me. And I'm not certain I'm willing to risk changing what is, right now, a pretty perfect life. And you know what else? I guess I'm reluctant to share Luke. What if he loves me less when there's a baby to love as well?' She stood, smoothing the bedspread. 'My point is, I guess we all fear what we don't know.'

'My issue is more with fearing what I do know. Anyway,' Roni continued hurriedly, as interest flickered across Taylor's face, 'are you going to the meeting on Friday? Tracey tells me the official lamington laureate will be announced, and as she's insisting my name also go on the award, I'm worried about a rebellion. Would be nice to see a friendly face or two there.'

Taylor took some chemist-wrapped packages from her bag. 'I think most faces there are friendly. Well, with a couple of notable exceptions, I guess.'

'Who—' The rumble of a vehicle crossing the cattle grid throbbed through the room. 'That's Matt.'

Scritches stirred sleepily as Taylor tweaked aside the curtain. 'Reckon you're right. I'll let him in.'

'Actually,' Roni tried to push her hair into place, 'could you tell him I'm in the shower? I'll be five minutes if he wants to stick the kettle on. Of course, you're welcome to stay, too. Tracey brought a peach crumble.'

'How about I keep him company until you're finished in the bathroom? That way you don't have to rush. I wanted a chance to see how he's going, anyway. I rarely catch him alone.'

See how Matt was going? In a medical sense or as mates? She didn't have time to ponder it now, she needed to scrub away any hint of tears. Oddly, having shared the secrets she'd not even realised she kept, she felt lighter, her chest less constricted.

∾

His hair rumpled and face streaked with grime, Matt rubbed at reddened eyes as Taylor spoke to him, too low for Roni to hear the words. Taylor stood, then stooped to kiss his cheek. She glanced over at Roni. 'I'll get out of your way, then. I promise I'll swing by the meeting on Friday. Better pack my boxing gloves, just in case.'

'Boxing gloves?' Matt sounded weary, his blue eyes lacking a spark, though he reached for a smile as she returned from letting Taylor out.

'CWA thing.'

'Ah. I see. You're feeling better? You look good.' A flush crawled under his tan and he ducked his head as the cat jumped into his lap. 'Yeah, you too, Scritches.' He chucked the cat under the chin.

'Scritch is sooking about being locked in. He's going to have to get used to it because I'm never risking him outdoors. I can't go through that again.'

'Me either.'

'You look beat. Or did I breathe on you?'

Dust caked the weathered creases around Matt's eyes as he grimaced. 'A few eighteen-hour days will do that, but there's more rain coming, so I have to get it done. Not my favourite time of year.' He linked his hands above his head and cracked his back. 'I'm starting your back acres tomorrow, so I finished up early and put some gear down the sheds. Figured I'd duck in and check you're doing okay before I head home.'

Her teeth worried at a thumbnail as she leaned back against the sink, thinking. 'What time do you start in the morning?'

'About four, soon as there's a hint of light.' He glanced up at the kitchen clock. 'Too soon.'

'Then if your equipment's already here, why don't you stay the night? It'll mean a quicker start for you, right?'

Thunderous silence greeted her suggestion.

Matt pulled at his chin. 'Thing is,' he said eventually, 'I wouldn't be good company.'

'I know. Long day.'

'Not only that.'

'That's okay. I'm not big on conversation.'

'I'd noticed.' A slight smile tipped his lips, as though her reticence could be a good thing rather than a withdrawal. Still, he hadn't agreed, and, oh God, why did she even want him to? It was no skin off her nose if he wanted to waste time driving the slow, rutted roads between the properties.

He stood and reached for his akubra. 'I'm sorry, Roni. Tonight's just . . . not good. I have to get home.'

She turned quickly toward the sink, unnecessarily rinsing a cup from the drying rack. 'Fine.' Overwrought after the fortnight from hell, clearly she had read Matt completely wrong. But she didn't need him, and didn't need his rejection, either. 'I'll lock up after you.'

Lock him out.

❧

It rained that night. Though it was warm, she burrowed further under the quilt with Scritches. The rain drummed a soft melody on the roof then swirled along the gutters and tumbled through the downpipes, a lullaby too beautiful to sleep through. She wondered what the rain would mean for Matt's harvest. Maybe he would get to sleep in. He'd certainly looked like he needed it.

Except his appearance seemed worse than fatigue. He'd seemed . . . melancholy.

But she couldn't risk thinking about that, about him, so she thrust him from her mind.

Again.

Chapter Thirty-one

The rain turned to a solid downpour on Thursday, lightening to a morning mist on Friday, softening the sometimes harsh landscape. From the bedroom window she made out puddles reflecting the patches of blue sky between scudding clouds, the overblown roses in the garden bent under the weight of raindrops. 'C'mon, lazy cat. Up you get. Tracey will be here soon.'

She dressed and pulled on a pair of rubber boots from the row lining the hall. She'd found two pairs of socks had her nicely filling Marian's shoes. A piece of paper fluttered in the doorjamb and she tugged it free.

Sorry about the other night, Roni. My fault, not yours.
Matt

She snorted and crumpled the note, muting the voice in her head that suggested she had been disappointed. Then she slowly unclenched her fist and smoothed the page, folded it and slid it into her jeans pocket.

She tucked her chin down against the sharp breeze as she rounded the corner of the house, beneath the wisteria-covered pergola.

'Ow!' The breath exploded from her as she collided with a wooden post.

'Hey, you okay?'

She rubbed her chest as she looked up. 'Matt? What are you doing here? Or, rather, up there?'

Matt grabbed a horizontal beam, supported by the unfamiliar pole she had smacked into, and swung himself off the ladder, landing lithely alongside her. 'Rained out. Can't harvest for a few days so I thought maybe I could do something useful here.' He stepped back and swept a hand wide. The pergola was now neatly enclosed with lattice and mesh, creating dappled patches of sun and shade. 'I'll put a gate in each end, maybe a water feature for interest. Then you can add some climbing gear, whatever you fancy.'

'But . . . what is it?'

'Oh, sorry.' Matt put his palm on the small of her back, barely touching, as he guided her beneath the arbour. 'A cat run for Scritches. I've put fine mesh around the bottom so even the baby browns shouldn't be able to get in. I figured if I put a bench in here, you can sit and read your books and Scritch will still get the fresh air he's after. Otherwise, you might have a problem with him trying to escape, now he's had a taste of freedom.' He held his hands away from his narrow hips, a question. 'But I can pull it down if you like. It was only an idea.'

She shook her head. 'No! Don't pull it down. It's . . . amazing. But why?'

He lifted one shoulder. 'Didn't want him getting bitten again.'

'You do this for all your clients?'

'Only those I need to impress because they also happen to be my boss.'

'Thought you didn't really want this job?'

'Hmm. You may have me there. Okay, I did it because I'm kind of smitten.' His eyes were still bloodshot from fatigue but pierced her nonetheless before flickering toward the house. 'Scritches is a totally awesome cat.'

The cool air seared her nostrils. 'Seems he manages to cultivate himself some pretty special fans.' Her gaze roamed the enclosure, examining it more closely. Matt had installed ledges at various heights in the corners, and a small hammock was slung across one end.

Though she didn't look at him, she was aware that he rubbed at his chin, watching her every move. 'I can't—' Her tongue gummed to the roof of her mouth. Why? No need for nerves, Matt wasn't the sort to look for repayment for his favours. She tried again. 'I can't believe someone would do something this nice—no, I can't believe someone would even think of doing something this nice for me. I haven't . . . I really don't know what to say. Except thank you.' Gratitude came easily enough but, without practice, expressing it was another matter altogether.

'It was nothing.' He dismissed what must have been hours of labour while she slept. 'I just—' He turned slightly away, as if something in the farmyard needed checking. 'I just don't want to ever again see you as sad as you were the other day.'

'You should've taken the opportunity to sleep in.'

Only inches separated them as he turned to her. 'I'm having trouble sleeping.'

She froze. His gaze was both penetrating and intimate, and she couldn't respond. How did she express what she wasn't entirely certain she felt? All she knew for sure was that she was damaged, and there was something about Matt that called to her. Something . . . wounded. And maybe that was because she wanted to be a rescuer, not the rescued.

'Thank you.' She stood on tiptoe and brushed his lips with her own, then quickly stepped back, gesturing down the yard. 'I need to get to the chooks before they batter the door down.'

Matt matched his stride to her flustered steps, careful not to touch her.

What the hell had she done? He'd rebuffed her the other evening, and now she'd pretty much thrown herself at him. *Thank you.* That's all she'd needed to say. Say the words and leave it there. Shit.

She stumbled but, hands firmly wedged in his pockets, his face carved in stone, Matt didn't notice.

Or chose not to.

They worked through the coops in silence, feeding and cleaning, though Matt did the bulk of the work.

'Right, then.' He stacked the tools in the barrow of manure. 'I'll dump this, then finish the cat run and get out of your way.'

'Thanks.' She should have chosen another word. They both knew where that had led last time.

She headed indoors, taking out her frustration on her bread dough. She would plait this loaf, make it into a glazed wreath.

God, she was such an idiot. A kiss? Why the hell a kiss?

Her fingers slowed on the dough, pinching and twisting instead of plaiting as she closed her eyes.

She knew why she'd kissed him.

She liked him. Maybe more than liked, though how the hell would she know? But, despite the subtext she imagined into their conversations, the feeling was clearly one-sided, and she had just made their employer–employee relationship untenable.

A light tap at the back door jerked her head up. 'It's open.'

Matt appeared in the doorway, looking pretty much anywhere but at her.

She pressed her knuckles into the dough. 'Oh, I thought you were Tracey.'

'Ah.' The chin rub. 'She came by. I asked if she'd mind calling back a little later, and she said for you to catch up at her place before your meeting.'

Kneading automatically, she watched him warily.

'We need to talk,' he said finally.

Was she supposed to fire him, or would he give notice?

It would have been better if Tracey had been there to ease the situation. 'Yep.'

'I was thinking, seeing as it's too wet to harvest for a few days, I'll pick up that goat. Did you want to drop by mine and have a go at milking first?'

Her fingers stilled. 'You're sure I'm never going to be able to milk Baby?'

His lips twitched. 'I'm certain you won't get the result you want.'

'Guess I'm trapped, then. When were you thinking?'

His gaze met hers and suddenly she was soaring, lost in the arctic blue expanse.

Matt moved closer. 'How's Sunday morning? Looks like I can get a bit of quiet then.'

She nodded, flour covering the back of the chair she clutched.

'Right, then.' His eyes still hadn't left hers, and she was falling, the swooping sensation stealing her stomach.

'Flour.' His thumb brushed a smudge from her cheek.

His breath cooled her flushed skin.

Then he kissed her.

Not like she'd done. He took longer. The press of his firm lips against her cheek was more deliberate, more conscious. Yet the gesture wasn't inappropriate, or demanding, or anything it shouldn't be. Even though maybe she wanted it to be.

Then he gave a businesslike nod and left.

～

It wasn't like she'd never kissed a man. Hell, she even gave Rafe a peck on the cheek when they closed up for Christmas. But kissing Matt was . . . different. And the fact that he'd kissed her? She had no idea what that meant— if it meant anything. But, for the first time in her life, she wanted it to mean something.

She pulled up at the front of Tracey's house, tapping her horn then shaking her hands, trying to force her fingers to relax.

'So.' Tracey launched her appliquéd bag onto the rear seat and slid in, adjusting her flowing purple-shaded blouse around the seatbelt. 'I came by this morning.'

'Uh huh.'

'Matt sent me away.'

'I, uh, I heard.' She gave the almost-empty road far more attention than it required. The best thing about Settlers Bridge was that it was so small, it took only minutes to get anywhere. The football clubrooms were about two country-sized blocks from the main street; if she could briefly sidetrack Tracey, interrogation time would run out. 'Do you think many people will turn up to the meeting?'

'Bugger the meeting. I'm talking about far more interesting things.' Tracey screwed sideways in her seat. 'Like the fact that I had to give the two of you privacy.'

'We had, uh, farm stuff to discuss?' It should have been a statement, but it came out sounding like a question. A lame one.

She turned into the carpark and pulled into the nearest space, despite it being forty degrees; who needed the shade from the jacarandas, anyway? She scrambled from the car before Tracey could get fully into her interrogation.

'Here, love, you carry this.' Tracey passed her a container.

'We had to bring more lamingtons today?'

'No. But if we surprisingly happen to win, the others can taste what they need to live up to.' There was certainly no false modesty with Tracey.

'You should've let me know. I'd have helped,' Roni said, praying for the conversation to stay on cake.

'I figured you weren't up to baking this week.' Tracey lowered her voice as they entered the hall. 'Mind, I still want to know just what you were up to.'

The meeting followed the same form as the others, but after a couple of hours, the activities halted for the president to announce the contest winner. Amid a sharp crack of applause, Tracey wriggled a finger at her. 'Come on, love. Lucky we happened to have a big bake-up, isn't it? We've probably enough lamingtons to go around.'

'Coincidentally. Just like last year. And most years before that.' Christine pulled the edges of her thin cardigan closed, her lips pressed tight like a steel trap.

'It's always nice to share,' Tracey replied brightly.

'I'm surprised you won without Marian's patronage.'

'Proves Tracey's skill rather indisputably, doesn't it?' Taylor said. Roni had sagged with relief as she'd noticed her enter the hall. 'And I guess pairing her with Roni makes them unbeatable. Maybe we should enter as a team next year, Christine?'

'I'd rather have some chance of winning, thank you very much.' Christine stalked off, her expression sour enough to turn milk.

Taylor grinned. 'How are we, ladies? This tub of deliciousness doesn't look like you've been taking it easy, per doctor's orders.'

Tracey's gauzy sleeve wafted across the cakes. 'I assure you I've been taking it easy. Veronica, though, you might need to have a word with.'

'You did this, Roni?' Taylor gestured at the container. 'Impressive, but it means we can no longer be friends. I preferred you when your chickens were as well fed as mine.'

'That's not what I said,' Tracey chortled. 'She's been otherwise occupied. Bring that other tray round when you're ready, love.'

If her face were any warmer she would melt the chocolate off the sponges. Roni shook her head as Taylor lifted her eyebrows. 'Don't ask. She's got some weird thing going on in her head. I'd better take these cakes round.'

Christine sat almost nose-to-nose with a woman at the embroidery table. As the woman turned, her profile highlighted by a lamp, Roni recognised her. Fiona.

Well, time to build bridges, and all that stuff Marian espoused. 'Hi, ladies. Would either of you care for one of Tracey's lamingtons?'

Christine selected carefully, holding the lamington at eye level as though her judgment was required. 'Tracey's? I recall you entered as a team.' She picked off a fleck of coconut, examining it minutely.

Roni lowered the container, a buffer between them. 'We did. But Tracey happened to make this lot.'

'Not so certain of your prowess, then?' Christine said.

Fiona's glossed lips curled, although there was neither humour nor empathy in the expression. 'Don't be mean, Christine. Poor Veronica is only trying to fit in.'

'She has no reason to be uncertain.' A whiff of Avon heralded Tracey. 'Her lamingtons are first-rate. Like the rest of her baking, as Matt will no doubt attest.'

Fiona's nostrils flared, but she ignored Tracey. 'Of course, it's rather insensitive, forcing your way in where you don't belong. Especially right now.'

Roni stared at her, nonplussed. 'I was under the impression competition was encouraged.'

'Depends what you're competing for. Certain things belong to those who've put in the long-term effort.'

Tracey fluffed herself up like a bantam hen. 'No point going off like a frog in a sock, Fiona. You've had a fair shot.'

As Roni beat a hasty retreat, Taylor gave whispered encouragement. 'Run! You don't want to be in the middle of that if they kick off.'

Roni shook her head bemusedly. 'What's the deal? I thought small towns were supposed to be all love-thy-neighbour.'

'Sometimes there's too much of the loving stuff, and loyalties get tested.' Taylor gave a heavy sigh, frowning back toward the three other women. 'There's a lot of messy back-story. Best you just steer clear of Fiona.'

Roni snorted. 'Gladly.'

Taylor angled her toward an empty table. Apparently, it was too hot for the knitting group. 'Have you seen Matt since the other night? I'm a bit worried about him.'

'Worried? Why?'

'Oh, nothing to concern you. History.' She waved a vague hand.

'He came by today. Said it was too wet to harvest, so he built a cat run for Scritches.' And he kissed her. But she'd kissed him first, so did it even count?

'He did? Excellent.' Taylor looked far too pleased, considering she had barely met Scritches.

Roni tutted with sudden frustration. 'What is it about Matt that no one's saying? I thought I was the one with secrets, but I swear everyone in this town speaks in half sentences. I'm beginning to think I'm going nuts.'

The doctor glanced around the room, making sure they couldn't be overheard. 'Has he mentioned his brother?'

'The one who died?'

'Committed suicide. Yesterday was the second anniversary of his death. When Simon died, it kind of turned Matt's world upside down. He took on a lot of extra responsibilities.'

'The farm. He told me.'

'That. And other stuff. Anyway, I was worried how he would handle the anniversary.'

Roni sat quickly, resisting the temptation to touch her fingertips to where his lips had pressed to her cheek. As though she'd not relived the moment a hundred times. 'He seemed . . . distracted on Wednesday. But fine today.'

Rather more than fine, actually.

Chapter Thirty-two

What did one wear to milk a cow? Certainly nothing she owned, Roni decided as she surveyed the small mound of clothes on the bed. Scritches burrowed beneath them, purring happily.

Why did it even matter what she wore? Matt had seen her in trackies, in manure-covered jeans, even in her pyjamas. Now, a peck on the cheek and she suddenly cared how she looked?

She snatched up a pair of jeans—they just happened to be her best ones, eight-buck Levi's from the op shop—and added a tank and a button-through shirt over the top and ponytailed her hair. Then decided that, though impractical, loose hair looked better, particularly as it seemed to have picked up some natural sunstreaks, highlighting the soft, walnut-brown shades.

With a groan, she scrapped the whole look and dropped a soft floral dress over her head. The wide skirt flared from a narrow waist and the sweetheart neckline left a lot of her chest exposed. She quickly spiralled her wavy hair around her fingers and arranged a section over each shoulder.

Twenty minutes later, as she pulled into a yard similar in design to her own, though the stone sheds were fewer and less grand, she felt vaguely sick. Lucky she'd skipped breakfast, cleaning her teeth twice instead.

She chewed at her thumbnail, staring at the house. Should she make the move, kiss his cheek? A businesslike greeting, obviously. But if they saw each other more than once a week, wouldn't kissing each time be over the top?

She startled as her car door opened.

'Hey there. I was in the barn wait—'

Waiting? Had Matt been about to say waiting?

Clearly not, as he stood back, hiking a thumb toward a shed. 'This way. Daisy's in the stall.'

'Daisy? Not exactly original.' Clean-shaven, Matt wasn't wearing his hat, nor the sunglasses. She caught a whiff of fresh hay and a faint trace of aftershave.

'Not in the least,' he agreed. 'But not my choice.'

'Your mum's?'

'Mum's what?'

'Choice.'

'Oh. No, Mum doesn't have anything to do with the farm.'

'I assumed she lived here.'

'She moved into town after Dad died. There's something of a community of farm widows in Settlers Bridge. You probably run into most of them in the CWA. Not Mum's kind of thing, though.' He shoved open a wooden door and stood aside. As she brushed past him, his fingertips trailed across her forearm. 'You look amazing, by the way.' Before she could respond—not that she knew how—Matt gestured toward a cow in a stall. 'Seeing as you're about to get intimate, guess I'd better introduce you.'

She pressed her back to the stone wall. 'She's kind of huge. Is it safe?'

He grinned. 'Bigger than Baby, but she's a sweetheart. Roni, meet Daisy. Daisy, Roni.'

She shuffled forward to tentatively pat the rust-brown side of the cow, flinching as the beast swung her head and blew sweet breath and a string of drool in her direction.

'Sorry about that.' Matt wiped the silver saliva from her arm, then snatched his hand back. 'She's like Scritches: dribbles when she's in love. Okay, wash your hands. I brought warm water down for you. I know what you city softies are like.' He pointed to an old-school enamel bowl filled with suds.

'You reckon I'm soft?' She displayed her palms. She'd spent a good part of Saturday fixing the irrigation around the fruit trees and had the cuts and calluses to prove it.

Instead of laughing, Matt caught her hand, his thumb stroking across an undamaged portion. 'Ouch. Aren't you supposed to be taking it easy? No, you're definitely not soft.' He turned back to the cow, raising a cloud of dust as he thwacked her side. 'At least, only in a good way.'

If her heart thumped any faster she would pass out. She focused intently on washing her hands, then held them up like a surgeon ready to operate.

Matt grinned and dunked his own hands. 'Okay, so this is how we do it.' With the toe of his boot, he dragged a three-legged stool up to Daisy's side, then plopped a bucket under her. 'A quick wash for her ladyship and we're off.'

'Don't you have machines to do this stuff?' She cringed as he rinsed the cow's udder.

'Not for one cow. I only ended up with Daisy because Marian fancied producing her own milk, but it got too hard for her toward the end. If you can handle Daisy, you can always have her back, instead of a goat.'

'And I repeat, she's huge.'

Matt's voice muffled as he leaned into Daisy's side, but she was pretty sure he was laughing. 'Okay, all you need to do is grip at the top of the teat, then slide your fingers down in one smooth, firm movement.' White liquid jetted into the bucket as he spoke, Daisy contentedly chomping at the hay in her manger. 'Ready to give it a try?'

'Sure.' It looked easy enough, if a little too intimate.

She took the seat Matt vacated, the cow looming even larger from this position.

'Lean your head in against her flank. Hang on.' He pushed the back leg of her stool with his foot, skittering it forward. 'Okay, take her teat, right at the top, near her udder. Wrap your fingers around, then draw your hand down.'

Easier said than done. The teat felt kind of gross and lay flaccid in her hand. She changed her grip. No good. 'Maybe that one's empty?'

This time, Matt didn't hide his laugh. 'Feel free to try another.'

Nope. 'All duds.'

'Do you want me to help?'

'Well, I'm pretty sure Daisy does.'

'Poor girl's not used to being molested.'

Roni involuntarily stiffened, thrusting up from the stool. 'I can't do this.'

Matt's touch on her shoulder was light, reassuring. Not possessive, not holding her captive. 'You want to try it together?'

She sat and Matt dropped to his haunches behind her. 'Let's see if this'll work,' he said. 'Head against her side, take the teat. You might find it easier to use both hands.'

As she closed her fingers around the thick teats, Matt covered her hands with his own, his arms caging her. 'If you want to see what you're doing, rather than just feel it, lean back against me. I'll stop you from toppling off the stool.'

She needed to lean against him because her head was spinning, her skin electric where it touched his. She could feel the rise and fall of his chest against her back, the beat of his heart. Tingles of anticipation rippled down her neck as he spoke, his voice low in her ear.

'Relax your hands, let me do the work.'

Relax. Yeah, right. She could barely breathe.

Matt's hands set an easy rhythm that propelled jet after jet of milk into the bucket.

'Oh!' She twisted toward him. 'That's amaz—'

His face centimetres from hers, his pupils were huge, but he made no move to pull away. His right arm tightened around her and she nestled into the crook of his shoulder.

His breath washed warm over her cheek, his lips almost touching her skin. 'Roni, I—'

'No wonder you didn't want to take your mum to church today.'

Matt jerked back guiltily as the female voice, stripped of saccharine, sliced the air.

Roni kicked over the bucket as she snatched for balance.

Hands on her hips, lipstick cut a vicious pink slash across Fiona's face. 'Given your family, I suppose finding you here was inevitable, Veronica. Matthew, we brought your mother back with us. The kids are waiting in the house for you.'

Roni lurched to her feet. 'Kids?' Taylor had intimated that she would find trouble with Fiona—why the hell hadn't she simply said Matt was married to her? That he had kids? She'd have run a million miles. She whirled to face him, her voice a low snarl. 'You bastard.'

'Roni, listen,' he demanded.

'To what?' To him try to explain that his marriage was loveless, or nearly over, or on a break, or he had Fiona's permission or whatever fucking crap he wanted to spin? Hell, no. Even if any of that were true, he had kids. Kids who deserved a family, who needed parents to keep them safe. She backed away from him, coming up against the cow's side.

He seized her arm. 'It's not—'

'Leave me alone!' She grabbed the fingers he'd closed around her wrist and bent them straight back, like she'd learned in the self-defence classes. Beneath his tan, Matt's face went white with shock at the sickening crunch. But he reached for her with his other hand.

'Don't you fucking touch me!' she screamed. But the words weren't only for him. Fourteen-year-old Veronica had finally found her voice. Finally demanded, instead of begged.

Fiona hung onto Matt's good arm. 'Jesus, she's as mad as Marian. Let her go, Matthew.'

'No, Roni—'

His bulk blocked her escape. Ignoring the flare of pain in her stomach at the sudden movement, she shoved past the cow. Blood thundered in her ears, obscuring his words. Did his friends dislike Fiona so much that they'd schemed to help Matt cheat on her? Or did they believe Roni needed the bribe of his company to stay at Peppertree Crossing to keep Marian's precious dream alive? Was that why they'd said nothing?

From the corner of her eye, she saw Matt reach for her, but Fiona had latched on to him like a tick. Helping her escape.

When Matt had said he'd be in trouble for hanging around, drinking tea and enjoying her cooking, she had envisioned his sweet old mother waiting with dinner on the table for him. Not his wife.

When he'd said he could find a bit of quiet time today, she'd thought he meant a break from work, not from his kids.

He called after her as she pounded across the yard, her stupid sandals slowing her down, but she ignored him. He had deceived her into re-creating her mother's foul behaviour, and Fiona had every right to hate her.

She slammed the car into drive just as he reached the vehicle, his fist pounding the roof. She floored the accelerator, sped out of the yard and recklessly along the dirt roads, blinded by tears of fury and humiliation. She'd cried in front of him. He'd seen her at her most vulnerable. She'd allowed feelings for him. Dammit, she'd been so close to persuading herself that maybe she—no. Never that.

She couldn't go home yet; Peppertree Crossing was where he would come looking for her.

The suppressed anger of years erupting inside her, she was too furious to think clearly, almost too angry to see the road. Not that it mattered. A tree, a rock, maybe a farm truck coming the other way—it could all be over quickly.

She slowed the car and pulled over. Shoved the door open and bent double, her empty stomach convulsing. Retching, she spat bile into the dust, then sat back, trembling as she wiped her face with her ridiculous skirt.

She had to calm down. She had to be rational. She wouldn't leave Scritches alone. She wouldn't destroy her life for a man; any man. The burst of anger left her weak, hands shaking, heart racing. She hadn't done anything wrong, not really. A stupid, misplaced thankyou kiss the other day, that was all. Matt was the one in the wrong, not her.

Yet this hurt, it hurt so damn bad. She had persuaded herself he was good and safe and—oh God, she'd been so wrong, and she should have known, because nothing in her life was ever safe.

She started the engine again. Tracey would help her. Her sympathy, her motherly touch, would take away this new pain.

Except Tracey had known.

Tracey wasn't safe, either.

Pulling back onto the road, she drove aimlessly. Directionless. Until suddenly Taylor's driveway loomed in the windscreen.

Was Taylor safe? Biting at her lip, she replayed Taylor's conversations. Had the doctor tried to push her toward Matt, or had that been her imagination?

The car rattled over the cattle grid as she frantically tried to sort the memories. Surely Taylor had never said anything more than that Matt was a nice guy?

Yeah, a nice lying, cheating bastard.

Several cars littered Taylor's yard, and Roni clutched the steering wheel as she surveyed them. Could she walk into the darkened lounge room again, with no one to rescue her?

She thrust open the car door. She didn't need rescuing, and to hell with her dread of darkened rooms. Apparently, that wasn't the only place men tried to take advantage of her, so she might as well confront that fear head on.

'Hey, Roni, how're you doing?' Luke opened the door. 'Come on in. Tay's in the kitchen, threatening some poor, innocent cake.'

Luke had been in on it. Teasing Matt the other weekend, encouraging him. While his wife was home with the kids.

What story had Matt spun Fiona when he spent the night of the storm at her house? Why had he even been there instead of protecting his own family?

She nodded tersely at Luke and made her way straight to the kitchen.

Taylor glanced up, wisps of hair escaping her ponytail, icing sugar smeared across one cheek. 'Wow, I love that dress. And you have perfect timing; how the heck do I get this stuff to come out of the bag?'

When Roni didn't answer, she set aside the icing. 'Roni? What's wrong? Are you okay?'

'I just met Fiona. At Matt's place. Their place.'

'Ah.' Taylor picked up the bag again. 'I take it that's a euphemism for you had words? Or, knowing her, Fiona had all the words?'

'She had every right to, didn't she?' The accusation ripped from her on a wave of anguish and anger.

Taylor gave an amused snort. 'I'm sure she'd argue that's the case.'

Roni shook her head. 'You know the worst thing? I knew from the start Matt was out to screw me over.' She leaned her elbows on the high counter, covering her face with her palms as her fingers drove into her hair. 'I just didn't want to see it. I wanted to believe something good could actually happen in my life, without the something bad to balance it.'

'Why would Matt screw you over?' Taylor sounded perplexed.

Because he could. 'I don't know. The farm, I suppose.' Even though that made no sense, in light of what he'd shared. But the fact remained, he'd lied to her. They all had. 'Why the hell were you all acting like you were trying to set me up with Matt?'

Taylor splattered a dollop of icing on the cake. 'Because he's a nice guy. And matchmaking's pretty much a sport around here.' She spread the icing with a carving knife, her tone calm, as though what she'd said was perfectly reasonable. 'The guys are a couple of beers in—do you think they'll notice I'm hiding burned cake? Anyway, what's Fiona's issue? Beyond the obvious, I mean.' Sudden interest lit her face. 'Hey, did something, you know, happen, to set her off?'

They were all mad. Roni slumped on a stool as the unreality of the situation swept her. 'We nearly—well, I think we almost—'

'What?' Taylor shrieked.

'We almost kissed.' Waves of mortification swept her, hot and cold faster than a fever chill, and she kept her gaze nailed to the counter. 'And Fiona saw us.'

'That's one way to stick it up her. Good for you.'

She reeled back in disgust. 'What is wrong with you people? I would never have gone near him if I'd known about his wife.'

'Wife?' Icing dripped from the knife as Taylor stared at her. 'Wait. Is that what Fiona told you?'

'Yes. Well, no, she didn't have to. But she made it pretty bloody clear.'

Taylor waved the knife in her direction. 'Pretty clear in her own mind, maybe. She's not Matt's wife. He's never been married.'

'Oh, for God's sake, his significant other, then. I don't see the title makes any difference. The fact is, everyone, including him, let me think he was available.'

When she hadn't wanted to think about him at all.

'He *is* available. As far as I know, anyway. Hang on, I'll check. Luke? Hon!' Taylor yelled toward the hallway.

'Coming.' Luke appeared in the doorway, then crossed the room to dip his finger in the icing, one hand on Taylor's waist. 'Sweet. Not as sweet as you, though.' He nuzzled his wife's neck.

'Point of contention in here,' Taylor said. 'Is Matt seeing anyone at the moment?'

'Matty? You know he isn't.' He tilted his head in Roni's direction. 'Though he seems to be spending a lot of time at yours.'

'Fiona led Roni to believe that she and Matt are a thing.'

He snorted. 'Fiona? Matt would rather be a monk than go there. Take my word for it.' He swiped the icing and traced it across Taylor's lips.

Roni clutched at the edge of the counter. Nothing they said made any sense. 'But they have kids.'

Luke's eyes widened. 'Hell, no. What—'

Taylor pushed the plate of half-iced cake into his chest. 'Take this. Go.' She shooed him from the room and whirled to the sink, flipping the tap. 'Roni, are you okay? Here, drink.'

The glass knocked against her teeth as she tried to swallow.

'Okay, take a few deep breaths. Breathe in to my count. One. Two. Three. Now out, two, three.'

Roni concentrated on Taylor's calm voice, trying not to think. Except how could she not think?

'Okay, keep breathing like that, but listen to me. Matt doesn't have any kids. Fiona is his sister-in-law. The kids are hers and his brother Simon's. No, don't talk, keep breathing. Now, I'm not denying Fiona would like there to be something between her and Matt; rumour is she's been hot for him since they were at high school. But it's not happening.'

'He didn't play me?' The words came out jerky.

'Take another drink.' Taylor pressed the glass to her lips. 'I can't breach patient confidentiality by telling you anything that's not already common knowledge, but I will say that, after what happened to Matt, he'd be the last guy to ever play you.' She traced her finger through a cloud of icing sugar on the counter. 'Listen, Roni. You're safe with him. Like Luke, he's one of the guys you can trust.'

Trust. Easy to say, so much harder to do. No wonder it was one of the things Marian insisted she work on. 'So he's not married? No girlfriend? No kids?'

'Still no to all of the above. You want to call him?' Taylor pulled a phone from her jeans.

Roni shook her head, her teeth chattering as reaction set in. 'I—I—broke his fingers.'

Chapter Thirty-three

Taylor had insisted on driving her home once she'd calmed down, saying she would drop by Matt's on the way back to see if he required medical attention.

Medical attention because of what Roni had done to him. God.

Not that Taylor had judged her. When she'd explained, between hiccoughs and sobs, that Matt had grabbed her and she'd reacted, Taylor had seemed to understand there was more to the story.

But she couldn't face him again—except there was no way around it: after locking herself indoors for two days, ignoring Scritches' yowls as he raced to answer the familiar knock on the back door yesterday and again this morning, and skulking out to feed the animals when she was sure the farmyard was empty, she'd realised she couldn't run an eight-hundred-acre property alone. She either allowed Matt to farm it or she sold up and moved away. Somewhere. Or maybe . . . she had another idea. A vague plan. She tugged at Scritches' ears as he curled in her lap. No matter what, she had to face the mess caused by her inability to trust.

Her heart stumbled as she opened the back door and a note fell to the ground. She unfolded the paper with trembling fingers.

Roni,

I've organised the goat—yet to be named—to pick up on the weekend. I'm cropping your lower paddocks today if you want to come see how it's done?
Matt

She rubbed at her chest. Reread the letter. Ran her fingertips over the words, as though she could read his subtext like braille.

A chill rippled through her: Matt had obviously decided one of them needed to act like an adult. He was tying up loose ends and planned to show her how to run her machinery. Because he was quitting.

What the hell else had she expected? He'd made it clear he didn't want to farm the property and, in return for his honesty, she'd assaulted him.

She took a tremulous breath, moving to the kitchen to slide the letter carefully behind the breadboard with Marian's collection. Then she pulled a bunch of paper lunch bags from the drawer. She might have lost her dreams—all of them—but she couldn't destroy Marian's. 'We need him, Scritch.' As a farmer. She had cost them the chance of anything more.

The harvester slowly patrolled the circumference of the paddock beyond the gums at the bottom of the yard. It disappeared where the land dipped, then reappeared on the hillside, crawling back toward the house. Great blades churned in front of it, devouring the golden stalks.

Gripping the brown paper bag tighter, she marched down the yard, trying to look less terrified than she felt. She climbed through the wire fence and stood at the edge of the paddock, waiting.

The earth trembled, the noise deafening as Matt pulled up and swung the cab door open. Leaning down, he offered his left hand, his bandaged fingers sticking out awkwardly as he gripped the side of the vehicle with his right.

She pressed her lips hard together, then took his hand, and he hoisted her effortlessly into the towering machine.

'Morning, boss,' he nodded, resuming his seat.

She barely took in the huge cab, the dash like a jet cockpit, all dials and controls and levers. 'Look. I'm really sorry. I jumped to conclusions and overreacted.' The words came out in a garbled rush, despite her careful rehearsal.

He shrugged. 'From what Tay said, seems you had pretty good reason.'

She nudged her chin at his fingers. 'Still . . .'

He lifted them from the control panel, staring as though he'd not previously noticed them. 'Yeah, well . . . I'm glad you know how to look after yourself. Though, next time maybe remind me you're trained in martial arts instead of demonstrating.'

'Next time?'

He put the machine into gear, letting it lumber forward. 'We're partners; I'm sure to tick you off again someday.'

She nodded, biting her lips together to hold in her relief.

Matt caught her glance around the cab. 'Marian's equipment—your equipment—is prime. She always insisted on having the right tool for the job.'

He was walling her off again, making it clear they were on strictly business terms. Their relationship was right back where it had been when she arrived. Stilted mistrust and distrust. And it was her fault.

'Speaking of task-specific gear . . .' Matt reached into the pocket of his navy-blue cotton shirt and pulled out a pair of small, buff-coloured gloves. He held them toward her, his gaze on the paddock. 'You messed up your hands pretty bad doing that gardening.'

She pressed the obviously expensive, pliable new leather to her trembling lips, inhaling the scent. How was it that every time she thought she had his measure, Matt blindsided her? 'Thanks.' She held out her peace-offering. 'I thought you might be hungry.' She flinched as his gaze met hers, the blue eyes piercing her armour.

He took the bag and opened it. 'Carrot cake.' He huffed out a short laugh, then indicated a stand of trees in the distance. 'How about we stop over by that scrub? Make it a picnic?'

'I didn't bring a rug. Apparently, that's mandatory.'

'I'm sure we can find a way to make it work.' His gaze lingered on her, and she desperately wanted to believe he meant so much more than he said.

He put the paper sack alongside his seat and focused on the rows of crop in front of them. Rubbed his chin. His chest rose, then fell on an audible sigh, so close to a groan that she winced. 'Roni, I reckon we need to talk.'

She lifted her chin and met his eye. She would speak her piece, and if he said no, she would survive. She would find a way to manage the property, maybe even implement the new plan that was burgeoning inside her without him. But she would rather do it with him. 'You're right. I wanted to tell you—'

'There's never been anything between Fiona and me,' he interrupted. 'It's important you know that.'

'Important? Why?' Sudden hope pulsed strongly through her veins, but she needed more: she wanted reasons and reassurance—but she had no right to either.

'Because I want you to understand. I'm not big on talking, Roni. Guess that's a throwback to my roots. You jumped to conclusions because I didn't confide in you— which proves Marian right; things shouldn't be left unsaid.' He scowled at the tinted window, choosing his words. 'Truth is, Simon's death was my fault. I owe it to him to look after Fiona and the kids.'

Everything inside her coiled tight and hard, appalled at the weight of grief in his tone. She instinctively wanted to comfort him but she had no idea how.

Sorrow carved deep furrows in his cheeks. 'I know Fiona likes to come across as though we're together, and I've never pulled her up on it. Never had any reason to, until yesterday.'

She didn't dare ask him what that reason could be. 'How can your brother's suicide be your fault?'

Matt shook his head fractionally. 'Messy story. I'm not ready for that one yet.' He shot an apologetic glance at her. 'But one day, okay?'

One day. That sounded like a promise of a future, a concept that should scare the hell out of her, yet she could barely keep the jealousy from her voice. 'But Fiona does live with you?'

The muscle in Matt's jaw twitched, as though he clenched his teeth. 'We share the house. That's the extent of it. I barely see her. I'm trying to juggle work, plus your property, my property, and provide some kind of stability for the kids until she's ready to move on. That's why I've not been around here much. One of the reasons, anyway.'

'There are others?' she whispered. Matt was clearly not the man to pursue an uncomplicated relationship with. She should run. Not lean toward him.

'Were. But you've made me rethink them.' His eyes met hers, dark and serious, but then he grinned, breaking the tension. 'Mind, you've also made me rethink why I'm doing all the driving. Reckon the boss should know how to handle her own equipment.'

Her elbow hit the door as she jerked back. 'No, that's— oh.' Matt stood, and her entire focus was on the warmth snaking around her waist as he drew her closer to the illuminated control panel.

'Stand here. It's all computerised, so all you do is press this.' He leaned forward to indicate the control. The machine continued to trundle, the huge blade scything the paddock in front of them.

She stared forward for a few minutes. The cab was large enough that they didn't need to stand close, yet she could feel his chest against her back. The machine chugged steadily. 'I think I see why you prefer being a vet.'

Conscious of his every movement, every breath, she felt his shrug before he spoke. 'It's not all bad. The best bit is coming up . . . wait for it . . . any second now . . . right, time to get excited, here's the turn.' One arm wrapped around her waist so he wouldn't knock her over, he reached to the control panel again. He cornered the paddock then adjusted levers, setting the machine straight ahead once more. 'That's the highlight. The pressure's intense, right? And you have to be able to handle it four times every lap, or you're just not cut out for the job.' He didn't drop his arm.

She twisted to look back at him and wrinkled her nose. 'So today is the slow tour?'

He reached for the control panel. The combine blade ground to a halt. 'That was my plan.' He tightened his grip on her waist, turning her to face him. 'But now I'm thinking maybe sometimes going slow isn't all it's cracked up to be.'

His fingers brushed across her temple, pretending to chase a strand of hair she knew was caught tightly in her ponytail.

She was far too close, losing herself in the wilderness of his eyes as his roughened fingertips traced her jaw. There was nothing safe or familiar in this moment, and she couldn't breathe. Didn't want to breathe, if it would interrupt his exploration.

He leaned back a little, frowning at her. 'What is about you, Veronica Gates, that's messing me up so bad?' His knuckle stroked down her cheek, his voice low and puzzled. 'What did you come here looking for?'

She shook her head wordlessly. Maybe she had come looking for herself—yet that wasn't all she had found.

'I read you so wrong,' Matt's fingers continued their exploration, his eyes following the path they traced. 'I was sure you'd be like Denise. Cruise into town, find a loophole in Marian's crazy scheme and sell everything she'd built. Instead, you come in here and take over. You've got this kick-arse take-no-prisoners independence that blows me away—even when you're ripping me to shreds over something I didn't do. Or, you know, breaking my fingers.'

She winced.

'I should probably run like hell.' His mouth now only centimetres from hers, she could smell sweet coffee. 'God knows, I tried to back off. But then you gave me a glimpse of this vulnerability you hide. And that just—I don't know, it tears me apart.' The blue of his eyes endless, his forehead furrowed. 'It kills me that there's something in your past, something that hurt you even more than being abandoned. I want to fix it, but I don't know how.'

She pulled back, though she made no attempt to free herself from his loose grasp. 'You can't fix me.'

'You don't need fixing. I said fix *it*. I want to make whatever is wrong in your life right. I don't know what you're looking for, Roni. But if I can give it to you, here I am.'

Her heart hurt from wanting. 'There's too much you don't know about me.' Things she could never share. The strength Matt thought he saw was Marian's creation; she was nothing more than a scared woman trapped in her past, seeking safety in familiarity.

Except . . . what if she wasn't anymore? Hadn't Marian given her the tools, and she'd used them to liberate herself? She'd left her comfort zone, crossed the country alone, and created a new life for herself and Scritches. What Matt saw, what he liked and admired, was *her*.

He brushed his palm from her wrist to her shoulder, a welter of goosebumps shadowing the move. 'There's plenty we don't know about each other, and maybe that's how it should be. At least at the start. The unknown is our adventure.'

He was right: she didn't know him. He wasn't familiar. He wasn't safe. He wasn't predictable or mundane, or any of the things she had convinced herself were necessary in her life. And yet, maybe he could be everything she wanted.

If she could summon the courage to let herself find out.

She bunched her fists. Why the hell did this have to be so hard? Why couldn't she blindly leap, allow herself to fall helplessly, thoughtlessly in love, like everyone else seemed to?

Matt's fingers found the nape of her neck as his lips brushed the sensitive pulse in her throat. Not kissing, not biting. Just touching, as though he tasted and inhaled her, the warmth of his breath thrilling through her. She swayed toward him, her hands moving to his chest, keeping the safe distance between them, but also holding him close as her fear ebbed.

His lips traced her jaw, tiny kisses now, trailing fire. 'Tell me if it needs to be slower, Roni.'

She tipped her head back to allow him access. It didn't need to be slower. Because maybe he was perfect.

Matt jerked away, staring out of the side window. 'Damn it!' His neck corded and fury vibrated in his tone. 'What the hell does she want?'

A couple of hundred metres from them, a blue BMW had pulled up on the dirt track. A woman leaned back against the hood on her elbows, loose summer dress billowing around her legs.

'Who—?' Roni didn't need to finish the question. Her gaze flicked back to Matt and, for the first time, she truly knew what his anger looked like.

The words ground between his tight lips. 'Your mother.'

Chapter Thirty-four

Matt leaped from the cab, then turned to lift her down. When her feet were firmly on the ground, he squeezed her waist. 'Roni, this is your business, not mine. And maybe it's not my place to say, but the way Taylor explained it to me, your mother's a narcissist. She cares for no one but herself. She can't feel empathy. But don't you forget, no matter what she says, you're an amazing woman. You don't need Denise for anything.'

'Just as well, huh?' she murmured. Yet, though her mother had twice deserted her, now she had come back. Hope she didn't want to allow flared deep inside Roni.

Alongside the implied strength of Matt's towering presence, her hand in his, she picked her way across the furrows, the air thick with the fragrance of sun-ripened wheat.

'Denise.' Matt's tone was curt, and Roni instinctively moved closer to him. 'I thought you'd gone to Queensland.'

Coal black eyes flicked from Roni to him. 'Missed me, did you, Matthew?'

'Hardly. What do you want?'

'I don't think I require your permission to visit my daughter.'

My daughter. So there was still a chance they could have a relationship? She shouldn't want that, shouldn't need it, yet still she longed for connection. Her last chance to claim a family. Roni impulsively stepped forward, as though she could breach the chasm between them.

Matt's grip tightened, cautioning her. 'You know you're not welcome at Peppertree Crossing, Denise.'

The fine lines around Denise's lips deepened. 'It's not really your place to say, now, is it, Matthew? I guess that's pretty hard for you to take. Though it seems you're working your way around it.' She nodded at their linked hands, partially hidden behind Roni's hip. 'Didn't take you long to scope out the best angle, did it? I did warn you, Veronica. Remember? I came here specifically to tell you this would happen.'

She hadn't taken her eyes from Denise, hoping for some stirring of family, some bond to repair the damage her mother had done. Something more intimate and personal than the casually thrown word, *daughter*, which inferred ownership rather than love. Yet, as her mother sought to tear apart the tiny, fragile, growing something she had with Matt, a something so new, so precious that she dare not try to name it, a wave of sorrow and loss washed through her, drowning the last of her most secret childhood dreams.

But with the death came freedom; her mother was toxic, and Roni owed her nothing. 'Are you done, Denise?'

The woman straightened momentarily, but then deliberately lounged back against the car again. A blur of white fluff, Bonnie dashed from passenger seat to driver's seat, leaping up against the steering wheel and yipping furiously. 'I thought we'd grown closer than that, Veronica. Aren't you going to call me Mum?'

'No.'

'Why not?'

'Off the top of my head, I can't think of a less appropriate title.'

The groomed eyebrows lifted a millimetre. 'I suppose we've nothing in common other than a dash of blood.' Denise's snakelike glance flicked to Matt, a taunting sneer on her painted lips. 'Well, something in common.'

'Why are you here?' She didn't have to grow up on a farm to know how to cut through bullshit.

'To protect your interests, darling. I cautioned you that some people around here aren't as open as I am. They like to keep their bad behaviour under wraps, whereas I'm unconcerned with what people think.'

Matt stiffened. 'Denise. Be very careful what you say.'

Denise flicked her fingers dismissively. 'Down, boy. You don't have your protector here anymore. Have you wondered, Veronica, how little old farm boy here got to be a vet?'

'I already know.'

Denise sneered. 'You know that your aunt used *our* money to put him through school? How do you imagine he persuaded her to do that? Do you think that maybe, as she got older, Marian questioned the choices she'd made? After all, he's not too bad, is he?' Her lascivious gaze caressed Matt from head to foot. 'If anyone was going to turn my sister, it'd be him.'

Matt's voice was low and dangerous, as though he barely restrained his anger. 'Haven't you done enough damage, Denise?'

'Oh, I don't think I'm the one causing harm, am I? Veronica, don't you find it intriguing that Matthew had a . . . how can I say this nicely? A *relationship* with your aunt, yet here he is, holding your hand like a teenager? Of course, I told you before that I'm not immune to his charms myself.' She pulled a strand of her hair forward, toying with it coquettishly. 'Maybe he didn't leap straight from Marian to you. In fact, this little triangle must be almost incestuous. Though it's not a triangle, is it, considering our history? Goodness me, so many tangled webs. Let me see,' she drew lines in the air. 'Marian, Andrew, me, Matthew, Fiona, Simon. And, of course, now you, Veronica. So complicated. Yet it seems the common denominator is always Matthew, doesn't it?'

Roni staggered back, the rutted ground crumbling beneath her feet, fear and denial squeezing at her chest. She had deliberately pushed Denise's insinuation from her mind and turned a deaf ear to the whispers of gossip. She hadn't wanted to know the truth. Her fingers turned to ice, sliding from Matt's grip. She shot a desperate glance up at him, and his eyes met hers steadily. He shook his head fractionally and interlaced his fingers with hers, his thumb caressing the back of her hand.

Denise would destroy them if she allowed it. But Marian had urged her to learn to trust. And she trusted Marian's judgment and, above all others, Tracey's.

She moved closer to Matt.

A smile haunted Denise's lips. 'Nicely played, Matthew. But so many secrets, aren't there? It must be difficult to keep them all straight.' She snapped toward Roni. 'Do you realise he's living with Fiona? From the day her husband died, actually.'

'Don't you bring them into this,' Matt growled, his grip on Roni's hand painful.

Roni realised that the poison her mother spewed was made more dangerous because it was seasoned with grains of truth. She laced her voice with sarcasm. 'Fascinating rundown. Now we're all caught up, what exactly do you want?'

Denise slammed a hand on the hood of the car. 'My share, Veronica. Your aunt cheated me. I should have had Andrew's estate. After all, I was far more wife to him than Marian was, in the ways that really count. And I've kept his dirty little secret all these years.'

So that's all she was? A dirty little secret? 'The way I understand it, Marian paid you to keep that secret.'

Denise slapped the comment away with a wild gesture. 'Not enough! She always implied there'd be more. I want a share of Peppertree Crossing. It was my parents' property, just as much as it was hers.'

'Derek Prescott tells me you've already exhausted the legal avenues to argue your case.'

'Prescott's an old fool,' Denise snapped.

'Fine. Have your solicitor contact my old fool, and enjoy paying to hash it out again.' Roni released Matt's hand and took a step toward her mother, lowering her voice menacingly. 'Because I swear, you're never getting a single acre of this land. Your own sister didn't want you on it, and now I'm telling you I don't want you here. Get off my property, Denise.'

Shock flashed across her mother's face. 'But I thought we—'

'There is no "we". You forfeited that right every day of the past twenty-nine years. You're a stranger to me, and certainly not one I care to get to know any better.'

'Don't you realise what this is?' Denise's painted nails flashed as she pointed at Matt. 'You're the new poor little rich girl in town, and he's going to drain you. Has he hit you up for a share of the property yet? Suggested a variation to the farming agreement?'

'No.' She knew with certainty Matt had no intention of taking advantage of her. 'And he won't.'

'He will!' Denise's hysterical screech startled a raucous murder of crows from the nearby scrub. 'His brother was just the damn same. It's all about the money.'

'Let it go, Denise. Haven't you hurt enough people?'

Matt's tone was flat and exhausted, as though the pain he hid had become too heavy.

Spittle flecked the corners of Denise's mouth. 'Simon wanted me, he loved me. He was going to leave that bitch Fiona, but then he discovered Marian had control of all the money that should have been mine. She stole him from me, just like she did with Andrew. You don't realise, Veronica, how much she interfered in people's lives, how she controlled them. Even dead, she still wins; you're just her new puppet.' Her voice disjointed and her fists clenched, her eyes were wild.

Matt stepped up. 'Denise, you have to calm down. You're going to hurt yourself. You know it's all over.'

Tears studded Denise's eyes, spilling as she shook her head, her tone suddenly pathetic. 'It can't be over. It can't. There's no one left who loves me. I thought . . . I thought maybe my daughter would love me. Would need me.'

Roni recognised Denise's manipulation, yet still her heart twisted. She wanted her mother to want her. But she sure as hell didn't need her. She lifted her chin to indicate the paddocks, but placed a palm against her heart. 'There's nowhere here for you.'

Denise scowled at Roni's hand, her face hardening. 'Fine. You're no better than your aunt. I don't give a damn about any of you, and even less about this godforsaken dump. I'm going to Europe. You don't have to come, I'll go alone. Just give me the money. It's rightfully mine, anyway.'

A one-way ticket and they'd be shot of her. How could she resist? 'I'll talk to Derek. But I can't promise anything.'

Except that she wouldn't hesitate to get an intervention order to keep this woman away from Peppertree Crossing.

Denise snapped upright. 'Talking isn't enough. You owe it to me, Veronica. You ruined my life. All this should have been mine.' She waved a hand, encompassing both Matt and the property. 'You never should have been born, you know. No one wanted you. Not me, not your father. And my sister, ha, she only wanted you as her latest plaything. You were no more important to her than an orphaned lamb.'

'Enough!' Matt strode to the BMW and wrenched open the door. 'Get the hell off this property, Denise. You either move now or I'll bloody well move you.'

Denise slipped back to ingratiating like a switch had been flicked. 'Of course. I know you must be busy, Veronica. When you have some time, let's catch up for coffee again. That was a lovely afternoon.'

As Denise settled behind the wheel, Bonnie on her lap licking eagerly at her face, Matt slammed the door, the set of his shoulders making it clear he held back unimaginable fury.

Roni sagged as the car disappeared in a cloud of dust. She hadn't realised how tense she was until the adrenaline evaporated, leaving her knees weak and her lips quivering.

Matt's hands moved to her upper arms, supporting her. 'Are you okay?'

She nodded, blinking furiously, then dashed a hand across her face as the tears spilled. 'Sorry. I'm being stupid. I don't care about her, I really don't. It's not like I had any expectations.'

'It's okay to hurt, Roni. There's no prize for having the thickest skin.'

She dropped her chin so her face was hidden against his chest. 'If you let yourself start hurting, sometimes you can't find the way to turn it off.'

He was silent for a long moment. 'Everyone hurts. Sometimes you have to let it out, not close it up inside.' His chest rose unevenly against her cheek. 'I don't want any secrets between us, Roni. They're poison. Denise is . . . well, you saw for yourself. She's unstable. But what she said about Simon is true. Part of it, anyway. He was in love with her. Somehow, she worked her way into his life when he was at a low point. But he didn't kill himself because he discovered she had no money.'

'Then why?' She leaned back to look up at him.

'He killed himself because of me.' Matt's throat moved convulsively. 'What your mother said—'

'Don't call her that.' She never wanted to be associated with Denise in that way again.

He nodded. 'What Denise said, about her and me. It's a lie. She did kiss me once, when I was about eighteen. Cougar move. Anyway, she and Simon were fighting a couple of years ago, so she told him she was screwing me, that I was a better prospect because I had a profession and Marian's support.' His grip on her arms tightened. 'We weren't, Roni, you understand that? I loved my brother. And Simon truly loved Denise.' Lips compressed into a white line, he shook his head. 'I guess that's the tragedy of all this. Denise is so desperate for love that when she had it, she didn't recognise it.' He released her and rubbed a hand across his eyes. 'Anyway. She got her talons into Simon when he was vulnerable. The farm wasn't doing well—like most out here—and I reckon he was depressed. He talked like it was his responsibility to single-handedly end the drought, increase our yield and save the farm. I guess because Dad left it to him. In any case, Denise must have offered him some sort of reprieve from the darkness of his mind. Maybe the attention of a confident, attractive older woman made him feel more worthwhile. I don't know.' He shrugged, scowling into the distance as though a scene played before his eyes.

She could feel his pain, his inner turmoil, and she wanted to wrap her arms around him, to tell him it was all in the past; but she knew how the past had a habit of bleeding into the present. Perhaps talking was the best way for him to find healing.

He heaved out a heavy, uneven breath. 'I could never figure out what the lure was. I suppose Denise is very like Fiona in some respects, so perhaps he was attracted to dominant women. All I know is he could never see her for the manipulator she is. As far as he was concerned, she walked on water. Anyway, when she trotted out this crap about me, he believed her, drank himself stupid, then ploughed his ute into a tree.' His voice broke and he mashed his lips together for a moment before continuing more quietly. 'He left a note, just saying he was tired. And that he was sorry. But I know it was my fault; if I'd talked more, like Marian was always nagging me to, Simon would have known the truth. And he wouldn't have needed to hide in a bottle.'

'That's not your fault! We all have things we couldn't control—' She shuddered, breaking off. She couldn't go there. 'But I get it. It's not your fault, yet still you hurt.'

'Yeah. Well, like they say, time's supposed to heal.'

She screwed up her face. 'Can't say I've done much healing.' Yet, as Matt's penetrating gaze probed her secrets, it seemed that sharing might ease the weight of her memories.

'We'll work on it?' he asked softly.

She nodded but stepped away from him. 'But right now, there's a crop to work on.'

'Boss.' He mock-saluted, and she breathed easier. At least he understood where the boundaries lay, that she needed space. 'Want to do a couple more rounds on the header?'

She shook her head. 'I have to go into town.'

'No picnic?'

'The cake's all yours. I've got a few calls to make, and I need to see Tracey.'

Marian was right, she did need people in her life.

And, thanks to her aunt, she got to choose who those people were.

Chapter Thirty-five

'Door's open, love.'

The predictable sing-song call brought a smile to Roni's lips. She stepped over the tufted welcome mat and walked down the familiar hall, lined with pictures of her family.

Tracey was in the kitchen, her glasses perched on the end of her nose, the local newspaper spread open on the table. 'I'll pop the kettle on. Lamingtons are in the fridge. Though I have Anzacs if you prefer.'

Roni pressed her lips together for a moment, determined not to cry as the sense of belonging swelled within her. 'Do we have a biscuit bake-off before the Anzac Day fundraiser?'

'No, we always use the traditional recipe—wait! We?' Tracey was out of her seat, pastel fabric billowing around her like a gypsy angel. 'Anzac Day is months away. Do you mean . . . Are you . . .'

Roni pretended not to understand, shifting the biscuit tin from the counter to the centre of the table. 'I suppose we should focus on the lamington fundraiser for Christmas before we start on our strategy for the next contest.'

Tracey clutched at her arm, her eyes shining. 'Veronica! Stop messing with me. Do you mean you're staying?'

She nodded, the tears spilling. She made no effort to stop them. 'I'm staying.'

'Oh my. Oh my, oh my.' Tracey's arms were around her, her voice broken by sobs. 'Oh my, I was so afraid you wouldn't stay. I was worried you'd leave me and go back to Sydney. I wanted to slap that damn Christine Albright for being horrible to you. And Matthew Krueger—treading so carefully instead of telling you how he feels, because he's afraid you'd get the wrong idea. Oh!' She released Roni and stepped back, her hand flying to cover her mouth. 'Did Matt say anything? Only, I know Taylor spoke with him, and that he went to yours yesterday. And his fingers . . .'

'Of course you know.' There were no secrets around here. Not anymore.

'I swear, if he's not over at your place talking to you, that man's here or at Taylor's talking *about* you. So you're good? He's good?'

She lifted one shoulder. 'Yeah. I think so. We're . . . something, anyway. Maybe. We'll see. There's no rush, is there?'

'Yes. No, I mean, no, there's no rush. Oh, I'm just so happy, I don't know what I'm saying.' Tracey's corkscrew curls danced, defying the restraint of the bright pink scarf threaded through them. She flung her arms around Roni again. 'This is just the best news ever. You're so like Marian, having you around is like having a tiny piece of her back.'

'I need to ask you something about Marian.' Roni caught at Tracey's fluttering hands, holding them still. 'Denise came to visit again today.'

Tracey's countenance darkened. 'Oh, I do wish she would just disappear. Can't we throw a bucket of water over her or something?'

'That's what I want to ask you about. Not so much the bucket-of-water plan but the disappearing bit. I know Marian said she didn't want Denise to have anything from the estate, but you knew my aunt better than anyone alive, so I'll trust your judgment entirely. Denise wants to go to Europe. I want her to go. Would Marian have been terribly angry at the thought of the estate purchasing her a ticket? I mean, I know that, unfortunately, Denise won't stay gone forever, she's always going to find a way to be in my life.' Ironic, considering how she'd once longed for her mother's commitment. 'But this way I figure we at least get a bit of a breather from her. Is that too cowardly?'

Tracey sat slowly, her hands folded in an attitude of prayer. 'For all that Marian complained about Denise, she did love her sister. That's why she kept funding her. If you choose to buy her a ticket, or a house, or a one-way trip to the moon—which would, incidentally, be my preference— you'll be doing exactly what Marian had always done, and would have continued to do.'

Roni exhaled. 'So you're all right with that part of my plan?'

'It's none of my business, love.'

'Yes, it is. I respect your opinion. You're going to have to get used to me bringing all my mum problems to you.'

Tracey's fingers fluttered to clutch her beads. 'I hope you mean that in the way I think you mean it. I've never been a mum before.'

Roni smiled shyly. 'And I've never been a daughter before. But I'd like to try.'

Tracey's hug was a promise of a forever home.

∞

Derek Prescott was rather more circumspect; she could almost imagine him leaning back in his leather chair, staring out over the harbour as he considered the proposal she put to him by phone. 'You can certainly gift Denise whatever you choose, but you can't stipulate she stay away from you, or from the property.' His words held a note of caution. 'Not without a court order. However, from what Marian told me of her sister's mental state, should you choose to follow that path I think we will find little resistance within the legal system.'

For a moment she was tempted. A clean cut.

Except it would never be clean. Maybe she was incapable of abandoning her mother despite having been abandoned by her. 'No. I don't want to cause her trouble. I want . . .' She paused, almost embarrassed to admit what she wanted. 'I want her to be happy. I can see she has problems, but she's still my . . . well, she's still related to me. And that puts her in a group of about, let's see . . . one person. Although, apparently, I do have a bunch of cousins on my father's side, but I think he would have preferred they didn't know about my heritage.'

'Your father?'

She glanced at the phone as though she would be able to see the surprise that echoed in the lawyer's voice. Marian had truly kept her promise; it seemed even Derek Prescott didn't know the full truth of her identity. She didn't owe her father a thing, and he'd never taken responsibility for his actions. His humiliation and regret weren't a fair penalty, but Marian had chosen to protect him, and she owed Marian . . . everything. Although she didn't agree with Marian's decision, she would honour her aunt's choice.

She ignored Derek's implied question. 'So I can gift Denise the money to go on the trip?'

'You can gift her whatever you want. Although Marian didn't include Denise in her will, wanting to be certain that Peppertree Crossing became entirely yours, she did establish a family trust that provides an annuity for Denise and keeps Jim Smithton on a retainer. Very generous funding, I must say, although it seems Denise burns through it quickly.'

Across the room, from where she had been pretending not to listen to Derek's booming voice, Tracey snorted.

Roni flashed her a grin. Though Derek only confirmed what Tracey had already told her, still it was a relief to find that she and Marian were on the same page; family were family, no matter what.

She returned to the property later than she had hoped, multiple cups of tea being required to lubricate the lengthy phone consultation with Derek, and then more tea when Tracey drove her over to discuss her proposal with Jim Smithton. She discovered that Ella was, in fact, his wife, not one of his greyhounds, and that his sons, with a little encouragement from their parents, were in complete agreement that playing online games and doing a few hours' work at the supermarket were probably not the career paths they wanted.

Though it was dark, she was disappointed not to see Matt in the paddocks as she drove up to the house. He was the person she was most eager to share her idea with. Born from a notion that had formed weeks earlier, as she worried about what would become of her growing menagerie if she left the farm, it was now a plan, down on paper thanks to Derek Prescott's business acumen.

Scritches yowled as she reached the back door, informing her he had been shut inside for far too long and would like time in his new cat run.

An envelope fluttered in the doorjamb, and she tried to control a surge of excitement. The note could be one of the promised 'hidden' letters from Marian, delivered by a faithful friend. But, as much as she craved the missives that connected her with the family she could never know, a single line from Matt would hold more promise of a future than any inheritance could offer.

She crossed to the kitchen, flipped on the kettle and sat. Scritches jumped onto the table. She'd read that squirting a cat with water would break that particular bad habit but, as Scritches still shared her shower, it was unlikely to work on him. Besides, they both knew he was king here. He padded over, butting his head up under her chin, making sure she didn't forget him, despite the distraction in her hand.

'You know I'll always love you, Scritch.' But there was no reason for him to be the only one. She unfolded the note.

Roni,

I've learned the stupidity of keeping my mouth shut, of thinking my intentions are obvious, and I'm not willing to risk losing you by staying silent. But talking doesn't come easy, so I figure I'll take a page out of Marian's book and put my thoughts in writing.

Marian did a number on both of us. She was a master manipulator with a long-term plan for everything. Maybe she did intend for me only to mentor you. I guess we'll never know. Yet I hope she wanted more, as when she set her heart on something the universe had a tendency to fall into line—and I'd really appreciate that kind of backing right now because I'm way beyond the point of wanting to share only my knowledge with you.

There's an eclipse tonight. I know how you value your security, but if you're prepared to see where this thing between us could go, leave your door unlocked. Matt

The letter was everything she could want, yet it terrified her. Despite her plans and desires, dare she let Matt beyond her defences? She had worked so hard to be capable. To be strong. Unbreakable.

But Marian's overarching message was that she needed to step from the imagined safety of solitude and take a chance to find true happiness.

She heaved a tremulous breath and unlocked her door.

∾

Scritches raced to the sunroom, his paws still nowhere near as fast as her heartbeat. She stood, remaining in the kitchen. 'It's open.' The words probably weren't loud enough for Matt to hear but still he entered. Stood awkwardly inside the doorway.

She looked at the table.

He looked at her looking at the table.

Scritches swung his head, gazing from one to the other. Then he decided the silence had stretched too long, yowled and stuck his claws into Matt's moleskins, trying to pull his way up.

'Ouch! He's really not big on jumping, is he?'

'Likes to play it cautious.'

'Smart.' Matt hauled the cat up against his chest.

'Maybe not always.'

'Do you think he'll change?'

She bit the inside of her cheek. 'This new environment might help.'

His eyes on her, Matt didn't even glance at the cat that neither of them was actually talking about. He slid the backpack from his shoulder and dropped it onto the table.

'I figured it was my turn to bring the picnic. But you never said whether you like liverwurst.'

'I think it'll grow on me.' She waved a hand toward the bench beneath the etched glass cupboards. 'Lamingtons for dessert okay?'

'No need for them to grow on me. I'm already sold.'

She caught her bottom lip between her teeth and stuck her hands in her back pockets. Why had she ever thought she wanted him to talk more? This wordplay was excruciating. If he'd sweep her into his arms and kiss her it would ease the tension. Maybe. But he wasn't that kind of guy. He wouldn't make a move until she made her permission clear.

She took a ragged breath and stepped toward him. 'Down you get, Scritch. I believe that's my space you're occupying.'

Matt dropped Scritches onto the yellow cushion. His hands found her hips, drawing her close. Still he didn't kiss her. 'You read my letter?'

She nodded.

'Want to talk?'

She stayed silent. Perhaps she should have written her thoughts down, but committing her secrets to paper would make them more real.

Matt waited a beat, then nodded. 'I set up a hammock on the verandah. You bring the rug. I've got the rest covered.' He pressed his lips to her hair, then released her. 'The eclipse is almost full.'

He knew that her secrets belonged in the dark.

She collected the rug from their library picnic and made her way onto the front verandah. As she lowered onto the hammock strung between the verandah poles, the webbing tilted crazily and she gasped. Matt grinned and swung himself in, almost tipping her out. As she squealed and clutched at the woven ropes, he stretched on his back, extending one arm to invite her into the safety of his embrace. 'Trick is to relax and go with the ride.'

Though the summer night air was balmy, still she had to try not to tremble as she settled against him. He smelled good; sunshine and a subtle, spicy cologne. His arm wrapped loosely around her. Secure. Reassuring.

They lay in silence as the last sliver of the huge, silvery moon slipped into shadow, the sky sprinkled with sparkling pinpricks. Diamonds on a celestial picnic rug. The hooting barn owls and chirping cicadas fell silent. The tiny nocturnal animals foraging beneath the night-scented lavenders paused, and the world held its breath.

Matt's question came soft but firm in the absolute privacy of their safe cocoon. 'What is it that scares you, Roni?'

For someone who could be positively monosyllabic, he had a hell of a way of opening a conversation. Her instinct was to shrug off his question. Instead, she lay quiet, trying to find words to match her emotions. 'I guess . . . I'm afraid of disappointing you. That I won't be who you seem to think I am. I've never had to live up to anyone's expectations.'

The hammock rocked beneath them. 'I get that.'

She stole a glance at his face but could see little as the sky shifted from purple to black.

Silence again. Long minutes, which could have been oppressive, but as darkness enveloped them the lack of judgment freed her. It was time to share at least one of her secrets. 'The thing is, I failed the one person who did depend on me.' The memory sliced at her heart, and her words trembled. 'And I don't know if I can live with that again.'

Matt's fingers caressed her arm, slow strokes from wrist to elbow. 'Was it your fault?'

'No. I don't think so, anyway. It ended, but it wasn't my choice.'

A tiny crescent of moon appeared, reborn in the void of night.

Matt's breath stirred her hair as he turned to face her. 'Sometimes it hurts to love. But sometimes it hurts more to stay.'

'It wasn't like that. I've never been in love.'

'But you said—'

'I was pregnant. I lost the baby.' The admission tore at her heart, yet the wound seemed to lessen the weight in her chest. But she wasn't sure she was ready to let go of the grief. It was all she had left of Roo. 'The thing is, love is a lie. It's an excuse for people—for life—to hurt you. You know there's no such thing as a happily ever after in real life, right?' Even as she whispered the words, she wanted him to persuade her otherwise, to tell her that he would never be reckless with her heart, that she would always be safe.

Instead of rushing to provide empty promises and placation, Matt's words were measured, his thumb stroking her clenched knuckles. 'What about Marian and Tracey? And Luke and Taylor? Do you think they aren't happy?'

'Marian hid her love for Tracey, scared of judgment, so how happy could they have been? And Taylor has things she's scared of, too.'

'Maybe that's the point. We're all scared. But sometimes we just have to close our eyes and jump.' Matt's steel gaze glinted as the heavens blossomed above them. 'Roni, I'm not great with words, I don't know all the right things to say. Hell, I have trouble saying much at all. But I am good at listening. When you're ready to tell me what it is that hurt you so badly, I'll be right here.' He let go of her hand, his fingertips tracing the curve of her cheek. 'I'm not going anywhere. I swear, if you fall, I'll catch you.'

She wanted that to be true more than he could possibly imagine. But her happiness wasn't his job. 'I don't need saving, Matt. I can look after myself.'

'I wouldn't have it any other way.'

She believed him. This strong, reserved man wouldn't control or manipulate her, instead he would support and enable her. One day, she would be able to tell him her secrets. But right now, she needed him to kiss her.

As though he could read her mind, Matt shook his head, a smile playing at the corners of his mouth. 'Not yet.'

'Why?'

'I'm waiting for the shadows to disappear.' He lifted his chin toward the moon, an enormous silver orb now, hanging low in the sky and lighting the farmyard in shades of ice blue. 'I want to see you when I kiss you.'

Her heart swelled. Matt was the one man who could help banish her own shadows. She pressed close to his warmth, his breath whispering across her face as his hands explored her curves and hollows. He was all heat and strength, and, for the first time in her life, she was all longing.

The ghost of a caressing breeze swayed the hammock. Marian was right. If she wanted to truly live, she had to embrace risk.

As Matt's lips descended on hers, she murmured, 'Let's close our eyes and jump . . . and see how high we soar.'

Epilogue

Although Matt's footfalls were silent on the lush winter grass behind her, she knew he approached. As always, she had an absolute awareness of his presence.

One of his hands moved to the small of her back, the other resting on the high mound of her belly. 'You're not overdoing it, are you?'

She covered his hand with hers, loving the slight leatheriness of his skin, the knowledge that his palms were worn and callused. From working on their property. Their dream.

'You know the doctor said exercise is good for us.' She probably should be more worried: twins had a reputation of coming early, and she only had a month to go. But with Taylor Hartmann monitoring her pregnancy every step of the way, she felt only joy and anticipation.

'I know,' Matt's lips pressed against her ear. 'But I suspect Taylor wasn't imagining you in the middle of the farmyard, building your empire.'

'I don't think overseeing the tradies really counts as building,' she laughed, waving a hand toward the largest of the sheds. Although the exterior hadn't changed, still strong and solid—like her man—the interior was now warm and soft, a safe harbour. She'd had a nest of small rooms created, each fully lined and air-conditioned. Each to be fitted out to the personal preference of the occupant.

She had shared all her secrets and her new dream with Matt that night on the hammock almost two years ago. With the land making only a marginal return on sheep and crops, she had a vision for Peppertree Crossing, one that would free Matt to follow his true passion and would nurture her love of animals.

With their father's encouragement, Jim Smithton's sons had been eager to become farmhands, and Matt trained them to work that scaled-back side of the businesses.

Then, together, she and Matt created The Peaceful Paws.

She would never be Marian, but she could adopt Marian's qualities and strengths, her determination to see a dream to fruition. Now, with the opening of their pet retirement home, that dream was reality.

With Scritches winding around their legs, Roni nestled against her husband. Goat and Baby let out a barnyard chorus as a candy-apple-red car bounced over the cattle grid, an explosion of grey fur dashing toward them the second Tracey opened the door.

Matt fondled the dog's ears. 'Good boy, Bear. Go find Tess and play.'

Bear swiped the vet's hand with a long tongue, then bounded off in search of Matt's collie.

'We're going to have to watch out for favouritism,' Roni teased. 'Everyone requires the same level of attention.'

'But some need a little extra love,' Matt murmured into her hair as Tracey drifted toward them, clutching a fistful of buttercup-yellow soursobs.

He was right. She had a good business head. She would charge for animals to spend their last years living here in happiness and luxury when their owners could no longer care for them. But she would also set aside a portion of the funds and space to take in unwanted, neglected and abandoned animals.

Because everything deserved someone to love them.

Acknowledgements

There is an old African proverb, 'It takes a village to raise a child.' In this case, it took a village to create a book. There are so many people to thank, I'm terrified of inadvertently omitting someone.

First, Taylor, aka 'The Kid' in my social media feeds. Starting with a title as a concept, Taylor and I brainstormed the original version of this book. Taylor spent hours listening to me—or, in true teen style, arguing with me—as we worked through the plot. We suffered for the art together, dedicating uncountable calories (okay, the bathroom scales disagree!) to picnicking on liverwurst and lamingtons at The Farm to mentally set the scene. I swear I was applying the literary version of method acting. True sacrifice. Nothing at all to do with delicious food.

Wonderful Australian author Sandie Docker has shared much of the adventure with me from way back when we were trying to win agents for our first manuscripts (ha, that sounds ever so Hollywood). Finding well-deserved success with her women's fiction titles, Sandie pens the most beautifully descriptive work I've read. Trying to gently steer me away from a tendency to write 'dark', she provides incredibly thorough critiques. Thanks for always being there, Sandie.

American author Marty Mayberry has been a long-time writing friend and a staunch champion of many of my titles, always ready with an encouraging word about how much she loved a particular story. Together we've waded through the depths of the publishing journey and surmounted some decent-sized hills.

Syed M. Masood gave up his writing time to exchange critiques, despite having debuts in both adult and young adult fiction in 2020. James Ormonde, Lindsay Landgraf Hess and Tessa Kelly provided fabulous feedback, while Michelle Parsons, a well-loved champion of Australian writers, overlooked my appalling punctuation (maybe I should rethink free grammar apps) to beta read and provide encouragement.

To the seemingly-vast, well-organised team at Allen & Unwin, including the submissions editors who pulled my manuscript from the slush pile and sent that first, heart-stopping, life-changing 'we might be interested' email; the structural editor, Christa Munns; the copyeditor, Claire de Medici; the proofreader, Simone Ford; the publicity team; and the designer, Nada Backovic, who produced a cover that is the absolute embodiment of *The Farm at Peppertree Crossing*: thank you.

Of course, hugs to my wonderful (and not-at-all-terrifying, despite my fears) publisher, Annette Barlow, who took a chance on me and somehow manages to shoot across *just* the right warm fuzzies at *just* the right moment. And to my editor, Courtney Lick—I can't even imagine how many times you've read this story, and I know I still owe you that coffee I promised. Thanks for always being only a message away. And for not being the least fazed by my sometimes odd sense of humour.

To Stephen, purveyor of replacement laptops and provider of time, even though you can't fathom my passion: thank you.

And my love to my parents, Lawrie and Chris, who enlivened countless visits to Flinders Hospital with an unwavering interest in my publishing exploits—even when it was only a handful of hours since you last asked. I should probably warn you that I have a coin jar going with a long-term plan for The Farm to one day be mine!

Finally, my heartfelt thanks to that other person. You know who you are. No, I didn't forget you: see, you have a paragraph all to yourself.

The Wattle Seed Inn

PR executive Gabrielle Moreau knows she has an easy life, but when her business partner claims she lacks career passion she takes ownership of a dilapidated pub in a tiny riverside settlement to prove she can be a success without falling back on her privilege.

Eighteen months ago, Settlers Bridge stonemason Hayden Paech had it all: a job he loved, good mates and a close family. All he needed was the right woman to come along and he was ready to settle down. But one poor choice stole that chance and he'll never risk caring for anyone again.

Living at Wurruldi Hotel for . . . goodness, so many years, Ilse has seen more changes of ownership than she can recall. Clinging to her failing memories, she's tired of trying to protect the property her grandparents built. With the arrival of the elegant Gabrielle Moreau, however, it seems that finally an owner may recognise the importance of recapturing the grace and dignity of Ilse's past.

For Ilse to find peace, Hayden forgiveness and Gabrielle her true passion, three aching hearts must reveal their secrets.

Read on for the first chapter of
The Wattle Seed Inn

1

Gabrielle

'The place must be haunted,' the conveyancer said, shaking his head as Gabrielle signed the transfer paperwork.

'Why is that?' She underlined *Moreau* with a sweeping ink stroke.

The conveyancer tapped the original title, the document apparently a rarity since the Titles Office joined the twenty-first century and switched to computer-generated documentation. Gabrielle's ex-fiancé, Brendan, had splashed enough cash to somehow make the parchment appear when they purchased the hotel three years ago. Which was particularly ironic, given that he often accused her of buying her way through life.

'Fourth transfer in thirteen years. Unlucky number,' the conveyancer observed. 'Before that, the same family held it for over a hundred and thirty years.'

Gabrielle knew he was fishing for information, specifically about why this was the second transfer in three years, with the property being changed from joint ownership to hers alone. But she wasn't about to delve into the details of the demise of her decade-long relationship, to talk about the way she and Brendan had been drifting: not so much apart, as moored in a sticky morass of wealth and lack of expectation. Life was too easy, too familiar, too . . . perfect? But when Brendan accused her of lacking passion, her achievements and partnership in their marketing company a product of her parents' affluence and influence rather than her drive, she had finally woken from the daydream of wealth and privilege. Gabrielle had traded her share in their Adelaide apartment for Brendan's portion of the country hotel and now the Wurruldi Hotel was hers, as evidenced by the title deed, and it was here she planned to prove that her creativity trumped his supposed passion.

She set the pen down, pushing the papers back across the desk. 'I guess that family had the best of it, when Wurruldi was a paddle-steamer trading port. Progress—and, I suppose, roads—killed the town along with the trade. There's just the pub and a handful of cottages there now.'

'Looks like the river's going the same way,' the conveyancer muttered. 'Unless we get a bigger water allocation from upriver, it'll be ruined. Nothing but carp left in there.'

'Hopefully not,' Gabrielle said, refusing to let his doom and gloom sway her. 'In any case, I'm taking the premises in a different direction. Those roads that ruined the pub decades ago mean it's now perfectly placed for a bed-and-breakfast set-up.' She pointed in the general direction of the mountain range to the east of Adelaide, punctuating the air with her Chanel blush-nude nails. 'World-class wine regions within ninety minutes in three directions. The Barossa Valley pours a fortune into promotions and commands a massive tourist market. South, there's the Fleurieu Peninsula and McLaren Vale wineries, and the Adelaide Hills are also on the town's doorstep. So, Wurruldi is the perfect hub for holidaymakers. Backed up by the right marketing, a bed-and-breakfast there will be a guaranteed winner.'

'And that marketing is what Small & Sassy does, right?' the conveyancer asked, leaning forward, his eyebrows raised.

Gabrielle swallowed her irritation. *Small* was a nod to Brendan's surname, which unsurprisingly he despised and was hellbent on disproving; *Sassy* was for her role in the firm they'd started together straight out of uni. She knew that alliteration was a tool that should never be underestimated, and she could adopt the required personality at will. Or at Brendan's will: he was the one who viewed every interaction as a chance to network.

'I'm PR,' she said. 'I handle our clients' public persona, help shape the perception of their image.' She watched the conveyancer's eyes glaze over as he reached for his pen and rolled it between thumb and forefinger, though he kept his slightly unfocused gaze on her. 'Brendan does the marketing,' she wrapped up swiftly. It had taken her a bachelor's degree to realise that the unfamiliar necessity to stick to budgets and spreadsheets was never going to sit well with her, but adding a postgrad in communications had been the perfect way to complement Brendan's indisputable skills and build their niche business. She had a practised talent for reinventing, camouflaging and selling—people, at least. Now, she had to hope her abilities would translate to revitalising an old hotel that had seen better days, so she could prove Brendan wrong: success didn't need passion, it needed a plan.

∾

Rather than take the main road through Settlers Bridge to the south, Gabrielle took a scenic route from the north, past the tiny wineries and through the gum-studded hills of Eden Valley. She hadn't paid much attention when Brendan drove them out to Wurruldi three years ago, and now she almost missed the unmarked turn-off that led from the bitumen onto a potholed dirt lane. It looked like the roads department had also missed it for quite some time.

The road wound for a couple of kilometres between paddocks filled with oatmeal-coloured grass and studded with granite boulders the size of caravans, then, without warning, it took a hard right. On Gabrielle's left was a breathtakingly sheer drop of hundreds of feet. Far below threaded the mighty Murray River, while directly opposite soared a vast apricot-toned cliff, the twin of the one she edged along. It was as though a rift had appeared in the earth, cracking the land apart as the khaki waters forced through the crevasse.

Yet another unmarked turn led her onto a series of tight switchbacks sliced into the cliff face. She took her time, her foot pressing on the brake until finally she reached the bottom of the steep descent and breathed a tremulous sigh of relief as the track levelled out onto a wide river flat. While her inexperience with country driving made the road seem particularly treacherous, Gabrielle recognised that the dirt track was part of the isolated, rural charm of the tiny, almost hidden town.

A forest of river red gums dwarfed her car, the leafy canopy making lacy dapples of the last of the day's light. The road wound across the broadening flats, the opposite side of the river still sharply defined by stark cliffs. Within a kilometre she was following a spit of land between the river and lagoons landscaped with the bleached skeletons of trees, victims of salinity caused by upriver locks interfering with the natural cycle of flood and drought.

Wurruldi might only be fifteen kilometres off the main road—according to her GPS, though she had doubts— but this stark, ominous beauty was a world away from her city life. For the right clientele, that could be turned into a selling point. Gabrielle would have to get on to the council about fixing up the road, though; there was a fine line between offering tranquillity and isolation, and being inaccessible in some banjo-playing backwater.

Her grip on the wheel eased as she reached the town-limit sign, an ancient, unofficial-looking piece of tin. *Wurruldi.* No population count.

She turned left, along the outside of the wattle-tree–lined boundary of her property. On the opposite side of the road was what constituted the township: a small, multiple-doored construction of stone and tin sat in the middle of a paddock. Low in one window was a faded sign: *South Australia's favourite. Amscol ice cream. 'It's a food, Not a fad.'* In the opposite corner a hand-painted poster, the curling, yellowed edges cradling decades' worth of fly husks, declared *Wurruldi Postal Agency*.

Almost on the river's edge, the road came to a junction. Gabrielle pulled up facing the rusting remnants of a massive pulley system. To the right, beyond the shop-cum-post office, four symmetrical sandstone cottages sat precariously close to the low banks of the river. To the left the road hooked, leading back up the inside boundary of her property.

Directly in front of her, a pair of pelicans floated across the olive satin towards a flat-bedded ferry moored among the moulting willows below the far cliff. The front of the punt drifted mesmerisingly from side to side, catching the sharp breeze—or perhaps swayed by invisible currents. She buzzed down her window, taking deep breaths of the rich, dank odour. The pelicans changed tack, effortlessly moving upstream, past an ancient timber dock, until they were hidden by the golden late-autumn willow fronds.

When they had disappeared, Gabrielle nodded decisively, put the car back into gear and made a sharp left U-turn onto a broad, crushed-limestone driveway. From here, this was her property. Thigh-high grass and weeds tangled in dying bushes almost hid the low drystone wall that separated the driveway from the public road.

Staring in appalled fascination, she let the car crawl two hundred metres, to where the driveway curved in a majestic swoop between the pub and a wooden horse trough, before running in a mirror image down the far side of the vast block. When Gabrielle had visited with Brendan to check out the potential investment, she'd told him she could imagine Shire horses clopping up the pristine concourse, pulling drays laden with trade goods—or perhaps barrels of beer—as women in long skirts reclined in lawn chairs on the soft grass beneath the lacy canopy of an imposing, multi-trunked jacaranda that stood proud in the centre of the area. Brendan had laughed and pointed out that dreaming didn't equate to passion. Maybe she should have seen the warning signs back then, but they had been together so long they were accustomed to one another. No, almost immune to one another. It had taken a long time for words, or even deeds, to burrow deep enough to hurt beyond a passing sting.

Pulling up, Gabrielle clambered slowly from the blue Audi S5 convertible, reluctant to face the magnitude of the task before her. Even Brendan's silver tongue would have trouble marketing this. Deep, crusted ruts scabbed the driveway, and rubble was scattered across the burr-covered yard. The century-old hitching rail and rough-hewn water trough that had fired her imagination were now a pile of splintered kindling.

She groaned, then recoiled as the noise startled a burst of rosellas from gums overhanging the stone wall. They shot skyward like fireworks, an explosion of colour in the drabness, and she turned to follow their flight above the high-peaked roof of the hotel. The Wurruldi Hotel.

Her hotel.

Resting her hands on narrow hips, Gabrielle slowed her slightly panicked breathing. Although the bones of the two-storey stone structure remained the same as when she and Brendan purchased it, the signs of insidious rot couldn't be overlooked. Unease wormed through her stomach. The best PR campaign in the world couldn't positively influence the impression this ruin would make on clients.

Beneath a hooded tin roof, three recessed doors were scarcely visible through the utilitarian square posts of the timber-railed balcony. Wooden-framed casement windows, softened only slightly by beige scrim netting, gazed sightlessly at the river.

The deep balcony created a darkly shaded verandah over the lower level, but Gabrielle could make out *Gentlemen's Bar* and *Ladies' Lounge* stylishly rendered in peeling gold-leaf above two of the windows. Arching over the centrally placed door, *1884* was clearly legible but the name of the licensee had flaked away, becoming a few dots and dashes of glitter and the odd, almost indecipherable, letter. As though to invite customers, the doorway was generous, wide enough to fit a broad-shouldered farmer on his way in for a pint or two after tying his horse to the nearby hitching post.

Not that anyone would be tethering a horse anymore; Gabrielle waved a fly away as she tried to dispel the disillusionment that pulled her mouth into a tight line. Other than location, the place was nothing like she remembered, and the damage worse than she had imagined.

Slowly, her gaze travelled across the front of the building. Gabrielle recalled the property boasting stately, park-like gardens, a pleasing blend of form and function that appealed to her artistic nature. But now the rose bushes sticking out from the weeds bordering the pub were covered in mottled, mouldy leaves, the branches blackened with canker. The odd small, struggling flower clung to life well beyond its season.

The worst thing wasn't the sad state of the property, but the fact that much of it was her fault. Some time back, in a surge of manic creativity and without revisiting the property, Brendan had pushed through the required council approvals to remodel the upstairs space to fit his vision of a boutique ale house where they could occasionally weekend. But other than that, their development intentions had been buried beneath the demands of their business. Although the estate agent said a woman was available, they never managed to get around to hiring someone to maintain the property. Out of sight, out of mind, the best-laid plans, and all that stuff: living and working in the thriving urban heart of Adelaide, it was impossible to imagine the abandoned property would slowly turn in on itself, crumbling with neglect.

The earthquake, however, had not been her fault. South Australia had a history of small quakes, averaging around four on the Richter scale, but they rarely caused much beyond minor damage. Now she had to deal with the consequences of both her inaction and the fact that the world had rubbed up the tectonic plates the wrong way a few months earlier.

Gabrielle pinched the bridge of her nose, trying to ease the tension without messing up her eye make-up. 'Can't make plans until I see how bad the damage is,' she muttered, taking slight reassurance from the sound of a voice, even her own. She considered checking if anyone was home, over in the cottages, but decided the news that she planned on developing their graveyard-quiet village of four houses, one deserted multi-purpose shop and a derelict pub into a thriving tourist mecca might not go down well.

She snorted: they'd probably laugh her out of town.

Taking a deep breath, Gabrielle started along the tree-lined passage on the southern side of the building. 'Oh!' she yelped, thrusting a hand out to steady herself as the heel of the over-the-knee leather boots she'd picked up in Rome caught in a crack of the uneven slate. She swiped slime on her denim-clad thigh, glaring at the damp moss-covered stone wall, then wound a hand beneath her woollen layers to tug the vibrating mobile phone from her pocket. She scowled at the illuminated screen—it didn't matter how many public pronouncements they had made about staying friends over the past thirteen months, still Brendan's profile pic twisted her stomach with irrational annoyance.

With the Manawaiopuna Falls in the background, he was fully kitted out in hiking gear, a backpack over his shoulders, expensive carbon trekking poles in one hand. She wasn't sure how many years ago they had taken that trip— maybe four? It had been the Greek Islands last autumn,

Italy the year before that. What she did know was that the carefully cropped snap was, like all of Brendan's social media, a construct she had helped build; the image he currently required the world to have of him. The contrived outdoorsy theme was an indication he was wooing a client in the physical recreation field.

What the picture didn't reveal was the helicopter that dropped them at the Hawaiian waterfall, or the ubiquitous smoother tucked away in Brendan's pocket or palmed in his left hand, out of frame.

Last month, when he was chasing a corporate account, his profile had been a devastatingly handsome candid snap of him in a Tom Ford suit and open-necked shirt, his casually dishevelled hair cut in a fade above the AirPods permanently embedded in his ears.

Her own profile photo needed to be updated. Backlit by nightclub neon, cocktail in one hand, her French-polished nails caressing the hanging fronds of a potted bamboo, Gabrielle wore dramatic make-up and a black woven bamboo shirt dress, evocative of Audrey Hepburn. Small & Sassy had won the account for the clothing line and she handled their PR campaign with a heavy focus on the ecological sustainability of bamboo, environmental awareness and the innate ability of women to do good while looking good.

Like Brendan said, every point of contact was an opportunity to sell yourself.

The difference was that he enjoyed doing it.

'Hey, Brendan.' Gabrielle tried to keep the peevish sigh from her voice.

'Hi, Elle. How's it look?' Brendan's voice crackled down the line and she shifted the phone away from her ear, toggling it onto speaker.

'Like a crumbling ruin,' she exaggerated. Even without doing the loathed budget projections, Gabrielle knew that financially she had made a crap decision in taking this on. But emotionally? Finishing things with Brendan was the right call. They had a long history, and it would have been simple to stay with him, to tell herself she remained seduced by his urbane charm. But then life would have continued as it was, an endless loop of dissatisfied satisfaction.

'If it's too far gone, sell for land value. Recoup your losses and come back to work.'

The practised calm of Brendan's deep voice should be soothing, but instead he had her hackles up in an instant. After so many years together, how could he not realise how much his thinly veiled directions irritated her? Besides, quitting would be easy, she had the financial reserves to take the hit. But accepting a loss on the place would reinforce his accusation that she wasn't passionate, that she wasn't driven to see the project through.

Brendan didn't need proof that he was right, that instead of enhancing life, money was an anaesthetic. With everything so easily attainable, there was no edge, no fear of failure to spice a venture. And without fear of failure, it was impossible to cultivate passion.

Gabrielle tipped her head back, focusing on a lone gunmetal-grey cloud scudding overhead. The pelicans soared high above now, drifting in circles over the wetlands, their outstretched wings wider than the span of her arms. Tempted to lose herself in their hypnotic laziness, Gabrielle shook her head. *Focus*. At least she hadn't let her need to escape persuade her to sell her share of their business; rather, she had stepped back into a consultancy role.

As she strode from the passage into a brick-paved courtyard Gabrielle forced cheerfulness into her tone, as though a tight smile would evidence a positive attitude. If Brendan doubted her ability to follow through with her plan, that made her all the more determined. 'I'll work it out.'

'At least come back here after you've had a look around today, Elle. There's no point roughing it. You said you'd use the apartment as your base.'

The designer-furnished, fully serviced apartment in the city that was now all his. Just like this ruin was all hers. And, with the chill breeze gusting the musty odour of rotting vegetation from the river's edge, it didn't seem like such a fair trade. 'Actually, *you* said that.' Sharing the apartment hadn't been a problem for the first months post–break-up—after all, their relationship had never fallen into the hot-and-steamy category, they'd always been better suited as friends than lovers—but she was woman enough to feel irritation at the sight of the latest pocket-sized brunette or blonde draped all over her ex—and all over her bespoke handmade Molmic lounge suite.

Brendan's Molmic, now.

'I'm only going to have a quick look around the outside, then I'll head in to Settlers Bridge to pick up the key,' she said.

'You didn't go to the agent first?'

'I came the back way.'

By now he should know that she preferred a tactile approach to her job, getting to know her clients and their products before she calculated the best way to build and maintain their image. Today, she had needed to put herself in the place of her guests-to-be, and taking the scenic route had been mandatory to her process.

Brendan grunted. 'The agent will be closed now.' Gabrielle knew the rustle of fabric meant he'd turned his wrist to check his Tag Heuer. 'I said you'd left it too late to head down tonight.'

It had taken her a few years to recognise that Brendan's overbearing attitude wasn't one of protection, but of possession. 'And I told you that I needed to finish up the KPI report for Ormandes' campaign before I clocked off.' Collating data and statistics was her least favourite part of the job, and she'd dragged her heels. 'Anyway, the agent is leaving the keys in a lock box for me.' She crossed her fingers against the bad luck her lie could bring. 'Got to go.'

Brendan was right, though, she had left her run too late to make a decent assessment of the property. Already, purple dusk lay in plump pillows beneath the trees bordering the courtyard. But this was the first weekend she'd had clear for months. The PR business involved too many crazy hours, too many events, too many functions; all of which Brendan loved. He thrived on the stimulation of being constantly surrounded by people, always in the spotlight, putting on a performance. And he liked to party, even though he knew that drugs were her kryptonite. Had been since Amelie had hit a downward spiral and overdosed on a cocktail of pre-scriptions and illegals when they were seventeen.

Losing her sister had taught her to numb herself: without passion, there couldn't be pain. But there was no risk of pain in rescuing this ruin; she would only do it to prove to Brendan she could be successful in her own right, that she didn't need to fall back on the cushion of money. The cushion that had suffocated Amelie.

Gabrielle shook off her thoughts. It was time to add photos to the margin sketches and notes she had doodled. To create a brand for this property, she needed to connect with it, to clarify her vague ideas of what it could become.

Ideas that seemed more far-fetched by the second, she thought morosely as she kicked a clod of mud from the red-brick pavers. As though moving one lump of clay would make any appreciable difference to the derelict, forlorn look of the property. All it did was spray dirt across the fawn leather of her boots.

Gabrielle stepped back to look up at the rear of the building. While she had thought the front stark, the back had neither balcony nor verandah to soften the no-frills presentation. Snapping photos from various angles, she worked quickly in the dying light.

Across the courtyard, the building jutted out at a one-and-a-half storey right angle. A sloping verandah shaded narrow rectangular windows, while on the upper level, which must be a loft rather than another floor, small, square, uncurtained windows let in the light. At the end of the building, disappearing in the twilight, she could just make out a door in the same olive shade as the winter river. Although the barn style was different to the main building, the stonework was complimentary. She decided that the extension, which she recalled as being a large kitchen and new wet areas, had likely been commissioned by one of the recent owners; those who had been chased off by the ghosts of the conveyancer's imagination. A frisson rippled across her skin as the breeze billowed a dirty grey curtain from the window above, and she rubbed briskly at her arms through her sweater, huddling deeper into the alpaca wool afghan wrap.

Peering up, Gabrielle realised that the curtain fluttered where the window *had* been. While some of the mullioned panes reflected rainbows of the last of the muted ochre sun filtering through the hedge of wattles, others had exploded, leaving jagged shards of glass in twisted frames as the only deterrent to looters. Deep cracks creased the pale sandstone walls, and dark frown lines ran from above the central door to the forehead of the second storey. Dirty runnels gouged the mortar beneath the windows like tear stains, and the once-cheery trims were disjointed and splintered, held together with scabbed burgundy blood.

A sense of overwhelming desolation seized Gabrielle. An inanimate object couldn't die, yet it seemed that was exactly what had happened to the hotel.

She shook off the notion, looking around for something to relieve the oppression. The faded red-brick quoins on each corner of the building added a dash of colour in the face of the pervading grimness, and high above her, the second floor looked across the large courtyard to a vista of gum-studded wetlands beyond the wattle-tree hedge.

She set her jaw. The state of the property following the earthquake shouldn't come as a shock, but close up, the damage to the building looked far worse than it had in the photos the insurance company emailed a few months back. She and Brendan had taken the settlement in cash so they could rebuild to suit their needs—or at least, that had been the plan. Brendan had been in favour of modernising, capitalising on the property's location and outlook rather than on the dated infrastructure, but obviously she couldn't do that now. Gabrielle had to find something different, something *more*, to prove to Brendan that despite everything material in her life coming easily, she had vision and ability enough to not need his touted *passion*. She would find a point of difference, something to set the Wurruldi Hotel aside from the mundane bed-and-breakfast enterprises dotting the state. At the moment, she had a stellar location. And not much more.

Gabrielle wrapped her arms around herself, the enormity of the task suddenly daunting. What had she got herself into? With no real renovating experience, she'd signed up to prove her independence by making over a ruin? And why even bother? Brendan's interest, beyond his initial ego-driven taunt, would be limited, and Wurruldi was too far off the beaten track for any of her old crowd to visit. Siri's maps existed only to guide them to the nearest open bar.

A crow cawed in the tree overhead, echoed by more of his coven further along the river. Gabrielle shivered. The crumbling façade, undermined walls and missing windows vastly diminished any charm she had imagined in this venture. Realising she had been frowning unseeingly up at the building, Gabrielle snapped a few more pictures, then turned away. Against the wattle-tree hedge at the rear of the courtyard stood a row of stone outbuildings separated into pairs by five-metre spaces. Although she and Brendan hadn't bothered to investigate them when they had made their impromptu and unresearched decision to purchase the property, at her desk she had toyed with the notion of converting them into tiny cottages to house the overflow of tourists her campaign would attract. But now she saw that a combination of time and the earthquake had hit the smaller buildings hard. A pile of roofing iron created a funeral pyre alongside the corpse of a rusted vehicle in what the real-estate agent claimed had been a stable.

Gabrielle carefully navigated the mud-slicked pavers as she skirted fallen branches of the red gum that shaded the courtyard, the hardened amber sap shattering to release an earthy, resinous scent beneath her tread.

Orange bunting sectioned off one pair of buildings, a handwritten sign in a plastic sleeve reading, *Caution: Unstable*. She circled the sheds, stumbling through the scrubby saltbush at the rear. The back wall tilted outward, far enough that it would cast a shadow if the encroaching darkness hadn't already made the scene grim.

Rusted triangular hinge plates clutched at a wooden door that leaned drunkenly ajar. She edged closer and peered into the gloom beyond. Stone and mortar had tumbled from the rear wall, forming a pyramid on the dirt floor. The breach was plugged with a scrabble of twigs and twine and the odd piece of litter. The floor immediately below was centimetres-deep in bird mess.

Shit. Literally. Why had she imagined she could turn these feral hovels into accommodation? She flicked on her torch app and tentatively pushed at the final door. It gave reluctantly, creaking open.

'Oh!' She eased a step further into the room, peering around with renewed interest. With a ceiling of rusted pressed-metal tiles, each decorated with a stylised floral cross in the centre of an ornately curlicued border, and with papered walls, it seemed that, unlike the other sheds, this had once been inhabited. Under her feet, old lino cracked like bones, the pieces shifting to reveal a different layer beneath.

The iPhone's torch beam was too feeble to probe far into the gloom, but as Gabrielle's eyes adjusted, she could make out a few details. A plush armchair dwarfed a chequerboard cigar humidor, the spindly legs poised to dance across the room as soon as she turned her back. Against the side wall, almost consumed by the luscious darkness, stood a long sideboard. She couldn't see into it, but glass refracted her light in patchy flashes through the grime.

As Gabrielle took another step, something moved in the dim recesses and a chill rushed towards her. She lurched back across the stone hearth and into the last of the watery evening light. Gooseflesh prickled her arms as she clutched them tight across her chest and gave a nervous giggle. Prying around in the dusk made her feel like a trespasser, and if she was going to let a breeze and the rustle of a possum spook her, it was time to call it a night.

In daylight the project would seem more achievable, the property would look less abandoned.

It had to.

Otherwise, she had made the biggest mistake of her life.